JEROME,
A POOR MAN

MORE WILDSIDE CLASSICS

Please see www.wildsidepress.com for a complete list!

JEROME, A POOR MAN

MARY E. WILKINS

WILDSIDE PRESS

JEROME, A POOR MAN

This edition published 2005 by Wildside Press, LLC.
www.wildsidepress.com

CHAPTER I

One morning in early May, when the wind was cold and the sun hot, and Jerome about twelve years old, he was in a favorite lurking-place of his, which nobody but himself knew.

Three fields' width to the northward from the Edwardses' house was a great rock ledge; on the southern side of it was a famous warm hiding-place for a boy on a windy spring day. There was a hollow in the rock for a space as tall as Jerome, and the ledge extended itself beyond it like a sheltering granite wing to the westward.

The cold northwester blowing from over the lingering Canadian snow-banks could not touch him, and he had the full benefit of the sun as it veered imperceptibly south from east. He lay there basking in it like some little animal which had crawled out from its winter nest. Before him stretched the fields, all flushed with young green. On the side of a gentle hill at the left a file of blooming peach-trees looked as if they were moving down the slope to some imperious march music of the spring.

In the distance a man was at work with plough and horse. His shouts came faintly across, like the ever-present notes of labor in all the harmonies of life. The only habitation in sight was Squire Eben Merritt's, and of that only the broad slants of shingled roof and gray end wall of the barn, with a pink spray of peach-trees against it.

Jerome stared out at it all, without a thought concerning it in his brain. He was actively conscious only of his own existence, which had just then a wondrously pleasant savor for him. A sweet exhilarating fire seemed leaping through every vein in his little body. He was drowsy, and yet more fully awake than he had been all winter. All his pulses tingled, and his thoughts were overborne by the ecstasy in them. Jerome had scarcely felt thoroughly warm before, since last summer. That same little, tight, and threadbare jacket had been his thickest garment all winter. The wood had been stinted on the hearth, the coverings on his bed; but now the full privilege of the spring sun was his, and the blood in this little meagre human plant, chilled and torpid with the winter's frosts, stirred and flowed like that in any other. Who could say that the bliss of renewed vitality which the boy felt, as he rested there in his snug rock, was not identical with that of the springing grass and the flowering peach-trees? Who could say that he was more to all intents and purposes, for that minute, than the rock-honeysuckle opening its red cups on the ledge over his head? He was conscious of no more memory or forethought.

Presently he shut his eyes, and the sunlight came in a soft rosy glow through his closed lids. Then it was that a little girl came across the fields, clambering cautiously over the stone walls, lest she should tear her gown, stepping softly over the green grass in her little morocco shoes, and finally stood still in front of the boy sitting with his eyes closed in the hollow of the rock. Twice she opened her mouth to speak, then shut it again. At last she gained courage.

"Be you sick, boy?" she inquired, in a sweet, timid voice.

Jerome opened his eyes with a start, and stared at the little quaint figure standing before him. Lucina wore a short blue woollen gown; below it her starched white pantalets hung to the tops of her morocco shoes. She wore also a white tier, and over that a little coat, and over that a little green cashmere shawl sprinkled with palm leaves, which her mother had crossed over her bosom and tied at her back for extra warmth. Lucina's hood was of quilted blue silk, and her smooth yellow curls flowed from under it quite down to her waist. Moreover, her mother had carefully arranged four, two on each side, to escape from the frill of her hood in front and fall softly over her pink cheeks. Lucina's face was very fair and sweet — the face of a good and gentle little girl, who always minded her mother and did her daily tasks.

Her dark blue eyes, set deeply under seriously frowning childish brows, surveyed Jerome with innocent wonder; her pretty mouth drooped anxiously at the corners. Jerome knew her well enough, although he had never before exchanged a word with her. She was little Lucina Merritt, whose father had money and bought her everything she wanted, and whose mother rigged her up like a puppet, as he had heard his mother say.

"No, ain't sick," he said, in a half intelligible grunt. A cross little animal poked into wakefulness in the midst of its nap in the sun might have responded in much the same way. Gallantry had not yet developed in Jerome. He saw in this pretty little girl only another child, and, moreover, one finely shod and clothed, while he went shoeless and threadbare. He looked sulkily at her blue silk hood, pulled his old cap down with a twitch to his black brows, and shrugged himself closer to the warm rock.

The little girl eyed his bare toes. "Be you cold?" she ventured.

"No, ain't cold," grunted Jerome. Then he caught sight of something in her hand — a great square of sugar-gingerbread, out of which she had taken only three dainty bites as she came along, and in spite of himself there was a hungry flash of his black eyes.

Lucina held out the gingerbread. "I'd just as lives as not you had it," said she, timidly. "It's most all there. I've just had three teenty bites."

Jerome turned on her fiercely. "Don't want your old gingerbread," he cried. "Ain't hungry — have all I want to home."

The little Lucina jumped, and her blue eyes filled with tears. She turned away without a word, and ran falteringly, as if she could not see for tears, across the field; and there was a white lamb trotting after her. It had appeared from somewhere in the fields, and Jerome had not noticed it. He remembered hearing that Lucina Merritt had a cosset lamb that followed her everywhere. "Has everything," he muttered — "lambs an' everything. Don't want your old gingerbread."

Suddenly he sprang up and began feeling in his pocket; then he ran like a deer after the little girl. She rolled her frightened, tearful blue eyes over her shoulder at him, and began to run too, and the cosset lamb cantered faster at her heels; but Jerome soon gained on them.

"Stop, can't ye?" he sang out. "Ain't goin' to hurt ye. What ye 'fraid of?" He laid his hand on her green-shawled shoulders, and she stood panting, her little face looking up at him, half reassured, half terrified, from her blue silk hood-frills and her curls.

"Like sas'fras?" inquired Jerome, with a lordly air. An emperor about to bestow a largess upon a slave could have had no more of the very grandeur of beneficence in his mien.

Lucina nodded meekly.

Jerome drew out a great handful of strange articles from his pocket, and they might, from his manner of handling them, have been gold pieces and jewels. There were old buttons, a bit of chalk, and a stub of slate-pencil. There were a horse-chestnut and some grains of parched sweet-corn and a dried apple-core. There were other things which age and long bondage in the pocket had brought to such passes that one could scarcely determine their identities. From all this Jerome selected one undoubted treasure — a great jagged cut of sassafras root. It had been nicely scraped, too, and looked white and clean.

"Here," said Jerome.

"Don't you want it?" asked Lucina, shyly.

"No — had a great piece twice as big as that yesterday. Know where there's lots more in the cedar swamp. Here, take it."

"Thank you," said Lucina, and took it, and fumbled nervously after her little pocket.

"Why don't you eat it?" asked Jerome, and Lucina took an

obedient little nibble.

"Ain't that good and strong?"

"It's real good," replied Lucina, smiling gratefully.

"Mebbe I'll dig you some more some time," said Jerome, as if the cedar swamp were a treasure-chest.

"Thank you," said the little girl. Then she timidly extended the gingerbread again. "I only took three little bites, an' it's real nice, honest," said she, appealingly.

But she jumped again at the flash in Jerome's black eyes.

"Don't want your old gingerbread!" he cried. "Ain't hungry; have more'n I want to eat to home. Guess my folks have gingerbread. Like to know what you're tryin' to give me victuals for! Don't want any of your old gingerbread!"

"It ain't old, honest," pleaded Lucina, tearfully. "It ain't old — Hannah, she just baked it this morning." But the boy was gone, pelting hard across the field, and all there was for the little girl to do was to go home, with her sassafras in her pocket and her gingerbread in her hand, with an aromatic savor on her tongue and the sting of slighted kindness in her heart, with her cosset lamb trotting at heel, and tell her mother.

Jerome did not return to his nook in the rock. As he neared it he heard the hollow note of a horn from the northwest.

"S'pose mother wants me," he muttered, and went on past the rock ledge to the west, and climbed the stone wall into the first of the three fields which separated him from his home. Across the young springing grass went Jerome — a slender little lad moving with an awkward rustic lope. It was the gait of the homely toiling men of the village which his young muscles had caught, as if they had in themselves powers of observation and assimilation. Jerome at twelve walked as if he had held plough-shares, bent over potato hills, and hewn wood in cedar swamps for half a century. Jerome's feet were bare, and his red rasped ankles showed below his hitching trousers. His poor winter shoes had quite failed him for many weeks, his blue stockings had shown at the gaps in their sides which had torn away from his mother's strong mending. Now the soles had gone, and his uncle Ozias Lamb, who was a cobbler, could not put in new ones because there was not strength enough in the uppers to hold them. "You can't have soles in shoes any more than you can in folks, without some body," said Ozias Lamb. It seemed as if Ozias might have made and presented some new shoes, soles and all, to his needy nephew, but he was very poor, and not young, and worked painfully to make every cent count. So Jerome went barefoot after the soles parted from his shoes; but he did not care, because it was spring and the snow was gone. Jerome had, moreover, a curious disregard of physical discomfort for a boy who could take such delight in sheer existence in a sunny hollow of a rock. He had had chilblains all winter from the snow-water which had soaked in through his broken shoes; his heels were still red with them, but not a whimper had he made. He had treated them doggedly himself with wood-ashes, after an old country prescription, and said nothing, except to reply, "Doctorin' chilblains," when his mother asked him what he was doing.

Jerome also often went hungry. He was hungry now as he loped across the field. A young wolf that had roamed barren snow-fields all winter might not have felt more eager for a good meal than Jerome, and he was worse off, because he had no natural prey. But he never made a complaint.

Had any one inquired if he were hungry, he would have flown at him as he had done at little Lucina Merritt when she offered him her gingerbread. He knew, and all his family knew, that the neighbors thought they had not enough to eat, and the knowledge so stung their pride that it made them defy the fact itself. They would not own to each other that they were hungry; they denied it fiercely to their own craving stomachs.

Jerome had had nothing that morning but a scanty spoonful of corn-meal porridge, but he would have maintained stoutly that he had eaten a good breakfast. He took another piece of sassafras from his pocket and chewed it as he went along. After all, now the larder of Nature was open and the lock of the frost on her cupboards was broken, a boy would not fare so badly; he could not starve. There was sassafras root in the swamps — plenty of it for the digging; there were young winter-green leaves, stinging pleasantly his palate with green aromatic juice; later there would be raspberries and blackberries and huckleberries. There were also the mysterious cedar apples, and the sour-sweet excrescences sometimes found on swamp bushes. These last were the little rarities of Nature's table which a boy would come upon by chance when berrying and snatch with delighted surprise. They appealed to his imagination as well as to his tongue, since they belonged not to the known fruits in his spelling-book and dictionary, and possessed a strange sweetness of fancy and mystery beyond their woodland savor. In a few months, too, the garden would be grown and there would be corn and beans and potatoes. Then Jerome's lank outlines would begin to take on curves and the hungry look would disappear from his face. He was a handsome boy, with a fearless outlook of black eyes from his lean, delicate face, and a thick curling crop of fair hair which the sun had bleached like straw. Always protected from the weather, Jerome's hair would have been brown; but his hats failed him like his shoes, and often in the summer season were crownless. However, his mother mended them as long as she was able. She was a thrifty woman, although she was a semi-invalid, and sat all day long in a high-backed rocking-chair. She was not young either; she had been old when she married and her children were born, but there was a strange element of toughness in her — a fibre either of body or spirit that kept her in being, like the fibre of an old tree.

Before Jerome entered the house his mother's voice saluted him. "Where have you been, Jerome Edwards?" she demanded. Her voice was querulous, but strongly shrill. It could penetrate every wall and door. Ann Edwards, as she sat in her rocking-chair, lifted up her voice, and it sounded all over her house like a trumpet, and all her household marched to it.

"Been over in the pasture," answered Jerome, with quick and yet rather defiant obedience, as he opened the door.

His mother's face, curiously triangular in outline, like a cat's, with great hollow black eyes between thin parted curtains of black false hair, confronted him when he entered the room. She always sat face to the door and window, and not a soul who passed or entered escaped her for a minute. "What have you been doing in the pasture?" said she.

"Sittin'."

"Sittin'?"

"I've been sitting on the warm side of the big rock a little while," said Jerome. He looked subdued before his mother's gaze, and yet not abashed. She always felt sure that there was some hidden reserve of rebellion in Jerome, coerce him into obedience as she might. She never really governed him, as she did her daughter Elmira, who stood washing dishes at the sink. But she loved Jerome better, although she tried not to, and would not own it to herself.

"Do you know what time it is?" said she, severely.

Jerome glanced at the tall clock in the corner. It was nearly ten. He glanced and made no reply. He sometimes had a dignified masculine way, beyond his years, of eschewing all unnecessary words. His mother saw him look at the time; why should he speak? She did not wait for him. "'Most ten o'clock," said she, "and a great boy twelve years old lazing round on a rock in a pasture when all his folks are working. Here's your mother, feeble as she is, workin' her fingers to the bone, while you're doing nothing a whole forenoon. I should think you'd be ashamed of yourself. Now you take the spade and go right out and go to work in the garden. It's time them beans are in, if they're going to be. Your father has had to go down to the wood-lot and get a load of wood for Doctor Prescott, and here 'tis May and the garden not planted. Go right along." All the time Jerome's mother talked, her little lean strong fingers flew, twirling bright colored rags in and out. She was braiding a rug for this same Doctor Prescott's wife. The bright strips spread and twirled over her like snakes, and the balls where-in the rags were wound rolled about the floor. Most women kept their rag balls in a basket when they braided, but Ann Edwards worked always in a sort of untidy fury.

Jerome went out, little hungry boy with the winter chill again creeping through his veins, got the spade out of the barn, and set to work in the garden. The garden lay on the sunny slope of a hill which rose directly behind the house; when his spade struck a stone Jerome would send it rolling out of his way to the foot of the hill. He got considerable amusement from that, and presently the work warmed him.

The robins were singing all about. Every now and then one flew out of the sweet spring distance, lit, and silently erected his red breast among some plough ridges lower down. It was like a veritable transition from sound to sight.

Below where Jerome spaded, and upon the left, stretched long waving plough ridges where the corn was planted. Jerome's father had been at work there with the old white horse that was drawing wood for him today. Much of the garden had to be spaded instead of ploughed, because this same old white horse was needed for other work.

As Jerome spaded, the smell of the fresh earth came up in his face. Now and then a gust of cold wind, sweet with unseen blossoms, smote him powerfully, bending his slender body before it like a sapling. A bird flashed past him with a blue dazzle of wings, and Jerome stopped and looked after it. It lit on the fence in front of the house, and shone there in the sunlight like a blue precious stone. The boy gazed at it, leaning on his spade. Jerome always looked hard out of all his little open windows of life, and saw every precious thing outside his daily grind of hard, toilsome childhood which came within his sight.

The bird flew away, and Jerome spaded again. He knew that he must finish so much before dinner or his mother would scold. He was not afraid of his mother's sharp tongue, but he avoided provoking it with a curious politic and tolerant submission which he had learned from his father. "Mother ain't well, you know, an' she's high-sperited, and we've got to humor her all we can," Abel Edwards had said, confidentially, many a time to his boy, who had listened sagely and nodded.

Jerome obeyed his mother with the patient obedience of a superior who yields because his opponent is weaker than he, and a struggle beneath his dignity, not because he is actually coerced. Neither he nor his father ever answered back or contradicted; when her shrill voice waxed loudest and her vituperation seemed to fairly hiss in their ears, they sometimes looked at each other and exchanged a solemn wink of understanding and patience. Neither ever opened mouth in reply.

Jerome worked fast in his magnanimous concession to his mother's will, and had accomplished considerable when his sister opened the kitchen window, thrust out her dark head, and called in a voice shrill as her mother's, but as yet wholly sweet, with no harsh notes in it: "Jerome! Jerome! Dinner is ready."

Jerome whooped in reply, dropped his spade, and went leaping down the hill. When he entered the kitchen his mother was sitting at the table and Elmira was taking up the dinner. Elmira was a small, pretty girl, with little, nervous hands and feet, and eager black eyes, like her mother's. She stretched on tiptoe over the fire, and ladled out a steaming mixture from the kettle with an arduous swing of her sharp elbow. Elmira's sleeves were rolled up and her thin, sharply-jointed, girlish arms showed.

"Don't you know enough, without being told, to lift that kettle off the fire for Elmira?" demanded Mrs. Edwards of Jerome.

Jerome lifted the kettle off the fire without a word.

"It seems sometimes as if you might do something without being told," said his mother. "You could see, if you had eyes to your head, that your sister wa'n't strong enough to lift that kettle off, and was dippin' it up so's to make it lighter, an' the stew 'most burnin' on."

Jerome made no response. He sniffed hungrily at the savory steam arising from the kettle. "What is it?" he asked his sister, who stooped over the kettle sitting on the hearth, and plunged in again the long-handled tin dipper.

Mrs. Edwards never allowed any one to answer a question when she could do it herself. "It's a parsnip stew," said she, sharply. "Elmira dug some up in the old garden-patch, where we thought they were dead. I put in a piece of pork, when I'd ought to have saved it. It's good 'nough for anybody, I don't care who 'tis, if it's Doctor Prescott, or Squire Merritt, or the minister. You'd better be thankful for it, both of you."

"Where's father?" said Jerome.

"He 'ain't come home yet. I dun'no' where he is. He's been gone long enough to draw ten cords of wood. I s'pose he's potterin' round somewheres — stopped to talk to somebody, or something. I ain't going to wait any longer. He'll have to eat his dinner cold if he can't get home."

Elmira put the dish of stew on the table. Jerome drew his chair up. Mrs. Edwards grasped the long-handled dipper preparatory to distributing the savory mess, then suddenly stopped and turned to Elmira.

"Elmira," said she, "you go into the parlor an' git the china bowl with pink flowers on it, an' then you go to the chest in the spare bedroom an' get out one of them fine linen towels."

"What for?" said Elmira, wonderingly.

"No matter what for. You do what I tell you to."

Elmira went out, and after a little reappeared with the china bowl and the linen towel. Jerome sat waiting, with a kind of fierce resignation. He was almost starved, and the smell of the stew in his nostrils made him fairly ravenous.

"Give it here," said Mrs. Edwards, and Elmira set the bowl before her mother. It was large, almost large enough for a punchbowl, and had probably been used for one. It was a stately old dish from overseas, a relic from Mrs. Edwards's mother, who had seen her palmy days before her marriage. Mrs. Edwards had also in her parlor cupboard a part of a set of blue Indian china which had belonged to her mother. The children watched while their mother dipped the parsnip stew into the china bowl. Elmira, while constantly more amenable to her mother, was at the moment more outspoken against her.

"There won't be enough left for us," she burst forth, excitedly.

"I guess you'll get all you need; you needn't worry."

"There won't be enough for father when he comes home, anyhow."

"I ain't a mite worried about your father; I guess he won't starve."

Mrs. Edwards went on dipping the stew into the bowl while the children watched. She filled it nearly two-thirds full, then stopped, and eyed the girl and boy critically. "I guess you'd better go, Elmira," said she. "Jerome can't unless he's all cleaned up. Get my little red cashmere shawl, and you can wear my green silk pumpkin hood. Yours don't look nice enough to go there with."

"Can't I eat dinner first, mother?" pleaded Elmira, pitifully.

"No, you can't. I guess you won't starve if you wait a little while. I ain't 'goin' to send stew to folks stone-cold. Hurry right along and get the shawl and hood. Don't stand there lookin' at me."

Elmira went out forlornly.

Mrs. Edwards began pinning the linen towel carefully over the bowl.

"Let Elmira stay an' eat her dinner. I'd just as lives go. Don't care if I don't ever have anythin' to eat," spoke up Jerome.

His mother flashed her black eyes round at him. "Don't you be saucy, Jerome Edwards," said she, "or you'll go back to your spadin' without a mouthful! I told your sister she was goin', an' I don't want any words about it from either of you."

When Elmira returned with her mother's red cashmere shawl pinned carefully over her childish shoulders, with her sharply pretty, hungry-eyed little face peering meekly out of the green gloom of the great pumpkin hood, Mrs. Edwards gave her orders. "There," said she, "you take this bowl, an' you be real careful and don't let it fall and break it, nor slop the stew over my best shawl, an' you carry it down the road to Doctor Prescott's; an' whoever comes to the door, whether it's the hired girl, or Lawrence, or the hired man, you ask to see Mis' Doctor Prescott. Don't you give this bowl to none of the others, you mind. An' when Mis' Doctor Prescott comes, you courtesy an' say, 'Good-mornin', Mis' Prescott. Mis' Abel Edwards sends you her compliments, and hopes you're enjoyin' good health, an' begs you'll accept this bowl of parsnip stew. She thought perhaps you hadn't had any this season.'"

Mrs. Edwards repeated the speech in a little, fine, mincing voice, presumably the one which Elmira was to use. "Can you remember that?" she asked, sharply, in her natural tone.

"Yes, ma'am."

"Say it over."

Poor little Elmira Edwards said it over like a parrot, imitating her mother's fine, stilted tone perfectly. In truth, it was a formula of presentation which she had often used.

"Don't you forget the 'compliments,' an' 'I thought she hadn't had any parsnip stew this season.'"

"No, ma'am."

"Take the bowl up, real careful, and carry it stiddy."

Elmira threw back the ends of the red cashmere shawl, lifted the big bowl in her two small hands, and went out carrying it before her. Jerome opened the door, and shut it after her.

"Now I guess Mis' Doctor Prescott won't think we're starvin' to death here, if her husband has got a mortgage on our house," said Mrs. Edwards. "I made up my mind that time she sent over that pitcher of lamb broth that I'd send her somethin' back, if I lived. I wouldn't have taken it anyhow, if it hadn't been for the rest of you. I guess I'll let folks know we ain't quite beggars yet."

Jerome nodded. A look of entire sympathy with his mother came into his face. "Guess so too," said he.

Mrs. Edwards threw back her head with stiff pride, as if it bore a crown. "So far," said she, "nobody on this earth has ever give me a thing that I 'ain't been able to pay 'em for in some way. I guess there's a good many rich folks can't say 's much as that."

"Guess so too," said Jerome.

"Pass over your plate; you must be hungry by this time," said his mother. She heaped his plate with the stew. "There," said she, "don't you wait any longer. I guess mebbe you'd better set the dish down on the hearth to keep warm for Elmira and your father first, though."

"Ain't you goin' to eat any yourself?" asked Jerome.

"I couldn't touch a mite of that stew if you was to pay me for it. I never set much by parsnip stew myself, anyway."

Jerome eyed his mother soberly. "There's enough," said he. "I've got all I can eat here."

"I tell you I don't want any. Ain't that enough? There's plenty of stew if I wanted it, but I don't. I never liked it any too well, an' today seems as if it fairly went against my stomach. Set it down on the hearth the way I told you to, an' eat your dinner before it gets any colder."

Jerome obeyed. He ate his plate of stew; then his mother obliged him to eat another. When Elmira returned she had her fill, and there was plenty left for Abel Edwards when he should come home.

Jerome, well fed, felt like another boy when he returned to his task in the garden. "Guess I can get this spadin' 'most done this afternoon," he said to himself. He made the brown earth fly around him. He whistled as he worked. As the afternoon wore on he began to wonder if he could not finish the garden before his father got home. He was sure he had not come as yet, for he had kept an eye on the road, and besides he would have heard the heavy rattle of the wood-wagon. "Father 'll be real tickled when he sees the garden all done," said Jerome, and he stopped whistling and bent all his young spirit and body to his work. He never thought of feeling anxious about his father.

At five o'clock the back door of the Edwards house opened. Elmira came out with a shawl over her head and hurried up the hill. "Oh, Jerome," she panted, when she got up to him. "You must stop working, mother says, and go right straight off to the ten-acre lot. Father 'ain't come home yet, an' we're dreadful worried about him. She says she's afraid something has happened to him."

Jerome stuck his spade upright in the ground and stared at her. "What does she s'pose has happened?" he said, slowly. Jerome had no imagination for disasters.

"She thinks maybe he's fell down, or some wood's fell on him, or Peter's run away."

"Peter wouldn't ever run away; it's much as ever he'll walk lately, an' father don't ever fall down."

Elmira fairly danced up and down in the fresh mould. She caught her brother's arm and twitched it and pushed him fiercely. "Go along, go along!" she cried. "Go right along, Jerome Edwards! I tell you something dreadful has happened to father. Mother says so. Go right along!"

Jerome pulled himself away from her nervous clutch, and collected himself for flight. "He was goin' to carry that wood to Doctor Prescott's," said he, reflectively. "Ain't any sense goin' to the ten-acre lot till I see if he's been there."

"It's on the way," cried Elmira, frantically. "Hurry up! Oh, do hurry up, Jerome! Poor father! Mother says he's — fell — down —" Elmira crooked her little arm around her face and broke into a long wail as she started down the hill. "Poor — father — oh — oh — poor — father!" floated back like a wake of pitiful sound.

CHAPTER II

Jerome started, and once started he raced. Long-legged, light-flanked, long-winded, and underfed, he had the adaptability for speed of a little race-horse. Jerome Edwards was quite a famous boy in the village for his prowess in running. No other boy could equal him. Marvellous stories were told about it. "Jerome Edwards, he can run half a mile in five minutes any day, yes he can, sir," the village boys bragged if perchance a cousin from another town came a-visiting and endeavored to extol himself and his comrades beyond theirs. In some curious fashion Jerome, after he had out-speeded all the other boys, furnished them with his own victories for a boast. They seemed, in exulting over the glory of this boy of their village, to forget that the glory came only through their defeat. It was national pride on a very small and childish scale.

Jerome, swift little runner that he was, ran that day as he had never run before. The boys whom he met stood aside hastily, gaped down the road behind him to see another runner laboring far in the rear, and then, when none appeared, gaped after his flying heels.

"Wonder what he's a-runnin' that way fur?" said one boy.

"Ain't nobody a-tryin' to ketch up with him, fur's I can see," said another.

"Mebbe his mother's took worse, an' he's a-runnin' fur the doctor," said a third, who was Henry Judd, a distant cousin of Jerome's.

The boys stood staring even when Jerome was quite out of sight. Jerome had about three-quarters of a mile to run to Doctor Prescott's house. He was almost there when he caught sight of a team coming. "There's father, now," he thought, and stood still, breathing hard. Although Jerome's scanty food made him a swift runner, it did not make him a strong one.

The team came rattling slowly on. The old white horse which drew it planted his great hoofs lumberingly in the tracks, nodding at every step.

As it came nearer, Jerome, watching, gave a quick gasp. The wagon contained wood nicely packed; the reins were wound carefully around one of the stakes; and there was no driver. Jerome tried to call out, tried to run forward, but he could not. He could only stand still, watching, his boyish face deadly white, his eyes dilating. The old white horse came on, dragging his load faithfully and steadily towards his home. He never swerved from his tracks except once, when he turned out carefully for a bad place in the road, where the ground seemed to be caving in, which Abel Edwards had always avoided with a loaded team. There was something awful about this old animal, with patient and laborious stupidity in every line of his plodding body, obeying still that higher intelligence which was no longer visible at his guiding-reins, and perhaps had gone out of sight forever. It had all the uncanny horror of a headless spectre advancing down the road.

Jerome collected himself when the white horse came along-side. "Whoa! Whoa, Peter!" he gasped out. The horse stopped and stood still, his great forefeet flung stiffly forward, his head and ears and neck hanging as inertly as a broken tree-bough with all its leaves drooping.

The boy stumbled weakly to the side of the wagon and stretched himself up on tiptoe. There was nothing there but the wood. He stood a minute, thinking. Then he began searching for the hitching-rope in the front of the wagon, but he could not find it. Finally he led the horse to the side of the road, unwound the reins from the stake, and fastened him as well as he could to a tree.

Then he went on down the road. His knees felt weak under him, but still he kept up a good pace. When he reached the Prescott place he paused and looked irresolutely a moment through the trees at the great square mansion-house, with its green, glancing window-panes.

Then he ran straight on. The ten-acre wood-lot which be-longed to his father was about a half mile farther. It was a birch and chestnut wood, and was full of the green shimmer of new leaves and the silvery glistening of white boughs as delicate as maidens' arms. There was a broad cart-path leading through it. Jerome entered this directly when he reached the wood. Then he began calling. "Father!" he called. "Father! father!" over and over again, stopping between to listen. There was no sound in re-sponse; there was no sound in the wood except the soft and elu-sive rustling of the new foliage, like the rustling of the silken garments of some one in hiding or some one passing out of sight. It brought also at this early season a strange sense of a presence in the wood. Jerome felt it, and called with greater importunity: "Father! father! father, where be you? Father!"

Jerome looked very small among the trees — no more than a little pale child. His voice rang out shrill and piteous. It seemed as much a natural sound of the wood as a bird's, and was indeed one of the primitive notes of nature: the call of that most helpless human young for its parent and its shield.

Jerome pushed on, calling, until he came to the open space where his father had toiled felling trees all winter. Cords of wood were there, all neatly piled and stacked. The stumps between them were sending out shoots of tender green. "Father! father!" Jerome called, but this time more cautiously, hushing his voice a little. He thought that his father might be lying there among the stumps, injured in some way. He remembered how a log had once fallen on Samuel Lapham's leg and broken it when he was out alone in the woods, and he had lain there a whole day before anybody found him. He thought something like that might have happened to his father. He searched everywhere, peering with his sharp young eyes among the stumps and between the piles of wood. "Mebbe father's fainted away," he muttered.

Finally he became sure that his father was nowhere in the clearing, and he raised his voice again and shouted, and hallooed, and listened, and hallooed again, and got no response.

Suddenly a chill seemed to strike Jerome's heart. He thought of the pond. Little given as he was to forebodings of evil, when once he was possessed of one it became a certainty.

"Father's fell in the pond and got drowned," he burst out with a great sob. "What will mother do?"

The boy went forward, stumbling half blindly over the stumps. Once he fell, bruising his knee severely, and picked himself up, sobbing piteously. All the child in Jerome had asserted itself.

Beyond the clearing was a stone wall that bounded Abel Edwards's property. Beyond that was a little grove of old thick-topped pine-trees; beyond that the little woodland pond. It was very shallow in places, but it never dried up, and was said to have deep holes in it. The boys told darkly braggart stories about this pond. They had stood on this rock and that rock with poles of fabulous length; they had probed the still water of the pond, and "never once hit the bottom, sir." They had flung stones with all their might, and, listening sharply forward like foxes, had not heard them "strike bottom, sir."

One end of this pond, reaching up well among the pine-trees, had the worst repute, and was called indeed a darkly significant name — the "Dead Hole." It was confidently believed by all the village children to have no bottom at all. There was a belief current among them that once, before they were born, a man had been drowned there, and his body never found.

They would stand on the shore and look with horror, which yet gave somehow a pleasant titillation to their youthful spirits, at this water which bore such an evil name. Their elders did not need to caution them; even the most venturesome had an awe of the Dead Hole, and would not meddle with it unduly.

Jerome climbed over the stone wall. The land on the other side belonged to Doctor Prescott. He went through the grove of pine-trees and reached the pond — the end called the Dead Hole. He stood there looking and listening. It was a small sheet of water; the other shore, swampy and skirted with white-flowering bushes and young trees, looked very near; a cloying, honey sweetness came across, and a silvery smoke of mist was beginning to curl up from it. The frogs were clamorous, and every now and then came the bass boom of a bull-frog. A red light from the westward sun came through the thin growth opposite, and lay over the pond and the shore. Little swarms of gnats danced in it.

A swarm of the little gauzy things, so slight and ephemeral that they seemed rather a symbolism of life than life itself, whirled before the boy's wild, tearful eyes, and he moved aside and looked down, and then cried out and snatched something from the ground at his feet. It was the hat Abel Edwards had worn when he left home that morning. Jerome stood holding his father's hat, gazing at it with a look in his face like an old man's. Indeed, it may have been that a sudden old age of the spirit came in that instant over the boy. He had not before conceived of anything but an accident happening to his father; now all at once he saw plainly that if his father, Abel Edwards, had come to his death in the pond it must have been through his own choice. "He couldn't have fell in," muttered Jerome, with stiff lips, looking at the gently curving shore and looking at the hat.

Suddenly he straightened himself, and an expression of desperate resolution came into his face. He set his teeth hard; somehow, whether through inherited instincts or through impressions he had got from his mother, he had a firm conviction that suicide was a horrible disgrace to the dead man himself and to his family.

"Nobody shall ever know it," the boy thought. He nodded fiercely, as if to confirm it, and began picking up stones from the shore of the pond. He filled the crown of the hat with them, got a string out of his pocket, tied it firmly around the crown, making a strong knot; then he swung his arm back at the shoulder, brought it forward with a wide sweep, and flung the hat past the middle of the Dead Hole.

"There," said Jerome; "guess nobody 'll ever know now. There ain't no bottom to the Dead Hole." The boy hurried out of the woods and down the road again. When he reached the Prescott house a man was just coming out of the yard, following the path from the south door. When he came up to Jerome he eyed him curiously; then he grasped him by the shoulder.

"Sick?" said he.

"No," said Jerome.

"What on airth makes you look so?"

"Father's lost."

"Lost — where's he lost? What d'ye mean?"

"Went to get a load of wood for Doctor Prescott this mornin', an' 'ain't got home."

"Now, I want to know! Didn't I see his team go up the road a few minutes ago?"

Jerome nodded. "Met it, an' he wa'n't on," said he.

"Lord!" cried the man, and stared at him. He was a middle-aged man, with a small wiry shape and a gait like a boy's. His name was Jake Noyes, and he was the doctor's hired man. He took care of his horse, and drove for him, and some said helped him compound his prescriptions. There was great respect in the village for Jake Noyes. He had a kind of reflected glory from the doctor, and some of his own.

Jerome pulled his shoulder away. "Got to be goin'," said he.

"Stop," said Jake Noyes. "This has got to be looked into. He must have got hurt. He must be in the woods where he was workin'."

"Ain't. I've been there," said Jerome, shortly, and broke away.

"Where did ye look?"

"Everywhere," the boy called back. But Jake followed him up.

"Stop a minute," said he; "I want to know. Did you go as fur 's the pond?"

"What should I want to go to the pond for, like to know?" Jerome looked around at him fiercely.

"I didn't know but he might have fell in the pond; it's pretty near."

"I'd like to know what you think my father would jump in the pond for?" Jerome demanded.

"Lord, I didn't say he jumped in. I said fell in."

"You know he couldn't have fell in. You know he would have had to gone in of his own accord. I'll let you know my father wa'n't the man to do anything like that, Jake Noyes!" The boy actually shook his puny fist in the man's face. "Say it again, if ye dare!" he cried.

"Lord!" said Jake Noyes, with half comical consternation. He screwed up one blue eye after a fashion he had — people said he had acquired it from dropping drugs for the doctor — and looked with the other at the boy.

"Say it again an' I'll kill ye, I will!" cried Jerome, his voice breaking into a hoarse sob, and was off.

"Be ye crazy?" Jake Noyes called after him. He stood staring at him a minute, then went into the house on a run.

Jerome ran to the place where he had left his father's team, untied the horse, climbed up on the seat, and drove home. He could not go fast; the old horse could proceed no faster than a walk with a load. When he came in sight of home he saw a blue flutter at the gate. It was Elmira's shawl; she was out there watching. When she saw the team she came running down the road to meet it. "Where's father?" she cried out. "Jerome, where's father?"

"Dun'no'," said Jerome. He sat high above her, holding the reins. His pale, set face looked over her head.

"Jerome — haven't you — seen — father?"

"No."

Elmira burst out with a great wail. "Oh, Jerome, where's father? Jerome, where is he? Is he killed? Oh, father, father!"

"Keep still," said Jerome. "Mother 'll hear you."

"Oh, Jerome, where's father?"

"I tell you, hold your tongue. Do you want to kill mother, too?"

Poor little Elmira, running alongside the team, wept convulsively. "Elmira, I tell you to keep still," said Jerome, in such a voice that she immediately choked back her sobs.

Jerome drew up the wood-team at the gate with a great creak. "Stand here 'side of the horse a minute," he said to Elmira. He swung himself off the load and went up the path to the house. As he drew near the door he could hear his mother's chair. Ann Edwards, crippled as she was, managed, through some strange manipulation of muscles, to move herself in her rocking-chair all about the house. Now the jerking scrape of the rockers on the uncarpeted floor sounded loud. When Jerome opened the door he saw his mother hitching herself rapidly back and forth in a fashion she had when excited. He had seen her do so before, a few times.

When she saw Jerome she stopped short and screwed up her face before him as if to receive a blow. She did not ask a question.

"I met the team comin' home," said Jerome.

Still his mother said nothing, but kept that cringing face before a coming blow.

"Father wa'n't on it," said Jerome.

Still his mother waited.

"I hitched the horse," said Jerome, "and then I went up to the ten-acre lot, and I looked everywhere. He ain't there."

Suddenly Ann Edwards seemed to fall back upon herself before his eyes. Her head sank helplessly; she slipped low in her chair.

Jerome ran to the water-pail, dipped out some water, and sprinkled his mother's face. Then he rubbed her little lean hands with his hard, boyish palm. He had seen his mother faint before. In fact, he had been all prepared for it now.

Presently she began to gasp and struggle feebly, and he knew she was coming to. "Feel better?" he asked, in a loud voice, as if she were miles away; indeed, he had a feeling that she was. "Feel better, mother?"

Mrs. Edwards raised herself. "Your — father has fell down and died," she said. "There needn't anybody say anything else. Wipe this water off my face. Get a towel." Jerome obeyed.

"There needn't anybody say anything else," repeated his mother.

"I guess they needn't, either," assented Jerome, coming with the towel and wiping her face gently. "I'd like to hear anybody," he added, fiercely.

"He's fell down — and died," said his mother. She made sounds like sobs as she spoke, but there were no tears in her eyes.

"I s'pose I ought to go an' take the horse out," said Jerome.

"Well."

"I'll send Elmira in; she's holdin' him."

"Well."

Jerome lighted a candle first, for it was growing dark, and went out. "You go in and stay with mother," he said to Elmira, "an' don't you go to cryin' an' makin' her worse — she's been faintin' away. Any tea in the house?"

"No," said the little girl, trying to control her quivering face.

"Make her some hot porridge, then — she'd ought to have something. You can do that, can't you?"

Elmira nodded; she dared not speak for fear she should cry.

"Go right in, then," said Jerome; and she obeyed, keeping her face turned away. Her childish back looked like an old woman's as she entered the door.

Jerome unharnessed the horse, led him into the barn, fed him, and drew some water for him from the well. When he came out of the barn, after it was all done, he saw Doctor Prescott's chaise turning into the yard. The doctor and Jake Noyes were in it. When the chaise stopped, Jerome went up to it, bobbed his head and scraped his foot. A handsome, keenly scowling face looked out of the chaise at him. Doctor Seth Prescott was over fifty, with a smooth-shaven face as finely cut as a woman's, with bright blue eyes under bushy brows, and a red scratch-wig. Before years and snows and rough winds had darkened and seamed his face, he had been a delicately fair man. "Has he come yet?" he demanded, peremptorily.

Jerome bobbed and scraped again. "No, sir."

"You didn't see a sign of him in the woods?"

Jerome hesitated visibly.

The doctor's eyes shone more sharply. "You didn't, eh?"

"No, sir," said Jerome.

"Does your mother know it?"

"Yes, sir."

"How is she?"

"She fainted away, but she's better."

The doctor got stiffly out of the chaise, took his medicine-chest, and went into the house. "Stay here till I come out," he ordered Jerome, without looking back.

"The doctor's goin' to send a posse out lookin' with lanterns," Jake Noyes told Jerome.

Jerome made a grunt, both surly and despairing, in response. He was leaning against the wheel of the chaise; he felt strangely weak.

"Mebbe we'll find him 'live an' well," said Jake, consolingly.

"No, ye won't."

"Mebbe 'twon't be nothin' wuss than a broken bone noway, an' the doctor, he can fix that."

Jerome shook his head.

"The doctor, he's goin' to do everything that can be done," said Jake. "He's sent Lawrence over to East Corners for some ropes an' grapplin'-hooks."

Then Jerome roused himself. "What for?" he demanded, in a furious voice.

Jake hesitated and colored. "Mebbe I hadn't ought to have said that," he stammered. "Course there ain't no need of havin' 'em. It's just because the doctor wants to do everything he can."

"What for?"

"Well — you know there's the pond — an' —"

"Didn't I tell you my father didn't go near the pond?"

"Well, I don't s'pose he did," said Jake, shrewdly; "but it won't do no harm to drag it, an' then everybody will know for sure he didn't."

"Can't drag it anyhow," said Jerome, and there was an odd accent of triumph in his voice. "The Dead Hole 'ain't got any bottom."

Jake laughed. "That's a darned lie," said he. "I helped drag it myself once, forty year ago; a girl by the name of 'Lizy Ann Gooch used to live 'bout a mile below here on the river road, was missin'. She wa'n't there; found her bones an' her straw bonnet in the swamp two years afterwards, but, Lord, we dragged the Dead hole — scraped bottom every time."

Jerome stared at him, his chin dropping.

"Of course it ain't nothin' but a form, an' we sha'n't find him there any more than we did 'Lizy Ann," said Jake Noyes, consolingly.

Doctor Prescott came out of the house, and as he opened the door a shrill cry of "There needn't anybody say anything else" came from within.

"Now you'd better go in and stay with your mother," ordered Doctor Prescott. "I have given her a composing powder. Keep her as quiet as possible, and don't talk to her about your father."

Doctor Prescott got into his chaise and drove away up the road, and Jerome went in to his mother. For a while she kept her rocking-chair in constant motion; she swung back and forth or hitched fiercely across the floor; she repeated her wild cry that her husband had fallen down and died, and nobody need say anything different; she prayed and repeated Scripture texts. Then she succumbed to the Dover's powder which the doctor had given her, and fell asleep in her chair.

Jerome and Elmira dared not awake her that she might go to bed. They sat, each at a window, staring out into the night, watching for their father, or some one to come with news that his body was found — they did not know which. Now and then they heard the report of a gun, but did not know what it meant. Sometimes Elmira wept a little, but softly, that she might not waken her mother.

The moon was full, and it was almost as light as day outside. When a little after midnight a team came in sight they could tell at once that it was the doctor's chaise, and Jake Noyes was driving. The boy and girl left the windows and stole noiselessly out of the house. Jake drew up at the gate. "You'd better go in an' go to bed, both on you," he said. "We'll find him safe an' sound somewheres tomorrow. There's nigh two hundred men an' boys out with lanterns an' torches, an' firin' guns for signals. We'll find him with nothing wuss than a broken bone to-morrow. We've dragged the whole pond, an' he ain't there, sure."

CHAPTER III

The pond undoubtedly partook somewhat of the nature of an Eastern myth in this little New England village. Although with the uncompromising practicality of their natures the people had given it a name so directly significant as to make it lose all poetical glamour, and render it the very commonplace of ghastliness, it still appealed to their imaginations.

The laws of natural fancy obtained here as everywhere else, although in small and homely measure. The village children found no nymphs in the trees of their New England woods. If there were fauns among them, and the children took their pointed ears for leaves as they lay sleeping in the undergrowth, they never knew it. They had none of these, but they had their pond, with its unfathomable depth. They could not give that up for any testimony of people with ropes and grappling-hooks. Had they not sounded it in vain with farther-reaching lines?

Not a boy in the village believed that the bottom of that famous Dead Hole had once been touched. Jerome Edwards certainly did not. Then, too, they had not brought his father's hat to light — or, if they had, had made no account of it.

Some of the elders, as well as the boys, believed in their hearts that the pond had not, after all, been satisfactorily examined, and that Abel Edwards might still lie there. "Ever since I can remember anything, I've heard that pond in that place 'ain't got any bottom,'" one old man would say, and another add, with triumphant conclusion, "If he ain't there, where is he?"

That indeed was the question. All solutions of mysteries have their possibilities in the absence of proof. No trace of Abel Edwards had been found in the woodland where he had been working, and no trace of him for miles around. The search had been thorough. Other ponds of less evil repute had also been dragged, and the little river which ran through the village, and two brooks of considerable importance in the spring. If Able Edwards had taken his own life, the conclusion was inevitable that his body must lie in the pond, which had always been reported unfathomable, and might be, after all.

"The way I look at it is this," said Simon Basset one night in the village store. He raised the index-finger of his right hand, pointed it at the company, shook it authoritatively as he spoke, as if to call ocular attention also to his words. "Ef Abel Edwards did make 'way with himself any other way than by jumping into the Dead Hole, *what* did he do with his remains? He couldn't bury himself nohow." Simon Basset chuckled dryly and looked at the others with conclusive triumph. His face was full of converging lines of nose and chin and brows, which seemed to bring it to a general point of craft and astuteness. Even his grizzled hair slanted forward in a stiff cowlick over his forehead, and his face bristled sharply with his gray beard. Simon Basset was the largest land-owner in the village, and the dust and loam of his own acres seemed to have formed a gray grime over all his awkward home-spun garb. Never a woman he met but looked apprehensively at his great, clomping, mud-clogged boots.

It was believed by many that Simon Basset never removed a suit of clothes, after he had once put it on, until it literally dropped from him in rags. He was also said to have argued, when taken to task for this most untidy custom, that birds and animals never shifted their coats until they were worn out, and it behooved men to follow their innocent and natural habits as closely as possible.

Simon Basset, sitting in an old leather-cushioned armchair in the midst of the lounging throng, waited for applause after his conclusive opinion upon Abel Edwards's disappearance; but there were only affirmative grunts from a few. Many had their own views.

"I ain't noways clear in my mind that Abel did kill himself," said a tall man, with a great length of thin, pale whiskers falling over his breast. He had a vaguely elongated effect, like a shadow, and had, moreover, a way of standing behind people like one. When he spoke everybody started and looked around at him.

"I'd like to know what you think did happen to him, Adoniram Judd," cried Simon Basset.

"I don't think Abel Edwards ever killed himself," repeated the tall man, solemnly. His words had weight, for he was a distant relative of the missing man.

"Do you know of anybody that had anything agin him?" demanded Simon Basset.

"No, I dun'no' 's I do," admitted the tall man.

"Then what in creation would anybody want to kill him for? Guess they wouldn't be apt to do it for anything they would get out of Abel Edwards." Simon Basset chuckled triumphantly; and in response there was a loud and exceedingly bitter laugh from a man sitting on an old stool next to him. Everybody started, for the man was Ozias Lamb, Abel Edwards's brother-in-law.

"What ye laughin' at?" inquired Simon Basset, defiantly; but he edged his chair away a little at the same time. Ozias Lamb had the reputation of a very high temper.

"Mebbe," said Ozias Lamb, "somebody killed poor Abel for his mortgage. I dun'no' of anything else he had." Ozias laughed again. He was a stout, squat man, leaning forward upon his knees as he sat, with a complete subsidence of all his muscles, which showed that it was his accustomed attitude. Just in that way had Ozias Lamb sat and cobbled shoes on his lapboard for nearly forty years. He was almost resolved into a statue illustrative of his own toil. He never stood if he could help it; indeed, his knees felt weak under him if he tried to do so. He sank into the first seat and settled heavily forward into his one pose of life.

All the other men looked rather apprehensively at him. His face was all broadened with sardonic laughter, but his blue eyes were fierce under his great bushy head of fair hair. "Abel Edwards has been lugging of that mortgage 'round for the last ten years," said he, "an' it's been about all he had to lug. It's been the meat in his stomach an' the hope in his heart. He 'ain't been a-lookin' forward to eatin', but to payin' up the interest money when it came due; he 'ain't been a-lookin' forward to heaven, but to clearin' off the mortgage. It's been all he's had; it's bore down on his body and his soul, an' it's braced him up to keep on workin'. He's been a-livin' in this Christian town for ten years a-carryin' of this fine mortgage right out in plain sight, an' I shouldn't be a mite surprised if somebody see it an' hankered arter it. Folks are so darned anxious in this 'ere Christian town to get holt of each other's burdens!"

Simon Basset edged his chair away still farther; then he spoke. "Don't s'pose you expected folks to up an' pay Abel Edwards's mortgage for him," he said.

"No, I didn't," returned Ozias Lamb, and the sardonic curves around his mouth deepened.

"An' I don't s'pose you'd expect Doctor Prescott to make him a present of it," said Jake Noyes, suddenly, from the outskirts of the group. He had come in for the doctor's mail, and was lounging with one great red-sealed missive and a religious newspaper in his hand.

"No," said Ozias Lamb, "I shouldn't never expect the doctor to make a present to anybody but himself or the Lord or the meetin'-house."

A general chuckle ran over the group at that. Doctor Prescott was regarded in the village as rather parsimonious except in those three directions.

Jake Noyes colored angrily and stepped forward. "I ain't goin' to hear no nonsense about Doctor Prescott," he exclaimed. "I won't stan' it from none of ye. I give ye fair warnin'. I don't eat no man's flapjacks an' hear him talked agin within swing of my fists if I can help it."

The storekeeper and postmaster, Cyrus Robinson, had been leaning over his counter between the scales and a pile of yellow soap bars, smiling and shrewdly observant. Now he spoke, and the savor of honey for all was in his words.

"It's fust-rate of you, Jake, to stand up for the doctor," said he. "We all of us feel all wrought up about poor Abel. I understand the doctor's goin' to be easy with the widder about the mortgage. I thought likely he would be. Sometimes folks do considerable more good than they get credit for. I shouldn't be surprised if Doctor Prescott's left hand an' his neighbors didn't know all he did."

Ozias Lamb turned slowly around and looked at the storekeeper. "Doctor Prescott's a pretty good customer of yours, ain't he?" he inquired.

There was a subdued titter. Cyrus Robinson colored, but kept his pleasant smile. "Everybody in town is a good customer," said he. "I haven't any bad customers."

"P'r'aps 'cause you won't trust 'em," said Ozias Lamb. This time the titter was audible. Cyrus Robinson's business caution was well known.

The storekeeper said no more, turned abruptly, took a key from his pocket, went to the little post-office in the corner, and locked the door. Then he began putting up the window-shutters.

There was a stir among the company, a scraping of chairs and stools, and a shuffling of heavy feet, and they went lingeringly out of the store. Cyrus Robinson usually put up his shutters too early for them. His store was more than a store — it was the nursery of the town, the place where her little commonweal was evolved and nurtured, and it was also her judgment-seat. There her simple citizens formed their simple opinions upon town government and town officials, upon which they afterwards acted in town meeting. There they sat in judgment upon all men who were not within reach of their voices, and upon all crying evils of the times which were too mighty for them to struggle against. This great country store of Cyrus Robinson's — with its rank odors of molasses and spices, whale oil, and West India rum; with its counters, its floor, its very ceiling heaped and hung with all the paraphernalia of a New England village; its clothes, its food, and its working-utensils — was also in a sense the nucleus of this village of Upham Corners. There was no tavern. Although this was the largest of the little cluster of Uphams, the tavern was in the West Corners, and the stages met there. However, all the industries had centred in Upham Corners on account of its superior water privileges: the grist-mill was there, and the saw-mill. People from the West and East Corners came to trade at Robinson's store, which was also a factory in a limited sense. Cyrus Robinson purchased leather in considerable quantities, and employed several workmen in a great room above the store to cut out the rude shoes worn in the country-side. These he let out in lots to the towns-folk to bind and close and finish, paying them for their work in store goods, seldom in cash, then selling the shoes himself at a finely calculated profit.

Robinson had, moreover, several spare rooms in his house adjoining the store, and there, if he were so disposed, he could entertain strangers who wished to remain in Upham overnight, and neither he nor his wife was averse to increasing their income in that way. Cyrus Robinson was believed by many to be as rich as Doctor Prescott and Simon Basset.

When the men left the store that night, Simon Basset's, Jake Noyes's, and Adoniram Judd's way lay in the same direction. They still discussed poor Abel Edwards's disappearance as they went along. Their voices were rising high, when suddenly Jake Noyes gave Simon Basset a sharp nudge. "Shut up," he whispered; "the Edwards boy's behind us."

And indeed, as he spoke, Jerome's little light figure came running past them. He was evidently anxious to get by without notice, but Simon Basset grasped his arm and brought him to a standstill.

"Hullo!" said he. "You're Abel Edwards's boy, ain't you?"

"I can't stop," said Jerome, pulling away. "I've got to go home. Mother's waiting for me."

"I don't s'pose you've heard anything yet from your father?"

"No, I 'ain't. I've got to go home."

"Where've you been, Jerome?" asked Adoniram Judd.

"Up to Uncle Ozias's to get Elmira's shoes." Jerome had the stout little shoes, one in each hand.

"I don't s'pose you've formed any idee of what's become of your father," said Simon Basset.

Jerome, who had been pulling away from his hold, suddenly stood still, and turned a stern little white face upon him.

"He's dead," said he.

"Yes, of course he's dead. That is, we're all afraid he is, though we all hope for the best; but that ain't the question," said Simon Basset. "The question is, how did he die?"

Jerome looked up in Simon Basset's face. "He died the same way you will, some time," said he. And with that Simon Basset let go his arm suddenly, and he was gone.

"Lord!" said Jake Noyes, under his breath. Simon Basset said not another word; his grandfather, his uncle, and a brother had all taken their own lives, and he knew that the others were thinking of it. They all wondered if the boy had been keen-witted enough to give this hard hit at Simon intentionally, but he had not. Poor little Jerome had never speculated on the laws of heredity; he had only meant to deny that his father had come to any more disgraceful end than the common one of all mankind. He did not dream, as he raced along home with his sister's shoes, of the different construction which they had put upon his words, but he felt angry and injured.

"That Sim' Basset pickin' on me that way," he thought. A wild sense of the helplessness of his youth came over him. "Wish I was a man," he muttered — "wish I was a man; I'd show 'em! All them men talkin' — sayin' anything — 'cause I'm a boy."

Just before he reached home Jerome met two more men, and he heard his father's name distinctly. One of them stretched out a detaining hand as he passed, and called out, "Hullo! you're the Edwards boy?"

"Let me go, I tell you," shouted Jerome, in a fury, and was past them with a wild flourish of heels, like a rebellious colt.

"What in creation ails the boy?" said the man, with a start aside; and he and the other stood staring after Jerome.

When Jerome got home and opened the kitchen door he stood still with surprise. It was almost ten o'clock, and his mother and Elmira had begun to make pies. His mother had pushed herself up to the table and was mixing the pastry, while Elmira was beating eggs.

Mrs. Edwards looked around at Jerome. "What you standin' there lookin' for?" said she, with her sharp, nervous voice. "Put them shoes down, an' bring that quart pail of milk out of the pantry. Be careful you don't spill it."

Jerome obeyed. When he set the milk-pail on the table, Elmira gave him a quick, piteously confidential glance from under her tearful lids. Elmira, with her blue checked pinafore tied under her chin, sat in a high wooden chair, with her little bare feet curling over a round, and beat eggs with a wooden spoon in a great bowl.

"What you doin'?" asked Jerome.

Her mother answered for her. "She's mixin' up some custard for pies," said she. "I dun'no' as there's any need of you standin' lookin' as if you never saw any before."

"Never saw you makin' custard-pies at ten o'clock at night before," returned Jerome, with blunt defiance.

"Do you s'pose," said his mother, "that I'm goin' to let your father go off an' die all alone an' take no notice of it?"

"Dun'no' what you mean?"

"Don't you know it's three days since he went off to get that wood an' never come back?"

Jerome nodded.

"Do you s'pose I'm goin' to let it pass an' die away, an' folks forget him, an' not have any funeral or anything? I made up my mind I'd wait until nine o'clock tonight, an' then, if he wa'n't found, I wouldn't wait any longer. I'd get ready for the funeral. I've sent over for Paulina Maria and your aunt B'lindy to come in an' help. Henry come over here to see if I'd heard anything, and I told him to go right home an' tell his mother to come, an' stop on the way an' tell Paulina Maria. There's a good deal to do before two o'clock tomorrow afternoon, an' I can't do much myself; somebody's got to help. In the mornin' you'll have to take the horse an' go over to the West Corners, an' tell Amelia an' her mother an' Lyddy Stokes's folks. There won't be any time to send word to the Greens over in Westbrook. They're only second-cousins anyway, an' they 'ain't got any horse, an' I dun'no' as they'd think they could afford to hire one. Now you take that fork an' go an' lift the cover off that kettle, an' stick it into the dried apples, an' see if they've begun to get soft."

Ann Edwards's little triangular face had grown plainly thinner and older in three days, but the fire in her black eyes still sparkled. Her voice was strained and hoarse on the high notes, from much lamentation, but she still raised it imperiously. She held the wooden mixing-bowl in her lap, and stirred with as desperate resolution, compressing her lips painfully, as if she were stirring the dregs of her own cup of sorrow.

Pretty soon there were voices outside and steps on the path. The door opened, and two women came in. One was Paulina Maria, Adoniram Judd's wife; the other was Belinda, the wife of Ozias Lamb.

Belinda Lamb spoke first. She was a middle-aged woman, with a pretty faded face. She wore her light hair in curls, which fell over her delicate, thin cheeks, and her blue eyes had no more experience in them than a child's, although they were reddened now with gentle tears. She had the look of a young girl who had been out like a flower in too strong a light, and faded out her pretty tints, but was a young girl still. Belinda always smiled an innocent girlish simper, which sometimes so irritated the austere New England village women that they scowled involuntarily back at her. Paulina Maria Judd and Ann Edwards both scowled without knowing it now as she spoke, her words never seeming to disturb that mildly ingratiating upward curve of her lips.

"I've come right over," said she, in a soft voice; "but it ain't true what Henry said, is it?"

"What ain't true?" asked Ann, grimly.

"It ain't true you're goin' to have a funeral?" Tears welled up afresh in Belinda's blue eyes, and flowed slowly down her delicate cheeks, but not a muscle of her face changed, and she smiled still.

"Why can't I have a funeral?"

"Why, Ann, how can you have a funeral, when there ain't — when they 'ain't found him?"

"I'd like to know why I can't!"

Belinda's blue, weeping eyes surveyed her with the helpless bewilderment of a baby. "Why, Ann," she gasped, "there won't be any — remains!"

"What of that? I guess I know it."

"There won't be nothin' for anybody to go round an' look at; there won't be any coffin — Ann, you ain't goin' to have any coffin when he ain't found, be you?"

"Be you a fool, Belindy Lamb?" said Ann. A hard sniff came from Paulina Maria.

"Well, I didn't s'pose you was," said Belinda, with meek abashedness. "Of course I knew you wasn't — I only asked; but I don't see how you can have a funeral no way, Ann. There won't be any coffin, nor any hearse, nor any procession, nor —"

"There'll be mourners," broke in Ann.

"They're what makes a funeral," said Paulina Maria, putting on an apron she had brought. "Folks that's had funerals knows."

She cast an austere glance at Belinda Lamb, who colored to the roots of her fair curls, and was conscious of a guilty lack of funeral experience, while Paulina Maria had lost seven children, who all died in infancy. Poor Belinda seemed to see the other woman's sternly melancholy face in a halo of little coffins and funeral wreaths.

"I know you've had a good deal more to contend with than I have," she faltered. "I 'ain't never lost anybody till poor — Abel." She broke into gentle weeping, but Paulina Maria thrust a broom relentlessly into her hand.

"Here," said she, "take this broom an' sweep, an' it might as well be done tonight as any time. Of course you 'ain't got your spring cleanin' done, none of it, Ann?"

"No," replied Mrs. Edwards; "I was goin' to begin next week."

"Well," said Paulina Maria, "if this house has got to be all cleaned, an' cookin' done, in time for the funeral, somebody's got to work. I s'pose you expect some out-of-town folks, Ann?"

"I dare say some 'll come from the West Corners. I thought I wouldn't try to get word to Westbrook, it's so far; but mebbe I'd send to Granby — there's some there that might come."

"Well," said Paulina Maria, "I shouldn't be surprised if as many as a dozen came, an' supper 'll have to be got for 'em. What are you goin' to do about black, Ann?"

"I thought mebbe I could borrow a black bonnet an' a veil. I guess my black bombazine dress will do to wear."

"Mis' Whitby had a new one when her mother died, an' didn't use her mother's old one. I don't believe but what you can borrow that," said Paulina Maria. She was moving about the kitchen, doing this and that, waiting for no commands or requests. Jerome and Elmira kept well back out of her way, although she had not half the fierce impetus that their mother sometimes had when hitching about in her chair. Paulina Maria, in her limited field of action, had the quick and unswerving decision of a general, and people marshalled themselves at her nod, whether they would or no. She was an example of the insistence of a type. The prevailing traits of the village women were all intensified and fairly dominant in her. They kept their houses clean, but she kept hers like a temple for the footsteps of divinity. Marvellous tales were told of Paulina Maria's exceeding neatness. It was known for a fact that the boards of her floors were so arranged that they could be lifted from their places and cleaned on their under as well as upper sides. Could Paulina Maria have cleaned the inner as well as the outer surface of her own skin she would doubtless have been better satisfied. As it was, the colorless texture of her thin face and hands, through which the working of her delicate jaws and muscles could be plainly seen, gave an impression of extreme purity and cleanliness. "Paulina Maria looks as ef she'd been put to soak in rain-water overnight," Simon Basset said once, after she had gone out of the store. Everybody called her Paulina Maria — never Mrs. Judd, nor Mrs. Adoniram Judd.

The village women were, as a rule, full of piety. Paulina Maria was austere. She had the spirit to have scourged herself had she once convicted herself of wrong; but that she had never done. The power of self-blame was not in her. Paulina Maria had never labored under conviction of sin; she had had no orthodox conversion; but she set her slim unswerving feet in the paths of righteousness, and walked there with her head up. In her the uncompromising spirit of Puritanism was so strong that it defeated its own ends. The other women were at times inflexible; Paulina Maria was always rigid. The others could be severe; Paulina Maria might have conducted an inquisition. She had in her possibilities of almost mechanical relentlessness which had never been tested in her simple village life. Paulina Maria never shirked her duty, but it could not be said that she performed it in any gentle and Christlike sense. She rather attacked it and slew it, as if it were a dragon in her path. That night she was very weary. She had toiled hard all day at her own vigorous cleaning. Her bones and muscles ached. The spring languor also was upon her. She was not a strong woman, but she never dreamed of refusing to go to Ann Edwards's and assist her in her sad preparations.

She and Belinda Lamb remained and worked until midnight; then they went home. Jerome had to escort them through the silent village street — he had remained up for that purpose. Elmira had been sent to bed. When the boy came home alone along the familiar road, between the houses with their windows gleaming with blank darkness in his eyes, with no sound in his ears save the hoarse bark of a dog when his footsteps echoed past, a great strangeness of himself in his own thoughts was upon him.

He had not the feminine ability to ease descent into the depths of sorrow by catching at all its minor details on the way. He plunged straight down; no questions of funeral preparations or mourning bonnets arrested him for a second. "My father is dead," Jerome told himself; "he jumped into the pond and drowned himself, and here's mother, and Elmira, and the mortgage, and me."

This poor little *me* of the village boy seemed suddenly to have grown in stature, to have bent, as it grew, under a grievous burden, and to have lost all its childish carelessness and childish ambition. Jerome saw himself in the likeness of his father, bearing the mortgage upon his shoulders, and his boyish self never came fully back to him afterwards. The mantle of the departed, that, whether they will or not, covers those that stand nearest, was over him, and he had henceforth to walk under it.

CHAPTER IV

The next morning Paulina Maria and Belinda Lamb returned to finish preparations, and Jerome was sent over to the West Corners to notify some relatives there of the funeral service. Just as he was starting, it was decided that he had better ride some six miles farther to Granby, and see some others who might think they had a claim to an invitation.

"Imogen Lawson an' Sarah were always dreadful touchy," said Mrs. Edwards. "They'll never get over it if they ain't asked. I guess you'd better go there, Jerome."

"Yes, he had," said Paulina Maria.

"It's a real pleasant day, an' I guess they'll enjoy comin'," said Belinda. Paulina Maria gave her a poke with a hard elbow, that hurt her soft side, and she looked at her wonderingly.

"Enjoy!" repeated Ann Edwards, bitterly.

"I dun'no' what you mean," half whimpered Belinda.

"No, I don't s'pose you do," returned Ann. "There's one thing about it — folks can always tell what *you* mean. You don't mean nothin', an' never did. You couldn't be put in a dictionary. Noah Webster couldn't find any meanin' fer you if he was to set up all night." A nervous sob shook Mrs. Edwards's little frame. She was almost hysterical that morning. Her black eyes were brightly dilated, her mouth tremulous, and her throat swollen.

Paulina Maria grasped Belinda by the shoulder. "You'd better get the broom an' sweep out the wood-shed," said she, and Belinda went out with a limp flutter of her cotton skirts and her curls.

Jerome rode the old white horse, that could only travel at a heavy jog, and he did not get home until noon — not much in advance of the funeral guests he had bidden. They had directly left all else, got out what mourning-weeds they could muster, and made ready.

When Jerome reached home, he was immediately seized by Paulina Maria. "Go right out and wash your face and hands real clean," said she, "and then go up-stairs and change your clothes. I've laid them out on the bed. When you get to the neckerchief, you come down here, and I'll tie it for you; it's your father's. You've got to wear somethin' black, to be decent."

Jerome obeyed. All the incipient masculine authority in him was overwhelmed by this excess of feminine strength. He washed his face and hands faithfully, and donned his little clean, coarse shirt and his poor best garments. Then he came down with the black silk neckerchief, and Paulina Maria tied it around his boyish neck.

"His father thought so much of that neckerchief," said Mrs. Edwards, catching her breath. "It was 'most the only thing he bought for himself for ten year that he didn't actually need."

"Jerome is the one to have it," said Paulina Maria, and she made the black silk knot tight and firm.

An hour before the time set for the funeral Ann Edwards was all dressed and ready. They had drawn her chair into the front parlor, and there she sat in state. She wore the borrowed black bonnet and veil. The decent black shawl and gown were her own. The doctor's wife had sent over some black silk gloves, and she wore them. They were much too large. Ann crossed her tiny hands, wrinkled over with the black silk, with long, empty black silk fingers dangling in her lap, over a fine white linen handkerchief. She had laid her gloved hands over the handkerchief with a gesture full of resolution. "I sha'n't give way," she said to Paulina Maria. That meant that, although she took the handkerchief in obedience to custom, it would not be used to dry the tears of affliction.

Ann's face, through the black gloom of her crape veil, revealed only the hard lines of resolution about her mouth and the red stain of tears about her eyes. She held now her emotions in check like a vise.

Jerome and poor little Elmira, whom Paulina Maria had dressed in a little black Canton-crape shawl of her own, sat on either side. Elmira wept now and then, trying to stifle her sobs, but Jerome sat as immovable as his mother.

The funeral guests arrived, and seated themselves solemnly in the rows of chairs which had been borrowed from the neighbors. Adoniram Judd and Ozias Lamb had carried chairs for a good part of the forenoon. Nearly all the village people came; the strange circumstances of this funeral, wherein there was no dead man to carry solemnly in the midst of a long black procession to his grave, had attracted many. Then, too, Abel Edwards had been known to them all since his childhood, and well liked in the main, although the hard grind of his daily life had of late years isolated him from his old mates.

Men sat there with stiff bowed heads, and glances of solemn furtiveness at new-comers, who had played with Abel in his boyhood, and to whom those old memories were more real than those of the last ten years. Abel Edwards, in the absence both of his living soul and his dead body, was present in the minds of many as a sturdy, light-hearted boy.

The people of Upham Corners assembled there together, dressed in their best, displaying their most staid and decorous demeanor, showed their fortunes in life plainly enough. Generally speaking, they were a poor and hard-working folk — poorer and harder working than the average people in villages. Upham Corners, from its hilly site, freely intersected with rock ledges, was not well calculated for profitable farming. The farms therein were mortgaged, and scarcely fed their tillers. The water privileges were good and mills might have flourished, but the greater markets were too far away, and few workmen could be employed.

Most of the women at poor Abel Edwards's funeral were worn and old before their prime, their mouths sunken, wearing old women's caps over their locks at thirty. Their decent best gowns showed that piteous conservation of poverty more painful almost than squalor.

The men were bent and gray with the unseen, but no less tangible, burdens of life. Scarcely one there but bore, as poor Abel Edwards had borne, a mortgage among them. It was a strange thing that although all of the customary mournful accessories of a funeral were wanting, although no black coffin with its silent occupant stood in their midst, and no hearse waited at the door, yet that mortgage of Abel Edwards's — that burden, like poor Christian's, although not of sin, but misfortune, which had doubled him to the dust — seemed still to be present.

The people had the thought of it ever in their minds. They looked at Ann Edwards and her children, and seemed to see in truth the mortgage bearing down upon them, like a very shadow of death.

They looked across at Doctor Seth Prescott furtively, as if he might perchance read their thoughts, and wondered if he would foreclose.

Doctor Prescott, in his broadcloth surtout, with his black satin stock muffling richly his stately neck, sat in the room with the mourners, directly opposite the Edwards family. His wife was beside him. She was a handsome woman, taller and larger than her husband, with a face of gentlest serenity set in shining bands of auburn hair. Mrs. Doctor Prescott looked like an empress among the other women, with her purple velvet pelisse sweeping around her in massive folds, and her purple velvet bonnet with a long ostrich plume curling over the side — the purple being considered a sort of complimentary half mourning. Squire Eben Merritt's wife, Abigail, could not approach her, although she was finely dressed in black satin, and a grand cashmere shawl from overseas. Mrs. Eben Merritt was a small and plain-visaged little woman; people had always wondered why Squire Eben Merritt had married her. Eben Merritt had not come to the funeral. It was afterwards reported that he had gone fishing instead, and people were scandalized, and indignantly triumphant, because it was what they had expected of him. Little Lucina had come with her mother, and sat in the high chair where they had placed her, with her little morocco-shod feet dangling, her little hands crossed in her lap, and her blue eyes looking out soberly and anxiously from her best silk hood. Once in a while she glanced timidly at Jerome, and reflected how he had given her sassafras, and how he hadn't any father.

When the singing began, the tears came into her eyes and her lip quivered; but she tried not to cry, although there were smothered sobs all around her. There was that about the sweet, melancholy drone of the funeral hymn which stirred something more than sympathy in the hearts of the listeners. Imagination of like bereavements for themselves awoke within them, and they wept for their own sorrows in advance.

The minister offered a prayer, in which he made mention of all the members of poor Abel's family, and even distant relatives. In fact, Paulina Maria had furnished him with a list, which he had studied furtively during the singing. "Don't forget any of 'em, or they won't like it," she had charged. So the minister, Solomon Wells, bespoke the comfort and support of the Lord in this affliction for all the second and third cousins upon his list, who bowed their heads with a sort of mournful importance as they listened.

Solomon Wells was an elderly man, tall, and bending limberly under his age like an old willow, his spare long body in nicely kept broadcloth sitting and rising with wide flaps of black coat-tails, his eyes peering forth mildly through spectacles. He was a widower of long standing. His daughter Eliza, who kept his house, sat beside him. She resembled her father closely, and herself looked like an old person anywhere but beside him. There the juvenility of comparison was hers.

Solomon Wells, during the singing, before he offered prayer, had cast sundry perplexed glances at a group of strangers on his right, and then at his list. He was quite sure that they were not mentioned thereon. Once he looked perplexedly at Paulina Maria, but she was singing hard, in a true strong voice, and did not heed him. The strangers sat behind her. There was a large man, lumbering and uncomfortable in his best clothes, a small woman, and three little girls, all dressed in blue delaine gowns and black silk mantillas and blue bonnets.

The minister had a strong conviction that these people should be mentioned in his prayer. He gave his daughter Eliza a little nudge, and looked inquiringly at them and at her, but she shook her head slightly — she did not know who they were. Her father had to content himself with vaguely alluding in his petition to all other relatives of this afflicted family.

During the eulogy upon the departed, which followed, he made also casual mention of the respect in which he was held by strangers as well as by his own towns-people. The minister gave poor Abel a very good character. He spoke at length of his honesty, industry, and sobriety. He touched lightly upon the unusual sadness of the circumstances of his death. He expressed no doubt; he gave no hints of any dark tragedy. "Don't speak as if you thought he killed himself; if you do, it'll make her about crazy," Paulina Maria had charged him. Ann, listening jealously to every word, could take no exception to one. Solomon Wells was very mindful of the feelings of others. He seemed at times to move with a sidewise motion of his very spirit to avoid hurting theirs.

After dwelling upon Abel Edwards's simple virtues, fairly dinning them like sweet notes into the memories of his neighbors, Solomon Wells, with a sweep of his black coat-skirts around him, sat down. Then there was a solemn and somewhat awkward pause. The people looked at each other; they did not know what to do next. All the customary routine of a funeral was disturbed. The next step in the regular order of funeral exercises was to pass decorously around a coffin, pause a minute, bend over it with a long last look at the white face therein; the next, to move out of the room and take places in the funeral procession. Now that was out of the question; they were puzzled as to further proceedings.

Doctor Seth Prescott made the first move. He arose, and his wife after him, with a soft rustle of her silken skirts. They both went up to Ann Edwards, shook hands, and went out of the room. After them Mrs. Squire Merritt, with Lucina in hand, did likewise; then everybody else, except the relatives and the minister and his daughter.

After the decorous exit of the others, the relatives sat stiffly around the room and waited. They knew there was to be a funeral supper, for the fragrance of sweet cake and tea was strong over all the house. There had been some little doubt concerning it among the out-of-town relatives: some had opined that there would be none, on account of the other irregularities of the exercises; some had opined that the usual supper would be provided. The latter now sniffed and nodded triumphantly at the others — particularly Amelia Stokes's childish old mother. She, half hidden in the frills of a great mourning-bonnet and the folds of a great black shawl, kept repeating, in a sharp little gabble, like a child's: "I smell the tea, 'Melia — I do, I smell it. Yes, I do — I told ye so. I tell ye, I smell the tea."

Poor Amelia Stokes, who was a pretty, gentle-faced spinster, could not hush her mother, whisper as pleadingly as she might into the sharp old ear in the bonnet-frills. The old woman was full of the desire for tea, and could scarcely be restrained from following up its fragrant scent at once.

The two Lawson sisters sat side by side, their sharp faces under their black bonnets full of veiled alertness. Nothing escaped them; they even suspected the truth about Ann's bonnet and gloves. Ann still sat with her gloved hands crossed in her lap and her black veil over her strained little face. She did not move a muscle; but in the midst of all her restrained grief the sight of the large man, the woman, and the three girls in the blue thibets, the black silk mantillas, and the blue bonnets filled her with a practical dismay. They were the relatives from Westbrook, who had not been bidden to the funeral. They must have gotten word in some irregular manner, and the woman held her blue-bonneted head with a cant of war, which Ann knew well of old.

For a little while there was silence, except for Paulina Maria's heavy tramp and the soft shuffle of Belinda Lamb's cloth shoes out in the kitchen. They were hurrying to get the supper in readiness. Another appetizing odor was now stealing over the house, the odor of baking cream-of-tartar biscuits.

Suddenly, with one accord, as if actuated by one mental impulse, the little woman, the large man, and the three girls arose and advanced upon Ann Edwards. She grasped the arm of her chair hard, as if bracing herself to meet a shock.

The little woman spoke. Her eyes seemed full of black sparks, her voice shook, red spots flamed out in her cheeks. "We'll bid you good-bye now, Cousin Ann," said she.

"Ain't you going to stay and have some supper?" asked Ann. Her manner was at once defiant and conciliatory.

Then the little woman made her speech. All the way from her distant village, in the rear gloom of the covered wagon, she had been composing it. She delivered it with an assumption of calm dignity, in spite of her angry red cheeks and her shaking voice. "Cousin Ann," said the little woman, "me and mine go nowhere

where we are not invited. We came to the funeral — though you didn't see fit to even tell us when it was, and we only heard of it by accident from the butcher — out of respect to poor Abel. He was my own second-cousin, and our folks used to visit back and forth a good deal before he was married. I felt as if I must come to his funeral, whether I was wanted or not, because I know if he'd been alive he'd said to come; but staying to supper is another thing. I am sorry for you, Cousin Ann; we are all sorry for you in your affliction. We all hope it may be sanctified to you; but I don't feel, and 'Lisha and the girls don't feel, as if we could stay and eat victuals in a house where we've been shown very plainly we ain't wanted."

Then Ann spoke, and her voice was unexpectedly loud. "You haven't any call to think you wasn't all welcome," said she. "You live ten miles off, and I hadn't a soul to send but Jerome, with a horse that can't get out of a walk. I didn't know myself there'd be a funeral for certain till yesterday. There wasn't time to send for you. I thought of it, but I knew there wouldn't be time to get word to you in season for you to start. You might, as long as you're a professing Christian, Eloise Green, have a little mercy in a time like this." Ann's voice quavered a little, but she set her mouth harder.

The large man nudged his wife and whispered something. He drew the back of his rough hand across his eyes. The three little blue-clad girls stood toeing in, dangling their cotton-gloved hands.

"I thought you might have sent word by the butcher," said the little woman. Her manner was softer, but she wanted to cover her defeat well.

"I couldn't think of butchers and all the wherewithals," said Ann, with stern dignity. "I didn't think Abel's relations would lay it up against me if I didn't."

The large man's face worked; tears rolled down his great cheeks. He pulled out a red handkerchief and wiped his eyes.

"You'd ought to had a white handkerchief, father," whispered the little woman; then she turned to Ann. "I'm sure I don't want to lay up anything," said she.

"I don't think you have any call to," responded Ann. "I haven't anything more to say. If you feel like staying to supper I shall be glad to have you, but I don't feel as if I had strength to urge anybody."

The large man sobbed audibly in his red handkerchief. His wife cast an impatient glance at him. "Well, if that is the way it was, of course we shall all be happy to stay and have a cup of tea," said she. "We've got a long ride before us, and I don't feel quite as well as common this spring. Of course I didn't understand how it happened, and I felt kind of hurt; it was only natural. I see how it was, now. 'Lisha, hadn't you better slip out and see how the horse is standing?" The little woman thrust her own white handkerchief into her husband's hand as he started. "You put that red one under the wagon seat," she whispered loud in his ear. Then she and the little girls in blue returned to their chairs. The rest of the company had been listening with furtive attention. Jerome had been trembling with indignation at his mother's side. He looked at the large man, and wondered impatiently why he did not shake that small woman, since he was able. There was as yet no leniency on the score of sex in the boy. He would have well liked to fly at that little wrathful body who was attacking his mother, and also blaming him for not riding those ten miles to notify her of the funeral. He scowled hard at her and the three little girls after they had returned to their seats. One of the girls, a pretty child with red curls, caught his frown, and stared at him with scared but fascinated blue eyes.

Supper was announced shortly. Belinda Lamb, instigated by Paulina Maria, stood in the door and said, with melancholy formality, "Will you come out now and have a little refreshment before you go home?"

Ann did not stir. The others went out lingeringly, holding back for politeness' sake; she sat still with her black veil over her face and her black gloved hands crossed in her lap. Paulina Maria came to her and tried to induce her to remove her bonnet and have some tea with the rest, but she shook her head. "I want to just sit here and keep still till they're gone," said she.

She sat there. Some of the others came and added their persuasions to Paulina Maria's, but she was firm. Jerome remained beside his mother; Elmira had been bidden to go into the other room and help wait upon the company.

"There's room for Jerome at the table, if you ain't coming," said Paulina Maria to Ann; but Jerome answered for himself.

"I'll wait till that crowd are gone," said he, with a fierce gesture.

"You wouldn't speak that way if you were my boy," said Paulina Maria.

Jerome muttered under his breath that he wasn't her boy. Paulina Maria cast a stern glance at him as she went out.

"Don't you be saucy, Jerome Edwards," Ann said, in a sharp whisper through her black veil. "She's done a good deal for us."

"I'd like to kill the whole lot!" said the boy, clinching his little fist.

"Hold your tongue! You're a wicked, ungrateful boy!" said his mother; but all the time she had a curious sympathy with him. Poor Ann was seized with a strange unreasoning rancor against all that decorously feeding company in the other room. There are despairing moments, when the happy seem natural enemies of the miserable, and Ann was passing through them. As she sat there in her gloomy isolation of widowhood, her black veil and her dark thoughts coloring her whole outlook on life, she felt a sudden fury of blindness against all who could see. Had she been younger, she would have given vent to her emotion like Jerome. Her son seemed the very expression of her own soul, although she rebuked him.

The people were a long time at supper. The funeral cake was sweet to their tongues, and the tea mildly exhilarating. When they came at last to bid farewell to Ann there was in their faces a pleasant unctuousness which they could not wholly veil with sympathetic sorrow. The childish old lady was openly hilarious. "That was the best cup o' tea I ever drinked," she whispered loud in Ann's ear. Jerome gave a scowl of utter contempt at her. When they were all gone, and the last covered wagon had rolled out of the yard, Ann allowed Paulina Maria to divest her of her bonnet and gloves and bring her a cup of tea. Jerome and Elmira ate their supper at one end of the disordered table; then they both worked hard, under the orders of Paulina Maria, to set the house in order. It was quite late that night before Jerome was at liberty to creep off to his own bed up in the slanting back chamber. Paulina Maria and Belinda Lamb had gone home, and the bereaved family were all alone in the house. Jerome's boyish heart ached hard, but he was worn out physically, and he soon fell asleep.

About midnight he awoke with a startling sound in his ears. He sat up in bed and listened, straining ears and eyes in the darkness. Out of the night gloom and stillness below came his mother's voice, raised loud and hoarse in half accusatory prayer, not caring who heard, save the Lord.

"What hast thou done, O Lord?" demanded this daring and pitiful voice. "Why hast thou taken away from me the husband of my youth? What have I done to deserve it? Haven't I borne patiently the yoke Thou laidst upon me before? Why didst Thou try so hard one already broken on the wheel of Thy wrath? Why didst Thou drive a good man to destruction? O Lord, give me back my husband, if Thou art the Lord! If Thou art indeed the

Almighty, prove it unto me by working this miracle which I ask of Thee! Give me back Abel! give him back!"

Ann's voice arose with a shriek; then there was silence for a little space. Presently she spoke again, but no longer in prayer — only in bitter, helpless lament. She used no longer the formal style of address to a Divine Sovereign; she dropped into her own common vernacular of pain.

"It ain't any use! it ain't any use!" she wailed out. "If there is a God He won't hear me, He won't help me, He won't bring him back. He only does His own will forever. Oh, Abel, Abel, Abel! Oh, my husband! Where are you? where are you? Where is the head that I've held on my breast? Where are the lips I have kissed? I couldn't even see him laid safe in his grave — not even that comfort! Oh, Abel, Abel, my husband, my husband! my own flesh and my own soul, torn away from me, and I left to draw the breath of life! Abel, Abel, come back, come back, come back!"

Ann Edwards's voice broke into inarticulate sobs and moans; then she did not speak audibly again. Jerome lay back in his bed, cold and trembling. Elmira, in the next chamber, was sound asleep, but he slept no more that night. A revelation of the love and sorrow of this world had come to him through his mother's voice. He was shamed and awed and overwhelmed by this glimpse of the nakedness of nature and that mighty current which swept him on with all mankind. The taste of knowledge was all at once upon the boy's soul.

CHAPTER V

The next morning Jerome arose at dawn, and crept downstairs noiselessly on his bare feet, that he might not awake his mother. However, still as he was, he had hardly crossed the threshold of the kitchen before his mother called to him from her bedroom, the door of which stood open.

"Who's that?" called Ann Edwards, in a strained voice; and Jerome knew that she had a wild hope that it was his father's step she heard instead of his. The boy caught his breath, hesitating a second, and his mother called again: "Who's that? Who's that out in the kitchen?"

"It's only me," answered Jerome, with that most pitiful of apologies in his tone — the apology for presence and very existence in the stead of one more beloved.

His mother drew a great shuddering sigh. "Come in here," she called out, harshly, and Jerome went into the bedroom and stood beside her bed. The curtain was not drawn over the one window, and the little homely interior was full of the pale dusk of dawn. This had been Ann Edwards's bridal chamber, and her children had been born there. The face of that little poor room was as familiar to Jerome as the face of his mother. From his earliest memory the high bureau had stood against the west wall, near the window, and a little round table, with a white towel and a rosewood box on it, in the corner at the head of the great high-posted bedstead, which filled the rest of the room, with scant passageway at the foot and one side. Ann's little body scarcely raised the patchwork quilt on the bed; her face, sunken in the feather pillows, looked small and weazened as a sick child's in the dim light. She reached out one little bony hand, clutched Jerome's poor jacket, and pulled him close. "What's goin' to be done?" she demanded, querulously. "What's goin' to be done? Do you know what's goin' to be done, Jerome Edwards?"

The boy stared at her, and her sharply questioning eyes struck him dumb.

Ann Edwards had always been the dominant spirit in her own household. The fact that she was so, largely on masculine sufferance, had never been fully recognized by herself or others. Now, for the first time, the stratum of feminine dependence and helplessness, which had underlain all her energetic assertion, was made manifest, and poor little Jerome was spurred out of his boyhood into manhood to meet this new demand.

"What's goin' to be done?" his mother cried again. "Why

don't you speak, Jerome Edwards?"

Then Jerome drew himself up, and a new look came into his face. "I've been thinkin' of it over," he said, soberly, "an' — I've got a plan."

"What's goin' to be done?" Ann raised herself in bed by her clutch at her son's arm. Then she let go, and rocked herself to and fro, hugging herself with her little lean arms, and wailing weakly. "What's goin' to be done? Oh, oh! what's goin' to be done? Abel's dead, he's dead, and Doctor Prescott, he holds the mortgage. We 'ain't got any money, or any home. What's goin' to be done? What's goin' to be done? Oh, oh, oh, oh!"

Jerome grasped his mother by the shoulder and tried to force her back upon her pillows. "Come, mother, lay down," said he.

"I won't! I won't! I never will. What's goin' to be done? What's goin' to be done?"

"Mother, you lay right down and stop your cryin'," said Jerome; and his mother started, and hushed, and stared at him, for his voice sounded like his father's. The boy's wiry little hands upon her shoulders, and his voice like his father's, constrained her strongly, and she sank back; and her face appeared again, like a thin wedge of piteous intelligence, in the great feather pillow.

"Now you lay still, mother," said Jerome, and to his mother's excited eyes he looked taller and taller, as if in very truth this sudden leap of his boyish spirit into the stature of a man had forced his body with it. He straightened the quilt over his mother's meagre shoulders. "I'm goin' to start the fire," said he, "and put on the hasty-pudding, and when it's all ready I'll call Elmira, and we'll help you up."

"What's goin' to be done?" his mother quavered again; but this time feebly, as if her fierce struggles were almost hushed by contact with authority.

"I've got a plan," said Jerome. "You just lay still, mother, and I'll see what's best."

Ann Edwards's eyes rolled after the boy as he went out of the room, but she lay still, obediently, and said not another word. An unreasoning confidence in this child seized upon her. She leaned strongly upon what, until now, she had held the veriest reed — to her own stupefaction and with doubtful content, but no resistance. Jerome seemed suddenly no longer her son; the memory of the time when she had cradled and swaddled him failed her. The spirit of his father awakened in him filled her at once with strangeness and awed recognition.

She heard the boy pattering about in the kitchen, and, in spite of herself, the conviction that his father was out there, doing the morning task which had been his for so many years, was strong upon her.

When at length Jerome and Elmira came and told her breakfast was ready, and assisted her to rise and dress, she was as unquestioningly docile as if the relationship between them were reversed. When she was seated in her chair she even forbore, as was her wont, to start immediately with sharp sidewise jerks of her rocker, but waited until her children pushed and drew her out into the next room, up to the breakfast-table. There were, moreover, no sharp commands and chidings as to the household tasks that morning. Jerome and Elmira did as they would, and their mother sat quietly and ate her breakfast.

Elmira kept staring at her mother, and then glancing uneasily at Jerome. Her pretty face was quite pale that morning, and her eyes looked big. She moved hesitatingly, or with sharp little runs of decision. She went often to the window and stared down the road — still looking for her father; for hope dies hard in youth, and she had words of triumph at the sight of him all ready upon her tongue. Her mother's strange demeanor frightened her, and made her almost angry. She was too young to grasp any but the more familiar phases of grief, and revelations of character were to her revolutions.

She beckoned her brother out of the room the first chance she got, and questioned him.

"What ails mother?" she whispered, out in the woodshed, holding to the edge of his jacket and looking at him with piteous, scared eyes.

Jerome stood with his shoulders back, and seemed to look down at her from his superior height of courageous spirit, though she was as tall as he.

"She's come to herself," said Jerome.

"She wasn't ever like this before."

"Yes, she was — inside. She ain't anything but a woman. She's come to herself."

Elmira began to sob nervously, still holding to her brother's jacket, not trying to hide her convulsed little face. "I don't care, she scares me," she gasped, under her breath, lest her mother hear. "She ain't any way I've ever seen her. I'm 'fraid she's goin' to be crazy. I'm dreadful 'fraid mother's goin' to be crazy, Jerome."

"No, she ain't," said Jerome. "She's just come to herself, I tell you."

"Father's dead and mother's crazy, and Doctor Prescott has

got the mortgage," wailed Elmira, in an utter rebellion of grief.

Jerome caught her by the arm and pulled her after him at a run, out of the shed, into the cool spring morning air. So early in the day, with no stir of life except the birds in sight or sound, the new grass and flowering branches and blooming distances seemed like the unreal heaven of a dream; and, indeed, nothing save their own dire strait of life was wholly tangible and met them but with shocks of unfamiliar things.

Jerome, out in the yard, took his sister by both arms, piteously slender and cold through their thin gingham sleeves, and shook her hard, and shook her again.

"Jerome Edwards, what — you doin' — so — for?" she gasped.

"'Ain't you got anything to you? 'Ain't you got anything to you at all?" said Jerome, fiercely.

"I — don't know what you mean! Don't, Jerome — don't! Oh, Jerome, I'm 'fraid you're crazy, like mother?"

"'Ain't you got enough to you," said Jerome, still shaking her as if she had not spoken, "to control your feelin's and do up the housework nice, and not kill mother?"

"Yes, I will — I'll be just as good as I can. You know I will. Don't, Jerome! I 'ain't cried before mother this mornin'. You know I 'ain't."

"You cried loud enough, just now in the shed, so she could hear you."

"I won't again. Don't, Jerome!"

"You're 'most a grown-up woman," said Jerome, ceasing to shake his sister, but holding her firm, and looking at her with sternly admonishing eyes. "You're 'most as old as I be, and I've got to take care of you all. It's time you showed it if there's anything to you."

"Oh, Jerome, you look just like father," whispered Elmira, suddenly, with awed, fascinated eyes on his face.

"Now you go in and wash up the dishes, and sweep the kitchen, and make up the beds, and don't you cry before mother or say anything to pester her," said Jerome.

"What you goin' to do, Jerome?" Elmira asked, timidly.

"I'm goin' to take care of the horse and finish plantin' them beans first."

"What you goin' to do then?"

"Somethin' — you wait and see." Jerome spoke with his first betrayal of boyish weakness, for a certain importance crept into his tone.

Elmira instinctively recognized it, and took advantage of it.

"Ain't you goin' to ask mother, Jerome Edwards?" she said.

"I'm goin' to do what's best," answered Jerome; and again that uncanny gravity of authority which so awed her was in his face.

When he again bade her go into the house and do as he said, she obeyed with a longing, incredulous look at him.

Jerome had not eaten much breakfast; indeed, he had not finished when Elmira had beckoned him out. But he said to himself that he did not want any more — he would go straight about his tasks.

Jerome, striking out through the dewy wind of foot-path towards the old barn, heard suddenly a voice calling him by name. It was a voice as low and heavy as a man's, but had a nervous feminine impulse in it. "Jerome!" it called. "Jerome Edwards!"

Jerome turned, and saw Paulina Maria coming up the road, walking with a firm, swaying motion of her whole body from her feet, her cotton draperies blowing around her like sheathing-leaves.

Jerome stood still a minute, watching her; then he went back to the house, to the door, and stationed himself before it. He stood there like a sentinel when Paulina Maria drew near. The meaning of war was in his shoulder, his expanded boyish chest, his knitted brows, set chin and mouth, and unflinching eyes; he needed only a sword or gun to complete the picture.

Paulina Maria stopped, and looked at him with haughty wonder. She was not yet intimidated, but she was surprised, and stirred with rising indignation.

"How's your mother this morning, Jerome?" said she.

"Well 's she can be," replied Jerome, gruffly, with a wary eye upon her skirts when they swung out over her advancing knee; for Paulina Maria was minded to enter the house with no further words of parley. He gathered himself up, in all his new armor of courage and defiance, and stood firm in her path.

"I'm going in to see your mother," said Paulina Maria, looking at him as if she suspected she did not understand aright.

"No, you ain't," returned Jerome.

"What do you mean?"

"You ain't goin' in to see my mother this mornin'."

"Why not, I'd like to know?"

"She's got to be kept still and not see anybody but us, or she'll be sick."

"I guess it won't hurt her any to see me." Paulina Maria turned herself sidewise, thrust out a sharp elbow, and prepared to force herself betwixt Jerome and the door-post like a wedge.

"You stand back!" said Jerome, and fixed his eyes upon her face.

Paulina Maria turned pale. "What do you mean, actin' so?" she said, again. "Did your mother tell you not to let me in?"

"Mother's got to be kept still and not see anybody but us, or she'll be sick. I ain't goin' to have anybody come talkin' to her today," said Jerome, with his eyes still fixed upon Paulina Maria's face.

Paulina Maria was like a soldier whose courage is invincible in all tried directions. Up to all the familiar and registered batteries of life she could walk without flinching, and yield to none; but here was something new, which savored perchance of the uncanny, and a power not of the legitimate order of things. There was something frightful and abnormal to her in Jerome's pale face, which did not seem his own, his young eyes full of authority of age, and the intimation of repelling force in his slight, childish form.

Paulina Maria might have driven a fierce watch-dog from her path with her intrepid will; she might have pushed aside a stouter arm in her way; but this defence, whose persistence in the face of apparent feebleness seemed to indicate some supernatural power, made her quail. From her spare diet and hard labor, from her cleanliness and rigid holding to one line of thought and life, the veil of flesh and grown thin and transparent, like any ascetic's of old, and she was liable to a ready conception of the abnormal and supernatural.

With one half stern, half fearful glance at the forbidding child in her path, she turned about and went away, pausing, however, in the vantage-point of the road and calling back in an indignant voice, which trembled slightly, "You needn't think you're goin' to send folks home this way many times, Jerome Edwards!" Then, with one last baffled glance at the pale, strange little figure in the Edwards door, she went home, debating grimly with herself over her weakness and her groundless fear.

Jerome waited until she was out of sight, gave one last look down the road to be sure no other invaders were approaching his fortress, and then went on to the barn. When he rolled back the door and entered, the old white horse stirred in his stall and turned to look at him. There was something in the glance over the shoulder of that long white face which caused the heart of the boy to melt within him. He pressed into the stall, flung up his little arms around the great neck, and sobbed and sobbed, his face hid against the heaving side.

The old horse had looked about, expecting to see Jerome's father coming to feed and harness him into the wood-wagon, and Jerome knew it, and there was something about the consciousness of loss and sorrow of this faithful dumb thing which smote him in a weaker place than all human intelligence of it.

Abel Edwards had loved this poor animal well, and had set great store by his faithful service; and the horse had loved him, after the dumb fashion of his kind, and, indeed, not sensing that he was dead, loved him still, with a love as for the living, which no human being could compass. Jerome, clinging to this dumb beast, to which alone the love of his father had not commenced, by those cruel and insensible gradations, to become the memory which is the fate, as inevitable as death itself, of all love when life is past, felt for the minute all his new strength desert him, and relapsed into childhood and clinging grief. "You loved him, didn't you?" he whispered between his sobs. "You loved poor father, didn't you, Peter?" And when the horse turned his white face and looked at him, with that grave contemplation seemingly indicative of a higher rather than a lower intelligence, with which an animal will often watch human emotion, he sobbed and sobbed again, and felt his heart fail him at the realization of his father's death, and of himself, a poor child, with the burden of a man upon his shoulders. But it was only for a few minutes that he yielded thus, for the stature of the mind of the boy had in reality advanced, and soon he drew himself up to it, stopped weeping, led the horse out to the well, drew bucket after bucket of water, and held them patiently to his plashing lips. Then a neighbor in the next house, a half acre away, looking across the field, called her mother to see how much Jerome Edwards looked like his father. "It gave me quite a turn when I see him come out, he looked so much like his father, for all he's so small," said she. "He walked out just like him; I declare, I didn't know but he'd come back."

Jerome, leading the horse, walked back to the barn in his father's old tracks, with his father's old gait, reproducing the dead with the unconscious mimicry of the living, while the two women across the field watched him from their window. "It ain't a good sign — he's got a hard life before him," said the older of the two, who had wild blue eyes under a tousle of gray hair, and was held in somewhat dubious repute because of spiritualistic tendencies.

"Guess he'll have a hard life enough, without any signs — most of us do. He won't have to make shirts, anyhow," rejoined her daughter, who had worn out her youth with fine stitching of linen shirts for a Jew peddler. Then she settled back over her needle-work with a heavy sigh, indicative of a return from the troubles of others to her own.

Jerome fed the old horse, and rubbed him down carefully. "Sha'n't be sold whilst I'm alive," he assured him, with a stern nod, as he combed out his forelock, and the animal looked at him again, with that strange attention which is so much like the attention of understanding.

After his tasks in the barn were done Jerome went out to the sloping garden and finished planting the beans. He could see Elmira's smooth dark head passing to and fro before the house windows, and knew that she was fulfilling his instructions.

He kept a sharp watch upon the road for other female friends of his mother's, who, he was resolved, should not enter.

"Them women will only get her all stirred up again. She's got to get used to it, and they'll just hinder her," he said, quite aloud to himself, having in some strange fashion discovered the truth that the human mind must adjust itself to its true balance after the upheaval of sorrow.

After the beans were planted it was only nine o'clock. Jerome went soberly down the garden-slope, stepping carefully between the planted ridges, then into the house, with a noiseless lift of the latch and glide over the threshold; for Elmira signalled him from the window to be still.

His mother sat in her high-backed rocker, fast asleep, her sharp eyes closed, her thin mouth gaping, an expression of vacuous peace over her whole face, and all her wiry little body relaxed. Jerome motioned to Elmira, and the two tiptoed out across the little front entry to the parlor.

"How long has she been asleep?" whispered Jerome.

"'Most an hour. You don't s'pose mother's goin' to die too, do you, Jerome?"

"Course she ain't."

"I never saw her go to sleep in the daytime before. Mother don't act a mite like herself. She 'ain't spoke out to me once this mornin'," poor little Elmira whimpered; but her brother hushed her, angrily.

"Don't you know enough to keep still — a great big girl like you?" he said.

"Jerome, I have. I 'ain't cried a mite before her, and she couldn't hear that," whispered Elmira, chokingly.

"Mother's got awful sharp ears, you know she has," insisted Jerome. "Now I'm goin' away, and don't you let anybody come in here while I'm gone and bother mother."

"I'll have to let Cousin Paulina Maria and Aunt Belinda in, if they come," said Elmira, staring at him wonderingly. Neither she nor her mother knew that Paulina Maria had already been there and been turned away.

"You just lock the house up, and not go to the door," said Jerome, decisively.

Elmira kept staring at him, as if she doubted her eyes and ears. She felt a certain awe of her brother. "Where you goin'?" she inquired, half timidly.

"I'll tell you when I get back," replied Jerome. He went out with dignity, and Elmira heard him on the stairs. "He's goin' to dress up," she thought.

She sat down by the window, well behind the curtain, that any one approaching might not see her, and waited. She had wakened that morning as into a new birth of sense, and greeted the world with helpless childish weeping, but now she was beginning to settle comfortably into this strange order of things. Her face, as she sat thus, wore the ready curves of smiles instead of tears. Elmira was one whose strength would always be in dependence. Now her young brother showed himself, as if by a miracle, a leader and a strong prop, and she could assume again her natural attitude of life and growth. She was no longer strange to herself in these strange ways, and that was wherein all the bitterness of strangeness lay.

When Jerome came down-stairs, in his little poor best jacket and trousers and his clean Sunday shirt, she stood in the door and looked at him curiously, but with a perfect rest of confidence.

Jerome looked at her with dignity, and yet with a certain childish importance, without which he would have ceased to be himself at all. "Look out for mother," he whispered, admonishingly, and went out, holding his head up and his shoulders back, and feeling his sister's wondering and admiring eyes upon him, with a weakness of pride, and yet with no abatement of his strength of purpose, which was great enough to withstand self-recognition.

The boy that morning had a new gait when he had once started down the road. The habit of his whole life — and, more than that, an inherited habit — ceased to influence him. This new exaltation of spirit controlled even bones and muscles.

Jerome, now he had fairly struck out in life with a purpose of his own, walked no longer like his poor father, with that bent shuffling lope of worn-out middle age. His soul informed his whole body, and raised it above that of any simple animal that seeks a journey's end. His head was up and steady, as if he bore a treasure-jar on it, his back flat as a soldier's; he swung his little arms at his sides and advanced with proud and even pace.

Jerome's old gaping shoes were nicely greased, and he himself had made a last endeavor to close the worst apertures with a bit of shoemaker's thread. He had had quite a struggle with himself, before starting, regarding these forlorn old shoes and another pair, spick and span and black, and heavily clamping with thick new soles, which Uncle Ozias Lamb had sent over for him to wear to the funeral.

"He sent 'em over, an' says you may wear 'em to the funeral, if you're real careful," his aunt Belinda had said, and then added, with her gentle sniff of deprecation and apology: "He says you'll have to give 'em back again — they ain't to keep. He says he's got so behindhand lately he 'ain't got any tithes to give to the Lord. He says he 'ain't got nothing that will divide up into ten parts, 'cause he 'ain't got more'n half one whole part himself." Belinda Lamb repeated her husband's bitter saying out of his heart of poverty with a scared look, and yet with a certain relish and soft aping of his defiant manner.

"I don't want anybody to give when I can't give back again," Ann had returned. "Ozias has always done full as much for us as we've done for him." Then she had charged Jerome to be careful of the shoes, and not stub the toes, so his uncle would have difficulty in selling them.

"I'll wear my old shoes," Jerome had replied, sullenly, but then had been borne down by the chorus of feminine rebuke and misunderstanding of his position. They thought, one and all, that he was wroth because the shoes were not given to him, and the very pride which forbade him to wear them constrained him to do so.

However, this morning he had looked at them long, lifted them and weighed them, turning them this way and that, put them on his feet and stood contemplating them. He was ashamed to wear his old broken shoes to call on grand folks, but he was too proud and too honest, after all, to wear these borrowed ones.

So he stepped along now with an occasional uneasy glance at his feet, but with independence in his heart. Jerome walked straight down the road to Squire Eben Merritt's. The cut across the fields would have been much shorter, for the road made a great curve for nearly half a mile, but the boy felt that the dignified highway was the only route for him, bent on such errands, in his best clothes.

CHAPTER VI

Squire Eben Merritt's house stood behind a file of dark pointed evergreen trees, which had grown and thickened until the sunlight never reached the house-front, which showed, in consequence, green patches of moss and mildew. One entering had, moreover, to turn out, as it were, for the trees, and take a circuitous route around them to the right to the front-door path, which was quite slippery with a film of green moss.

There had been, years ago, a gap betwixt the trees — a gate's width — but now none could enter unless the branches were lopped, and Eben Merritt would not allow that. His respect for that silent file of sylvan giants, keeping guard before his house against winds and rains and fierce snows, was greater than his hospitality and concern for the ease of guests. "Let 'em go round — it won't hurt 'em," he would say, with his great merry laugh, when his wife sometimes suggested that the old gateway should be repaired. However, it was only a few times during the year that the matter disturbed her, for she was not one to falter long at the small stumbling-blocks of life; a cheerful skip had she over them, or a placid glide aside. When she had the minister's daughter and other notable ladies to tea, who held it due to themselves to enter the front door, she was somewhat uneasy lest they draggle their fine petticoats skirting the trees, especially if the grass was dewy or there was snow; otherwise, she cared not. The Squire's friends, who often came in muddy boots, preferred the east-side door, which was in reality good enough for all but ladies coming to tea, having three stone steps, a goodly protecting hood painted green, with sides of lattice-work, and opening into a fine square hall, with landscape-paper on the walls, whence led the sitting-room and the great middle room, where the meals were served.

Jerome went straight round to this side door and raised the knocker. He had to wait a little while before any one came, and looked about him. He had been in Squire Eben Merritt's east yard before, but now he had a sense of invasion which gave it new meanings for him. A great straggling rose-vine grew over the hood of the door, and its young leaves were pricking through the lattice-work; it was old and needed trimming; there were many long barren shoots of last year. However, Squire Merritt guarded jealously the freedom of the rose, and would not have it meddled with, arguing that it had thriven thus since the time of his grandfather, who had planted it; that this was its natural condition of growth, and it would die if pruned.

Jerome looked out of this door-arbor, garlanded with the old rose-vine, into a great yard, skirted beyond the driveway with four great flowering cherry-trees, so old that many of the boughs would never bud again, and thrust themselves like skeleton arms of death through the soft masses of bloom out into the blue. One tree there was which had scarcely any boughs left, for the winds had taken them, and was the very torso of a tree; but Squire Eben Merritt would not have even that cut, for he loved a tree past its usefulness as faithfully as he loved an animal. "Well do I remember the cherries I used to eat off that tree, when I was so high," Eben Merritt would say. "Many a man has done less to earn a good turn from me than this old tree, which has fed me with its best fruit. Do you think I'll turn and kill it now?"

He had the roots of the old trees carefully dug about and tended, though not a dead limb lopped. Nurture, and not surgery, was the doctrine of Squire Merritt. "Let the earth take what it gave," he said; "I'll not interfere."

Jerome had heard these sayings of Squire Merritt's about the trees. They had been repeated, because people thought such ideas queer and showing lack of common-sense. He had heard them unthinkingly, but now, standing on Squire Merritt's door-step, looking at his old tree pensioners, whom he would not desert in their infirmity, he remembered, and the great man's love for his trees gave him reason, with a sudden leap of faith, to believe in his kindness towards him. "I'm better than an old tree," reasoned Jerome, and raised the knocker again boldly and let it fall with a great brazen clang. Then he jumped and almost fell backward when the door was flung open suddenly, and there stood Squire Merritt himself.

"What the devil —" began Squire Merritt; then he stopped and chuckled behind his great beard when he saw Jerome's alarmed eyes. "Hullo," said he, "who have we got here?" Eben Merritt had a soft place in his heart for all small young creatures of his kind, and always returned their timid obeisances, when he met them, with a friendly smile twinkling like light through his bushy beard. Still, like many a man of such general kindly bearings, he could not easily compass details, and oftener than not could not have told which child he greeted.

Eben Merritt, outside his own family, was utterly impartial in magnanimity, and dealt with broad principles rather than individuals. Now he looked hard at Jerome, and could not for the life of him tell what particular boy he was, yet recognized him fully in the broader sense of young helplessness and timid need. "Speak up," said he; "don't be scared. I know all the children, and I don't know one of 'em. Speak up like a man."

Then Jerome, stung to the resolution to show this great Squire, Eben Merritt, that he was not to be classed among the children, but was a man indeed, and equivalent to those duties of one which had suddenly been thrust upon him, looked his questioner boldly in the face and answered. "I'm Jerome Edwards," said he; "and Abel Edwards was my father."

Eben Merritt's face changed in a minute. He looked gravely at the boy, and nodded with understanding. "Yes, I know now," said he; "I remember. You look like your father." Then he added, kindly, but with a scowl of perplexity as to what the boy was standing there for, and what he wanted: "Well, my boy, what is it? Did your mother send you on some errand to Mrs. Merritt?"

Jerome scraped his foot, his manners at his command by this time, and his old hat was in his hand. "No, sir," said he; "I came to see you, sir, if you please, sir, and mother didn't send me. I came myself."

"You came to see me?"

"Yes, sir," Jerome scraped again, but his black eyes on the Squire's face were quite fearless and steady.

Squire Eben Merritt stared at him wonderingly; then he cast an uneasy glance at his fishing-pole, for he had come to the door with his tackle in his hands, and he gave a wistful thought to the brooks running through the young shadows of the spring woods, and the greening fields, and the still trout-pools he had meant to invade with no delay, and from which this childish visitor, bound probably upon some foolish errand, would keep him. Then he found his own manners, which were those of his good old family, courteous alike to young and old, and rich and poor.

"Well, if you've come to see me, walk in, sir," cried Squire Merritt, with a great access of heartiness, and he laid his fishing-tackle carefully on the long mahogany table in the entry, and motioned Jerome to follow him into the room on the left.

Jerome had never been inside the house before, but this room had a strangeness of its own which made him feel, when he entered, as if he had crossed the border of a foreign land. It was typically unlike any other room in the village. Jerome, whose tastes were as yet only imitative and departed not from the lines to which they had been born and trained, surveyed it with astonishment and some contempt. "No carpet," he thought, "and no hair-cloth sofa, and no rocking-chair!"

He stared at the skins of bear and deer which covered the

floor, at the black settle with a high carven back, at a carved chest of black oak, at the smaller pelts of wolf and fox which decorated walls and chairs, at a great pair of antlers, and even a noble eagle sitting in state upon the top of a secretary. Squire Merritt had filled this room and others with his trophies of the chase, for he had been a mighty hunter from his youth.

"Sit down, sir," he told Jerome, a little impatiently, for he longed to be away for his fishing, and the stupid abstraction from purpose which unwonted spectacles always cause in childhood are perplexing and annoying to their elders, who cannot leave their concentration for any sight of the eyes, if they wish.

He indicated a chair, at which Jerome, suddenly brought to himself, looked dubiously, for it had a fine fox-skin over the back, and he wondered if he might sit on it or should remove it.

The Squire laughed. "Sit down," he ordered; "you won't hurt the pelt." And then he asked, to put him at his ease, "Did you ever shoot a fox, sir?"

"No, sir."

"Ever fire a gun?"

"No, sir."

"Want to?"

"Yes, sir."

Jerome did not respond with the ready eagerness which the Squire had expected. He had suddenly resolved, in his kindness and pity towards his fatherless state, knowing well the longings of a boy, to take him out in the field and let him fire his gun, and change, if he could, that sad old look he wore, even if he fished none that day; but Jerome disappointed him in his purpose. "He hasn't much spirit," he thought, and stood upon the hearth, before the open fireplace, and said no more, but waited to hear what Jerome had come for.

The Squire was far from an old man, though he seemed so to the boy. He was scarcely middle-aged, and indeed many still called him the "young Squire," as they had done when his father died, some fifteen years before. He was a massively built man, standing a good six feet tall in his boots; and in his boots, thick-soled, and rusty with old mud splashes, reaching high above his knees over his buckskin breeches, Squire Eben Merritt almost always stood. He was scarcely ever seen without them, except in the meeting-house on a Sunday — when he went, which was not often. There was a tradition that he in his boots, just home from a quail sortie in the swamp, had once invaded the best parlor, where his wife had her lady friends to tea, and which boasted a real

Turkey carpet — the only one in town.

Eben Merritt in these great hunting-boots, clad as to the rest of him in stout old buckskin and rough coat and leather waistcoat, with his fair and ruddy face well covered by his golden furze of beard, which hung over his breast, lounged heavily on the hearth, and waited with a noble patience, eschewing all desire of fishing, until this pale, grave little lad should declare his errand.

But Jerome, with the great Squire standing waiting before him, felt suddenly tongue-tied. He was not scared, though his heart beat fast; it was only that the words would not come.

The Squire watched him kindly with his bright, twinkling blue eyes under his brush of yellow hair. "Take your time," said he, and threw one arm up over the mantel-shelf, and stood as if it were easier for him than to sit, and indeed it might have been so, for from his stalking of woods and long motionless watches at the lair of game, he had had good opportunities to accustom himself to rest at ease upon his feet.

Jerome might have spoken sooner had the Squire moved away from before him and taken his eyes from his face, for sometimes too ardent attention becomes a citadel for storming to a young and modest soul. However, at last he turned his own head aside, and his black eyes from the Squire's keen blue eyes, and would then have spoken had not the door opened suddenly and little Lucina come in on a run and stopped short a minute with timid finger to her mouth, and eyes as innocently surprised as a little rabbit's.

Lucina, being unhooded today, showed all her shower of shining yellow curls, which covered her little shoulders and fell to her childish waist. Her fat white neck and dimpled arms were bare and gleaming through the curls, and she wore a lace-trimmed pinafore, and a frock of soft blue wool scalloped with silk around the hem, revealing below the finest starched pantalets, and little morocco shoes.

Squire Eben laughed fondly, to see her start and hesitate, as a man will laugh at the pretty tricks of one he loves. "Come here, Pretty," he cried. "There's nothing for you to be afraid of. This is only poor little Jerome Edwards. Come and shake hands with him," and bade her thus, thinking another child might encourage the boy.

With that Lucina hesitated no longer, but advanced, smiling softly, with the little lady-ways her mother had taught her, and held out her white morsel of a hand to the boy. "How do you do?" she said, prettily, though still a little shyly, for she was mindful how her gingerbread had been refused, and might not this strange poor boy also thrust the hand away with scorn? She said that, and looking down, lest that black angry flash of his eyes startle her again, she saw his poor broken shoes, and gave a soft little cry, then made a pitiful lip, and stared hard at them with wide eyes full of astonished compassion, for the shoes seemed to her much more forlorn than bare feet.

Jerome's eyes followed hers, and he sprang up suddenly, his face blazing, and made out that he did not see the proffered little hand. "Pretty well," he returned, gruffly. Then he said to the Squire, with no lack of daring now, "Can I see you alone, sir?"

The Squire stared at him a second, then his great chest heaved with silent laughter and his yellow beard stirred as with a breeze of mirth.

"You don't object to my daughter's presence?" he queried, his eyes twinkling still, but with the formality with which he might have addressed the minister.

Jerome scowled with important indignation. Nothing escaped him; he saw that Squire Merritt was laughing at him. Again the pitiful rebellion at his state of boyhood seized him. He would have torn out of the room had it not been for his dire need. He looked straight at the Squire, and nodded stubbornly.

Squire Merritt turned to his little daughter and laid a tenderly heavy hand on her smooth curled head. "You'd better run away now and see mother, Pretty," he said. "Father has some business to talk over with this gentleman."

Little Lucina gave a bewildered look up in her father's face, then another at Jerome, as if she fancied she had not heard aright, then she went out obediently, like the good and gentle little girl that she was.

When the door closed behind her, Jerome began at once. Somehow, that other child's compassion in the midst of her comfort and security had brought his courage up to the point of attack on fate.

"I want to ask you about the mortgage," said Jerome.

The Squire looked at him with quick interest. "The mortgage on your father's place?"

"Yes, sir."

"Doctor Prescott holds it?"

"Yes, sir."

"How much is it?"

"A thousand dollars." Jerome said that with a gasp of horror and admiration at the vastness of it. Sometimes to him that thousand dollars almost represented infinity, and seemed more than the stars of heaven. His childish brain, which had scarcely contemplated in verity more than a shilling at a time of the coin of the realm, reeled at a thousand dollars.

"Well?" observed Squire Merritt, kindly but perplexedly. He wondered vaguely if the boy had come to ask him to pay the mortgage, and reflected how little ready money he had in pocket, for Eben Merritt was not thrifty with his income, which was indeed none too large, and was always in debt himself, though always sure to pay in time. Chances were, if Squire Merritt had had the thousand dollars to hand that morning, he might have thrust it upon the boy, with no further parley, taken his rod and line, and gone forth to his fishing. As it was, he waited for Jerome to proceed, merely adding that he was sorry that his mother did not own the place clear.

The plan that the boy unfolded, clumsily but sturdily to the end, he had thought out for himself in the darkness of the night before. The Squire listened. "Who planned this out?" he asked, when Jerome had finished.

"I did."

"Who helped you?"

"Nobody did."

"Nobody?"

"No, sir."

Suddenly Squire Eben Merritt seated himself in the chair which Jerome had vacated, seized the boy, and set him upon his knee. Jerome struggled half in wrath, half in fear, but he could not free himself from that strong grasp. "Sit still," ordered Squire Eben. "How old are you, my boy?"

"Goin' on twelve, sir," gasped Jerome.

"Only four years older than Lucina. Good Lord!"

The Squire's grasp tightened tenderly. The boy did not struggle longer, but looked up with a wonder of comprehensiveness in the bearded face bent kindly over his. "He looks at me the way father use to," thought Jerome.

"What made you come to me, my boy?" asked the Squire, presently. "Did you think I could pay the mortgage for you?"

Then Jerome colored furiously and threw up his head. "No, *sir*," said he, proudly.

"Why, then?"

"I came because you are a justice of the peace, and know what law is, and —"

"And what?"

"I've always heard you were pleasanter-spoken than he was."

The Squire laughed. "Pleasant words are cheap coin," said he. "I wish I had something better for your sake, child. Now let me see what it is you propose. That wood-lot of your father's, you say, Doctor Prescott has offered three hundred dollars for."

"Yes, sir."

The Squire whistled. "Didn't your father think it was worth more than that?"

"Yes, sir, but he didn't think he could get any more. He said —"

"What did he say?"

"He said that a poor seller was the slave of a rich buyer; but I think —" Jerome hesitated. He was not used yet to expressing his independent thought.

"Go on," said the Squire.

"I think it works both ways, and the poor man is the slave either way, whether he buys or sells," said the boy, half defiantly, half timidly.

"I guess you're about right," said the Squire, looking at him curiously. "Ever hear your uncle Ozias Lamb say anything like that?"

"No, sir."

"Thought it yourself, eh?"

"Yes, sir."

"Well, let's get to business now," said the Squire. "What you want is this, if I understand it. You want Doctor Prescott to buy that wood-lot of your father's for three hundred dollars, or whatever over that sum he will agree to, and you don't want him to pay you money down, but give you his note for it, with interest at six per cent., for as long a term as he will. You did not say give you a note, because you did not know about it, but that is what you want."

Jerome nodded soberly. "I know father paid interest at six per cent., and it was sixty dollars a year, and I know it would be eighteen dollars if it was three hundred dollars instead of a thousand. I figured it out on my slate," he said.

"You are right," said the Squire, gravely. "Now you think that will bring your interest down to forty-two dollars a year, and maybe you can manage that; and if you cannot, you think that Doctor Prescott will pay you cash down for the wood-lot?"

The boy seemed to be engaged in an arithmetical calculation. He bent his brows, and his lips moved. "That would be over seven years' interest money, at forty-two dollars a year, anyway," he said at length, looking at the Squire with shrewdly innocent eyes.

Suddenly Eben Merritt burst into a great roar of laughter, and struck the boy a kindly slap upon his small back.

"By the Lord Harry!" cried he, "you've struck a scheme worthy of the Jews. But you need good Christians to deal with!"

Jerome started and stared at him, half anxiously, half resentfully. "Ain't it right, sir?" he stammered.

"Oh, your scheme is right enough; no trouble about that. The question is whether Doctor Prescott is right."

Eben Merritt burst into another roar of laughter as he arose and set the boy on his feet. "I am not laughing at you, my boy," he said, though Jerome's wondering, indignant eyes upon his face were, to his thinking, past humorous.

Then he laid a hand upon each of the boy's little homespun shoulders. "Go and see Doctor Prescott, and tell him your plan, and — if he does not approve of it, come here and let me know," he said, and seriously enough to suit even Jerome's jealous self-respect.

"Yes, sir," said Jerome.

"And," added the Squire, "you had better go a little after noon — you will be more likely to find him at home."

"Yes, sir."

"Are you afraid to go out alone after dark?" asked the Squire.

"No, sir," replied Jerome, proudly.

"Well, then," said the Squire, "come and see me this evening, and tell me what Doctor Prescott says."

"Yes, sir," replied Jerome, and bobbed his head, and turned to go. The Squire moved before him with his lounging gait, and opened the door for him with ceremony, as for an honored guest.

Out in the south entry, with her back against the opposite wall, well removed from the south-room door, that she might not hear one word not intended for her ears, stood Lucina waiting, with one little white hand clinched tight, as over a treasure. When her father came out, following Jerome, she ran forward to him, pulled his head down by a gentle tug at his long beard, and whispered. Squire Eben laughed and smoothed her hair, but looked at her doubtfully. "I don't know about it, Pretty," he whispered back.

"Please, father," she whispered again, and rubbed her soft cheek against his great arm, and he laughed again, and looked at her as a man looks at the apple of his eye.

"Well," said he, "do as you like, Pretty." With that the little Lucina sprang eagerly forward before Jerome, who, hardly certain whether he were dismissed or not, yet eager to be gone, was edging towards the outer door, and held out to him her little hand curved into a sweet hollow like a cup of pearl, all full of silver coins.

Jerome looked at her, gave a quick, shamed glance at the little outstretched hand, colored red, and began backing away.

But Lucina pressed forward, thrusting in his very face her little precious cup of treasure. "Please take this, boy," said she, and her voice rang soft and sweet as a silver flute. "It is money I've been saving up to buy a parrot. But a parrot is a noisy bird, mother says, and maybe I could not love it as well as I love my lamb, and so its feelings would be hurt. I don't want a parrot, after all, and I want you to take this and buy some shoes." So said little Lucina Merritt, making her sweet assumption of selfishness to cover her unselfishness, for the noisy parrot was the desire of her heart, and to her father's eyes she bore the aspect of an angel, and he swallowed a great sob of mingled admiration and awe and intensest love. And indeed the child's face as she stood there had about it something celestial, for every line and every curve therein were as the written words of purest compassion; and in her innocent blue eyes stood self-forgetful tears.

Even the boy Jerome, with the pride of poverty to which he had been born and bred, like a bitter savor in his heart, stared at her a moment, his eyes dilated, his mouth quivering, and half advanced his hand to take the gift so sweetly offered. Then all at once the full tide of self rushed over him with all its hard memories and resolutions. His eyes gave out that black flash of wrath, which the poor little Lucina had feared, yet braved and forgot through her fond pity, he dashed out the back of his hand so roughly against that small tender one that all the silver pieces were jostled out to the floor, and rushed out of the door.

Squire Eben Merritt made an indignant exclamation and one threatening stride after him, then stopped, and caught up the weeping little Lucina, and sought to soothe her as best he might.

"Never mind, Pretty; never mind, Pretty," he said, rubbing his rough face against her soft one, in a way which was used to make her laugh. "Father 'll buy you a parrot that will talk the roof off."

"I don't — want a parrot, father," sobbed the little girl. "I want the boy to have shoes."

"Summer is coming, Pretty," said Squire Eben, laughingly and caressingly, "and a boy is better off without shoes than with them."

"He won't — have any — for next winter."

"Oh yes, he shall. I'll fix it so he shall earn some for himself before then — that's the way, Pretty. Father was to blame. He ought to have known better than to let you offer money to him. He's a proud child." The Squire laughed. "Now, don't cry any more, Pretty. Run away and play. Father's going fishing, and he'll bring you home some pretty pink fishes for your supper. Don't cry any more, because poor father can't go while you cry, and he has been delayed a long time, and the fishes will have eaten their dinner and won't bite if he doesn't hurry."

Lucina, who was docile even in grief, tried to laugh, and when her father set her down with a great kiss, which seemed to include her whole rosy face pressed betwixt his two hands, picked up her rejected silver from the floor, put it away in the little box in which she kept it, and sat down in a window of the south room to nurse her doll. She nodded and laughed dutifully when her father, going forth at last to the still pools and the brook courses, with his tackle in hand, looked back and nodded whimsically at her.

However, her childish heart was sore beyond immediate healing, for the wounds received from kindness spurned and turned back as a weapon against one's self are deep.

CHAPTER VII

In every household which includes a beloved child there is apt to be one above another, who acts as an intercessor towards furthering its little plans and ends. Little Lucina's was her father. Her mother was no less indulgent in effect, but she was anxiously solicitous lest too much concession spoil the child, and had often to reconcile a permission to her own conscience before giving it, even in trivial matters.

Therefore little Lucina, having in mind some walk abroad or childish treasure, would often seek her father, and, lifting up her face like a flower against his rough-coated breast, beg him, in that small, wheedling voice which he so loved, to ask her mother that she might go or have; for well she knew, being astute, though so small and innocent and gentle, that such a measure was calculated to serve her ends, and allay her mother's scruples through a shift of responsibility.

However, today, since her father was away fishing, Lucina was driven to seek other aid in the carrying out of a small plan which she had formed for her delectation.

Right anxiously the child watched for her father to come home to the noonday dinner; but he did not come, and she and her mother ate alone. Then she stole away up-stairs to her little dimity-hung chamber, opening out of her parents' and facing towards the sun, and all twinkling and swaying with little white tassels on curtains and covers and counterpane, in the draught, as she opened the door. Then she went down on her knees beside her bed and prayed, in the simplicity of her heart, which would seek a Heavenly Father in lieu of an earthly one, for all her small desires, and think no irreverence: "Our Father, who art in heaven, please make mother let me go to Aunt Camilla's this afternoon. Amen."

Then she rose, with no delay for lack of faith, and went straight down to her mother, and proffered her request timidly, and yet with a confidence as of one who has a larger voice of authority at her back.

"Please, mother, may I go over to Aunt Camilla's this afternoon?" asked little Lucina.

And her mother, not knowing what principle of childish faith was involved, hesitated, knitting her small, dark face, which had no look like Lucina's, perplexedly.

"I don't know, child," said she.

"Please, mother!"

"I am afraid you'll trouble your aunt, Lucina."

"No, I won't, mother! I'll take my doll, and I'll play with her real quiet."

"I am afraid your aunt Camilla will have something else to do."

"She can do it, mother. I won't trouble her — I won't speak to her — honest! Please, mother."

"You ought to sit down at home this afternoon and do some work, Lucina."

"I'll take over my garter-knitting, mother, and I'll knit ten times across."

It happened at length, whether through effectual prayer, or such skilful fencing against weak maternal odds, that the little Lucina, all fresh frilled and curled, with her silk knitting-bag dangling at her side, and her doll nestled to her small mother-shoulder, stepping with dainty primness in her jostling starched pantalets, lifting each foot carefully lest she hit her nice morocco toes against the stones, went up the road to her aunt Camilla's.

Miss Camilla Merritt lived in the house which had belonged to her grandfather, called the "old Merritt house" to distinguish it from the one which her father had built, in which her brother Eben lived. Both, indeed, were old, but hers was venerable, and claimed that respect which extreme age, even in inanimate things, deserves. And in a way, indeed, this old house might have been considered raised above the mere properties of wood and brick and plaster by such an accumulation of old memories and associations, which were inseparable from its walls, to something nearly sentient and human, and to have established in itself a link 'twixt matter and mind.

Never had any paint touched its outer walls, overlapped with silver-gray shingles like scales of a fossil fish. The door and the great pillared portico over it were painted white, as they had been from the first, and that was all. A brick walk, sunken in mossy hollows, led up to the front door, which was only a few feet from the road, the front yard being merely a narrow strip with great poplars set therein. Lucina had always had a suspicion, which she confided to no one, being sensitive as to ridicule for her childish theories, that these poplars were not real trees. Even the changing of the leaves did not disarm her suspicion. Sometimes she dug surreptitiously around the roots with a pointed stick to see what she could discover for or against it, and always with a fearful excitement of daring, lest she topple the tree over, perchance, and destroy herself and Aunt Camilla and the house.

Today Lucina went up the walk between the poplars, recognizing them as one recognizes friends oftentimes, not as their true selves, but as our conception of them, and knocked one little lady-like knock with the brass knocker. She never entered her aunt Camilla's house without due ceremony.

Aunt Camilla's old woman, who lived with her, and performed her household work as well as any young one, answered the knock and bade her enter. Lucina followed this portly old-woman figure, moving with a stiff wabble of black bombazined hips, like some old domestic fowl, into the east room, which was the sitting-room.

The old woman's name was lost to memory, inasmuch as she had been known simply as 'Liza ever since her early childhood, and had then hailed from the town farm, with her parentage a doubtful matter.

There was about this woman, who had no kith nor kin, nor equal friends, nor money, nor treasures, nor name, and scarce her own individuality in the minds of others, a strange atmosphere of silence, broken seldom by uncouth, stammering speech, which always intimidated the little Lucina. She had, however, a way of expanding, after long stares at her, into sudden broad smiles which relieved the little girl's apprehension; and, too, her rusty black bombazine smelled always of rich cake — a reassuring perfume to one who knew the taste of it.

Lucina's aunt Camilla was a nervous soul, and liked not the rattle of starched cotton about the house. Her old serving-woman must go always clad in woollen, which held the odors of cooking long.

Lucina sat down in a little rocking-chair, hollowed out like a nest in back and seat, which was her especial resting-place, and 'Liza went out, leaving the rich, fruity odor of cake behind her, saying no word, but evidently to tell her mistress of her guest. There were no blinds on this ancient house, but there were inside shutters in fine panel-work at all the windows. These were all closed except at the east windows. There between the upper panels were left small square apertures which framed little pictures of the blue spring sky, slanted across with blooming peach boughs; for there was a large peach orchard on the east side of the house. Lucina watched these little pictures, athwart which occasionally a bird flew and raised them to life. She held her doll primly, and her little work-bag still dangled from her arm. She would not begin her task of knitting until her aunt appeared and her visit was fairly in progress.

Over against the south wall stood a clock as tall as a giant man, and giving in the half light a strong impression of the presence of one, to an eye which did not front it. Lucina often turned her head with a start and looked, to be sure it was only the clock which sent that long, dark streak athwart her vision. The clock ticked with slow and solemn majesty. She was sure that sixty of those ticks would make a minute, and sixty times the sixty an hour, if she could count up to that and not get lost in such a sea of numbers; but she could not tell the time of day by the clock hands.

Lucina was a quick-witted child, but seemed in some particulars to have a strange lack of curiosity, or else an instinct to preserve for herself an imagination instead of acquiring knowledge. She was either obstinately or involuntarily ignorant as yet of the method of telling time, and the hands of the clock were held before its face of mystery for concealment rather than revelation to her. But she loved to sit and watch the clock, and she never told her mother what she thought about it. Directly in front of Lucina, as she sat waiting, hanging over the mantel-shelf between the east windows, was a great steel engraving of the Declaration of Independence. Lucina looked at the cluster of grave men, and was innocently proud and sure that her father was much finer-looking than any one of them, and, moreover, doubted irreverently if any one of them could shoot rabbits or catch fish, or do anything but sign his name with that stiff pen. Lucina was capable of an agony of faithfulness to her own, but of loyalty in a broad sense she knew nothing, and never would, having in that respect the typical capacity only of women.

The east-room door had been left ajar. Presently a soft whisper of silk could be heard afar off; but before that even a delicate breath of lavender came floating into the room. Many sweet and subtly individual odors seemed to dwell in this old house, preceding the mortal inhabitants through the doors, and lingering behind them in rooms where they had stayed.

Lucina started when the lavender breath entered the room, and looked up as if at a ghostly herald. She toed out her two small morocco-shod feet more particularly upon the floor, she smoothed down her own and her doll's little petticoats, and she also made herself all ready to rise and courtesy.

After the lavender sweetness came the whisper of silk flounces, growing louder and louder; but there was no sound of footsteps, for Aunt Camilla moved only with the odor and rustle of a flower. No one had ever heard her little slippered feet; even her high heels never tapped the thresholds. She had a way of advancing her toes first and making the next step with a tilt, so soft that it was scarcely a break from a glide, and yet clearing the floor as to her slipper heels.

Lucina knew her aunt Camilla was coming down the stairs by the rustling of her silk flounces along the rails of the banisters, like harp-strings; then there was a cumulative whisper and an entrance.

Lucina rose, holding her doll like a dignified little mother, and dropped a courtesy.

"Good-afternoon," said Aunt Camilla.

"Good-afternoon," returned Lucina.

"How do you do?" asked Aunt Camilla.

"Pretty well, I thank you," replied Lucina.

"How is your mother?"

"Pretty well, I thank you."

"Is your father well?"

"Yes, ma'am; I thank you."

During this dialogue Aunt Camilla was moving gently forward upon her niece. When she reached her she stooped, or rather drooped — for stooping implies a bend of bone and muscle, and her graceful body seemed to be held together by integuments like long willow leaves — and kissed her with a light touch of cool, delicate lips. Aunt Camilla's slender arms in their pointed lilac sleeves and lace undersleeves waved forward as with a vague caressing intent. Soft locks of hair and frilling laces in her cap and bosom hung forward like leaves on a swaying bough, and tickled Lucina's face, half smothered in the old lavender fragrance.

Lucina colored innocently and sweetly when her aunt kissed her, and afterwards looked up at her with sincerest love and admiration and delight.

Camilla Merritt was far from young, being much older than her brother, Lucina's father; but she was old as a poem or an angel might be, with the lovely meaning of her still uppermost and most evident. Camilla in her youth had been of a rare and delicate beauty, which had given her fame throughout the country-side, and she held the best of it still, as one holds jewels in a worn casket, and as a poem written in obsolete language contains still its first grace of thought. Camilla's soft and slender body had none of those stiff, distorted lines which come from resistance to the forced attitudes of life. Her body and her soul had been amenable to all discipline. She had leaned sweetly against her crosses, instead of straining away from them with fierce cramps and agonies of resistance. In every motion she had the freedom of utter yielding, which surpasses the freedom of action. Camilla's graduated flounces of lilac silk, slightly faded, having over it a little spraying mist of gray, trimmed her full skirt to her slender waist, girdled with a narrow ribbon fastened with a little clasp set with amethysts. A great amethyst brooch pinned the lace at her throat. She wore a lace cap, and over that, flung loosely, draping her shoulders and shading her face with its soft mesh, a great shawl or veil of fine white lace wrought with sprigs. Camilla's delicately spare cheeks were softly pink, with that elderly bloom which lacks the warm dazzle of youth, yet has its own late beauty. Her eyes were blue and clear as a child's, and as full of innocent dreams — only of the past instead of the future. Her blond hair, which in turning gray had got a creamy instead of a silvery lustre, like her old lace, was looped softly and disposed in half-curls over her ears. When she smiled it was with the grace and fine dignity of ineffable ladyhood, and yet with the soft ignorance, though none of the abandon, of childhood. Camilla was like a child whose formal code and manners of life had been fully prescribed and learned, but whose vital copy had not been quite set.

Lucina loved her aunt Camilla with a strange sense of comradeship, and yet with awe. "If you can ever be as much of a lady as your aunt Camilla, I shall be glad," her mother often told her. Camilla was to Lucina the personification of the gentle and the genteel. She was her ideal, the model upon which she was to form herself.

Camilla was so unceasingly punctilious in all the finer details of living that all who infringed upon them felt her mere presence a reproach. Children were never rough or loud-voiced or naughty when Miss Camilla was near, though she never admonished otherwise than by example. As for little Lucina, she would have felt shamed for life had her aunt Camilla caught her toeing in, or stooping, or leaving the "ma'am" off from her yes and no.

Camilla, this afternoon, did what Lucina had fondly hoped she might do — proposed that they should sit out in the arbor in the garden. "I think it is warm enough," she said; and Lucina assented with tempered delight.

It was a very warm afternoon. Spring had taken, as she will sometimes do in May, being apparently weary of slow advances, a sudden flight into summer, with a wild bursting of buds and a great clamor of wings and songs.

Miss Camilla got a yellow Canton crêpe shawl, that was redolent of sandalwood, out of a closet, but she did not put it over her shoulders, the outdoor air was so soft. She needed nothing but her lace mantle over her head, which made her look like a bride of some old spring. Lucina followed her through the hall, out of the back door, which had a trellis and a grape-vine over it, into the garden. The garden was large, and laid out primly in box-bordered beds. There were even trees of box on certain corners, and it looked as if the box would in time quite choke out the flowers. Lucina, who was given to sweet and secret fancies, would often sit with wide blue eyes of contemplation upon the garden, and discover in the box a sprawling, many-armed green monster, bent upon strangling out the lives of the flowers in their beds.

"Why don't you have the box trimmed, Aunt Camilla?" she would venture to inquire at such times; and her aunt Camilla, looking gently askance at the flush of excitement, which she did not understand, upon her niece's cheek, would reply:

"The box has always been there, my dear."

Long existence proved always the sacredness of a law to Miss Camilla. She was a conservative to the bone.

The arbor where the two sat that afternoon was of the kind one sees in old prints where lovers sit in chaste embrace under a green arch of eglantine. However, in Miss Camilla's arbor were no lovers, and instead of eglantine were a honeysuckle and a climbing rose. The rose was not yet in bloom, and the honeysuckle's red trumpets were not blown — their parts in the symphony of the spring were farther on; over the arbor there was only a delicate prickling of new leaves, which cast a lacelike shadow underneath. A bench ran around the three closed sides of the arbor, and upon the bench sat Lucina and her aunt Camilla, in her spread of lilac flounces. Camilla held in her lap a little portfolio of papier-mâché, and wrote with a little gold pencil on sheets of gilt-edged paper. Camilla always wrote when she sat in the arbor, but nobody ever knew what. She always carried the finely written sheets into the house, and nobody knew where she put them afterwards. Camilla's long, thin fingers, smooth and white as ivory, sparkled dully with old rings. Some large amethysts in fine gold settings she wore, one great yellow pearl, a mourning-ring of hair in a circlet of pearls for tears, and some diamond bands in silver, which gave out cold white lights only as her hands moved across the gilt-edged paper.

As for Lucina, she had set up her doll primly in a corner of the arbor, and was knitting her stent. It might have seemed difficult to understand what the child found to enjoy in this quiet entertainment, but in childhood all situations which appeal to the imagination give enjoyment, and most situations which break the routine of daily life do so appeal. Then, too, Camilla's quiet persistence in her own employment gave a delightful sense of equality and dignity to the child. She would not have liked it half as well had her aunt stooped to entertain her and brought out toys and games for her amusement. However, there was entertainment to come, to which she looked forward with gratification, as that placed her firmly on the footing of an honored guest. The minister's daughter or the doctor's wife could not be treated better or with more courtesy.

Aunt Camilla wrote with pensive pauses of reflection, and Lucina knitted until her stent was finished. Then she folded up the garter neatly, quilted in the needles as she had been taught, and placed it in her little bag. Then she took up her doll protectingly and soothingly, and held her in her lap, with the great china head against her small bosom. Lucina's doll was very large, and finely attired in stiff book-muslin and pink ribbons. She wore also pink morocco shoes on her feet, which stood out strangely at sharp right angles. Lucina sometimes eyed her doll-baby's feet uncomfortably. "I guess she will outgrow it," she told herself, with innocent maternal hypocrisy early developed.

When Lucina laid aside her work and began nursing her doll her aunt looked up from her writing. "Are you enjoying yourself, dear?" she inquired.

"Yes, ma'am."

"Would you like to run about the garden?"

"No, thank you, ma'am; I will sit here and hold my doll. It is time for her nap. I will hold her till she goes to sleep."

"Then you can run about a little," suggested Miss Camilla, gravely, without a smile. She respected Lucina's doll, as she might have her baby, and the child's heart leaped up with gratitude. An older soul which needs not to make believe to re-enter childhood is a true comrade for a child.

"Yes, ma'am," replied Lucina. "I will lay her down on the bench here when she falls asleep."

"You can cover her up with my shawl," said Miss Camilla, gravely still, and naturally. Indeed, to her a child with a doll was as much a part and parcel of the natural order of things as a mother with an infant. Outside all of it herself, she comprehended and admitted it with the impartiality of an observer. "Then you can run in the garden," she added, "and pick a bouquet if you wish. There is not much in bloom now but the heart's-ease and the flowering almond and the daffodils, but you can make a bouquet of them to take home to your mother."

"Thank you, ma'am," said Lucina.

However, she was in no hurry to take advantage of her aunt's permission. She sat quietly in the warm and pleasant arbor, holding her doll-baby, with the afternoon sun sifting through the young leaves, and making over them a shifting dapple like golden water, and felt no inclination to stir. The spring languor was over even her young limbs; the sweet twitter of birds, the gathering birdlike flutter of leaves before a soft swell of air, the rustle of her aunt's gilt-edged paper, an occasional hiss of her silken flounces, grew dim and confused. Lucina, as well as her doll, fell asleep, leaning her pretty head against the arbor trellis-work. Camilla did not disturb her; she had never in her life disturbed the peace or the slumber of any soul. She only gazed at her now and then, with gentle, half abstracted affection, then wrote again.

Presently, stepping with that subtlest silence of motion through the quiet garden, came a great yellow cat. She rubbed against Miss Camilla's knees with that luxurious purr of love and comfort which is itself a completest slumber song, then made a noiseless leap to a sunny corner of the bench, and settled herself there in a yellow coil of sleep. Presently there came another, and another, and another still — all great cats, and all yellow, marked in splendid tiger stripes, with eyes like topaz — until there were four of them, all asleep on the sunny side of the arbor. Miss Camilla's yellow cats were of a famous breed, well represented in the village; but she had these four, which were marvels of beauty.

Another hour wore on. Miss Camilla still wrote, and Lucina and the yellow cats slept. Then it was four o'clock, and time for the entertainment to which Lucina had looked forward.

There was a heavy footstep on the garden walk and a rustling among the box borders. Then old 'Liza loomed up in the arbor door, darkening out the light. Little Lucina stirred and woke, yet did not know she woke, not knowing she had slept. To her thinking she had sat all this time with her eyes wide open, and the sight of her aunt Camilla writing and the leaf shadows on the arbor floor had never left them. She saw the yellow cats with some surprise, but cats can steal in quietly when one's eyes are turned. Had Lucina dreamed she had fallen asleep when an honored guest of her lady aunt, she would have been ready to sink with shame. Blindness to one's innocent shortcomings seems sometimes a special mercy of Providence.

Lucina straightened herself with a flushed smile, gave just one glance at the great tray which old 'Liza bore before her; then looked away again, being fully alive to the sense that it is not polite nor ladylike to act as if you thought much of your eating and drinking.

Old 'Liza set the tray on a little table in the midst of the arbor, and immediately odors, at once dainty and delicate, spicy, fruity, and aromatically soothing, diffused themselves about. The four yellow cats stirred; they yawned, and stretched luxuriously; then, suddenly fully awake to the meaning of those savory scents which had disturbed their slumbers, sat upright with eager jewel eyes upon the tray.

"Take the cats away, 'Liza," said Miss Camilla.

Old 'Liza advanced grinning upon the cats, gathered them up, two under each arm, and bore them away, moving out of sight between the box borders like some queer monster, with her wide humping flanks of black bombazine enhanced by four angrily waving yellow cat tails, which gave an effect of grotesque wrath to the retreat.

Lucina looked, in spite of her manners, at the tray when it was on the table before her very face and eyes. It was covered with a napkin of finest damask, whose flower pattern glistened like frostwork, and upon it were ranged little cups and saucers of pink china as thin and transparent as shells, a pink sugar-bowl to match, a small silver teapot under a satin cozy, a silver cream-jug, a plate of delicate bread-and-butter, and one of fruit-cake.

"You will have a cup of tea, will you not, dear?" said Aunt Camilla.

"If you please; thank you, ma'am," replied Lucina, striving to look decorously pleased and not too delighted at the prospect of the fruit-cake. Tea and bread-and-butter presented small attractions to her, but she did love old 'Liza's fruit-cake, made after a famous receipt which had been in the Merritt family for generations.

Miss Camilla removed the cozy and began pouring the tea. Lucina took a napkin, being so bidden, spread it daintily over her lap, and tucked a corner in her neck. The feast was about to commence, when a loud, jovial voice was heard in the direction of the house:

"Camilla! Camilla! Lucina, where are you all?"

"That's father!" cried Lucina, brightening, and immediately Squire Eben Merritt came striding down between the box-ridges, and Jerome Edwards was at his heels.

"Well, how are you, sister?" Squire Eben cried, merrily; and in the same breath, "I have brought another guest to your tea-drinking, sister."

Jerome bobbed his head, half with defiant dignity, half in utter shyness and confusion at the sight of this fine, genteel lady and her wonderful tea equipage. But Miss Camilla, having welcomed her brother with gentle warmth, greeted this little poor Jerome with as sweet a courtesy as if he had been the Governor, and bade Lucina run to the house and ask 'Liza to fetch two more cups and saucers and two plates, and motioned both her guests to be seated on the arbor bench.

Squire Eben laughed, and glanced at his great mud-splashed boots, his buckskin, his fishing-tackle, and a fine string of spotted trout which he bore. "A pretty knight for a lady's bower I am!" said he.

"A lady never judges a knight by his outward guise," returned Camilla, with soft pleasantry. She adored her brother.

Eben laughed, deposited his fish and tackle on the bench near the door, and flung himself down opposite them, at a respectful distance from his sister's silken flounces, with a sigh of comfort. "I have had a hard tramp, and would like a cup of your tea," he admitted. "I've been lucky, though. 'Twas a fine day for trout, though I would not have thought it. I will leave you some for your breakfast, sister; have 'Liza fry them brown in Indian meal."

Then, following Miss Camilla's remonstrating glance, he saw little Jerome Edwards standing in the arbor door, through which his entrance was blocked by the Squire's great legs and his fishing-tackle, with the air of an insulted ambassador who is half minded to return to his own country.

The Squire made room for him to pass with a hearty laugh. "Bless you, my boy!" said he, "I'm barring out the guest I invited myself, am I? Walk in — walk in and sit down."

Jerome, half melted by the Squire's genial humor, half disposed still to be stiffly resentful, hesitated a second; but Miss Camilla also, for the second time, invited him to enter, with her gentle ceremony, which was the subtlest flattery he had ever known, inasmuch as it seemed to set him firmly in his own esteem above his poor estate of boyhood; and he entered, and seated himself in the place indicated, at his hostess's right hand, near the little tea-table.

Jerome, hungry boy as he was, having the spicy richness of that wonderful fruit-cake in his nostrils, noted even before that the lavender scent of Miss Camilla's garments, which seemed, like a subtle fragrance of individuality and life itself, to enter his thoughts rather than his senses. The boy, drawn within this atmosphere of virgin superiority and gentleness, felt all his defiance and antagonism towards his newly discovered pride of life shame him.

The great and just bitterness of wrath against all selfish holders of riches that was beginning to tincture his whole soul was sweetened for the time by the proximity of this sweet woman in her silks and laces and jewels. Not reasoning it out in the least, nor recognizing his own mental attitude, it was to him as if this graceful creature had been so endowed by God with her rich apparel and fair surroundings that she was as much beyond question and envy as a lily of the field. He did not even raise his eyes to her face, but sat at her side, at once elevated and subdued by her gentle politeness and condescension. When Lucina returned, and 'Liza followed with the extra cups and plates, and the tea began, he accepted what was proffered him, and ate and drank with manners as mild and grateful as Lucina's. She could scarcely taste the full savor of her fruit-cake, after all, so occupied she was in furtively watching this strange boy. Her blue eyes were big with surprise. Why should he take Aunt Camilla's cake, and even her bread-and-butter, when he would not touch the gingerbread she had offered him, nor the money to buy shoes? This young Lucina had yet to learn that the proud soul accepts from courtesy what it will not take from love or pity.

CHAPTER VIII

That day had been one of those surprises of life which ever dwell with one. Jerome in it had discovered not only a new self, but new ways. He had struck paths at right angles to all he had followed before. They might finally verge into the old again, but for that day he saw strange prospects. Not the least strange of them was this tea-drinking with the Squire and the Squire's sister and the Squire's daughter in the arbor. He found it harder to reconcile that with his past and himself than anything else. So bewildered was he, drinking tea and eating cake, with the spread of Miss Camilla's lilac flounces brushing his knee, and her soft voice now and then in his ear, that he strove to remember how he happened to be there at all, and that shock of strangeness which obliterates the past wellnigh paralyzed his memory.

Yet it had been simple enough, as paths to strange conclusions always are. He had returned home from Squire Eben's that morning, changed his clothes, and resumed his work in the garden.

Elmira had questioned him, but he gave her no information. He had an instinct, which had been born in him, of secrecy towards womankind. Nobody had ever told him that women were not trustworthy with respect to confidences; he had never found it so from observation; he simply agreed within himself that he had better not confide any but fully matured plans, and no plans which should be kept secret, to a woman. He had, however, besides this caution, a generous resolution not to worry Elmira or his mother about it until he knew. "Wait till I find out; I don't know myself," he told Elmira.

"Don't you know where you've been? You can tell us that," she persisted, in her sweet, querulous treble. She pulled at his jacket sleeve with her little thin, coaxing hand, but Jerome was obdurate. He twitched his jacket sleeve away.

"I sha'n't tell you one thing, and there is no use in your teasin'," he said, peremptorily, and she yielded.

Elmira reported that their mother was sitting still in her rocking-chair, with her head leaning back and her eyes shut. "She seems all beat out," she said, pitifully; "she don't tell me to do a thing."

The two tiptoed across the entry and stood in the kitchen door, looking at poor Ann. She sat quite still, as Elmira had said, her head tipped back, her eyes closed, and her mouth slightly parted. Her little bony hands lay in her lap, with the fingers limp in utter nerveless relaxation, but she was not asleep. She opened her eyes when her children came to the door, but she did not speak nor turn her head. Presently her eyes closed again.

Jerome pulled Elmira back into the parlor. "You must go ahead and get the dinner, and make her some gruel, and not ask her a question, and not bother her about anything," he whispered, sternly. "She's resting; she'll die if she don't. It's awful for her. It's bad 'nough for us, but we don't know what 'tis for her."

Elmira assented, with wide, scared, piteous eyes on her brother.

"Go now and get the dinner," said Jerome.

"There's lots left over from yesterday," said Elmira, forlornly. "Shall we have anything after that's gone?"

"Have enough while I've got two hands," returned Jerome, gruffly. "Get some potatoes and boil 'em, and have some of that cold meat, and make mother the gruel."

Elmira obeyed, finding a certain comfort in that. Indeed, she belonged assuredly to that purely feminine order of things which gains perhaps its best strength through obedience. Give Elmira a power over her, and she would never quite fall.

Elmira went about getting dinner, tiptoeing around her mother, who still sat sunken in her strange apathy of melancholy or exhaustion, it was difficult to tell which, while Jerome spaded and dug in the garden, in the fury of zeal which he had inherited from her.

Elmira had dinner ready early, and called Jerome. When he went in he found her trying to induce her mother to swallow a bowl of gruel. "Won't you take it, mother?" she was pleading, with tears in her eyes; but her mother only lifted one hand feebly and motioned it away; she would not raise her head or open her eyes.

"Give me that bowl," said Jerome. He held it before his mother, and slipped one hand behind her neck, constraining her gently to raise her head. "Here, mother," said he, "here's your gruel."

She resisted faintly, and shook her weak, repelling hand again. "Sit up, mother, and drink your gruel," said Jerome, and his mother's eyes flew wide open at that, and stared up in his face with eager inquiry; for again she had that wild surmise that her lost husband spoke to her.

"Drink it, mother," said Jerome, again meeting her half delirious gaze fully; and Ann seemed to see his father looking at her from his son's eyes, through his immortality after the flesh. She raised herself at once, held out her trembling hands for the bowl, and drank the gruel to the last drop. Then she gave the empty bowl to Jerome, leaned her head back, and closed her eyes again.

After dinner Jerome changed his clothes for his poor best for the second time, and set forth to Doctor Prescott's. Elmira's wistful eyes followed him as he went out, but he said not a word. He threw back his shoulders and stepped out with as much boldness of carriage as ever.

"How smart he is!" Elmira thought, watching him from the window.

However, it was true that his heart quaked within him, supported as he was by the advice and encouragement of Squire Merritt. Doctor Prescott had been the awe and the terror of all his childhood. Nobody knew how in his childish illnesses — luckily not many — he had dreaded and resented the advent of this great man, who represented to him absolute monarchy, if not despotism. He never demurred at his noxious doses, but swallowed them at a gulp, with no sweet after-morsel as an inducement, yet, strangely enough, never from actual submissiveness, but rather from that fierce scorn and pride of utter helplessness which can maintain a certain defiance to authority by depriving it of that victory which comes only from opposition.

Jerome swallowed castor-oil, rhubarb, and the rest with a glare of fierce eyes over spoon and a triumphant understanding with himself that he took it because he chose, and not because the doctor made him. It was odd, but Doctor Prescott seemed to have some intuition of the boy's mental attitude, for, in spite of his ready obedience, he had always a singular aversion to him. He was much more amenable to pretty little Elmira, who cried pitifully whenever he entered the house, and had always to be coaxed and threatened to make her take medicine at all. No one would have said, and Doctor Prescott himself would not have believed, that he, in his superior estate of age and life, would have stooped to dislike a child like that, thus putting him upon a certain equality of antagonism; but in truth he did. Doctor Prescott scarcely ever knew one boy from another when he met him upon the street, but Jerome Edwards he never mistook, though he never stirred his stately head in response to the boy's humble bob of courtesy. Once, after so meeting and passing the boy, he heard an audacious note of defiance at his back, with a preliminary sniff of scorn: "Hm! wonder if he thinks he was born grown up, with money in his pockets; wonder if he thinks he owns this whole town?" The doctor never turned to resent this sarcastic soliloquy whereby the boy's suppressed democracy asserted itself, but the next time he saw Jerome's father he told him he had better look to his son's manners, and Jerome had been called to account.

However, when he had repeated his speech which had given offence, he had only been charged to keep his thoughts to himself in future. "I'll think 'em, anyhow," said Jerome, with unabated defiance.

"You'll pay proper respect to your elders," said his father.

"You'll think what we tell you to," said his mother, but the eyes of the two met. Doctor Prescott might hold the mortgage and exact his pound of flesh, these poor backs might bend to the yoke, but there was no cringing in the hearts of Abel Edwards and his wife. It was easy to see where Jerome got his spirit.

However, spirit needs long experience and great strength to assert itself fully at all times before long-recognized power. Jerome, going up the road to Doctor Prescott's, felt rather a fierce submission and obligatory humility than defiance. He felt as if this great man held not only himself, but his mother and sister, their lives and fortunes, at his disposal. Awe of the reigning sovereign was upon him, but it was the surly awe of the peasant whose mouth is stopped by force from questions.

It was not long before Jerome, going along the country road, came to the beginning of Doctor Prescott's estate. He owned long stretches of fields along the main street of the village, comprising many fine house-lots, which, however, people were too poor to buy. Doctor Prescott fixed such high prices to his house-lots that no one could pay them. However, people thought he did not care to sell. He liked being a large land-owner, like an English lord, and feeling that he owned half the village, they said.

Moreover, his acres brought him a fair income. They were sowed to clover and timothy, and barley and corn, and gave such hay and such crops as no others in town.

As Jerome passed these fair fields, either golden-green with the young grass, or ploughed in even ridges for the new seeds, set with dandelions like stars, or pierced as to the brown mould with emerald spears of grain, he scowled at them, and his mouth puckered grimly and piteously. He thought of all this land which Doctor Prescott owned; he thought of the one poor little bit of soil which he was going to offer him, to keep a roof over his head. Why should this man have all this, and he and his so little? Was it because he was better? Jerome shook his head vehemently. Was it because the Lord loved him better? Jerome looked up in the blue spring sky. The problem of the rights of the soil of the old earth was upon the boy, but he could not solve it — only scowl and grieve over it.

Past the length of the shining fields, well back from the road, with a fine curve of avenue between lofty pine-trees leading up to it, stood Doctor Prescott's house. It was much the finest one in the village, massively built of gray stone in large irregular blocks, veined at the junctions with white stucco; a great white pillared piazza stretched across the front, and three flights of stone steps led over smooth terraces to it; for it was raised on an artificial elevation above the road-level. Jerome, having passed the last field, reached the avenue leading to the doctor's house, and stopped a moment. His hands and feet were cold; there was a nervous trembling all over his little body. He remembered how once, when he was much younger, his mother had sent him to the doctor's to have a tooth pulled, how he stood there trembling and hesitating as now, and how he finally took matters into his own hands. A thrill of triumph shot over him even then, as he recalled that mad race of his away up the road, on and on until he came to the woods, and the tying of the offending tooth to an oak-tree by a stout cord, and the agonized but undaunted pulling thereat until his object was gained.

"I'd 'nough sight rather go to an oak-tree to have my tooth out than to Doctor Prescott," he had said, stoutly, being questioned on his return; and his father and mother, being rather taken at a loss by such defiance and disobedience, scarcely knew whether to praise or blame.

But there was no oak-tree for this strait. Jerome, after a minute of that blind groping and feeling, as of the whole body and soul, with which one strives to find some other way to an end than a hard and repugnant one, gave it up. He went up the avenue, holding his head up, digging his toes into the pine-needles, with an air of stubborn boyish bravado, yet all the time the nervous trembling never ceased. However, halfway up the avenue he came into one of those warmer currents which sometimes linger so mysteriously among trees, seeming like a pool of air submerging one as visibly as water. This warm-air bath was, moreover, sweetened with the utmost breath of the pine woods. Jerome, plunging into it, felt all at once a certain sense of courage and relief, as if he had a bidding and a welcome from old friends.

There are times when a quick conviction, from something like a special favor or caress of the great motherhood of nature, which makes us all as child to child, comes over one. "His pine-trees ain't any different from other folks' pine-trees," flashed through Jerome's mind.

CHAPTER IX

He went on straight round the house to the south-side door, whither everybody went to consult the doctor. He knocked, and in a moment the door opened, and a young girl with weak blue eyes, with a helpless droop of the chin, and mouth half opened in a silly smile, looked out at him. She was a girl whom Doctor Prescott had taken from the almshouse to assist in the lighter household duties. She was considered rather weak in her intellect, though she did her work well enough when she had once learned how.

Jerome bent his head with a sudden stiff duck to this girl. "Is Doctor Prescott at home?" he inquired.

"Yes, sir," replied the girl, with the same respectful courtesy and ceremony with which she might have greeted the Squire or any town magnate, instead of this poor little boy. Her mind was utterly incapable of the faculties of selection and discrimination. She applied one formula, unmodified, to all mankind.

"Can I see him a minute?" asked Jerome, gruffly.

"Yes, sir. Will you walk in?"

The girl, moving with a weak, shuffling toddle, like a child, led Jerome through the length of the entry to a great room on the north side of the house, which was the doctor's study and office. Two large cupboards, whose doors were set with glass in diamond panes in the upper panels, held his drugs and nostrums. Books, mostly ponderous volumes in rusty leather, lined the rest of the wall space. When Jerome entered the room the combined odor of those leather-bound folios and the doctor's drugs smote his nostrils, as from a curious brewing of theoretical and applied wisdom in one pot.

"Take a seat," said the girl, "and I will speak to the doctor." Then she went out, with the vain, pleased simper of a child who has said her lesson well.

Jerome sat down and looked about him. He had been in the room several times before, but his awe of it preserved its first strangeness for him. He eyed the books on the walls, then the great bottles visible through the glass doors on the cupboard shelves. Those bottles were mostly of a cloudy green or brown, but one among them caught the light and shone as if filled with liquid rubies. That was valerian, but Jerome did not know it; he only thought it must be a very strong medicine to have such a bright color. He also thought that the doctor must have mixed all those medicines from rules in those great books, and a sudden feverish desire to look into them seized him. However, neither his pride nor his timidity would have allowed him to touch one of those books, even if he had not expected the doctor to enter every moment.

He waited quite a little time, however. He could hear the far-off tinkle of silver and clink of china, and knew the family were at dinner. "Won't leave his dinner for me," thought Jerome, with an unrighteous bitterness of humility, recognizing the fact that he could not expect him to. "Might have planted an hour longer."

Then came a clang of the knocker, and this time the girl ushered into the study a clamping, red-faced man in a shabby coat. Jerome recognized him as a young farmer who lived three miles or so out of the village. He blushed and stumbled, with a kind of grim awkwardness, even before the simple girl delivering herself of her formula of welcome. He would not sit down; he stood by the corner of a medicine-cupboard, settling heavily into his boots, waiting.

When the girl had gone he looked at Jerome, and gave a vague and furtive "Hullo!" in simple recognition of his presence, as it were. He did not know who the boy was, never being easily certain as to identities of any but old acquaintances — not from high indifference and dislike, like the doctor, but from dulness of observation.

Jerome nodded in response to the man's salutation. "I can't ask the doctor before him," he thought, anxiously.

The man rested heavily, first on one leg, then on the other. "Been waitin' long?" he grunted, finally.

"Quite a while."

"Hope my horse 'll stan'," said the man; "headed towards home, an' load off."

"The doctor can tend to you first," Jerome said, eagerly.

The man gave a nod of assent. Thanks, as elegancies of social intercourse, were alarming, and savored of affectation, to him. He had thanked the Lord, from his heart, for all his known and unknown gifts, but his gratitude towards his fellow-men had never overcome his bashful self-consciousness and found voice.

Often in prayer-meeting Jerome had heard this man's fervent outpouring of the religious faith which seemed the only intelligence of his soul, and, like all single and concentrated powers, had a certain force of persuasion. Jerome eyed him now with a kind of pious admiration and respect, and yet with recollections.

"If I were a man, I'd stop colorin' up and actin' scared," thought the boy; and then they both heard a door open and shut, and knew the doctor was coming.

Jerome's heart beat hard, yet he looked quite boldly at the door. Somehow the young farmer's clumsy embarrassment had roused his own pride and courage. When the doctor entered, he stood up with alacrity and made his manners, and the young farmer settled to another foot, with a hoarse note of greeting.

The doctor said good-day, with formal courtesy, with his fine, keen face turned seemingly upon both of them impartially; then he addressed the young man.

"How is your wife today?" he inquired.

The young man turned purple, where he had been red, at this direct address. "She's pretty — comfortable," he stammered.

"Is she out of medicine?"

"Yes, sir. That's what I come for." With that the young man pulled, with distressed fumblings and jerks, a bottle from his pocket, which he handed to the doctor, who had in the meantime opened the door of one of the cupboards.

The doctor took a large bottle from the cupboard, and filled from that the one which the young man had brought. Jerome stood trembling, watching the careful gurgling of a speckled green liquid from one bottle to another. A strange new odor filled the room, overpowering all the others.

When the doctor gave the bottle to the young man, he shoved it carefully away in his pocket again, and then stood coloring more deeply and hesitating.

"Can ye take your pay in wood for this and the last two lots?" he murmured at length, so low that Jerome scarcely heard him.

But the doctor never lowered nor raised his incisive, high-bred voice for any man. His reply left no doubt of the question. "No, Mr. Upham," said Doctor Prescott. "You must pay me in money for medicine. I have enough wood of my own."

"I know ye have — consider'ble," responded the young man, in an agony, "but —"

"I would like the money as soon as convenient," said the doctor.

"I'm — havin' — dreadful — hard work to get — any money myself — lately," persisted the young man. "Folks — they promise, but — they don't pay, an' —"

"Never give or take promises long enough to calculate interest," interposed Doctor Prescott, with stern pleasantry; "that's my rule, young man, and it's the one I expect others to follow in their business dealings with me. Don't give and don't take; then you'll make your way in life."

Ozias Lamb had said once, in Jerome's hearing, that all the medicine that Doctor Prescott ever gave to folks for nothing was good advice, and he didn't know but then he sent the bill in to the Almighty. Jerome, who had taken this in, with a sharp wink of appreciation, in spite of his mother's promptly sending him out of the room, thinking that such talk savored of irreverence, and was not fit for youthful ears, remembered it now, as he heard Doctor Prescott admonishing poor John Upham.

"Know ye've got consider'ble," mumbled John Upham, who had rough lands enough for a village, but scarce two shillings in pocket, and a delicate young wife and three babies; "but — thought ye hadn't — no old apple-tree wood — old apple-tree wood — well seasoned — jest the thing for the parlor hearth — didn't know but —"

"I should like the money next week," said the doctor, as if he had not heard a word of poor John's entreaty.

The young man shook his head miserably. "Dun'no' as I can — nohow."

"Well," said the doctor, looking at him calmly, "I'm willing to take a little land for the medicine and that last winter's bill, when Johnny had the measles."

Then this poor John Upham, uncouth, and scarcely quicker-witted than one of his own oxen, but as faithful, and living up wholly to his humble lights, turned pale through his blushes, and stared at the doctor as if he could not have heard aright. "Take — my land?" he faltered.

Doctor Prescott never smiled with his eyes, but only with a symmetrical curving and lengthening of his finely cut, thin lips. He smiled so then. "Yes, I am willing to take some land for the debt, since you have not the money," said he.

"But — that was — father's land."

"Yes, and your father was a good, thrifty man. He did not waste his substance."

"It was grandfather's, too."

"Yes, it was, I believe."

"It has always been in our — family. It's the Upham — land. I can't part with it nohow."

"I will take the money, then," said Doctor Prescott.

"I'll raise it just as soon as I can, doctor," cried John Upham, eagerly. "I've got a man's note for twenty dollars comin' due in three months; he's sure to pay. An' — there's some cedar ordered, an' —"

"I must have it next week," said the doctor, "or —" He paused.

"I shall dislike to proceed to extreme measures," he added.

Then John Upham, aroused to boldness by desperation, as the very oxen will sometimes run in madness if the goad be sharp enough, told Doctor Prescott to his face, with scarce a stumble in his speech, that he owned half the town now; that his land was much more valuable than his, which was mostly swampy woodland and pasture-lands, bringing in scarcely enough income to feed and clothe his family.

"Sha'n't have 'nough to live on if I let any on't go," said John Upham, "an' you've got more land as 'tis than any other man in town."

Doctor Prescott did not raise or quicken his clear voice; his eyes did not flash, but they gave out a hard light. John Upham was like a giant before this little, neat, wiry figure, which had such a majesty of port that it seemed to throw its own shadow over him.

"We are not discussing the extent of my possessions," said Doctor Prescott, "but the extent of your debts." He moved aside, as if to clear the passage to the door, turning slightly at the same time towards his other caller, who was cold with indignation upon John Upham's account and terror upon his own.

Half minded he was, when John Upham went out, with his clamping, clumsy tread, with his honest head cast down, and no more words in his mouth for the doctor's last smoothly scathing remark, to follow him at a bound and ask nothing for himself; but he stood still and watched him go.

When John Upham had opened the door and was passing through, the doctor pursued him with yet one more bit of late advice. "It is poor judgment," said Doctor Prescott, "for a young man to marry and bring children into the world until he has property enough to support them without running into debt. You would have done better had you waited, Mr. Upham. It is what I always tell young men."

Then John Upham turned with the last turn of the trodden worm. "My wife and my children are my own!" he cried out, with a great roar. "It's between me and my Maker, my having 'em, and I'll answer to no man for it!" With that he was gone, and the door shut hard after him.

Then Doctor Prescott, no whit disturbed, turned to Jerome and looked at him. Jerome made his manners again. "You are the Edwards boy, aren't you?" said the doctor.

Jerome humbly acknowledged his identity.

"What do you want? Has your mother sent you on an errand?"

"No, sir."

"Well, what is it, then?"

"Please, sir, may I speak to you a minute?"

"Speak to me?"

"Yes, sir."

Doctor Prescott wore a massive gold watch-chain festooned across his fine black satin vest. He pulled out before the boy's wondering and perplexed eyes the great gold timepiece attached to it and looked at it. "You must be quick," said he. "I have to go in five minutes. I will give you five minutes by my watch. Begin."

But poor little Jerome, thus driven with such a hard check-rein of time, paled and reddened and trembled, and could find no words.

"One minute is gone," said the doctor, looking over the open face of his watch at Jerome. Something in his glance spurred on the frightened boy by arousing a flash of resentment.

Jerome, standing straight before the doctor, with a little twitching hand hanging at each side, with his color coming and going, and pulses which could be seen beating hard in his temples and throat, spoke and delivered himself of that innocently over-reaching scheme which he had propounded to Squire Eben Merritt.

It seems probable that mental states have their own reflective powers, which sometimes enable one to suddenly see himself in the conception of another, to the complete modification of all his own ideas and opinions. So little Jerome Edwards, even while speaking, began to see his plan as it looked to Doctor Prescott, and not as it had hitherto looked to himself. He began to understand and to realize the flaws in it — that he had asked more of Doctor Prescott than he would grant. Still, he went on, and the doctor heard him through without a word.

"Who put you up to this?" the doctor asked, when he had finished.

"Nobody, sir."

"Your mother?"

"No, sir."

"Did you ever hear your father propose anything like this?"

"No, sir."

"Who did? Speak the truth."

"I did."

"You thought out this plan yourself?"

"Yes, sir."

"Look at me."

Jerome, flushing with angry shame at his own simplicity as revealed to him by this other, older, superior intellect, yet defiant still at this attack upon his truth, looked the doctor straight in his keen eyes.

"Are you speaking the truth?"

"Yes, sir."

Still the doctor looked at him, and Jerome would not cast his eyes down, nor, indeed, could. He felt as if his very soul were being stretched up on tiptoe to the doctor's inspection.

"Children had better follow the wisdom of their elders," said the doctor. He would not even deign to explain to this boy the absurdity of his scheme.

He replaced the great gold watch in his pocket. "I will be in soon, and talk over matters with your mother," he said, turning away.

Jerome gave a gasp. He stumbled forward, as if to fall on his knees at the doctor's feet.

"Oh, sir, don't, don't!" he cried out.

"Don't what?"

"Don't foreclose the mortgage. It will kill mother."

"You don't know what you are talking about," said the doctor, calmly. "Children should not meddle in matters beyond them. I will settle it with your mother."

"Mother's sick!" gasped Jerome. The doctor was moving with his stately strut to the door. Suddenly the boy, in a great outburst of boldness, flung himself before this great man of his childhood and arrested his progress. "Oh, sir, tell me," he begged — "tell me what you're going to do!"

The doctor never knew why he stopped to explain and parley. He was conscious of no softening towards this boy, who had so repelled him with his covert rebellion, and had now been guilty of a much greater offence. An appeal to a goodness which is not in him is to a sensitive and vain soul a stinging insult. Doctor Prescott could have administered corporal punishment to this boy, who seemed to him to be actually poking fun at his dignity, and yet he stopped and answered:

"I am going to take your house into my hands," said Doctor Prescott, "and your mother can live in it and pay me rent."

"We can't pay rent any better than interest money."

"If you can't pay the rent, I shall be willing to take that wood-lot of your father's," said Doctor Prescott. "I will talk that over with your mother."

Jerome looked at him. There was a dreadful expression on his little boyish face. His very lips were white. "You are goin' to take our woodland for rents?"

"If you can't pay them, of course. Your mother ought to be glad she has it to pay with."

"Then we sha'n't have anything."

Doctor Prescott endeavored to move on, but Jerome fairly crowded himself between him and the door, and stood there, his pale face almost touching his breast, and his black eyes glaring up at him with a startling nearness as of fire.

"You are a wicked man," said the boy, "and some day God will punish you for it."

Then there came a grasp of nervous hands upon his shoulders, like the clamp of steel, the door was opened before him, and he was pushed out, and along the entry at arm's-length, and finally made to descend the south door-steps at a dizzy run. "Go home to your mother," ordered Doctor Prescott. Still, he did not raise his voice, his color had not changed, and he breathed no quicker. Births and deaths, all natural stresses of life, its occasional tragedies, and even his own bitter wrath could this small, equally poised man meet with calm superiority over them and command over himself. Doctor Seth Prescott never lost his personal dignity — he could not, since it was so inseparable from his personality. If he chastised his son, it was with the judicial majesty of a king, and never with a self-demeaning show of anger. He ate and drank in his own house like a guest of state at a feast; he drove his fine sorrel in his sulky like a war-horse in a chariot. Once, when walking to meeting on an icy day, his feet went from under him, and he sat down suddenly; but even his fall seemed to have something majestic and solemn and Scriptural about it. Nobody laughed.

Doctor Prescott expelling this little boy from his south door had the impressiveness of a priest of Bible times expelling an interloper from the door of the Temple. Jerome almost fell when he reached the ground, but collected himself after a staggering step or two as the door shut behind him.

The doctor's sulky was drawn up before the door, and Jake Noyes stood by the horse's head. The horse sprang aside — he was a nervous sorrel — when Jerome flew down the steps, and Jake Noyes reined him up quickly with a sharp "Whoa!"

As soon as he recovered his firm footing, Jerome started to run out of the yard; but Jake, holding the sorrel's bridle with one hand, reached out the other to his collar and brought him to a stand.

"Hullo!" said he, hushing his voice somewhat and glancing at the door. "What's to pay?"

"I told him he was a wicked man, and he didn't like it because it's true," replied Jerome, in a loud voice, trying to pull away.

"Hush up," whispered Jake, with a half whimsical, half uneasy nod of his head towards the door; "look out how you talk. He'll be out and crammin' blue-pills and assafœtidy into your mouth first thing you know. Don't you go to sassin' of your betters."

"He is a wicked man! I don't care, he is a wicked man!" cried Jerome, loudly. He glanced defiantly at the house, then into Jake's face, with a white flash of fury.

"Hush up, I tell ye," said Jake. "He'll be a-pourin' of castor-ile down your throat out of a quart measure, arter the blue-pills and the assafœtidy."

"I'd like to see him! He is a wicked man. Let me go!"

"Don't you go to callin' names that nobody but the Almighty has any right to fasten on to folks."

"Let me go!" Jerome wriggled under the man's detaining grasp, as wirily instinct with nerves as a cat; he kicked out viciously at his shins.

"Lord! I'd as lief try to hold a catamount," cried Jake Noyes, laughing, and released him, and Jerome raced out of the yard.

It was then about two o'clock. He should have gone home to his planting, but his childish patience was all gone. Poor little Jack had been worsted by the giant, and his bean-garden might as well be neglected. Human strength may endure heavy disappointments and calamities with heroism, but it requires superhuman power to hold one's hand to the grindstone of petty duties and details of life in the midst of them. Jerome had faced his rebuff without a whimper, and with a great stand of spirit, but now he could not go home and work in the garden, and tie his fiery revolt to the earth with spade and hoe. He ran on up the road, until he passed the village and came to his woodland. He followed the cart path through it, until he was near the boundary wall; then he threw himself down in the midst of some young brakes and little wild green things, and presently fell to weeping, with loud sobs, like a baby.

All day he had been strained up to an artificial height of manhood; now he had come down again to his helpless estate of boyhood. In the solitude of the woods there is no mocking, and no despite for helplessness and grief. The trees raising their heads in a great host athwart the sky, the tender plants beneath gathering into their old places with tumultuous silence, put to shame no outcry of any suffering heart of bird or beast or man. To these unpruned and mother-fastnesses of the earth belonged at first the wailing infancy of all life, and even now a vague memory of it is left, like the organ of a lost sense, in the heart oppressed by the grief of the grown world.

The boy unknowingly had fled to his first mother, who had soothed his old sorrow in his heart before he had come into the consciousness of it. Had Doctor Prescott at any minute surprised him, he would have faced him again, with no sign of weakening; but he lay there, curled up among the brakes as in a green nest, with his face against the earth, and her breath of aromatic moisture in his nostrils, and sobbed and wept until he fell asleep.

He had slept an hour and a half, when he wakened suddenly, with a clear "Hello!" in his ears. He opened his eyes and looked up, dazed, into Squire Eben Merritt's great blond face."

"Hullo!" said Squire Eben again. "I thought it was a woodchuck, and instead of that it's a boy. What are you doing here, sir?"

Jerome raised himself falteringly. He felt weak, and the confused misery of readjusting the load of grief under which one has fallen asleep was upon him. "Guess I fell asleep," he stammered.

"Guess you'd better not fall asleep in such a damp hole as this," said the Squire, "or the rheumatism will catch your young bones. Why aren't you home planting, sir? I thought you were a smart boy."

"He'll get it all; there ain't any use!" said Jerome, with pitiful doggedness, standing ankle-deep in brakes before the Squire. He rubbed his eyes, heavy with sleep and tears, and raised them, dull still, into the Squire's face.

"Who do you mean by he? Dr. Prescott?"

"Yes, sir."

"Then he didn't approve of your plan?"

"He's going to take our house, and let us live in it and pay rent, and if we can't pay he's going to take our wood-lot here —" Suddenly Jerome gave a great sob; he flung himself down wildly. "He sha'n't have it; he sha'n't — he never shall!" he sobbed, and clutched at the brakes and held them to his bosom, as if he were indeed holding some dear thing against an enemy who would wrest it from him.

Squire Eben Merritt, towering over him, with a long string of trout at his side, looked at him with a puzzled frown; then he reached down and pulled him to his feet with a mighty and gentle jerk. "How old are you, sir?" he demanded. "Thought you were a man; thought you were going to learn to fire my gun. Guess you haven't been out of petticoats long enough, after all!"

Jerome drew his sleeve fiercely across his eyes, and then looked up at the Squire proudly. "Didn't cry before him," said he.

Squire Eben laughed, and gave his back a hard pat. "I guess you'll do, after all," said he. "So you didn't have much luck with the doctor?"

"No, sir."

"Well, don't you fret. I'll see what can be done. I'll see him tonight myself."

Jerome looked up in his face, like one who scarcely dares to believe in offered comfort.

The Squire nodded kindly at him. "You leave it all to me," said he; "don't you worry."

Jerome belonged to a family in which there had been little demonstration of devotion and affection. His parents never caressed their children; he and his sister had scarcely kissed each other since their infancy. No matter how fervid their hearts might be, they had also a rigidity, as of paralyzed muscles, which forbade much expression as a shame and an affectation. Jerome had this tendency of the New England character from inheritance and training; but now, in spite of it, he fell down before Squire Eben Merritt, embraced his knees, and kissed his very feet in their great boots, and then his hand.

Squire Eben laughed, pulled the boy to his feet again, and bade him again to cheer up and not to fret. The same impulse of kindly protection which led him to spare the lives and limbs of old trees was over him now towards this weak human plant.

"Come along with me," said Squire Eben, and forthwith Jerome had followed him out of the woods into the road, and down it until they reached his sister's, Miss Camilla Merritt's, house, not far from Doctor Prescott's. There Squire Eben was about to part with Jerome, with more words of reassurance, when suddenly he remembered that his sister needed such a boy to weed her flower-beds, and had spoken to him about procuring one for her. So he had bidden Jerome follow him; and the boy, who would at that moment have gone over a precipice after him, went to Miss Camilla's tea-drinking in her arbor.

When he went home, in an hour's time, he was engaged to weed Miss Camilla's flower-garden all summer, at two shillings per week, and it was understood that his sister could weed as well as he when his home-work prevented his coming.

In early youth exaltation of spirit requires but slight causes; only a soft puff of a favoring wind will send up one like a kite into the ether. Jerome, with the prospect of two shillings per week, and that great, kindly strength of the Squire's underlying his weakness, went home as if he had wings on his feet.

"See that boy of poor Abel Edwards's dancin' along, when his father ain't been dead a week!" one woman at her window said to another.

CHAPTER X

Squire Eben Merritt had three boon companions — the village lawyer, Eliphalet Means; a certain John Jennings, the last of one of the village old families, a bachelor of some fifty odd, who had wasted his health and patrimony in riotous living, and had now settled down to prudence and moderation, if not repentance, in the home of his ancestors; and one Colonel Jack Lamson, also considered somewhat of a rake, who had possibly tendered his resignation rather than his reformation, and that perforce. Colonel Lamson also hailed originally from a good old stock of this village and county. He had gone to the wars for his country, and retired at fifty-eight with a limp in his right leg and a cane. Colonel Lamson, being a much-removed cousin of the lawyer's, kept bachelors' hall with him in a comfortable and untidy old mansion at the other end of the town, across the brook.

Many nights of a week these four met for an evening of whist or bezique, to the scandal of the steady-going folk of the town, who approved not of cards, and opined that the Squire's poor wife must feel bad enough to have such carousings at her house. But the Squire's wife, who had in herself a rare understanding among women of masculine good-fellowship, had sometimes, if the truth had been told, taken an ailing member's hand at cards when their orgies convened at the Squire's. John Jennings, being somewhat afflicted with rheumatic gout, was occasionally missing. Then did Abigail Merritt take his place, and play with the sober concentration of a man and the quick wit of a woman. Colonel Jack Lamson, whose partner she was, privately preferred her to John Jennings, whose overtaxed mental powers sometimes failed him in the memory of the cards; but being as intensely loyal to his friends as to his country, he never spoke to that effect. He only, when the little, trim, black-haired woman made a brilliant stroke of *finesse*, with a quick flash of her bright eyes and wise compression of lips, smiled privately, as if to himself, with face bent upon his hand.

Whether Abigail Merritt played cards or not, she always brewed a great bowl of punch, as no one but she knew how to do, and set it out for the delectation of her husband and his friends. The receipt for this punch — one which had been long stored in the culinary archives of the Merritt family, with the poundcake and other rich and toothsome compounds — had often, upon entreaty, been confided to other ambitious matrons, but to no purpose. Let them spice and flavor and add measures of fine strong liquors as they would, their punch had not that perfect harmony of results, which effaces detail, of Abigail Merritt's.

"By George!" Colonel Jack Lamson was wont to say, when his first jorum had trickled down his experienced throat — "By George! I thought I had drunk punch. There was a time when I thought I could mix a bowl of punch myself, but this is *punch.*"

Then John Jennings, holding his empty glass, would speak: "All we could taste in that last punch that Belinda Armstrong made at my house was lemon; and the time before that, allspice; and the time before that, raw rum." John Jennings's voice, somewhat hoarse, was yet full of sweet melancholy cadences; there was sentiment and pathos in his "lemon" and "allspice," which waxed almost tearful in his "raw rum." His worn, high-bred face was as instinct with gentle melancholy as his voice, yet his sunken black eyes sparkled with the light of youth as the fine aromatic fire of the punch penetrated his veins.

As for the lawyer, who was the eldest of the four, long, brown, toughly and dryly pliant as an old blade of marsh-grass, he showed in speech, look, nor manner no sign of enthusiasm, but he drank the punch.

That evening, after Jerome Edwards had run home with his prospects of two shillings a week and Squire Eben Merritt's assistance, the friends met at the Squire's house. At eight o'clock they came marching down the road, the three of them — John Jennings in fine old broadcloth and a silk hat, with a weak stoop in his shoulders, and a languid shakiness in his long limbs; the lawyer striding nimbly as a grasshopper, with the utter unconsciousness of one who pursues only the ultimate ends of life; and the colonel, halting on his right knee, and recovering himself stiffly with his cane, holding his shoulders back, breathing a little heavily, his neck puffing over his high stock, his face a purplish-red about his white mustache and close-cropped beard.

The Squire's wife had the punch-bowl all ready in the south room, where the parties were held. Some pipes were laid out there too, and a great jar of fine tobacco, and the cards were on the mahogany card-table — four packs for bezique. Abigail herself opened the door, admitted the guests, and ushered them into the south room. Colonel Lamson said something about the aroma of the punch; and John Jennings, in his sweet, melancholy voice, something gallant about the fair hands that mixed it; but Eliphalet Means moved unobtrusively across the room and dipped out for himself a glass of the beverage, and wasted not his approval in empty words.

The Squire came in shortly and greeted his guests, but he had his hat in his hand.

"I have to go out on business," he announced. "I shall not be long. Mrs. Merritt will have to take my place."

Abigail looked at him in surprise. But she was a most discreet wife. She never asked a question, though she wondered why her husband had not spoken of this before. The truth was he had forgotten his card-party when he had made his promise to Jerome, and then he had forgotten his promise to Jerome in thinking of his card-party, and little Lucina on her way to bed had just brought it to mind by asking when he was going. She had heard the promise, and had not forgotten.

"By the Lord Harry!" said the Squire, for he heard his friends down-stairs. Then, when Lucina looked at him with innocent wonder, he said, hurriedly, "Now, Pretty — I am going now," and went down to excuse himself to his guests.

Eliphalet Means, whose partner Abigail had become by this deflection, nodded, and seated himself at once in his place at table, the pleasant titillation of the punch in his veins and approval in his heart. He considered Abigail a better player than her husband, and began to meditate proposing a small stake that evening.

The Squire, setting forth on his errand to Doctor Prescott, striding heavily through the sweet dampness of the spring night, experienced a curious combination of amusement, satisfaction, and indignation with himself. "I'm a fool!" he declared, with more vehemence than he would have declared four aces in bezique; and then he cursed his folly, and told himself that if he kept on he would leave Abigail and the child without a penny. But then, after all, he realized that singularly warm glow of self-approval for a good deed which at once comforts and irradiates the heart in spite of all worldly prudence and wisdom.

That night the air was very heavy with moisture, which seemed to hold all the spring odors of newly turned earth, young grass, and blossoms in solution. Squire Eben moved through it as through a scented flood in which respiration was possible. Over all the fields was a pale mist, waving and eddying in such impalpable air currents that it seemed to have a sentient life of its own. These soft rises and lapses of the mist on the fields might seemingly have been due to the efforts of prostrate shadows to gather themselves into form. Beyond the fields, against the hills and woods and clear horizon, pale fogs arose with motions as of arms and garments and streaming locks. The blossoming trees stood out suddenly beside one with a white surprise rather felt than seen. The young moon and the stars shone dimly with scattering rays, and the lights in the house windows were veiled. The earth and sky and all the familiar features of the village had that effect of mystery and unreality which some conditions of the atmosphere bring to pass.

A strangely keen sense of the unstability of all earthly things, of the shadows of the tomb, of the dreamy half light of the world, came over Eben Merritt, and his generous impulse seemed suddenly the only lantern to light his wavering feet. "I'll do what I can for the poor little chap, come what will," he muttered, and strode on to Doctor Prescott's house.

Just before he reached it a horse and sulky turned into the yard, driven rapidly from the other direction. Squire Eben hastened his steps, and reached the south house door before the doctor entered. He was just ascending the steps, his medicine-case in hand, when he heard his name called, and turned around.

"I want a word with you before you go in, doctor," called the Squire, as he came up.

"Good-evening, Squire Merritt," returned the doctor, bowing formally on his vantage-ground of steps, but his voice bespoke a spiritual as well as material elevation.

"I would like a word with you," the Squire said again.

"Walk into the house."

"No, I won't come in, as long as I've met you. I have company at home. I haven't much to say —" The Squire stopped. Jake Noyes was coming from the barn, swinging a lantern; he waited until he had led the horse away, then continued. "It is just as well to have no witnesses," he said, laughing. "It is about that affair of the Edwards mortgage."

"Ah!" said the doctor, with a fencing wariness of intonation.

"I would like to inquire what you're going to do about it, if you have no objection. I have reasons."

The doctor gave a keen look at him. His face, as he stood on the steps, was on a level with the Squire's. "I am going to take the house, of course," he said, calmly.

"It will be a blow to Mrs. Edwards and the boy."

"It will be the best thing that could happen to him," said the doctor, with the same clear evenness. "That sick woman and boy are not fit to have the care of a place. I shall own it, and rent it to them."

Heat in controversy is sometimes needful to convince one's self as well as one's adversary. Doctor Prescott needed no increase of warmth to further his own arguments, so conclusive they were to his own mind.

"For how much, if I may ask? I am interested for certain reasons."

"Seventy dollars. That will amount to the interest money they pay now and ten dollars over. The extra ten will be much less than repairs and taxes. They will be gainers."

"What will you take for that mortgage?"

"Take for the mortgage?"

The Squire nodded.

The doctor gave another of his keen glances at him. "I don't know that I want to take anything for it," he said.

"Suppose it were made worth your while?"

"Nobody would be willing to make it enough worth my while to influence me," said the doctor. "My price for the transfer of a good investment is what it is worth to me."

"Well, doctor, what is it worth to you?" Squire Eben said, smiling.

"Fifteen hundred dollars," said the doctor.

The Squire whistled.

"I am quite aware that the mortgage is for a thousand only," the doctor said, and yet without the slightest meaning of apology, "but I consider when it comes to relinquishing it that it is worth the additional five hundred. I must be just to myself. Then, too, Mr. Edwards owed me a half year's interest. The fifteen hundred would cover that, of course."

"You won't take any less?"

"Not a dollar."

Squire Eben hesitated a second. "You know, I own that strip of land on the Dale road, on the other side of the brook," he said.

The doctor nodded, still with his eyes keenly intent.

"There are three good house-lots; that house of the Edwardses is old and out of repair. You'll have to spend considerable on it to rent it. My three lots are equal to that one house, and suppose we exchange. You take that land, and I take the mortgage on the Edwards place."

"Do you know what you are talking about?" Doctor Prescott said, sharply; for this plain proposition that he overreach the other aroused him to a show of fairness.

Squire Merritt laughed. "Oh, I know you'll get the best of the bargain," he returned.

Then the doctor waxed suspicious. This readiness to take the worst of a bargain while perfectly cognizant of it puzzled him. He wondered if perchance this easy-going, card-playing, fishing

Squire had, after all, some axe of policy to grind. "What do you expect to make out of it?" he asked, bluntly.

"Nothing. I am not even sure that I have any active hope of a higher rate of interest in the other world for it. I am not as sound in the doctrines as you, doctor." Squire Eben laughed, but the other turned on him sternly.

"If you are doing this for the sake of Abel Edwards's widow and her children, you are acting from a mistaken sense of charity, and showing poor judgment," said he.

Squire Eben laughed again. "You made no reply to my proposition, doctor," he said.

"You are in earnest?"

"I am."

"You understand what you are doing?"

"I certainly do. I am giving you between fifteen and sixteen hundred dollars' worth of land for a thousand."

"There is no merit nor charity in such foolish measures as this," said the doctor, half suspicious that there was more behind this, and not put to shame but aroused to a sense of superiority by such drivelling idiocy of benevolence.

"Dare say you're right, doctor," returned Squire Eben. "I won't even cheat you out of the approval of Heaven. Will you meet me at Means's office tomorrow, with the necessary documents for the transfer? We had better go around to Mrs. Edwards's afterwards and inform her, I suppose."

"I will meet you at Means's office at ten o'clock tomorrow morning," said the doctor, shortly. "Good-evening," and with that turned on his heel. However, when he had opened the door he turned again and called curtly and magisterially after Squire Eben: "I advise you to cultivate a little more business foresight for the sake of your wife and child," and Squire Eben answered back:

"Thank you — thank you, doctor; guess you're right," and then began to whistle like a boy as he went down the avenue of pines.

Through lack of remunerative industry, and easy-going habits, his share of the old Merritt property had dwindled considerably; he had none too much money to spend at the best, and now he had bartered away a goodly slice of his paternal acres for no adequate worldly return. He knew it all, he felt a half whimsical dismay as he went home, and yet the meaning which underlies the letter of a good action was keeping his heart warm.

When he reached home his wife, who had just finished her game, slid out gently, and the usual festivities began. Colonel

Lamson, warmed with punch and good-fellowship and tobacco, grew brilliant at cards, and humorously reminiscent of old jokes between the games; John Jennings lagged at cards, but flashed out now and then with fine wit, while his fervently working brain lit up his worn face with the light of youth. The lawyer, who drank more than the rest, played better and better, and waxed caustic in speech if crossed. As for the Squire, his frankness increased even to the risk of self-praise. Before the evening was over he had told the whole story of little Jerome, of Doctor Prescott and himself and the Edwards mortgage. The three friends stared at him with unsorted cards in their hands.

"You are a damned fool!" cried Eliphalet Means, taking his pipe from his mouth.

"No," cried Jennings, "not a damned fool, but a rare fool," and his great black eyes, in their mournful hollows, flashed affectionately at Squire Eben.

"And I say he's a damned fool. Men live in this world," maintained the lawyer, fiercely.

"Men's hearts ought to be out of the world if their heads are in it," affirmed John Jennings, with a beautiful smile. "I say he's a rare fool, and I would that all the wise men could go to school to such a fool and learn wisdom of his folly."

Colonel Jack Lamson, who sat at the Squire's left, removed his pipe, cleared his throat, and strove to speak in vain. Now he began with a queer stiffness of his lips, while his purplish-red flush spread to the roots of his thin bristle of gray hair.

"It reminds me of a story I heard. No, that is another. It reminds me —" And then the colonel broke down with a great sob, and a dash of his sleeve across his eyes, and recovered himself, and cried out, chokingly, "No, I'll be damned if it reminds me of anything I've ever seen or heard of, for I've never seen a man like you, Eben!"

And with that he slapped his cards to the table, and shook the Squire's hand, with such a fury of affectionate enthusiasm that some of his cards fluttered about him to the floor, like a shower of leaves.

As for Eliphalet Means, he declared again, with vicious emphasis, "He's a damned fool!" then rose up, laid his cards on top of the colonel's scattered hand, went to the punch-bowl and helped himself to another glass; then, pipe in mouth, went up to Squire Merritt and gave him a great slap on his back. "You are a damned fool, my boy!" he cried out, holding his pipe from his lips and breathing out a great cloud of smoke with the words; "but the wife and the young one and you shall never want a bite or a sup, nor a bed nor a board, on account of it, while old 'Liph Means has a penny in pocket."

And with that Eliphalet Means, who was old enough to be the Squire's father, and loved him as he would have loved a son, went back to his seat and dealt the cards over.

CHAPTER XI

Innocence and ignorance can be as easily hood-winked by kindness as by contumely.

This little Jerome, who had leaped, under the spur of necessity, to an independence of understanding beyond his years, allowed himself to be quite misled by the Squire as to his attitude in the matter of the mortgage. In spite of the momentary light reflected from the doctor's shrewder intelligence which had flashed upon his scheme, the Squire was able to delude him with a renewed belief in it, after he had informed him of the transfer of the mortgage-deed, which took place the next morning.

"I decided to buy that wood-lot of your father's, as your mother was willing," said the Squire; "and as I had not the money in hand to pay down, I gave my note to your mother for it, as you proposed the doctor should do, and allowed six per cent. interest."

Jerome looked at him in a bewildered way.

"Well, what is the matter? Aren't you as willing to take my note as the doctor's?" asked the Squire.

"Is it fair?" asked Jerome, hesitatingly.

"Fair to you?"

"No; to you."

"Of course it is fair enough to me. Why not?"

"The doctor didn't think it was," said the boy, getting more and more bewildered.

"Why didn't he?"

"I don't — know —" faltered Jerome; and he did not, for the glimmer of light which he had got from the doctor's worldly wisdom had quite failed him. He had seen quite clearly that it was not fair, but now he could not.

"Oh, well, I dare say it is fairer for me than for him," said the Squire, easily. "Probably he had the ready money; I haven't the ready money; that makes all the difference. Don't you see it does?"

"Yes — sir," replied Jerome, hesitatingly, and tried to think he saw; but he did not. A mind so young and immature as his is not unlike the gaseous age of planets, overlaid with great shifting masses of vapor, which part to disclose dazzling flame-points and incomparable gleams, then close again. Only time can accomplish a nearer balance of light in minds and planets.

Then, too, as the first strain of unwonted demands relaxed a little through use, Jerome's mental speed, which seemed to have taken him into manhood at a bound, slackened, and he even fell back somewhat in his tracks. He was still beyond what he had ever been before, for one cannot return from growth. He would never be as much of a child again, but he was more of a child than he had been yesterday.

His mother also had been instrumental towards replacing him in his old ways. Ann, after her day of crushed apathy, aroused herself somewhat. When the Squire, the lawyer, and Doctor Prescott came the next morning, she kept them waiting outside while she put on her best cap. She had a view of the road from her rocking-chair, and when she saw the three gentlemen advancing with a slow curve of progress towards her gate, which betokened an entrance, she called sharply to Elmira, who was washing dishes, "Go into the bedroom and get my best cap, quick," at the same time twitching off the one upon her head.

When poor little Elmira turned and stared, her pretty face quite pale, thinking her mother beside herself, she made a fierce, menacing gesture with her nervous elbow, and spoke again, in a whisper, lest the approaching guests hear: "Why don't you start? Take this old cap and get my best one, quick!" And the little girl scuttled into the bedroom just as the first knock came on the door. Ann kept the three dignitaries waiting until she adjusted her cap to her liking, and the knocks had been several times repeated before she sent the trembling Elmira to admit them and usher them into the best parlor, whither she followed, hitching herself through the entry in her chair, and disdainfully refusing all offers of assistance. She even thrust out an elbow repellingly at the Squire, who had sprung forward to her aid.

"No, thank you, sir," said she; "I don't need any help; I always go around the house so. I ain't helpless."

Ann, when she had brought her chair to a stand, sat facing the three callers, each of whose salutations she returned with a curtly polite bow. She had a desperate sense of being at bay, and that the hands of all these great men, whose supremacy she acknowledged with the futile uprearing of any angry woman, were against her. She eyed the lawyer, Eliphalet Means, with particular distrust. She had always held all legal proceedings as a species of quagmire to entrap the innocent and unwary. She watched while the lawyer took some documents from his bag and laid them on the table. "I won't sign a thing, nohow," she avowed to herself, and shut her mouth tight.

Squire Merritt discovered that besides dealing with his own scruples he had to overcome his beneficiary's.

It took a long time to convince Ann that she was not being

overreached and cheated. She seemed absolutely incapable of understanding the transfer of the mortgage note from Doctor Prescott to Squire Merritt.

"I've signed one mortgage," said she, firmly; "I put my name under my husband's. I ain't goin' to sign another."

"But nobody wants you to sign anything, Mrs. Edwards. The mortgage note is simply transferred to Squire Merritt here. We only want you to understand it," said Lawyer Means. He had a curiously impersonal manner of dealing with women, being wont to say that only a man who expected good sense in womenkind was surprised when he did not find it.

"I ain't goin' to put two mortgages on this place," said Ann, fronting him with the utter stupidity of obstinacy.

"Let me explain it to you, Mrs. Edwards," said Eliphalet Means, with no impatience. He regarded a woman as so incontrovertibly a patience-tryer, from the laws of creation, that he would as soon have waxed impatient with the structural order of things. He endeavored to explain matters with imperturbable persistency, but Ann was still unconvinced.

"I ain't goin' to sign my name to any other mortgage," said she.

Jerome, who had stood listening in the door, slid up to his mother and touched her arm. "Oh, mother," he whispered, "I know all about it — it's all right!"

Ann gave him a thrust with a little sharp elbow. "What do you know about it?" she cried. "I'm here to look out for you and your sister, and take care of what little we've got, an' I'm goin' to. Go out an' tend to your work."

"Oh, mother, do let me stay!"

"Go right along, I tell you." And Jerome, who was the originator of all this, went out helplessly, slighted and indignant. He did think the Squire might have interceded for him to stay, knowing what he knew. Even youth has its disadvantages.

But Squire Eben stood somewhat aloof, looking at the small, frail, pugnacious woman in the rocking-chair with perplexity and growing impatience. He wanted to go fishing that morning, and the vision of the darting trout in their still, clear pool was before him, like a vision of his own earthly paradise. He gave a despairing glance at Doctor Prescott, who had hitherto said little. "Can't you convince her it is all right? She knows you better than the rest of us," he whispered.

Doctor Prescott nodded, arose — he had been sitting apart — went to Mrs. Edwards, and touched her shoulder. "Mrs.

Edwards," said he — Ann gave a terrified yet wholly unyielding flash of her black eyes at him — "Mrs. Edwards, will you please attend to what we have come to tell you. I have transferred the mortgage note given me by your late husband to Squire Eben Merritt; there is nothing for you to sign. You will simply pay the interest money to him, instead of to me."

"You can tear me to pieces, if you want to," said Ann, "but I won't sign away what little my poor husband left to me and my children, for you or any other man."

"Look at me," said the doctor.

Ann never stirred her head.

"Look at me."

Ann looked.

"Now," said the doctor, "you listen and you understand. I can't waste any more time here. Squire Merritt has bought that mortgage which your husband gave me, and paid me for it in land. You have simply nothing to do with it, except to understand. Nobody wants you to sign anything."

Ann looked at him with some faint light of comprehension through her wild impetus of resistance. "I'd ruther it would stay the way it was before," said she. "My husband gave you the mortgage. He thought you were trustworthy. I'd jest as soon pay you interest money as Squire Merritt."

Then Eliphalet Means spoke dryly, still with that utter patience of preparation and expectation: "If Doctor Prescott retains this mortgage he intends to foreclose."

Ann looked at him, and then at Doctor Prescott. She gasped, "Foreclose!"

Doctor Prescott nodded.

"You mean to foreclose? You mean to take this place away from us?" Ann cried, shrilly. "You with all you've got, and we a widow and orphans! And you callin' yourself a good man an' a pillar of the sanctuary!"

Doctor Prescott's face hardened. "Your husband owed me for a half year's interest," he began, calmly.

"My husband didn't owe you any interest money. He paid you in work and wood."

"That was for medical attendance," proceeded the doctor, imperturbably. "He owed me half a year's interest. I considered it best for your interests, as well as mine, to foreclose, and should have done so had not Squire Merritt taken the matter out of my hands. I should advise him to a like measure, but he is his own best judge."

"Squire Merritt will not foreclose," said Eliphalet Means; "and he will be easy about the payments."

"Well," said Ann, with a strange, stony look, "I guess I understand. I'm satisfied."

Doctor Prescott gathered up his medicine-chest, bade the others a gruff, ceremonious good-morning, and went out. His sulky had been drawn up before the gate for some time, and Jake Noyes had been lounging about the yard.

The lawyer and the Squire lingered, as they had yet the business regarding the sale of the woodland to arrange.

Curiously enough, Ann was docile as one could wish about that. Whether her previous struggle had exhausted her or whether she began to feel some confidence in her advisers, they could not tell. She made no difficulty, but after all was adjusted she looked at the lawyer with a shrewd, sharp gleam in her eyes.

"Doctor Prescott can't get his claws on it now, anyhow," she said; "and he always wanted it, 'cause it joined his."

The Squire and the lawyer looked at each other. The Squire with humorous amazement, the lawyer with a wink and glance of wise reminder, as much as to say: "You know what I have always said about women. Here is a woman."

Jerome was digging out in his garden-patch, and Elmira, in her blue sunbonnet, was standing, full of scared questioning, before him, when the Squire came lounging up the slope and reported as before said, to the convincing of the boy in innocent credulity.

When he had finished, he laid hold on Elmira's little cotton sleeve and pulled her up to her brother, and stood before them with a kindly hand on a shoulder of each, smiling down at them with infinite good-humor and protection.

"Don't you worry now, children," he said. "Be good and mind your mother, and you'll get along all right. We'll manage about the interest money, and there'll be meal in the barrel and a roof over your heads as long as you want it, according to the Scriptures, I'll guarantee."

With that Squire Eben gave each a shake, to conceal, maybe, the tenderness of pity in him, which he might, in his hearty and merry manhood, have accounted somewhat of a shame to reveal, as well as tears in his blue eyes, and was gone down the hill with a great laugh.

Elmira looked after him. "Ain't he good?" she whispered. But as for Jerome, he stood trembling and quivering and looking down at a print the Squire's great boot had made in the soft mould. When Elmira had gone, he went down on his knees and kissed it passionately.

CHAPTER XII

Now the warfare of life had fairly begun for little Jerome Edwards. Up to this time, although in sorry plight enough as far as material needs went — scantily clad, scantily fed, and worked hard — he had as yet only followed at an easy pace, or skirted with merry play the march of the toilers of the world. Now he was in the rank and file, enlisted thereto by a stern Providence, and must lose his life for the sake of living, like the rest. No more idle hours in the snug hollow of the rock, where he seemed to pause like a bee on the sweets of existence itself that he might taste them fully, were there for Jerome. Very few chances he had for outspeeding his comrades in any but the stern and sober race of life, for this little Mercury had to shear the wings from his heels of youthful sport and take to the gait of labor. Very seldom he could have one of his old treasure hunts in swamps and woods, unless, indeed, he could perchance make a labor and a gain of it. Jerome found that sassafras, and snakeroot, and various other aromatic roots and herbs of the wilds about his house had their money value. There was an apothecary in the neighboring village of Dale who would purchase them of him; at the cheapest of rates, it is true — a penny or so for a whole peck measure, or a sheaf, of the largess of summer — but every penny counted. Poor Jerome did not care so much about his woodland sorties after they were made a matter of pence and shillings, sorely as he needed, and much as he wished for, the pence and shillings. The sense was upon him, a shamed and helpless one, of selling his birthright. Jerome had in the natural beauty of the earth a budding delight, which was a mystery and a holiness in itself. It was the first love of his boyish heart; he had taken the green woods and fields for his sweetheart, and must now put her to only sordid uses, to her degradation and his.

Sometimes, in a curious rebellion against what he scarcely knew, he would return home without a salable thing in hand, nothing but a pretty and useless collection of wild flowers and sedges, little swamp-apples, and perhaps a cast bird-feather or two, and meet his mother's stern reproof with righteously undaunted front.

"I don't care," he said once, looking at her with a meaning she could not grasp; nor, indeed, could he fathom it himself. "I ain't goin' to sell everything; if I do I'll have to sell myself."

"I'd like to know what you mean," said his mother, sharply.

"I mean I'm goin' to keep some things myself," said Jerome, and pattered up to his chamber to stow away his treasures, with his mother's shrill tirade about useless truck following him. Ann was a good taskmistress; there were, indeed, great powers of administration in the keen, alert mind in that little frail body. Given a poor house encumbered by a mortgage, a few acres of stony land, and two children, the elder only fourteen, she worked miracles almost. Jerome had shown uncommon, almost improbable, ability in his difficulties when Abel had disappeared and her strength had failed her, but afterwards her little nervous feminine clutch on the petty details went far towards saving the ship.

Had it not been for his mother, Jerome could not have carried out his own plans. Work as manfully as he might, he could not have paid Squire Merritt his first instalment of interest money, which was promptly done.

It was due the 1st of November, and, a day or two before, Squire Merritt, tramping across lots, over the fields, through the old plough ridges and corn stubble, with some plump partridges in his bag and his gun over shoulder, made it in his way to stop at the Edwards house and tell Ann that she must not concern herself if the interest money were not ready at the minute it was due.

But Ann laid down her work — she was binding shoes — straightened herself as if her rocking-chair were a throne and she an empress, and looked at him with an inscrutable look of pride and suspicion. The truth was that she immediately conceived the idea that this great fair-haired Squire, with his loud, sweet voice, and his loud, frank laugh and pleasant blue eyes, concealed beneath a smooth exterior depths of guile. She exchanged, as it were, nods of bitter confidence with herself to the effect that Squire Merritt was trying to make her put off paying the interest money, and pretending to be very kind and obliging, in order that he might the sooner get his clutches on the whole property.

All the horizon of this poor little feminine Ishmael seemed to her bitter fancy to be darkened with hands against her, and she sat on a constant watch-tower of suspicion.

"Elmira," said she, "bring me that stockin'."

Elmira, who also was binding shoes, sitting on a stool before the scanty fire, rose quickly at her mother's command, went into the bedroom, and emerged with an old white yarn stocking hanging heavily from her hand.

"Empty it on the table and show Squire Merritt," ordered her mother, in a tone as if she commanded the resources of the royal treasury to be displayed.

Elmira obeyed. She inverted the stocking, and from it jingled a shower of coin into a pitiful little heap on the table.

"There!" said Ann, pointing at it with a little bony finger. The smallest coins of the realm went to make up the little pile, and the Lord only knew how she and her children had grubbed them together. Every penny there represented more than the sweat of the brow: the sweat of the heart.

Squire Eben Merritt, with some dim perception of the true magnitude and meaning of that little hoard, gained partly through Ann's manner, partly through his own quickness of sympathy, fairly started as he looked at it and her.

"There's twenty-one dollars, all but two shillin's, there," said Ann, with hard triumph. "The two shillin's Jerome is goin' to have tonight. He's been splittin' of kindlin'-wood, after school, for your sister, this week, and she's goin' to pay him the same as she did for weedin'. You can take this now, if you want to, or wait and have it all together."

"I'll wait, thank you," replied Eben Merritt. For the moment he felt actually dismayed and ashamed at the sight of his ready interest money. It was almost like having a good deed thrust back in his face and made of no account. He had scarcely expected any payment, certainly none so full and prompt as this.

"I thought I'd let you see you hadn't any cause to feel afraid you wouldn't get it," said Ann, with dignity. "Elmira, you can put the money back in the stockin' now, and put the stockin' back under the feather-bed."

Squire Merritt felt like a great school-boy before this small, majestic woman. "I did not feel afraid, Mrs. Edwards," he said, awkwardly.

"I didn't know but you might," said she, scornfully; "people didn't seem to think we could do anything."

"All I wonder at is," said the Squire, rallying a little, "how you managed to get so much money together."

"Do you want to know? Well, I'll tell you. We've bound shoes, Elmira an' me, for one thing. We've took all they would give us. That wa'n't many, for the regular customers had to come first, and I didn't do any in Abel's lifetime — that is, not after I was sick. I used to a while before that. Abel wouldn't let me when we were first married, but he had to come to it. Men can't do all they're willin' to. I shouldn't have done anything but dress in silk, set an' rock, an' work scallops an' eyelets in cambric pocket-handkerchiefs, if Abel had had his say. After I was sick I quit workin' on boots, because the doctor he said it might hurt the muscles of my back to pull the needle through the leather; but there's somethin' besides muscles in backs to be thought of when it comes to keepin' body an' soul together. Two days after the funeral I sent Jerome up to Cyrus Robinson, and told him to ask him if he'd got some extra shoes to bind and close, and he come home with some. Elmira and me bound, and Jerome closed, and we took our pay in groceries. The shoes have fed us, with what we got out of the garden. Then Elmira and me have braided mats and pieced quilts and sewed three rag carpets, and Elmira picked huckleberries and blackberries in season, and sold them to your wife and Miss Camilla and the doctor's wife; and Lawyer Means bought lots of her, and the woman that keeps house for John Jennings bought a lot. Elmira picked bayberries, too, and sold 'em to the shoemaker for tallow; she sold a lot in Dale. Elmira did a good deal of the weeding in your sister's garden, so's to leave Jerome's time clear. Then once when the doctor's wife had company she went over to help wash dishes, and she give her three an' sixpence for that. Elmira said she give it dreadful kind of private, and looked round to be sure the doctor wa'n't within gunshot. She give her a red merino dress of hers, too, but she kept her till after nightfall, and smuggled her out of the back door, with it all done up under her arm, lest the doctor should see. They say she's got dresses she won't never put on her back again — silks an' satins an' woollens — because she's outgrown 'em, an' they're all hangin' up in closets gettin' mothy, an' the doctor won't let her give 'em away. But this dress she give Elmira wa'n't give away, for I sent her back next day to do some extra work to pay for it. I ain't beholden to nobody. Elmira swept and dusted the settin'-room and the spare chamber, and washed the breakfast an' dinner dishes, and I guess she paid for that old dress ample. It had been laid up with camphor in a cedar chest, but it had some moth holes in it. It wa'n't worth such a great sight, after all.

"Jerome he's worked smart, if I have had to drive him to it sometimes. He's wed and dug potatoes everywhere he could git a chance; he's helped 'bout hayin', an' he's split wood. He's sold some herbs and roots, too, over to Dale. Jake Noyes he put him up to that. He come in here one night an' talked to him real sensible. 'There's money 'nough layin' round loose right under your face an' eyes,' says he; 'all the trouble is you're apt to walk right past, with your nose up in the air. The scent for work an' wages ain't up in the air,' says he; 'it's on the ground.' Jerome he listened real sharp, an' the next day he went off an' got a good passel of boneset an' thoroughwort an' hardback, an' carried it over to Dale, an' sold it for a shilling.

"Elmira has done some spinnin', too; I can't spin much, but

she's done well enough. Your wife wants some linen pillow-shifts. Elmira can do the weavin', I guess, an' we can make 'em up together. I've got a job to make some fine shirts for you, too. Your wife come over to see about it this week. I dun'no' but she was gettin' kind of afraid you wouldn't git your interest money no other way; but she needn't have been exercised about it, if she was. We got this interest together without your shirts, an' I guess we can the next. It's been harder work than many folks in this town know anything about, but we've done it." Ann tossed her head with indescribable pride and bitterness. There was scorn of fate itself in the toss of that little head, with its black lace cap and false front, and her speech also was an harangue, reproachful and defiant, against fate, not against her earthly creditor; that she would have disdained.

Squire Eben, however, fully appreciating that, and taking the pictures of pitiful feminine and childish toil which she brought before his fancy as a shame to his great stalwart manhood, spending its strength in hunting and fishing and card-playing, looked at the woman binding shoes with painful jerks of little knotted hands — for she ceased not her work one minute for her words — and took the bitter reproach and triumphant scorn in her tone and gesture for himself alone.

He felt ashamed of himself, in his great hunting-boots splashed with swamp mud, his buckskins marred with woodland thorn and thicket, but not a mark of honest toil about him. Had he been in fine broadcloth he would not have felt so humiliated; for the useless labor of play cuts a sorrier figure in the face of genuine work for the great ends of life than idleness itself. He would not have been half so disgraced by nothing at all in hand as by that bag of game; and as for the money in that old stocking under the feather-bed, it seemed to him like the fruits of his own dishonesty.

The impulse was strong upon him, then and there, to declare that he would take none of that hoard.

"Now look here, Mrs. Edwards," said he, fairly coloring like a girl as he spoke, and smiling uneasily, "I don't want that money."

Ann looked at him with the look of one who is stung, and yet incredulous. Elmira gave a little gasp of delight. "Oh, mother!" she cried.

"Keep still!" ordered her mother. "I dun'no' what you mean," she said to Squire Merritt.

The Squire's smile deepened, but he looked frightened; his eyes fell before hers. "Why, what I say — I don't want this money, this time. I have all I need. Keep it over till the next half."

Squire Eben Merritt had a feeling as if something actually tangible, winged and clawed and beaked, and flaming with eyes, pounced upon him. He fairly shrank back, so fierce was Ann's burst of indignation; it produced a sense of actual contact.

"Keep it till next half?" repeated Ann. "Keep it till next half? What should we keep it till next half for, I'd like to know? It's your money, ain't it? We don't want it; we ain't beggars; we don't need it. I see through you, Squire Eben Merritt; you think I don't, but I do."

"I fear I don't know what you mean," the Squire said, helplessly.

"I see through you," repeated Ann. She had reverted to her first suspicion that his design was to gain possession of the whole property by letting the unpaid interest accumulate, but that poor Squire Eben did not know. He gave up all attempts to understand this woman's mysterious innuendoes, and took the true masculine method of departure from an uncomfortable subject at right angles, with no further ado.

He opened his game-bag and held up a brace of fat partridges. "Well," he said, laughing, "I want you to see what luck I've had shooting, Mrs. Edwards. I've bagged eight of these fellows today."

But Ann could not make a mental revolution so easily. She gave a half indifferent, half scornful squint at the partridges. "I dun'no' much about shootin'," said she, shortly. Ann had always been, in her own family, a passionate woman, but among outsiders she had borne herself with dignified politeness and formal gentility, clothing, as it were, her intensity of spirit with a company garb. Now, since her terrible trouble had come upon her, this garb had often slipped aside, and revealed, with the indecency of affliction, the struggling naked spirit of the woman to those from whom she had so carefully hidden it.

Once Ann would not have believed that she would have so borne herself towards Squire Merritt. The Squire laid the partridges on the table. "I am going to leave these for your supper, Mrs. Edwards," he said, easily; but he quaked a little, for this woman seemed to repel gifts like blows.

"Thank ye," said Ann, dryly, "but I guess you'd better take 'em home to your wife. I've got a good deal cooked up."

Elmira made a little expressive sound; she could not help it. She gave one horrified, wondering look at her mother. Not a morsel of cooked food was there on the bare pantry shelves. By-and-by a little Indian meal and water would be boiled for supper. There were some vegetables in the cellar, otherwise no food in the house. Ann lied.

Squire Eben Merritt then displayed what would have been tact in a keenly calculating and analytic nature. "Oh, throw them out for the dogs, if you don't want them, Mrs. Edwards," he returned, gayly. "I've got more than my wife can use here. We are getting rather tired of partridges, we have had so many. I stopped at Lawyer Means's on my way here and left a pair for him."

A sudden change came over Ann's face. She beamed with a return of her fine company manners. She even smiled. "Thank ye," said she; "then I will take them, if you are sure you ain't robbing yourself."

"Not at all," said the Squire — "not at all, Mrs. Edwards. You'd better baste them well when you cook them." Then he took his leave, with many exchanges of courtesies, and went his way, wondering what had worked this change; for a simple, benevolent soul can seldom gauge its own wisdom of diplomacy.

Squire Eben did not dream that his gift to one who was not needy had enabled him to give to one who was, by establishing a sort of equality among the recipients, which had overcome her proud scruples. On the way home he met Jerome, scudding along in the early dusk, having finished his task early. "Hurry home, boy," he called out, in that great kind voice which Jerome so loved — "hurry home; you've got something good for supper!" and he gave the boy, ducking low before him with the love and gratitude which had overcome largely the fierce and callous pride in his young heart, a hearty slap on the shoulder as he went past.

CHAPTER XIII

There was a good district school in the village, and Jerome, before his father's disappearance, had attended it all the year round; now he went only in winter. Jerome rose at four o'clock in the dark winter mornings, and went to bed at ten, getting six hours' sleep. It was fortunate that he was a hardy boy, with a wirily pliant frame, adapting itself, with no lesions, to extremes of temperature and toil, even to extremes of mental states. In spite of all his hardships, in spite of scanty food, Jerome thrived; he grew; he began to fill out better his father's clothes, to which he had succeeded. The first time Jerome wore his poor father's best coat to school — Ann had set in the buttons so it folded about him in ludicrous fashion, bringing the sleeves forward and his arms apparently into the middle of his chest — one of the big boys and two big girls at his side laughed at him, the boy with open jeers, the girls with covert giggles behind their hands. They were standing in front of the school-house at the top of the long hill when Jerome was ascending it with Elmira. It was late and cold, and only these three scholars were outside. The girls, who were pretty and coquettish, had detained this great boy, who was a man grown.

Jerome went up the long hill under this fire of covert ridicule. Elmira, behind him, began to cry, holding up one little shawled arm like a wing before her face. Jerome never lowered his proud head; his unwinking black eyes stared straight ahead at the three; his face was deadly white; his hands twitched at his sides.

The great boy was 'Lisha Robinson; the girls were the pretty twin daughters of a farmer living three miles away, who had just brought them to school on his ox-sled. Their two sweet, rosy faces, full of pitiless childish merriment for him, and half unconscious maiden wiles towards the young man at their side, towards whom they leaned involuntarily as they tittered, aroused Jerome to a worse frenzy than 'Lisha's face with its coarse leer.

All three started back a little as he drew near; there was something in his unwinking eyes which was intimidating. However, 'Lisha had his courage to manifest before these girls. "Say, Jerome," he shouted — "say, Jerome, got any room to spare in that coat? 'cause Abigail Mack is freezin'."

"Go 'long, 'Lisha," cried Abigail, sputtering with giggles, and giving the young man a caressing push with her elbow.

'Lisha, thus encouraged, essayed further wit. "Say, Jerome, s'pose you can fill out that coat of yours any quicker if I give ye half my dinner? Here's a half a pie I can spare. Reckon you don't have much to eat down to your house, 'cept chicken-fodder, and that ain't very fat'nin'.'"

Jerome came up. All at once through the glow of his black eyes flashed that spiritual lightning, evident when purpose is changed to action. The girls screamed and fled. 'Lisha swung about in a panic, but Jerome launched himself upon his averted shoulder. The girls, glancing back with terrified eyes from the school-house door, seemed to see the boy lift the grown man from the ground, and the two whirl a second in the air before they crashed down, and so declared afterwards. Jerome clung to his opponent like a wild-cat, a small but terrific body all made up of nerves and muscles and electric fire. He wound his arms with a violent jerk as of steel around 'Lisha's neck; he bunted him with a head like a cannon-ball; he twisted little wiry legs under the hollows of 'Lisha's knees. The two came down together with a great thud. The teacher and the scholars came rushing to the door. Elmira wailed and sobbed in the background. The slight boy was holding great 'Lisha on the ground with a strength that seemed uncanny.

'Lisha's nose was bleeding; he breathed hard; his eyes, upturned to Jerome, had a ghastly roll. "Let me — up, will ye?" he choked, faintly.

"Will you ever say anything like that again?"

"Let me up, will ye?" 'Lisha gave a convulsive gasp that was almost a sob.

"Jerome!" called the teacher. She was a young woman from another village, mildly and assentingly good, virtue having, like the moon, only its simply illuminated side turned towards her vision. Weakly blue-eyed and spectacled, hooked up primly in chaste drab woollen and capped with white muslin, though scarcely thirty, she stood among her flock and eyed the fierce combatants with an utter lack of command of the situation. She was a country minister's daughter, and had never taught until her father's death. This was her first school, and to its turbulent elements she brought only the precisely limited lore of a young woman's seminary of that day, and the experiences of early piety.

Looking at the struggling boys, she thought vaguely of that hymn of Isaac Watts's which treats of barking and biting dogs and the desirability of amity and concord between children, as if it could in some way be applied to heal the breach. She called again fruitlessly in her thin treble, which had been raised in public only in neighborhood prayer-meetings: "Jerome! Jerome Edwards!"

"Will you say it again?" demanded Jerome of his prostrate

adversary, with a sharp prod of a knee.

After a moment of astonished staring there was a burst of mirth among the pupils, especially the older boys. 'Lisha was not a special favorite among them — he was too good-looking, had too much money to spend, and was too much favored by the girls. In spite of the teacher's half pleading commands, they made a rush and formed a ring around the fighters.

"Go it, J'rome!" they shouted. "Give it to him! You're a fighter, you be. Look at J'rome Edwards lickin' a feller twice his size. Hi! Go it, J'rome!"

"Boys!" called the teacher. "Boys!"

Some of the smaller girls began to cry and clung to her skirts; the elder girls watched with dilated eyes, or laughed with rustic hardihood for such sights. Elmira still waited on the outskirts. Jerome paid no attention to the teacher or the shouting boys. "Will you say it again?" he kept demanding of 'Lisha, until finally he got a sulky response.

"No, I won't. Now lemme up, will ye?"

"Say you're sorry."

"I'm sorry. Lemme up!"

Jerome, without appearing to move, collected himself for a spring. Suddenly he was off 'Lisha and far to one side, with one complete bound of his whole body, like a cat.

'Lisha got up stiffly, muttering under his breath, and went round to the well to wash off the blood. He did not attempt to renew the combat, as the other boys had hoped he might. He preferred to undergo the ignominy of being worsted in fight by a little boy rather than take the risk of being pounced upon again with such preternatural fury. When he entered school, having washed his face, he was quite pale, and walked with shaking knees. Rather physical than moral courage had 'Lisha Robinson, and it was his moral courage, after all, which had been tested, as it is in all such unequal combats.

As for Jerome, he had to stand in the middle of the floor, a spectacle unto the school, folded in his father's coat, which had, alas! two buttons torn off, and a three-cornered rag hanging from one tail, which fluttered comically in the draught from the door; but nobody dared laugh. There was infinite respect, if not approbation, for Jerome in the school that day. Some of the big boys scowled, and one girl said out loud, "It's a shame!" when the teacher ordered him to stand in the floor. Had he rebelled, the teacher would have had no support, but Jerome took his place in the spot indicated, with a grave and scornful patience. The greatness of his triumph made him magnanimous. It was clearly evident to his mind that 'Lisha Robinson and not he should stand in the floor, and that he gained a glory of martyrdom in addition to the other.

Jerome had never felt so proud in his life as when he stood there, in his father's old coat, having established his right to wear it without remark by beating the biggest boy in school. He stood erect, equally poised on his two feet, looking straight ahead with a grave, unsmiling air. He looked especially at no one, except once at his sister Elmira. She had just raised her head from the curve of her arm, in which she had been weeping, and her tear-stained eyes met her brother's. He looked steadily at her, frowning significantly. Elmira knew what it meant. She began to study her geography, and did not cry again.

At recess the teacher went up to Jerome, and spoke to him almost timidly. "I am very sorry about this, Jerome," she said. "I am sorry you fought, and sorry I had to punish you in this way."

Jerome looked at her. "She's a good deal like mother," he thought. "You had to punish somebody," said he, "an' — *I'd* licked *him.*"

The teacher started; this reasoning confused her a little, the more so that she had an uneasy conviction that she had punished the lesser offender. She looked at the proud little figure in the torn coat, and her mild heart went out to him. She glanced round; there were not many scholars in the room. Elmira sat in her place, busy with her slate; a few of the older ones were in a knot near the window at the back of the room. The teacher slipped her hand into her pocket and drew out a lemon-drop, which she thrust softly into Jerome's hand. "Here," said she.

Jerome, who treated usually a giver like a thief, took the lemon-drop, thanked her, and stood sucking it the rest of the recess. It was his first gallantry towards womankind.

This teacher remained in the school only a half term. Some said that she left because she was not strong enough to teach such a large school. Some said because she had not enough government. This had always been considered a man's school during the winter months, but a departure had been made in this case because the female teacher was needy and a minister's daughter.

The place was filled by a man who never tempered injustice with lemon-drops, and ruled generally with fair and equal measure. He was better for the school, and Jerome liked him; but he felt sad, though he kept it to himself, when the woman teacher went away. She gave him for a parting gift a little volume, a treasure of her own childhood, purporting to be the true tale of an ungodly youth who robbed an orchard on the Sabbath day, thereby combining two deadly sins, and was drowned in crossing a brook on his way home. The weight of his bag of stolen fruit prevented him from rising, but he would not let go, and thereby added to his other crimes that of greediness. There was a frontispiece representing this froward hero, in a tall hat and little frilled trousers, with a bag the size of a slack balloon dragging on the ground behind him, proceeding towards the neighbor's apple-tree, which bore fruit as large as the thief's head upon its unbending boughs.

"There's a pretty picture in it," the teacher said, when she presented the book; she had kept Jerome after school for that purpose. "I used to like to look at it when I was a little girl." Then she added that she had crossed out the inscription, "Martha Maria Whittaker, from her father, Rev. Enos Whittaker," on the fly-leaf, and written underneath, "Jerome Edwards, from his teacher, Martha Maria Whittaker," and displayed her little delicate scratch.

Then the teacher had hesitated a little, and colored faintly, and looked at the boy. He seemed to this woman — meekly resigned to old-age and maidenhood at thirty — a mere child, and like the son which another woman might have had, but the missing of whom was a shame to her to contemplate. Then she had said good-bye to him, and bade him be always a good boy, and had leaned over and kissed him. It was the kiss of a mother spiritualized by the innocent mystery and imagination of virginity.

Jerome kept the little book always, and he never forgot the kiss nor the teacher, who returned to her native village and taught the school there during the summer months, and starved on the proceeds during the winter, until she died, some ten years later, being of a delicate habit, and finding no place of comfort in the world.

Jerome walked ten miles and back to her funeral one freezing day.

CHAPTER XIV

Jerome's mother never knew about the rent in his father's best coat, nor the fight. To do the boy justice, he kept it from her, neither because of cowardice nor deceit, but because of magnanimity. "It will just work her all up if she knew 'Lisha Robinson made fun of father's best coat, and it's tore," Jerome told Elmira, who nodded in entire assent.

Elmira sat up in her cold chamber until long after midnight, and darned the rent painfully by the light of a tallow candle. Then it was a comparatively simple matter, when one had to deal with a woman confined to a rocking-chair, to never give her a full view of the mended coat-tail. Jerome cultivated a habit of backing out of the room, as from an audience with a queen. The sting from his wounded pride having been salved with victory, he was unduly important in his own estimation, until an unforeseen result came from the affair.

There are many surprising complications from war, even war between two school-boys. One night, after school, Jerome went to Cyrus Robinson's for a lot of shoes which had been promised him two days before, and was told there were none to spare. Cyrus Robinson leaned over the counter and glanced around cautiously. It was not a busy time of day. Two old farmers were standing by the stove, talking to each other in a drone of extreme dialect, almost as unintelligible, except to one who understood its subject-matter, as the notes of their own cattle. The clerk, Samson Loud, was at the other end of the store, cleaning a molasses-barrel from its accumulated sugar. "Look-a-here," said Cyrus Robinson, beckoning Jerome with a hard crook of a seamed forefinger. The boy stood close to the counter, and uplifted to him his small, undaunted, yet piteously wistful face.

"Look-a-here," said Cyrus Robinson, in a whisper of furtive malice, leaning nearer, the point of his shelving beard almost touching Jerome's forehead; "I've got something to say to you. I 'ain't got any shoes to spare tonight; an', what's more, I 'ain't going to have any to spare in future. Boys that fight 'ain't got time enough to close shoes."

Jerome looked at him a moment, as if scarcely comprehending; then a sudden quiver as of light came over him, and Cyrus Robinson shrank back before his eyes as if his counter were a bulwark.

"I s'pose if your big boy had licked me 'cause he made fun of my father's coat, instead of me lickin' him, you'd have given me some more shoes!" cried the boy, with the dauntlessness of utter scorn, and turned and walked out of the store.

"You'd better take care, young man!" called Cyrus Robinson, in open rage, for the boy's clear note of wrath had been heard over the whole store. The two old farmers looked up in dull astonishment as the door slammed after Jerome, stared questioningly at the storekeeper and each other, then the thick stream of their ideas returned to its course of their own affairs, and their husky gabble recommenced.

Samson Laud raised his head, covered with close curls of light red hair, and his rasped red face out of the molasses-barrel, gave one quick glance full of acutest sarcasm of humor at Cyrus Robinson, then disappeared again into sugary depths, and resumed his scraping.

Jerome, on his homeward road, did not feel his spirit of defiance abate. "Wonder how we're going to pay that interest money now? Wonder how mother 'll take it?" he said; yet he would have fought 'Lisha Robinson over again, knowing the same result. He had not yet grown servile to his daily needs.

However, speeding along through the clear night, treading the snow flashing back the full moonlight in his eyes like a silver mirror, he dreaded more and more the meeting his mother and telling her the news. He slackened his pace. Now and then he stood still and looked up at the sky, where the great white moon rode through the hosts of the stars. Without analyzing his thoughts, the boy felt the utter irresponsiveness of all glory and all heights. Mocking shafts of moonlight and starlight and frostlight seemed glancing off this one little soul in the freezing solitude of creation, wherein each is largely to himself alone. What was it to the moon and all those shining swarms of stars, and that far star-dust in the Milky Way, whether he, Jerome Edwards, had shoes to close or not? Whether he and his mother starved or not, they would shine just the same. The triviality — even ludicrousness — of the sorrow of man, as compared with eternal things, was over the boy. He was maddened at the sting and despite of his own littleness in the face of that greatness. Suddenly a wild impulse of rebellion that was almost blasphemy seized him. He clinched a puny fist at a great star. "Wish I could make you stop shinin'," he cried out, in a loud, fierce voice; "wish I could do somethin'!"

Suddenly Jerome was hemmed in by a cloud of witnesses. Eliphalet Means, John Jennings, and Colonel Lamson had overtaken him as he stood star-gazing. They were on their way to punch and cards at Squire Merritt's. Jerome felt a hand on his shoulder, and looked up into John Jennings's long, melancholy countenance, instead of the shining face of the star. He saw the eyes of the others surveying him, half in astonishment, half in amusement, over the folds of their camlet cloaks.

"Want to make the star stop shining?" queried John Jennings, in his sweet drawl.

Jerome made no reply. His shoulder twitched under Mr. Jennings's hand. He meditated pushing between these interlopers and running for home. The New England constraint, to which he had been born, was to him as a shell of defence and decency, and these men had had a glimpse of him outside it. He was horribly ashamed. "S'pose they think I'm crazy," he reflected.

"Want to stop the star shining?" repeated John Jennings. "Well, you can."

Jerome, in astonishment, forgot his shame, and looked up into the man's beautiful, cavernous eyes.

"I'll tell you how. Don't look at it. I've stopped nearly all the stars I've ever seen that way." John Jennings's voice seemed to melt into infinite sadness and sweetness, like a song. The other men chuckled but feebly, as if scarcely knowing whether it were a jest or not. John Jennings took his hand from Jerome's shoulder, tossed the wing of his cloak higher over his face, and went on with his friends. However, when fairly on his way, he turned and called back, with a soft laugh, "I would let the star shine, though, if I were you, boy."

"Who was the boy?" Colonel Lamson asked the lawyer, as the three men proceeded.

"The Edwards boy."

"Well," said John Jennings, "'tis an unlucky devil he is, call him what you will, for he's born to feel the hammer of Thor on his soul as well as his flesh, and it is double pain for all such."

Jerome stood staring after John Jennings and his friends a moment; he had not the least conception what it all meant; then he proceeded at a good pace, arguing that the sooner he got home and told his mother and had it over, the better.

But he had not gone far before he saw some one else coming, a strange, nondescript figure, with outlines paled and blurred in the moonlight, looking as if it bore its own gigantic and heavy head before it in outstretched arms. Soon he saw it was his uncle Ozias Lamb, laden with bundles of shoes about his shoulders, bending forward under their weight.

Ozias halted when he reached Jerome. "Hullo!" said he; "that you?"

"Yes, sir," Jerome replied, deferentially. He had respect for his uncle Ozias.

"Where you goin'?"

"Home."

"'Ain't you been to Robinson's for shoes?"

"Yes, sir."

"Where be they, then?"

Jerome told him.

"I ain't surprised. I knew what 'twould be when I heard you'd fit 'Lisha," said Ozias. "You hit my calf, you hit me. It's natur'." Ozias gave a cynical chuckle; he shifted his load of shoes to ease his right shoulder. "'Lisha's big as two of you," he said. "How'd ye work it to fling him? Twist your leg under his, eh?"

Jerome nodded.

"That's a good trick. I larnt that when I was a boy. Well, I ain't surprised Robinson has shet down on the shoes. What ye goin' to do?"

"Dun'no'," replied Jerome; then he gave a weak, childish gesture, and caught his breath in a sob. He was scarcely more than a child, after all, and his uncle Ozias was the only remaining natural tower to his helplessness.

"O Lord, don't ye go to whimperin', big man like you!" responded Ozias Lamb, quickly. "Look at here —" Ozias paused a moment, pondering. Jerome waited, trying to keep the sobs back.

"Tell you what 'tis," said Ozias. "It's one of the cases where the sarpents and the doves come in. We've got to do a little manœuvrin'. Don't you fret, J'rome, an' don't you go to frettin' of your mother. I'll take an extra lot of shoes from Cy Robinson; he can think Belinda's goin' to bind — she never has — or he can think what he wants to; I ain't goin' to regulate his thinkin'; an' you come to me for shoes in future. Only you keep dark about it. Don't you let on to nobody, except your mother, an' she needn't know the whys an' wherefores. I've let out shoes before now. I'll pay a leetle more than Robinson. Tell her your uncle Ozias has taken all the shoes Robinson has got, and you're to come to him for 'em, an' to keep dark about it, an' let her think what she's a mind to. Women folks can't know everything."

"Yes, sir," said Jerome.

"You can come fer the shoes and bring 'em home after dark, so's nobody will see you," said Ozias Lamb, further.

So it befell that Jerome went for the work that brought him daily bread, like a thief, by night, oftentimes slipping his package of shoes under the wayside bushes at the sound of approaching footsteps. He was deceitfully reticent also with his mother, whom he let follow her own conclusion, that Cyrus Robinson had been dissatisfied with their work. "Guess he won't see as much difference with this work as he think he does," she would often say, with a bitter laugh. Jerome was silent, but the inborn straightforwardness of the boy made him secretly rebellious at such a course.

"It's lyin', anyhow," he said, sulkily, once, when he loaded the shoes on his shoulder, like a mason's hod, and was starting forth from his uncle's shop.

Ozias Lamb laughed the laugh of one who perverts humor, and makes a jest of the bitter instead of the merry things of life.

"It's got so that lies are the only salvation of the righteous," said Ozias Lamb, with that hard laugh of his. Then, with the pitilessness of any dissenting spirit of reform, who will pour out truths, whether of good or evil, to the benefit or injury of mankind, who will force strong meat as well as milk on babies and sucklings, he kept on, while the boy stood staring, shrinking a little, yet with young eyes kindling, from the bitter frenzy of the other.

"It's so," said Ozias Lamb. "You'll find it out for yourself, in the hard run you've got to hoe, without any help, but it's just as well for you to know it beforehand. You won't get bit so hard — forewarned's forearmed. Snakes have their poison-bags, an' bees have their stings; there ain't an animal that don't have horns or claws or teeth to use if they get in a hard place. Them that don't have weapons have wings, like birds. If they can't fight, they can fly away from the battle. But human beings that are good, and meek, and poor, and hard pushed, they hain't got any claws or any wings; though if they had 'twouldn't be right to use 'em to fight or get away, so the parsons say. They 'ain't got any natural weapons. Providence 'ain't looked out for them. All they can do, as far as I can see, is to steal some of the devil's own weapons to fight him with."

It was well that Jerome could not understand the half of his uncle's harangue, and got, indeed, only a general impression of the unjust helplessness of a meek and righteous man in the hands of adverse fate, compared with horned and clawed animals, and Ozias's system of defence did not commend itself to his understanding. He did not for a moment imagine that his uncle advised him to lie and steal to better his fortunes, and, indeed, nothing was further from the case. Ozias Lamb's own precepts never went into practice. He was scrupulously honest, and his word was as good as a bond. However, although Ozias had never told a lie in his life, he had perpetrated many subtleties of the truth. He was wily and secretive. "A man ain't a liar because he don't tell all he knows," he said.

When asking for more shoes from Cyrus Robinson, he had said nothing about his wife's working upon them, but he knew that was the inference, and he did not contradict it. He forbade Belinda to mention the matter in one way or another. "The sarpent has got to feed the widows an' the orphans," he said, "an' that's a good reason for bein' a sarpent."

As Ann and Elmira did most of their work on the shoes during the day, Jerome fell into the habit of doing his part, the closing, in his uncle's shop at night. Every evening he would load himself with the sheaf of bound shoes and hasten down the road. He liked to work in company with a man, rather than with his mother and Elmira; it gave him a sense of independence and maturity. He did not mind so much delving away on those hard leather seams while his mates were out coasting and skating, for he had the sensation of responsibility — of being the head of a family. Here he felt like a man supporting his mother and sister; at home he was only a boy, held to his task under the thumb of a woman.

Then, too, his uncle Ozias's conversation was a kind of pungent stimulant — not pleasant to the taste, not even recognizable in all its savors, yet with a growing power of fascination.

Ozias Lamb's shoemaker's shop was simply a little one-room building in the centre of the field south of his cottage house. He had in it a tiny box-stove, red-hot from fall to spring. When Jerome, coming on a cold night, opened the door, a hot breath scented with dried leather rushed in his face. Within sat his uncle on his shoemaker's bench, short and squat like an Eastern idol on his throne. His body was settled into itself with long habit of labor, his mind with contemplation. His high, bald forehead overshadowed his lower face like a promontory of thought; his eyes, even when he was alone, were full of a wise, condemning observation; his mouth was inclined always in a set smile at the bitter humor of things. The face of this elderly New England shoemaker looked not unlike some Asiatic conception of a deity.

Jerome always closed the door immediately when he entered, for Ozias dreaded a draught, having an inclination to rheumatism, and being also chilly, like most who sit at their labor. Then he would seat himself on a stool, and close shoes, and listen when his uncle talked, as he did constantly when once warmed to it. The little room was lighted by a whale-oil lamp on the wall. On some nights the full moonlight streamed in the three windows athwart the lamp-light. The room got hotter and closer. Ozias now and then, as he talked, motioned Jerome, who put another stick of wood in the stove. The whole atmosphere, spiritual and physical, seemed to grow combustible, and as if at any moment a word or a thought might cause a leap into flame. A spirit of anarchy and revolution was caged in that little close room, bound to a shoemaker's bench by the chain of labor for bread. The spirit was harmless enough, for its cage and its chain were not to be escaped or forced, strengthened as they were by the usage of a whole life. Ozias Lamb would deliver himself of riotous sentiments, but on that bench he would sit and peg shoes till his dying day. He would have pegged there through a revolution.

Jerome's eyes would gleam with responsive fire when his uncle, his splendid forehead flushing and swelling with turbid veins, said, in that dry voice of his, which seemed to gain in force without being raised into clamor: "What right has one man with the whole purse, while another has not a penny in his pocket? What right has one with the whole loaf, while another has a crumb? What right has one man with half the land in the village, while another can hardly make shift to earn his grave?"

Ozias would pause a second, then launch out with new ardor, as if Jerome had advanced an opposite argument. "Born with property, are they — inherited property? One man comes into the world with the gold all earned, or stolen — don't matter which — waiting for him. Shoes all made for him, no peggin' for other folks; carpets to walk on, sofas to lay on, china dishes to eat off of. Everything is all complete; don't make no odds if he's a fool, don't make no odds if he 'ain't no more sense of duty to his fellow-beings than a pig, it's all just as it should be. Everybody is cringin' an' bowin' an' offerin' a little more to the one that's got more than anybody else. It's 'Take a seat here, sir — do; this is more comfortable,' when he's set on feather cushions all day. There'll be a poor man standin' alongside that 'ain't had a chance to set down since he got out of bed before daylight, every bone in him achin' — stiff. There ain't no extra comfortable chairs pointed out to him. Lord, no! If there happens to be the soft side of a rock or a plank handy, he's welcome to take it; if there ain't, why let him keep his standin'; he's used to it. I tell ye, it's them that need to whom it should be given, and not them that's got it already. I tell ye, the need should always regulate the supply.

"I tell ye, J'rome, balance-wheels an' seesaws an' pendulums wa'n't give us for nothin' besides runnin' machinery and clocks. Everything on this earth means somethin' more'n itself, if we could only see it. They're symbols, that's what they be, an' we've got to work up from a symbol that we see to the higher thing that we don't see. Most folks think it's the other way, but it ain't.

"Now, J'rome, you look at that old clock there; it was one that b'longed to old Peter Thomas. I bought it when he broke up an' went to the poorhouse. Doctor Prescott he foreclosed on him 'bout ten years ago — you don't remember. He had his old house torn down, an' sowed the land down to grass. I s'pose I paid more'n the clock was worth, but I guess it kept the old man in snuff an' terbaccer a while. Now you look at that clock; watch that pendulum swingin'. Now s'pose we say the left is poverty — the left is the place for the goats an' the poor folks that poverty has made goats; an' the right is riches. See it swing, do ye? It don't no more'n touch poverty before it's rich; it don't get time to starve an' suffer. It don't no more'n touch riches before it's poor; it don't have time to forget, an' git proud an' hard. I tell ye, J'rome, it ain't even division we're aimin' at; we can't keep that if we get it till we're dead; it's — balance. We want to keep the time of eternity, jest the way that clock keeps the time of day."

Jerome looked at the clock and the pendulum swinging dimly behind a painted landscape on the glass door, and never after saw one without his uncle's imagery recurring to his mind. Always for him the pendulum swung into the midst of a cowering throng of beggars on the left, and into a band of purple-clad revellers on the right. Somehow, too, Doctor Seth Prescott's face always stood out for him plainly among them in purple.

Always, sooner or later, Ozias Lamb would seize Doctor Prescott and Simon Basset as living illustrations and pointed examples of the social wrongs. "Look at them two men," he would say, "to come down to this town; look at them. You've heard about cuttle-fishes, J'rome, 'ain't ye?"

Jerome shook his head, as he drew his waxed thread through.

"Well, I'll tell ye what they be. They're an awful kind of fish. I never see one, but Belinda's brother that was a sailor, I've heard him tell enough to make your blood run cold. They're all head an' eyes an' arms. Their eyes are big as saucers, an' they're made just to see things the cuttle-fishes want to kill; an' they've got a hundred arms, with suckin' claws on the ends, an' they jest search an' seek, search an' seek, with them dreadful eyes that ain't got no life but hate an' appetite, an' they stretch out an' feel, stretch out an' feel, with them hundred arms, till they git what they want, an' then they lay hold with all the suckers on them hundred arms, an' clutch an' wind, an' twist an' overlay, till, whether it's a drownin' sailor or a ship, you can't see nothin' but cuttle-fish, an' —"

Jerome stopped working, staring at him. He was quite pale. His imagination leaped to a glimpse of that frightful fish. "An' — what comes — then?" he gasped.

"The cuttle-fish — has got a beak," said Ozias. "By-an'-by there ain't nothin' but cuttle-fish."

Jerome saw quite plainly the monster writhing and coiling over a waste of water, and nothing else.

"Look at this town, an' look at Doctor Prescott, an' look at Simon Basset," Ozias went on, coming abruptly from illustration to object, with a vigor of personal spite. "Look at 'em. You can't see much of anything here but them two men. Much as ever you can see the meetin'-house steeple. There are a few left, so you can see who they be, like Squire Merritt an' Lawyer Means; but, Lord, they'd better not get too careless huntin' and fishin' and card-playin', or they'll git hauled in, partridges, cards, an' all. But I'll tell you what 'tis — about all that anybody can see in this town is the eyes an' the arms of them two men, a-suckin' and graspin'.

"Doctor Prescott, he's a church member, too, an' he gives tithes of his widders an' orphans to the Lord. That meetin'-house couldn't be run nohow without him. If they didn't have him to speak in the prayer-meetin's, an' give the Lord some information about the spiritooal state of this town on foreign missions, an' encourage Him by admittin' He'd done pretty well, as far as He's gone, why, we couldn't have no prayer-meetin's at all."

Most of us have our personal grievances, as a vantage-point for eloquence in behalf of the mass. Simon Basset had deprived Ozias Lamb, by shrewd management, of the old Lamb homestead; Doctor Prescott had been instrumental in hushing his voice in prayer and exhortation in prayer-meeting.

The village people were not slow to recognize a certain natural eloquence in Ozias Lamb's remarks; oftentimes they appealed to their own secret convictions; yet they always trembled when he arose and looked about with that strange smile of his. Ozias said once they were half scared on account of the Lord, and half on account of Doctor Prescott. Ozias was often clearly unorthodox in his premises — no one could conscientiously demur when Doctor Prescott, a church meeting having been called, presented for approval, the minister being acquiescent, a resolution that Brother Lamb be requested to remain quiet in the sanctuary, and not lift up his voice unto the Lord in public unless he could do so in accordance with the tenets of the faith, and to the spiritual edification of his fellow-Christians. The resolution was passed, and Ozias Lamb never entered the door of the meeting-house again, though his name was not withdrawn from the church books.

Therefore the cuttle-fish was a sort of Circean revenge upon Doctor Prescott and Simon Basset for his own private wrongs. It takes a god to champion wrongs which have not touched him in his farthest imaginings.

CHAPTER XV

Jerome Edwards, young as he was, had within him the noblest instinct of a reformer — that of deducting from all evils a first lesson for himself. He said to himself: "It is true, what Uncle Ozias says. It is wrong, the way things are. The rich have everything — all the land, all the good food, all the money; the poor have nothing. It is wrong." Then he said, "If ever I am rich I will give to the poor." This pride of good intentions, in comparison with others' deeds, gave the boy a certain sense of superiority. Sometimes he felt as if he could see the top of Doctor Prescott's head when he met him on the street.

Poor Jerome had few of the natural joys and amusements of boyhood; he was obliged to resort to his fertile and ardent imagination, or the fibre of his spirit would have been relaxed with the melancholy of age. While the other boys played in the present, whooping and frisking, as free of thought as young animals, Jerome worked and played in the future. Some air-castles he built so often that he seemed to fairly dwell in them; some dreams he dreamed so often that he went about always with them in his eyes. One fancy which specially commended itself to him was the one that he was rich, that he owned half the town, that in some manner Doctor Prescott's and Simon Basset's acres had passed into his possession, and he could give them away. He established all the town paupers in the doctor's clover. He recalled old Peter Thomas from the poorhouse, and set him at Doctor Prescott's front window in a broadcloth coat. An imbecile pauper by the name of Mindy Toggs he established in undisturbed possession of Simon Basset's house and lands.

Doctor Seth Prescott little dreamed when he met this small, shabby lad, and passed him as he might have passed some wayside weed, what was in his mind. If people, when they meet, could know half the workings of one another's minds, the recoils from the shocks might overbalance creation. But Doctor Prescott never saw the phantom paupers slouching through his clover-fields, and Simon Basset never jostled Mindy Toggs on his threshold. However, Mindy Toggs had once lived in Simon Basset's house.

As Jerome advanced through boyhood it seemed as if everything combined to strengthen, by outside example, the fancies and beliefs derived from Ozias Lamb's precepts and his own constantly hard and toilsome life. Jerome, on his very way to the district school, learned tasks of bitter realism more impressive to his peculiar order of mind than the tables and columns in the textbooks.

There was a short cut across the fields between the school-house and the Edwards house. Jerome and Elmira usually took it, unless the snow was deep, as by doing so they lessened the distance considerably.

The Edwards house was situated upon a road crossing the main highway of the village where the school-house stood. In the triangle of fields between the path which the Edwards children followed on their way to school and the two roads was the poor-house. It was a low, stone-basemented structure, with tiny windows, a few of them barred with iron, retreating ignominiously within thick walls; the very grovelling of mendicancy seemed symbolized in its architecture by some unpremeditatedness of art. It stood in a hollow, amid slopes of stony plough ridges, over which the old male paupers swarmed painfully with spades and shovels when spring advanced. When spring came, too, old pauper women and wretched, halfwitted girls and children squatted like toads in the green fields outside the ploughed ones, digging greens in company with grazing cows, and looked up with unexpected flashes of human life when footsteps drew near. There was a thrifty Overseer in the poorhouse, and the village paupers, unless they were actually crippled and past labor, found small repose in the bosom of the town. They grubbed as hard for their lodging and daily bread of charity, with its bitterest of sauces, as if they worked for hire.

Old Peter Thomas, for one, had never toiled harder to keep the roof of independence over his head than he toiled tilling the town fields. Old Peter, even in his age and indigence, had an active mind. Only one panacea was there for its workings, and that was tobacco. When the old man had — which was seldom — a comfortable quid with which to busy his jaws, his mind was at rest; otherwise it gnawed constantly one bitter cud of questioning, which never reached digestion. "Why," asked old Peter Thomas, toiling tobaccoless in the town fields — "why couldn't the town have give me work, an' paid me what I airned, an' let me keep my house, instead of sendin' of me here?"

Sometimes he propounded the question, his sharp old eyes twinkling out of a pitiful gloom of bewilderment, to the Overseer: "Say, Mr. Simms, what ye s'pose the object of it is? Here I be, workin' jest as hard for what's give as for what I used to airn." But he never got any satisfaction, and his mind never relaxed to ease, until in some way he got a bit of tobacco. Old Peter Thomas, none of whose forebears had ever been on the town, who had had in his youth one of the prettiest and sweetest girls in the village to wife, toiling hard with his stiff old muscles for no gain of independence, his mind burdened with his unanswered question, would almost at times have sold his soul for tobacco. Nearly all he had was given him by Ozias Lamb, who sometimes crammed a wedge of tobacco into his hand, with a hard and furtive thrust and surly glance aloof, when he jostled him on the road or at the village store. Old Peter used to loaf about the store, whenever he could steal away from the poorhouse, on the chance of Ozias and tobacco. Ozias was dearly fond of tobacco himself, but little enough he got, with this hungry old pensioner lying in wait. He always yielded up his little newly bought morsel of luxury to Peter, and went home to his shoes without it; however, nobody knew. "Don't ye speak on't," he charged Peter, and he eschewed fiercely to himself all kindly motives in his giving, considering rather that he was himself robbed by the great wrong of the existing order of things.

Jerome, who had seen his uncle cram tobacco into old Peter's hand, used sometimes to leave the path on his way to school, when he saw the delving old figure in the ploughed field, and discovered, even at a distance, that his jaws were still and his brow knotted, run up to him, and proffer as a substitute for the beloved weed a generous piece of spruce-gum. The old man always took it, and spat it out when the boy's back was turned.

Jerome used to be fond of storing up checker-berries and sassafras root, and doling them out to a strange small creature with wild, askant eyes and vaguely smiling mouth, with white locks blowing as straightly and coarsely as dry swamp grass, who was wont to sit, huddling sharp little elbows and knees together, even in severe weather, on a stone by the path. She had come into the world and the poorhouse by the shunned byway of creation. She had no name. The younger school-children said, gravely, and believed it, that she had never had a father; as for her mother, she was only a barely admitted and shameful necessity, who had come from unknown depths, and died of a decline, at the town's expense, before the child could walk. She had nothing save this disgraceful shadow of maternity, her feeble little body, and her little soul, and a certain half scared delight in watching for Jerome and his doles of berries and sassafras. One of Jerome's dearest dreams was the buying this child a doll like Lucina Merritt's, with a muslin frock and gay sash and morocco shoes. So much he thought about it that it fairly seemed to him sometimes, as he drew near the little thing, that she nursed the doll in her arms. He wanted to tell her what a beautiful doll she was to have when he was rich, but he was too awkward and embarrassed before his own kind impulses. He only bade her, in a rough voice, to hold her hands, and then dropped into the little pink cup so formed his small votive offering to childhood and poverty, and was off.

Occasionally Elmira had cookies given her by kind women for whom she did extra work, and then she saved one for the little creature, emulating her brother's example. There was one point on the way to school where Elmira liked to have her brother with her, and used often to wait for him at the risk of being late. Even when she was one of the oldest girls in school, almost a young woman, she scurried fast by this point when alone, and even when Jerome was with her did not linger. As for Jerome, he had no fear; but during his winters at the district school the peculiar bent of his mind was strengthened by the influence of this place.

The poorhouse in the hollow had its barn and out-buildings attached at right angles, with a cart-path leading thereto from the street; but at the top of the slope, on the other side of the schoolward path, stood a large, half ruinous old barn, used only for storing surplus hay. The door of this great, gray, swaying structure usually stood open, and in it, on an old wreck of a wheelbarrow, sat Mindy Toggs, in fair or foul weather.

Mindy Toggs's head, with its thick thatch of light hair reaching to his shoulders, had the pent effect of some monstrous mushroom cap over his meagre body, with its loosely hung limbs, which moved constantly with uncouth sprawls and flings, as if by some terrible machinery of diseased nerves. Poor Mindy Toggs's great thatched head also nodded and lopped unceasingly, and his slobbering chin dipped into his calico shirt-bosom, and he said over and over, in his strange voice like a parrot's, the only two words he was ever known to speak, "Simon Basset, Simon Basset."

Mindy Toggs was sixty years old, it was said. His past was as dim as his intellect. Nobody seemed to know exactly when Mindy Toggs was born, or just when he had come to the poorhouse. Nobody knew who either of his parents had been. Nobody knew how he got his name, but there was a belief that it had a folklore-like origin; that generations of Overseers ago an enterprising wife of one had striven to set his feeble wits to account in minding the pauper babies, and gradually, through transmission by weak and childish minds, his task had become his name. Toggs was held to be merely a reminiscence of some particularly ludicrous stage of his poorhouse costume.

Mindy Toggs had dwelt in the poorhouse ever since people could remember, with the exception of one year, when he was boarded out by the town with Simon Basset, and learned to speak his two words. Simon Basset had always had an opinion that work could be gotten out of Mindy Toggs. Nobody ever knew by what means he set himself to prove it; there had been dark stories; but one day Simon brought Mindy back to the poorhouse, declaring with a strange emphasis that he never wanted to set eyes on the blasted fool again, and Mindy had learned his two words.

It was said that the sight of Simon Basset roused the idiot to terrific paroxysms of rage and fear, and that Basset never encountered him if he could help it. However, poor Mindy was harmless enough to ordinary folk, sitting day after day in the barn door, looking out through the dusty shafts of sunlight, through spraying mists of rain, and often through the white weave of snow, repeating his two words, which had been dinned into his feeble brain, the Lord only knew by what cruelty and terror — "Simon Basset, Simon Basset."

Mindy Toggs was a terrifying object to nervous little Elmira Edwards, but Jerome used often to bid her run along, and stop himself and look at him soberly, with nothing of curiosity, but with indignant and sorrowful reflection. At these times poor Mindy, if he had only known it, drove his old master, who had illumined his darkness of mind with one cruel flash of fear, out of house and home, and sat in his stead by his fireside in warmth and comfort.

Jerome left school finally when he was seventeen; up to that time he attended all the winter sessions. During the winter, when Jerome was seventeen, a man came to the neighboring town of Dale, bought out the old shoe-factory and store there, and set up business on a more extensive scale, sending out work in large quantities. Many of the older boys left school on that account, Jerome among them; he had special inducements to do so, through his uncle Ozias Lamb.

"That man that bought out Bill Dickey, over in Dale, has been talkin' to me," Lamb told Jerome one evening. "Seems he's goin' to increase the business; he's laid in an extra lot of stock, and hired two more cutters, and he says he don't want to fool with so many small accounts, and he'd rather let some of it out in big lots. Says, if I'm willin', I can take as much as I can manage, and let it out myself for bindin' and closin', and he'll pay me considerable more on a lot than Robinson has, cash down. Now you see, J'rome, I'm gettin' older, and I can't do much more finishin' than I've been doin' right along. What I'm comin' at is this: s'pose I set another bench in here, and take the extra work, and you quit school and go into business. I can learn you all I know fast enough. You can nigh about make a shoe now — dun'no' but you can quite."

"I'd have to leave school," Jerome said, soberly.

"How much more book-learnin' do you think you need?" returned Ozias, with his hard laugh. "Don't you forget that all you came into this world for was to try not to get out of it through lack of nourishment, and to labor for life with the sweat of your brow. You don't need much eddication for that. It ain't with you as it was with Lawrence Prescott, who was too good to go to the district school, and had to be sent to Boston to have a minister fit him for college. You don't come of a liberal eddicated race. You've got to work for the breath of your nostrils, and not for the breath of your mind or your soul. You'll find you can't fight your lot in life, J'rome Edwards; you ain't got standin' room enough outside it."

"I don't want to fight my lot in life," Jerome replied, defiantly, "but I thought I'd go to school this winter."

"You won't grub a bit better for one more winter of schoolin'," said his uncle, "and there's another reason — your mother, she's gettin' older, an' Elmira, she's a good-lookin' girl, but she's gettin' wore to skin an' bones. They're both on 'em workin' too hard. You'd ought to try to have 'em let up a little more."

"I wouldn't have either of 'em lift a finger, if I could help it, the Lord knows!" Jerome cried, bitterly.

Ozias nodded, grimly. "Women wa'n't calculated to work as hard as men, nohow," he said. "Seems as if a man that's got hands, an' is willin', might be let to keep the worst of it off 'em, but he ain't. Seems as if I might have been able to do somethin' for Ann when Abel quit, but I wa'n't.

"There's one thing I've got to be thankful for, an' that is — a hard Providence ain't been able to hurt Belindy any more than it would a feather piller. She dints a little, and cries out when she's hurt, an' then she settles back again, smooth and comfortable as ever.

"I don't s'pose you'll understand it, J'rome, because you ain't come to thinking of such things yet, an' showed your sense that you ain't, but I took that very thing into account when I picked out my wife. There was another girl that I used to see home some, but, Lord, she was a high stepper! Handsome as a picture she was; there ain't a girl in this town today that can compare with her; but her head was up, an' her nose quiverin', an' her eyes shinin'. I knew she liked me pretty well, but, Lord, it was no use! Might as well have set a blooded mare to ploughin'. She was one of the sort that wouldn't have bent under hardship; she'd have broke. I knew well enough what a dog-life a wife of mine would have to lead — jest enough to keep body and soul together, an' no extras — an' I wa'n't goin' to drag her into it, an' I didn't. I knew just how she'd strain, an' work her pretty fingers to the bone to try to keep up. I made up my mind that if I married at all I'd marry somebody that wouldn't work more'n she could possibly help — not if we were poor as Job's off ox.

"So I looked 'round an' got Belindy. I spelled her out right the first time I see her. She 'ain't had nothin', but I dun'no' but she's been jest as happy as if she had. I 'ain't let her work hard; she 'ain't never bound shoes nor done anythin' to earn a dollar since I married her. Couldn't have kept the other one from doin' it."

"What became of her?" asked Jerome.

"Dead," replied Ozias.

Jerome asked nothing further. It ended in his leaving school and going to work. This course met with some opposition from his mother, who had madly ambitious plans for him. She had influenced Elmira to leave school the year before, that she might earn more, and thereby enable her brother to study longer, but he knew nothing of that.

However, a plan which Jerome formed for some evening lessons with the school-master appeased her. It savored of a private tutor like Lawrence Prescott's. Nobody knew how Ann Edwards had resented Doctor Prescott's sending his son to Boston to be fitted for college, while hers could have nothing better than a few terms at the district school. Her jealous bitterness was enhanced twofold because her poor husband was gone, and the memory of his ambition for his son stung her to sharper effort. Often the imagined disappointments of the dead, when they are still loved and unforgotten, weigh more heavily upon the living than their own. "I dun'no' what your father would have said if he'd thought Jerome had got to leave school so young," she told Elmira; and her lost husband's grievance in the matter was nearer her heart than her own.

Jerome's plan for evening lessons did not work long. The school-master to whom he applied professed his entire readiness, even enthusiasm, to further such a laudable pursuit of knowledge under difficulties; but he was young himself, scarcely out of college, and the pretty girls in his school swayed his impressionable nature into many side issues, even when his mind was set upon the main track. Soon Jerome found himself of an evening in the midst of a class of tittering girls, who also had been fired with zeal for improvement and classical learning, who conjugated *amo* with foolish blushes and glances of sugared sweetness at himself and the teacher. Then he left.

Jerome at that time felt absolutely no need of the feminine element in creation, holding himself aloof from it with a patient, because measureless, superiority. Sometimes in growth the mental strides into life ahead of the physical; sometimes it is the other way. At seventeen Jerome's mind took the lead of his body, and the imaginations thereof, though he was well grown and well favored, and young girls placed themselves innocently in his way and looked back for him to follow.

Jerome's cold, bright glances met theirs, full of the artless appeal of love and passion, shameless because as yet unrecognized, and then he turned away with disdain.

"I came here to learn Latin and higher algebra, not to fool with a pack of girls," he told the school-master, bluntly. The young man laughed and colored. He was honest and good; passion played over him like wildfire, not with any heat for injury, but with a dazzle to blind and charm.

He did not intend to marry until he had well established himself in life, and would not; but in the meantime he gave his resolution as loose a rein as possible, and conjugated *amo* with shades of meaning with every girl in the class.

"I don't see what I can do, Edwards," he said. "I cannot turn the girls out, and I could not refuse them an equal privilege with you, when they asked it."

Jerome gave the school-master a look of such entire comprehension and consequent scorn that he fairly cast down his eyes before him; then he went out with his books under his arm.

He paid for his few lessons with the first money he could save, in spite of the school-master's remonstrances.

After that Jerome went on doggedly with his studies by himself, and asked assistance from nobody. In the silent night, after his mother and sister were in bed, he wrestled all alone with the angel of knowledge, and half the time knew not whether he was smitten hip and thigh or was himself the victor. Many a problem in his higher algebra Jerome was never sure of having solved rightly; renderings of many lines in his battered old Virgil, bought for a sixpence of a past collegian in Dale, might, and might not, have been correct.

However, if he got nothing else from his studies, he got the discipline of mental toil, and did not spend his whole strength in the labor of his hands.

Jerome pegged and closed shoes with an open book on the bench beside him; he measured his steps with conjugations of Latin verbs when he walked to Dale with his finished work over shoulder; he studied every spare moment, when his daily task was done, and kept this up, from a youthful and unreasoning thirst for knowledge and defiance of obstacles, until he was twenty-one. Then one day he packed away all his old school-books, and never studied them again regularly; for something happened which gave his energy the force of reason, and set him firmly in a new track with a definite end in view.

CHAPTER XVI

One evening, not long after his twenty-first birthday, Jerome Edwards went to Cyrus Robinson's store on an errand.

When he entered he found a large company assembled, swinging booted legs over the counters, perched upon barrels and kegs, or tilting back in the old scooping armchairs around the red-hot stove. These last were the seats devoted to honor and age, when present, and they were worthily filled that night. Men who seldom joined the lounging, gossiping circle in the village store were there: Lawyer Means, John Jennings, Colonel Lamson, Squire Merritt, even Doctor Seth Prescott, and the minister, Solomon Wells.

The recent town-meeting, the elections and appropriations, accounted in some measure for this unusual company, though the bitter weather might have had something to do with it. Hard it was for any man that night to pass windows glowing with firelight, and the inward swing of hospitable doors; harder it was, when once within the radius of warmth and human cheer, to leave it and plunge again into that darkness of winter and death, which seemed like the very outer desolation of souls.

The Squire's three cronies had been on their way to cards and punch with him, but the winking radiance of the store windows had lured them inside to warm themselves a bit before another half mile down the frozen road; and once there, sunken into the battered hollows of the armchairs, within the swimming warmth from the stove, they had remained. Their prospective host, Squire Eben Merritt, also had shortly arrived, in quest of lemons for the brewing of his famous punch, and had been nothing loath to await the pleasure of his guests.

The minister had come in giddy, as if with strong drink, being unable, even with the steady gravity of his mind, to control the chilly trembling of his thin old shanks in their worn black broadcloth. His cloak was thin; his daughter had tied a little black silk shawl of her own around his neck for further protection; his mildly ascetic old face peered over it, fairly mouthing and chattering with the cold. He could scarcely salute the company in his customary reverend and dignified manner.

Squire Eben sprang up and place his own chair in a warmer corner for him, and the minister was not averse to settling therein and postponing for a season the purchase of a quarter pound of tea, and his shivering homeward pilgrimage.

Doctor Seth Prescott, who lived nearly across the way, had

come over after supper to prescribe for the storekeeper's wife, who had lumbago, and joined the circle around the stove, seeing within it such worthy companions as the lawyer and the Squire, and having room made promptly and deferentially for him.

The discussion had been running high upon the subject of town appropriations for the poor, until Doctor Prescott entered and the grating armchairs made place for him, when there was a hush for a moment. Ozias Lamb, hunched upon a keg on the out-skirts, smiled sardonically around at Adoniram Judd standing behind him.

"Cat's come," he said; "now the mice stop squeakin'." The men near him chuckled.

Simon Basset, who, having arrived first, had the choice of seats, and was stationed in the least rickety armchair the farthest from draughts, ceased for a moment the rotatory motion of lan-tern jaws and freed his mind upon the subject of the undue appro-priations for the poor.

"Ain't a town of this size in the State begins to lay out the money we do to keep them good-for-nothin' paupers," said he, and chewed again conclusively.

Doctor Prescott, not as yet condescending to speak, had made a slight motion and frown of dissent, which the minister at his elbow saw. Doctor Prescott was his pillar of the sanctuary, upholding himself and his pulpit from financial and doctrinal downfall — his pillar even of ideas and individual movements. Poor old Solomon Wells fairly walked his road of life attached with invisible leading-strings to Doctor Seth Prescott. He spoke when Simon Basset paused, and more from his mentor's volition than his own. "The poor ye have always with ye," said the minister, with pious and weighty dissent. Doctor Prescott nodded.

Ozias Lamb squinted slowly around with ineffable sarcasm of expression. He took in deliberately every detail of the two men — Doctor Seth Prescott, the smallest in physical stature of anybody there, yet as marked among them all as some local Napoleon, and the one whom a stranger would first have noted, and the old cler-gyman leaning towards him with a subtle inclination of mind as well as body; then he spoke as Jerome entered.

Jerome laid the empty sack, which he had brought for meal, on the counter, and stood about to listen with the rest. Squire Eben Merritt, having given his chair to the minister and squared up his great shoulders against a pile of boxes on the counter, was near him, and saluted him with a friendly nod, which Jerome returned with a more ardent flash of his black eyes than ever a girl had called forth yet. Jerome adored this kindly Squire, against whom he was always fiercely on his guard lest he tender him gratuitous favors, and his indebtedness to whom was his great burden of life.

His Uncle Ozias did not notice him or pause in his harangue. "The poor ye have always with ye, the poor ye have always with ye," he was repeating, with a very snarl of sarcasm. "I reckon ye do; an' why? Why is it that folks had the Man that give that sayin' to the world with 'em, and made Him suffer and die? It was the same reason for both. D'ye want to know what 'twas? Well, I'll tell ye — it don't take a very sharp mind to ferret that out. It don't even take college larnin'. It is because from the very foundation of this green airth the rich and the wicked and the proud have had the mastery over it, an' their horns have been exalted. The Lord knows they've got horns to their own elevation an' the hurt of others, as much as any horned animals, though none of us can see 'em sproutin', no matter how hard we squint."

With that Ozias Lamb gave a quick glance, pointed with driest humor, from under his bent brows at Simon Basset's great jumble of gray hair and Doctor Prescott's spidery sprawl of red wig. A subdued and half alarmed chuckle ran through the company. Simon Basset chewed imperturbably, but Doctor Seth Prescott's handsome face was pale with controlled wrath.

Ozias continued: "I tell ye that is the reason for all the sufferin', an' the wrongs, an' the crucifixion, on this earth. The rich are the reason for it all; the rich are the reason for the poor. If the money wa'n't in one pocket it would be in many; if the bread wa'n't all in one cupboard there wouldn't be so many empty; if all the garments wa'n't packed away in one chest there wouldn't so many go bare. There's money enough, an' food enough, an' clothes enough in this very town for the whole lot, an' it's the few that holds 'em that makes the paupers."

Doctor Seth Prescott's mouth was a white line of suppression. Some of the men exchanged glances of consternation. Cyrus Robinson's clerk, Samson Loud, leaning over the counter beside his employer, said, "I swan!" under his breath. As for Cyrus Robinson, he was doubtful whether or not to order this turbulent spirit out of his domain, especially since he was no longer a good customer of his, but worked for and traded with the storekeeper in Dale.

He looked around at his son Elisha, who was married now these three years to Abigail Mack, had two children, and a share in the business; but he got no suggestion from him. Elisha, who had grown very stout, sat comfortably on a half barrel of sugar inside the counter, sucking a stick of peppermint candy, unmoved by anything, even the entrance of his old enemy, Jerome. As Cyrus Robinson was making up his mind to say something, Doctor Seth Prescott spoke, coldly and magisterially, without moving a muscle in his face, which was like a fine pale mask.

"May I ask Mr. Lamb," he said, "how long, in his judgment, when the money shall have been divided and poured from one purse into many others, when the loaves shall have been distributed among all the empty cupboards, and when all the surplus garments have been portioned out to the naked, this happy state of equal possessions will last?"

"Well," replied Ozias Lamb, slowly, "I should say, takin' all things into consideration — the graspin' qualities of them that had been rich, and the spillin' qualities of them that had been poor, about fourteen hours an' three-quarters. I might make it twenty-four — I s'pose some might hang on to it overnight — but I guess on the whole it's safer to call it fourteen an' three-quarters."

"Well," returned Doctor Prescott, "what then, Mr. Lamb?"

"Give it back again," said Ozias, shortly.

Squire Eben Merritt gave a great shout of mirth. "By the Lord Harry," he cried, "that's an idea!"

"It is an entirely erroneous system of charity which you propose, Mr. Lamb," said Doctor Prescott; "such a constant disturbance and shifting of the property balance would shake the financial basis of the whole country. Our present system of one public charity, to include all the poor of the town, is the only available one, in the judgment of the ablest philanthropists in the country."

Ozias Lamb got off his keg, straightened his bowed shoulders as well as he was able, and raised his right hand. "You call the poorhouse righteous charity, do ye, Doctor Seth Prescott?" he demanded. "You call it givin' in the name of the Lord?"

Doctor Prescott made no response; indeed, Ozias did not wait for one. He plunged on in a very fury of crude oratory.

"It ain't charity!" he cried. "I tell ye what it is — it's a pushin' an' hustlin' of the poor off the steps of the temple, an' your own door-steps an' door-paths, to get 'em out of your sight an' sound, where your purple an' fine linen won't sweep against their rags, an' your delicate ears won't hear their groans, an' your delicate eyes an' nose won't see nor scent their sores; where you yourselves, with your own hands, won't have to nurse an' tend 'em. I tell ye, that rich man in Scriptur' was a damned fool not to start a poorhouse, an' not have Lazaruses layin' round his gate. He'd have been more comfortable, an' *mebbe* he'd have cheated hell so.

"You call it givin' — *givin'!* You call livin' in that house over there in the holler, workin' with rheumatic old joints, an' wearin' stiff old fingers to the bone, not for honest hire, but for the bread of charity, a gift, do ye? I tell ye, every pauper in that there house that's got his senses after what he's been through, knows that he pays for every cent he costs the town, either by the sweat of his brow an' the labor of his feeble hands, or by the independence of his soul."

Then Simon Basset spat, and shifted his quid and spoke. "Tell ye what 'tis, all of ye," said he — "it's mighty easy talkin' an' givin' away gab instead of dollars. I'll bet ye anything ye'll put up that there ain't one of ye out of the whole damned lot that 'ain't got any money that would give it away if he had it."

"I would," declared a clear young voice from the outskirts of the crowd. Everybody turned and looked, and saw Jerome beside Squire Merritt, his handsome face all eager and challenging. Jerome was nearly as tall as the Squire, though more slender, and there was not a handsomer young fellow in the village. He had, in spite of his shoemaking, a carriage like a prince, having overcome by some erectness of his spirit his hereditary stoop.

Simon Basset looked at him. "If ye had a big fortune left ye, s'pose ye'd give it all away, would ye?"

"Yes, sir, I would." Jerome blushed a little with a brave modesty before the concentrated fire of eyes, but he never unbent his proud young neck as he faced Simon Basset.

"S'pose ye'd give away every dollar?"

"Yes, sir, I would — every dollar."

"Lord!" ejaculated Simon Basset, and his bristling, grimy jaws worked again.

Squire Eben Merritt looked at Jerome almost as he might have done at his pretty Lucina. "By the Lord Harry, I believe you would, boy!" he said, under his breath.

"Such idle talk is not to the purpose," Doctor Seth Prescott said, with a stately aside to the minister, who nodded with the utter accordance of motion of any satellite.

But Simon Basset spoke again, and as he spoke he hit the doctor, who sat next him, a hard nudge in his broadcloth side with a sharp elbow. "Stan' ye any amount ye want to put up that that young bob-squirt won't give away a damned dollar, if he ever gits it to give," he said, with a wink of curious confidential scorn.

"I do not bet," replied the doctor, shortly.

"Lord! ye needn't be pertickler, doctor; it's safe 'nough," returned Simon Basset, with a sly roll of facetious eyes towards the company.

The doctor deigned no further reply.

"I'll stan' any man in this company anything he'll put up," cried Simon Basset, who was getting aroused to a singular energy.

Nobody responded. Squire Eben Merritt, indeed, opened his mouth to speak, then turned it off with a laugh. "I'd make the bet, boy," he whispered to Jerome, "if it were anybody else that proposed it, but that old —"

Simon Basset stood up; the men looked at him with wonder. His eyes glowed with strange fire. The lawyer eyed him keenly. "I should think from his face that the man was defending himself in the dock," he whispered to Colonel Lamson.

"I'll tell ye what I'll do, then," shouted Simon Basset, "if ye won't none of ye take me up. I'll be damned if I believe that any rich man on the face of this earth is capable of givin' away every dollar he's got, for the fear of the Lord or the love of his fellow-men. I'll be damned if I believe, if the Lord Almighty spoke to him from on high, and told him to, he'd do it, an' I'm goin' to prove that I don't believe it. I'll tell ye all what I'll do. Lawyer Means is here, an' he can take it down in black an' white, if he wants to, an' I'll sign it reg'lar an' have it witnessed. If that young man there," he pointed at Jerome, "ever comes into any property, an' gives away every dollar of it, I'll give away one quarter of all I've got in the world to the poor of this town, an' I'll take my oath on it.

"But there's more than that," continued Simon Basset. "I'll get a condition before I do it. I call on my fellow-townsman here — I won't say my fellow-Christian, 'cause he wouldn't think that much of a compliment — to do the same thing. If he'll do it, I will; if he won't, I won't." Simon Basset looked down at Doctor Prescott with malicious triumph. Everybody stared at the two men.

"Why don't ye speak up, doctor — hey?" asked Simon Basset, finally.

"Because I do not consider such an outrageous proposition worthy of consideration, Mr. Basset," returned the doctor, with a calm aside elevation of his clear profile, and not the slightest quickening of his even voice.

"Then ye don't believe there's a man livin' capable of givin' away his all for the Lord an' His poor any more'n I do, an' I calculate you jedge so from the workin's of your own heart an' knowin' what you'd do in like case, jest like me," said Simon Basset.

Doctor Prescott made a quick motion, and the color flashed over his thin face. "I made no such assertion," he said, hotly, for his temper at last was up over his icy bonds of will.

"Looks so," said Simon Basset.

"You have no right to make such a statement, sir," returned the doctor, and his lips seemed to cut the air like scissors.

"What is it, then?" returned the other. "Are you afraid the young fellow will come into property, an' then you'll have to give up too much to the Lord?"

The veins on Doctor Prescott's forehead swelled visibly as he looked at Simon Basset's hateful, bantering face.

"There's another thing I'm willin' to promise," continued Simon Basset. "If that young feller comes into money, an' gives it away, I'll do more than give away a quarter of my property — I'll believe anything after that. I'll get religion. But — I won't agree to do that unless you back me up, doctor. That ought to induce you — the prospect of savin' a brand from the burnin'; an' if I ain't a brand, I dun'no' who is."

"I tell you, sir, I'll have nothing to do with it!" shouted Doctor Prescott. The minister at his side looked pale and scared as a woman.

"Then," said Simon Basset, "it's settled. You an' me won't agree to no sech damn foolishness, because we both on us know that there's no sech Christian charity an' love as that in the world; an' if there should turn out to be, we're afraid we'd have to do likewise. I thought I was safe enough proposin' sech a plan, doctor."

There was a great shout of laughter, in spite of the respect for Doctor Prescott. In the midst of it the doctor sprang to his feet, looking as none of them had ever seen him look before. "Get a paper and pen and ink," he cried, turning to Lawyer Means; "draw up the document that this man proposes, and I will sign it!"

CHAPTER XVII

The paper which Lawyer Eliphalet Means, standing at the battered and hacked old desk whereon Cyrus Robinson made out his accounts, drew up with a sputtering quill pen — at which he swore under his breath — was as fully elaborated and as formal in every detail as his legal knowledge could make it. Apostrophizing it openly, before he began, as damned nonsense, he was yet not without a certain delight in the task. It was quite easy to see that Simon Basset, whatever motive he might have had in his proposition, was beyond measure terrified at its acceptance. With his bristling chin dropping nervously, and his forehead contracted with anxious wrinkles, he questioned Jerome.

"Look at here," he said, with a tight clutch on Jerome's sleeve, "I want to know, young man. There ain't no property anywheres in your family, is there? There ain't no second nor third nor fourth cousins out West anywheres that's got property?"

"No, there are not," said Jerome, impatiently shaking off his hand.

"Your father didn't have no uncle that had money?"

"I tell you there isn't a dollar in the family that I know of," cried Jerome. "I have nothing to do with all this, and I want you to understand it. All I said was, and I say it now, if in any way any money should ever fall to me, I would give it away; and I will, whether anybody else does or not."

"You don't mean money you earn; you mean money that falls to you —"

"I mean if ever I get enough money in a lump to make me rich," replied Jerome, doggedly.

"I want to know how much money you are goin' to call rich," demanded Simon Basset.

"Ten thousand dollars," replied Jerome, whose estimate of wealth was not large.

Simon Basset cried out with sharp protest at that, and Doctor Prescott evidently agreed with him.

"Any man might scrape together ten thousand dollars," said Basset. "Lord! he might steal that much."

The amount of wealth which the document should specify was finally fixed at twenty-five thousand dollars, which was, moreover, to come into Jerome's possession in full bulk and during the next ten years, or the obligation would be null and void.

Basset also insisted upon the stipulation that Jerome, in his giving, should not include his immediate family. "I've seen men shift their purses into women folks' pockets, an' take 'em out again, when they got ready, before now," he said. "I ain't goin' to have no such gum-game as that played."

That proposition met with some little demur, though not from Jerome.

"Might just as well say I wouldn't agree not to give mother and Elmira the moon, if it fell to me," he said to Squire Merritt.

The Squire nodded. "Let 'em put it any way they want to," he said; "it can't hurt you any. Means knows what he's about. I tell you that old fox of a Basset feels as if the dogs were after him." The Squire was highly amused, but Jerome did not regard it as quite a laughing matter. He wondered angrily if they were making fun of him, and would have flown out at the whole of them, with all his young impetuosity, had not Squire Eben restrained him.

"Easy, boy, easy," he whispered. "It won't do you any harm."

The instrument, as drawn up by Lawyer Means, also stipulated, at Simon Basset's insistence, that the said twenty-five thousand dollars should come into Jerome's possession within ten years from date, and be given away by him within one month's time after his acquisition of the same. Lawyer Means, without objection, filed carefully all Basset's precautionary conditions; then he proceeded to make it clearly evident, with no danger of quibble, that "in case the said Jerome Edwards should comply with all the said conditions, the said Doctor Seth Prescott and Simon Basset, Esquire, of Upham Corners, do covenant and engage by these presents to remise, release, give, and forever quitclaim, each of the aforesaid, one-quarter of the property of which he may at the time of the acquisition by the said Jerome Edwards of the said twenty-five thousand dollars, stand possessed, to all those persons of adult age residing within the boundaries of the town of Upham Corners who shall not own at the time of said acquisition homesteads free of encumbrance and the sum of twelve thousand dollars in bank, to be divided among the aforesaid in equal measure.

"In witness whereof we, the said Doctor Seth Prescott and Simon Basset, have hereunto set our hands and seals," etc.

This document, being duly signed, sealed, and delivered in the presence of the witnesses John Jennings, Eben Merritt, Esquire, and Cyrus Robinson, was stored away in the pocket of Lawyer Eliphalet Means's surtout, to be later locked safely in his iron box of valuables.

Simon Basset's writing lore was limited, being, many claimed, confined to the ability to sign his name, and even that seemed likely in this case to fail him. Simon Basset faltered as if he had forgotten either his name or his spelling, and it was truly a strange signature when done, full of sharp slants of rebellion and curves of indecision. As for Doctor Seth Prescott, who had sat aloof, with a fine withdrawn majesty, all through the discussion, when it was signified to him that everything was in readiness for his signature he arose, went to the desk amid a hush of attention, and signed his name in characters like the finest copper-plate. Then he went out of the store without a word, and the minister, forgetting his quarter of tea, slid after him as noiselessly as his shadow.

Lawyer Means, when once out in the frosty night with his three mates, bound at last for cards and punch, shook his long sides with husky merriment. "I tell you," he said, "if I were worth enough, I'd give every dollar of the twenty-five thousand to that boy before morning, just for the sake of seeing Prescott and Basset."

"Of course, when it comes to a question of legality, that document isn't worth the paper it's written on," the Colonel said, chuckling.

"Of course," replied the lawyer, dryly. "Basset didn't know it, though, nor Jerome, nor scarcely a soul in the store beside."

"Doctor Prescott did."

"I suppose so, or he wouldn't have signed."

"Do you think the boy would live up to his part of the bargain?" asked the Colonel, who, being somewhat gouty of late years, limped slightly on the frozen ground.

"I'd stake every cent I've got in the world on it," cried Squire Eben Merritt, striding ahead — "every cent, sir!"

"Well, there's no chance of his being put to the test," said Lamson.

"Chance!" exclaimed the lawyer. "Good heavens! You might as well talk of his chance of inheriting the throne of the Cæsars. I know the Edwards family, and I know Jerome's mother's family, root and branch, and there isn't five thousand dollars among them down to the sixth cousins; and as for the boy's accumulating it himself — where are the twenty-five thousand dollars in these parts for him to accumulate in ten years? You might as well talk of his discovering a gold-mine in that famous wood-lot. But I'll be damned if Basset wasn't as much scared as if the poor fellow had been jingling the gold in his pocket. If Jerome Edwards *does*, through the Lord or the devil, get twenty-five thousand dollars, I hope I shall be alive to see the fun."

"Hush," whispered John Jennings; "he is behind us, and I would not have such a generous young heart as that think itself spoken of lightly."

"Would he do it?" Colonel Lamson asked, short-winded and reflective.

"I'll be damned if he wouldn't!" cried the lawyer.

"By the Lord Harry, he would!" cried Squire Eben, each using his favorite oath for confirmation of his opinion.

Jerome, following in their tracks with his uncle Ozias, heard perfectly their last remarks, and lagged behind to hear no more, though his heart leaped up to second with fierce affirmation the lawyer and the Squire.

"Keep behind them," he whispered to Ozias; "I don't want to listen."

"Think you'd give it away if you had it, do ye?" his uncle asked, with his dry chuckle.

"I don't *think* — I *know*."

"How d'ye know?"

"I *know*."

"Lord!"

"You think I wouldn't, do you?" asked Jerome, angrily.

"I'd be more inclined to believe ye if I see ye more generous with what ye've got to give now."

Jerome started, and stared at his uncle's face, which, in the freezing moonlight, looked harder, and more possessed of an inscrutable bitterness of wisdom. "What d'ye mean?" he asked, sharply. "What on earth have I got to give, I'd like to know?"

Ozias Lamb tapped his head. "How about that?" he asked. "How about the strength you're puttin' into algebry an' Latin? You don't expect ever to learn enough to teach, do ye?"

Jerome shook his head.

"Well, then it's jest to improve your own mind. Improve your mind — what's that? What good is that goin' to do your fellow-bin's? I tell ye, Jerome, ye ain't givin' away what you've got to give, an' we ain't none of us."

"Maybe you're right," Jerome said, after a little.

After having left his uncle, he walked more slowly still. Soon the Squire and his friends were quite out of sight. The moonlight was very full and brilliant, the trees were crooked in hard lines, and the snow-drifts crested with white lights of ice; there was no softening of spring in anything, but the young man felt within him one of those flooding stirs of the spirit which every spring faintly symbolizes. A great passion of love and sympathy for the needy and oppressed of his kind, and an ardent defence of them, came upon Jerome Edwards, poor young shoemaker, going home with his sack of meal over his shoulder. Like a bird, which in the spring views every little straw and twig as towards his nest and purpose of love, Jerome would henceforth regard all powers and instrumentalities that came in his way only in their bearing upon his great end of life.

On reaching home that night he packed away his algebra and his Latin books on the shelf in his room, and began a new study the next evening.

CHAPTER XVIII

Seth Prescott was the only practising physician for some half dozen villages. His mud-bespattered sulky and his smart mare, advancing always with desperate flings of forward hoofs — which caused the children to scatter — were familiar objects, not only in the cluster of Uphams, but also in Dale and Granby, and the little outlying hamlet of Ford's Hill, which was nothing but a scattering group of farm-houses, with a spire in their midst, and which came under the jurisdiction of Upham. In all these villages people were wont to run from the windows to the doors when they saw the doctor's sulky whirl past, peer after it, up or down the road, to see where it might stop, and speculate if this old soul were about to leave the world, or that new soul to come into it.

One afternoon, not long before he was twenty-one, Jerome Edwards walked some three miles and a half to Ford's Hill to carry some shoes to a woman binder who was too lame to come for them herself. Jerome walked altogether of late years, for the white horse was dead of old age: but it was well for him, since he was saved thereby from the permanent crouch of the shoe-bench.

When, having left his shoes, he was returning down the steep street of the little settlement, he saw Doctor Prescott's sulky ahead of him. Then, just before it reached a small weather-beaten house on the right, he saw a woman rush out as if to stop it, and a man follow after her and pull her back through the door.

The sulky was driven past at a rapid pace; for the weather was sharp, and the doctor's mare stepped out well after standing. When Jerome reached the house the doctor was scarcely within hailing distance; but the woman was out again, calling after him frantically: "Doctor! Doctor! Doctor Prescott! Stop! Stop here! Doctor!"

Jerome sprang forward to offer his assistance in summoning him, but at that instant the man reappeared again and clutched the woman by the arm. "Come back, come back in the house, Laura," he gasped, faintly, and yet with wild energy.

Jerome saw then that the man was ghastly, staggering, and yellow-white, except for blazing red spots on the cheeks, and that his great eyes were bright with fever. Jerome knew him; he was a young farmer, Henry Leeds by name, and not long married. Jerome had gone to school with the wife, and called her familiarly by name. "What's the matter, Laura?" he asked.

"Oh, J'rome," she half sobbed, "do help me — do call the doctor. Henry's awful sick; I know he is. He'd ought to have the doctor, but he won't because it costs so much. Do call him; I can't make him hear."

Jerome opened his mouth to shout, but the sick man flew at him with an awful, piteous cry. "Don't ye, don't ye," he wailed out; "I tell ye not to, J'rome Edwards. I 'ain't got any money to pay him with."

"But you're sick, Henry," said Jerome, putting his hand on the man's shaking shoulder to steady him. "You'd better let me run after him — I can make him hear now. It won't cost much."

"Don't ye do it," almost sobbed the young farmer. "It costs us a dollar every time he comes so far, an' he'll say right off, the way he did about mother that last time she was sick — when she broke her hip — that he'd take up a little piece of land beforehand; it would jest pay his bill. He'll do that, an' I tell ye I 'ain't got 'nough land now to support me. I 'ain't got 'nough land now, J'rome."

The poor young wife was weeping almost like a child. "Do let him call the doctor, do let him, Henry," she pleaded.

"There's another thing, J'rome," half whispered the young man, turning his back on his wife and fastening mysterious bright eyes on Jerome's — "there's another thing. Laura, she'll have to have the doctor before long, you can see that, an' — there'll be another mouth to fill, an' I've been savin' up a little, an' it ain't goin' for *me* — I tell ye it ain't goin' for *me*, J'rome."

All the while poor Henry Leeds, in spite of hot red spots on his cheeks, was shivering violently, but stiffly, like a tree in a freezing wind. The doctor had whirled quite out of sight over the hill. "He's gone," wailed the wife — "he's gone, and Henry 'll die — oh, I know he'll die!"

Then Jerome, who had been standing bewildered, not knowing whether he should or should not run and call after the doctor, and listening first to one, then to the other, collected himself. "No, he isn't going to die, either," he said to the poor girl, who was very young; and he said it quite sharply, because he so pitied her in her innocent helplessness, and would give her courage even in a bitter dose. He asked her, furthermore, as brusquely as Doctor Prescott himself could have done, what medicine she had in the house. Then he bade her hasten, if she wished to help and not hurt her husband, to the nearest neighbor and beg some sweat-producing herbs — thoroughwort or sage or catnip — all of which he had heard were good for fever.

She went away, wrapped in the thick shawl which Jerome had found in a closet, and himself pinned over the wild fair head, under the quivering chin, while he quieted her with grave admo-

nitions, as if he were her father. Then he led poor Henry Leeds —
still crying out that he would not have the doctor — into his house
and his bedroom, and got him to bed, though it was a hard task.

"I tell you, Henry," pleaded Jerome, struggling with him to
loosen his neck-band, "you shall not have the doctor; I'll doctor
you myself."

"You don't know how — you don't know how, J'rome! She'll
say you don't know how; she'll send for him, an' then, when he's
got all my land, how am I goin' to get them a livin'?"

"I tell you, Doctor Prescott sha'n't darken your doors, Henry
Leeds, if you'll behave yourself," said Jerome, stoutly; "and I can
break up a fever as well as he can, if you'll only let me. Mother
broke up one for me, and I never forgot it. You let me get your
clothes off and get you into bed, Henry."

Jerome had had some little experience through nursing his
mother, but, more than that, had the natural instinct of helpful-
ness, balanced with good sense and judgment, which makes a
physician. Moreover, he worked with as fiery zeal as if he were a
surgeon in a battle-field. Soon he had Henry Leeds in his feather
bed, with all the wedding quilts and blankets of poor young Laura
piled over him. The fire was almost out, for the girl was a poor
house-keeper, and not shod by nature for any of the rough emer-
gencies of life. Jerome had the fire blazing in short space, and
some hot water and hot bricks in readiness.

Poor young Laura Leeds had to go almost half a mile for her
healing herbs, as the first neighbor was away from home and no
one came in answer to her knocks. By the time she returned, with
a stout neighboring mother at her side — both of them laden with
dried aromatic bouquets, and the visitor, moreover, clasping a
bottle or two of household panaceas, such as camphor and castor-
oil — Jerome had the sick man steaming in a circle of hot bricks,
and was rubbing him under the clothes with saleratus and water.

Jerome's proceedings might not have commended themselves
to a school of physicians; but he reasoned from the principle that
if remedies were individually valuable, a combination of them
would increase in value in the proportion of the several to one.
Sage and thoroughwort, sarsaparilla, pennyroyal, and burdock —
nearly every herb, in fact, in the neighbor's collection — were
infused into one black and eminently flavored tea, into which he
dropped a little camphor, and even a modicum of castor-oil.
Jerome afterwards wondered at his own daring; but then, with a
certainty as absolute as the rush of a stung animal to a mud bath —
as if by some instinct of healing born with him — he concocted

that dark and bitter beverage, and fed it in generous doses to the sick man. Nobody interfered with him. The neighbor, though older than Laura and the mother of several children, had never known enough to bring out their measles and loosen their colds. The herbs had been gathered and stored by her husband's mother, and for many a year hung all unvalued in her garret. Luckily Jerome, through his old gathering for the apothecary, knew them all.

Jerome set one of the neighbor's boys to Upham Corners to tell his mother of his whereabouts; then he remained all night with young Henry Leeds, and by dint of his medley of herbs, or his tireless bathing and nursing, or because the patient had great elasticity of habit, or because the fever was not, after all, of a dangerous nature, his treatment was quite successful.

Jerome went home the next morning, and returned late in the afternoon, to stay overnight again. The day after, the fever did not appear, and Henry Leeds was on the fair way to recovery. A few weeks later came the affair of the contract in Robinson's store, and Jerome grasped a new purpose from the two.

The next day, when he carried some finished shoes to Dale, he bought a few old medical books, the remnant of a departed doctor's library, which had been stowed away for years in a dusty corner of the great country store. This same store included in its stock such heterogeneous objects, so utterly irrelevant to one another and at such tangents of connection, that it seemed sometimes like a very mad-house of trade.

It was of this store that the story was told for miles around how one day Lawyer Means, having driven over with Colonel Lamson from Upham Corners, made a bet with him that he could not ask for anything not included in its stock of trade; and the Colonel had immediately gone in and asked for a skeleton; for he thought that he was thereby sure of winning his bet, and of putting to confusion his friend and the storekeeper. The latter, however, who was not the Bill Dickey of this time, but an unkempt and shrewd old man of an earlier date, had conferred with his own recollection for a minute, and asked, reflectively, of his clerk, "Lemme see, we've got a skeleton somewheres about, 'ain't we, Eph?" And had finally unearthed — not adjacent to the old doctor's medical books, for that would have been to much method in madness, but in some far-removed nook — a ghastly box, containing a reasonably complete little skeleton. Then was the laugh all on Colonel Jack Lamson, who had his bet to pay, and was put to hard shifts to avoid making his grewsome purchase, the article being offered exceedingly cheap on account of its unsalable properties.

"It's been here a matter of twenty-five year, ever sence the old doctor died. Them books, an' that, was cleaned out of his office, an' brought over here," the old storekeeper had said. "Let ye have it cheap, Colonel; call it a shillin'."

"Guess I won't take it today."

"Call it a sixpence."

"What in thunder do you suppose I want a skeleton for?" asked the Colonel, striding out, while the storekeeper called after him, with such a relish of his own wit that it set all the loafers to laughing and made them remember it:

"Guess ye'd find out if ye didn't have one, Colonel; an' I guess, sence natur's gin ye all the one she's ever goin' to, ye'll never have a chance to git another as cheap as this."

That same little skeleton was yet for sale when Jerome purchased his medical books at the price of waste-paper, and might possibly have been thrown into the bargain had he wished to study anatomy.

Jerome sought only to gain an extension of any old wife's knowledge of healing roots and herbs and the treatment of simple and common maladies. Surgery he did not meddle with, until one night, about a year later, when Jake Noyes, Doctor Prescott's man, came over secretly with a little whimpering dog in his arms.

"We run over this little fellar," he said to Jerome, when he had been summoned to the door, "an' his leg's broke, an' the doctor told me I'd better finish him up; guess he's astray; but" — Jake's voice dropped to a whisper — "I've heard what you're up to, an' I've brought a splint, an', if you say so, I'll show you how to set a bone."

So up in his little chamber, with his mother and Elmira listening curiously below, and a little whining, trembling dog for a patient, Jerome learned to set a bone. His first surgical case was nearly a complete success, moreover, for the little dog abode with him for many a year after that, and went nimbly and merrily on his four legs, with scarcely a limp.

Later on, Jake Noyes, this time with Jerome himself as illustration, gave him a lesson in bleeding and cupping, which was considered indispensable in the ordinary practice of that day. "Dun'no' what the doctor would say," Jake Noyes told Jerome, "an' I dun'no' as I much care, but I'd jest as soon ye'd keep it dark. Rows ain't favorable to the action of the heart, actin' has too powerful stimulants in most cases, an' I had an uncle on my mother's side that dropped dead. But I feel as if the doctor had ground the face of the poor about long enough; it's about time somebody dulled his grindstone a little. He's just foreclosed that last mortgage on John Upham's place, an' they've got to move. Mind ye, J'rome, I ain't sayin' this to anybody but you, an' I wouldn't say it to you if I didn't think mebbe you could do something to right what he'd done wrong. If he won't do it himself, somebody ought to for him. Tell ye what 'tis, J'rome, one way an' another, I think considerable of the doctor. I've lived with him a good many years now. I've got some books I'll let ye take any time. I calculate you mean to do your doctorin' cheap."

"Cheap!" replied Jerome, scornfully. "Do you think I would take any pay for anything I could do? Do you think *that's* what I'm after?"

Jake Noyes nodded. "Didn't s'pose it was, J'rome. Well, there'll be lots of things you can't meddle with; but there's no reason why you can't doctor lots of little ails — if folks are willin' — an' save 'em money. I'll learn ye all I know, on the doctor's account. I want it to balance as even as he thinks it does."

The result of it all was that Jerome Edwards became a sort of free medical adviser to many who were too poor to pay a doctor's fees, and had enough confidence in him. Some held strenuously to the opinion that "he knew as much as if he'd studied medicine." He was in requisition many of the hours when he was free from his shoemaker's bench; and never in the Uphams was there a sick man needing a watcher who did not beg for Jerome Edwards.

CHAPTER XIX

In these latter years Ann Edwards regarded her son Jerome with pride and admiration, and yet with a measure of disapproval. In spite of her fierce independence, a lifetime of poverty and struggle against the material odds of life had given a sordid taint to her character. She would give to the utmost out of her penury, though more from pride than benevolence; but when it came to labor without hire, that she did not understand.

"I 'ain't got anything to say against your watchin' with sick folks, an' nursin' of 'em, if you've got the spare time an' strength," she said to Jerome; "but if you do doctorin' for nothin' nobody 'll think anything of it. Folks 'll jest ride a free horse to death, an' talk about him all the time they're doin' of it. You might just as well be paid for your work as folks that go ridin' round in sulkies chargin' a dollar a visit. You want to get the mortgage paid up."

"It is almost paid up now, you know, mother," Jerome replied.

"How?" cried his mother, sharply. "By nippin' an' tuckin' an' pinchin', an' Elmira goin' without things that girls of her age ought to have."

"I don't complain, mother," said Elmira, with a sweet, bright glance at her brother, as she gave a nervous jerk of her slender arm and drew the waxed thread through the shoe she was binding.

"You'd ought to complain, if you don't," returned her mother. Then she added, with an air of severe mystery, "It might make a difference in your whole life if you did have more; sometimes it does with girls."

Jerome did not say anything, but he looked in a troubled way from his sister to his mother and back again. Elmira blushed hotly, and he could not understand why.

It was very early in a spring morning, not an hour after dawn, but they had eaten breakfast and were hurrying to finish closing and binding a lot of shoes for Jerome to take to his uncle's for finishing. They all worked smartly, and nothing more was said, but Ann Edwards had an air of having conclusively established the subject rather than dropped it. Jerome kept stealing troubled glances at his sister's pretty face. Elmira was a mystery to him, which was not strange, since he had not yet learned the letters of the heart of any girl; but she was somewhat of a mystery to her mother as well.

Elmira was then twenty-two, but she was very small, and looked no more than sixteen. She had the dreams and questioning wonder of extreme youth in her face, and something beyond that even, which was more like the wide-eye brooding and introspection of babyhood.

As one looking at an infant will speculate as to what it is thinking about, so Ann often regarded her daughter Elmira, sitting sewing with fine nervous energy which was her very own, but with bright eyes fixed on thoughts beyond her ken. "What you thinkin' about, Elmira?" she would question sharply; but the girl would only start and color, and look at her as if she were half awake, and murmur that she did not know. Very likely she did not; often one cannot remember dreams when suddenly recalled from them; though Elmira had one dream which was the reality of her life, and in which she lived most truly, but which she would always have denied, even to her own mother, to guard its sacredness.

When the shoes were done Jerome loaded himself with them, and, watching his chance, beckoned his sister slyly to follow him as he went out. Standing in the sweet spring sunlight in the dooryard, he questioned her. "What did mother mean, Elmira?" he said.

"Nothing," she replied, blushing shyly.

"What is it you want, Elmira?"

"Nothing. I don't want anything, Jerome."

"Do you want — a new silk dress or anything?"

"A new silk dress? No." Elmira's manner, when fairly aroused and speaking, was full of vivacity, in curious contrast to her dreaming attitude at other times.

"I tell you what 'tis, Elmira," said Jerome, soberly. "I want you to have all you need. I don't know what mother meant, but I want you to have things like other girls. I wish you wouldn't put any more of your earnings in towards the mortgage. I can manage that alone, with what I'm earning now. I can pay it up inside of two years now. I told you in the first of it you needn't do anything towards that."

"I wasn't going to earn money and not do my part."

"Well, take your earnings now and buy things for yourself. There's no reason why you shouldn't. I can earn enough for all the rest. There's no need of mother's working so hard, either. I can't charge for mixing up doses of herbs, as she wants me to, for I don't do it for anybody that isn't too poor to pay the doctor, but I earn enough besides, so neither of you need to work your fingers to the bone or go without everything. I'll give you some money. Get yourself a blue silk with roses on it; seems to me I saw one in meeting last Sunday."

Elmira laughed out with a sweet ring. Her black hair was

tossing in the spring wind, her whole face showed variations and under-meanings of youthful bloom and brightness in the spring light.

"'Twas Lucina Merritt wore the blue silk with roses on it; it rustled against your knee when she passed our pew," she cried. "She is just home from her young ladies' school, and she's as pretty as a picture. I guess you saw more than the silk dress, Jerome Edwards."

With that Elmira blushed, and dropped her eyes in a curious sensitive fashion, as if she had spoken to herself instead of her brother, who looked at her quite gravely and coolly.

"I saw nothing but the silk," he said, "and I thought it would become you, Elmira."

"I am too dark for blue," replied Elmira, fairly blushing for her own blushes. At that time Elmira was as a shy child to her own emotions, and Jerome's were all sleeping. He had truly seen nothing but the sweep of that lovely rose-strewn silk, and never even glanced at the fair wearer.

"Why not have a red silk, then?" he asked, soberly.

"I can't expect to have things like Squire Merritt's daughter," returned Elmira. "I don't want a new silk dress; I am going to have a real pretty one made out of mother's wedding silk; she's had it laid by all these years, and she says I may have it. It's as good as new. I'm going over to Granby this morning to get it cut. When Imogen and Sarah Lawson came over last week they told me about a mantua-maker there who will cut it beautifully for a shilling."

"Mother don't want to give up her wedding-dress."

"Women always have their wedding-dresses made over for their daughters," Elmira said, gravely.

"What color is it?"

"A real pretty green, with a little sheeny figure in it; and I am going to have a new ribbon on my bonnet."

"It's 'most ten miles to Granby; hadn't I better get a team and take you over?" said Jerome.

"No; it's a beautiful morning, and it will do me good to walk. I shall go to Imogen and Sarah's and rest, and have a bite of something before I come back too. I may not be home very early. You'd better run along, Jerome, and I've got to get ready."

Jerome gave his burden of shoes a hitch of final adjustment. "Well," said he, "I'd just as lief take you over, if you say so."

"I don't want to be taken over. I want to take myself over," laughed Elmira, and ran into the house before a flurry of wind.

That morning the wind was quite high, and though it was soft and warm, was hard to breast on a ten-mile stretch. Elmira's strength was mostly of nerve, and she had little staying power of muscle. Before she had walked three miles on the road to Granby she felt as if she were wading deeper and deeper against a mightier current of spring; the scent of the young blossoms suffocated her with sweet heaviness; the birds' songs rang wearily in her ears. She sat down on the stone wall to rest a few moments, panting softly. She laid her parcel of silk on the wall beside her and folded her hands in her lap. The day was so warm she had put on, for the first time that spring, her pink muslin gown, which had served her for a matter of eight seasons, and showed in stripes of brighter color around the skirt where the tucks had been let out to accommodate her growth. Her pink skirts fluttered around her as she sat there, smiling straight ahead out of the pink scoop of a sunbonnet like her dress, with a curious sweet directness, as if she saw some one whom she loved — as, indeed, she did. Elmira, full of the innocent selfishness of youth, saw such a fair vision of her own self clad in her mother's wedding silk, with loving and approving eyes upon her, that she could but smile.

Elmira rested a few minutes, then gathered up her parcel and started again on her way. She reached the place in the road where the brook willows border it on either side, and on the east side the brook, which is a river in earliest spring, flows with broken gurgles over a stony bed, and slackened her pace, thinking she would walk leisurely there, for the young willows screened the sun like green veils of gossamer, and the wind did not press her back so hard, and then she heard the trot, trot of a horse's feet behind her.

She did not look around, but walked more closely to the side of the road and the splendid east file of willows. The trot, trot of the horse's feet came nearer and nearer, and finally paused alongside of her; then a man's voice, half timid, half gayly daring, called, "Good-day, Miss Elmira Edwards!"

With that Elmira gave a great start, though not wholly of surprise; for the imagination of a maid can, at the stimulus of a horse's feet, encompass nearly all realities within her dreams. Then she looked up, and Doctor Prescott's son Lawrence was bending over from his saddle and smiling into her pink face in her pink sunbonnet.

"Good-day," she returned, softly, and courtesied with a dip of her pink skirts into a white foam of little way-side weedy flowers, and then held her pink sun-bonnet slanted downward, and would not look again into the young man's eager face.

"It is a full year since I have seen you, and not a glimpse of your face did I get this time, and yet I knew, the minute I came in sight of you, who it was," said he, gayly; still, there was a loving and wistful intonation in his voice.

"Small compliment to me," returned Elmira, with a pretty spirit, though she kept her pink bonnet slanted, "to know me by a gown and bonnet I have had eight years."

"But 'twas *your* gown and bonnet," said the young man, and Elmira trembled and took an uneven step, though she strove to walk in a dignified manner beside Lawrence Prescott on his bay mare. The mare was a spirited creature, and he had hard work to rein her into a walk. "Let me take your bundle," he said.

"It is not heavy," said she, but yielded it to him.

Lawrence Prescott was small and slight, but held himself in the saddle with a stately air. He was physically like his father, but his mother's smile parted his fine-cut lips, and her expression was in his blue eyes.

Upham people had not seen much of Lawrence since he was a child, for he had been away at a preparatory school before entering college, and many of his vacations had not been spent at home. Now he was come home to study medicine with his father and prepare to follow in his footsteps of life. The general opinion was that he would never be as smart. Many there were, even of those who had come in sore measure under Doctor Seth Prescott's autocratic thumb, who held in dismay the prospect of the transference of his sway to his son.

"Guess you'll see how this town will go down when the old doctor's gone and the young one's here in his place," they said. It is the people who make tyranny possible.

"How far are you going?" asked Lawrence, of Elmira flitting along beside his dancing mare.

"Oh, a little way," said she, evasively.

"How far?" There was something of his father's insistence in Lawrence's voice.

"To Granby," replied Elmira then, and tried to speak on unconcernedly. She was ashamed to let him know how far she had planned to walk because of her poverty.

"Granby!" cried Lawrence, with a whistle of astonishment; "why, that is seven miles farther! You are not going to walk to Granby and back to day?"

"I like to walk," said Elmira, timidly.

"Why, but it is a warm day, and you are breathing short now." Lawrence pulled the mare up with a sharp whoa. "Now I'll tell you what I'll do," he said. "You sit down here on that stone and rest, and I'll ride back home and put the mare into the chaise, and I'll drive you over there."

"No, thank you; I'd rather walk," said Elmira, all touched to bliss by his solicitude, but resolved in her pride of poor maidenhood that she would not profit by it.

"Let him go back and get the chaise, and have all the town talking because Lawrence Prescott caught me walking ten miles to get a dress cut? I guess I won't!" she told herself.

"You are just the same as ever; you would never let anybody do anything for you unless you paid them for it," said Lawrence, half angrily. Then he added, bending low towards her, "But you would pay me, measure pressed down and running over, by going with me — you know that, Elmira."

Elmira lost her step again, and her voice trembled a little, though she strove to speak sharply. "I like to walk," said she.

"And I tell you you're all tired out now," said Lawrence. "I can see you pant for breath. Don't you know, I am going to be a doctor, like father? Let me go back, and you wait here."

Elmira shook her pink bonnet decidedly.

"Well, then," said Lawrence, "I tell you what you must do." He slipped off the mare as he spoke. "Now," he said, and there was real authority in his voice, "you've got to ride. It's a man's saddle, and you won't sit so very secure, but I'll lead the mare, and you'll be safe enough."

Elmira shrank back. "Oh, I can't," said she.

"Yes, you can. Whoa, Betty. She's gentle enough, for all she's nervous, and she's used to a lady's riding her. The daughter of the man who sold her to father used to scour the country on her. Come, put your foot in my hand and jump up!"

"What would people say?"

"There isn't a house for a good mile, and I'll let you get down before you reach it if you want to; but I don't see what harm it would be if the whole town saw us. Come." Lawrence smiled with gentle importunity at her, and held his hand, and Elmira could not help putting her little foot in it and springing to the bay mare's back in obedience to his bidding.

Elmira, fluttering like a pink flower on the back of the bay mare, who really ambled along gently enough with Lawrence's hand on her bridle, journeyed for the next mile as one in a happy dream. She was actually incredulous of the reality of it all. She was half afraid that the jolt of the bay mare would wake her from slumber; she kept her eyes closed in the recesses of her sunbonnet. Here was Lawrence Prescott, about whom she had dreamed ever since she was a child, come home, grown up and grand, grander than any young man in town, grand as a prince, and not forgetting her, knowing her at a glance, even when her face was hidden, and making her ride lest she get over-tired. She had scarcely seen him, to speak to him, since she was sixteen. Doctor Prescott had kept his son very close when he was home on his vacations, and not allowed him to mingle much with the village young people. That summer when Elmira was sixteen there had been company in the doctor's house, and she had been summoned to assist in the extra work. Somehow time had hung idly on young Lawrence's hands that summer; the guests in the house were staid elderly folk and no company for him. There was also much sickness in the village, and his father was not as watchful as usual. It happened that Lawrence, for lack of other amusement, would often saunter about the domestic byways of the house, and had a hand in various tasks which brought him into working partnership with pretty, young Elmira — such as stemming currants or shelling pease and beans. On several occasions, also, he and Elmira had roamed the pastures in search of blackberries for tea. Once when they were out together, and had been picking a long time from one fat bush, neither saying a word — for a strange silence which abashed them both, though they knew not why, had come between them — the girl, moved thereto by some quick impulse of maidenly concealment and shame which she did not herself understand, made some light and trivial remark about the size of the fruit, which would well have acquit her had not her little voice broken with utter self-betrayal of innocent love and passion. And then young Lawrence, with a quick motion, as of fire which leaps to flame after a long smoulder, flung an arm about her, with a sigh of "Oh, Elmira!" and kissed her on her mouth.

Then they had quickly stood apart, as if afraid of each other, and finished picking their berries and gone home soberly, with scarce a word. But all the time it was as if invisible cords, which no stretching could thin or break, bound them together, and when they entered the house Doctor Prescott's wife, Lydia, looked at them both with a gentle, yet keen and troubled air. That night, when Elmira went home, she said to her softly that since the baking was all done for the week, and the guests were to leave in three days, and the weather was so warm, and she looked tired, she need not come again. But she drew her to her gently, as she spoke, with one great mother-arm, pressed the little dark head of the girl against her breast, and kissed her. Lydia Prescott was a large woman, shaped like a queen, but she was softer in her ways than Elmira's own mother.

When the girl had gone she turned to her son, who had seen her caress, and blushed and thrilled as if he had given it himself. "You must remember you are very young, Lawrence," said she; "you must remember that a man has no right to follow his mind until he has proved it, and you must remember your father."

And Lawrence had blushed and paled a little, and said, "Yes, mother," soberly, and gone away up-stairs to his own chamber, where he had some wakeful hours, and when he fell asleep often started awake again, with his heart throbbing in his side with that same joyful pain as when he kissed pretty Elmira.

As for Elmira, she did not sleep at all, and came down in the morning with young eyes like stars of love, which no dawn could dim. For six years the memory of that kiss, which had never been repeated, for Elmira had never seen Lawrence alone since, had been to her her sweetest honey savor of life. Lucky it was for her that young Lawrence, if the taste had not been in his heart as in hers during his busy life in other scenes, had still the memory of its sweetness left.

When they had passed through the avenue of brook willows, and the brook itself had wound away through fields spotted as with emeralds and gold, and then had passed some pasture-lands where red cattle were grazing, and then came to a little stretch of pines, beyond which the white walls of a house glimmered, Lawrence held up his arms to Elmira. "It isn't necessary," said he, "but if you don't want to ride my horse, with me leading him, past the houses there, why, I'll take you down, as I said."

And with that Elmira slipped down, and Lawrence had kissed her again, and she had not chidden him, and was following after him, trembling and quite pale, except for the reflection of her pink sunbonnet, while he rode slowly ahead.

When the cluster of houses were well passed he stopped and lifted her again to the mare's saddle, and the old shyness of the blackberry-field was over both of them again as they went on their way. In truth, Lawrence was sorely bewildered betwixt his impulse of young love and innocent conviction that his honor ought to be pledged with the kiss, since they were boy and girl no longer, and his memory of his father and what he might decree for him. As for Elmira, she was much troubled in mind lest she ought to rebuke the young man for his boldness, but could not bring herself so to do, not being certain that she had not kissed him back and been as guilty as he.

The young couple went so all the way to Granby, striving now and then, with casual talk, each to blind the other as to perturbation of spirit. Lawrence lifted her from the saddle when Granby village came in sight, but he did not kiss her again. Indeed, Elmira kept her head well down that he might not; but he asked if he might call and see her, and she said yes, and the next Wednesday evening was mentioned, that day being Thursday. Then she fluttered up the Granby street to Imogen and Sarah Lawson's with her mother's wedding silk, and Lawrence Prescott rode back to Upham. Much he would have liked to linger and take Elmira back as she had come, or else drive over for her later with a chaise, but she had refused.

"Imogen and Sarah can have one of their neighbors' horses and wagons whenever they like," said she, "and they will carry me home if I want them to."

A strange maidenly shyness of her own bliss and happiness, which she longed to repeat, was upon her. She had not told Lawrence what her errand in Granby was. The truth was that she had planned her new gown because Lawrence had come home, and she was anxious to wear it to meeting in the hope that he might admire her in it. Should she betray this artless preening and trimming of her maiden plumage, which, though, like a bird's, an open secret of nature, must nevertheless be kept sacred by an impulse of modest concealment and deceit towards the one for whose sake it all was?

CHAPTER XX

They who have sensitive palates for all small, sweet, but secondary savors of life that come in their way, and no imaginative desires for others, are contented in spirit. When also small worries and affairs, even those of their neighbors in lieu of their own, serve them as well as large ones to keep their minds to a healthy temper of excitement and zest of life, there is no need to pity them for any lack of full experience.

Imogen and Sarah Lawson, the two elderly single sisters whom Elmira Edwards sought in Granby that day, were in a way happier than she, all flushed with her hope of young love, for they held in certain tenure that which they had. They were sitting stitching on fine linen shirts in the little kitchen of the cottage house in which they had been born. There was a broad slant of sunlight athwart the floor, a great cat purred in a rocking-chair, the clock ticked, a pot of greens boiled over the fire. They seemed to look out of a little secure home radiance of peace at Elmira when she entered, all glowing and tremulous with sweet excitement which she strove hard to conceal.

No romances had there been in the lives of the Lawson sisters, and no repining over the lack of them. They had, in their youth, speculated as to what husbands the Lord might provide for them, and looked about for them with furtive alertness. When He provided none, they stopped speculating, and went on as sharply askant as hens at any smaller good pecks life might have for them.

The Lawson sisters had always been considered dressy. They owned their house and garden, also several acres which yielded fair crops of hay, and some good woodland. They earned considerable money making fine shirts for a little Jew peddler who let out work in several neighboring villages, and were enabled to devote the greater part of that to their wardrobes. They were said to always buy everything of the best — the finest muslins, the stiffest silks, the richest ribbons. Each of the sisters possessed several silk gowns, a fine cashmere shawl, and a satin pelisse; each had two beautiful bonnets, one for winter and one for summer, and each possessed the value of her fine apparel to the uttermost, and realized from it a petty, perhaps, but no less comforting, illumination of spirit. Many of the lights of happiness of this world are feeble and even ignoble, but one must see to live, and even a penny dip is exalted if it save one from the darkness of despair. It is not given to every one to light his way with a sun, or a full moon, or even a star.

The two Lawson sisters, Imogen and Sarah, greeted Elmira

with a shrill feminine clamor of hospitality, as was their wont, examined her mother's wedding silk with critical eyes and fingers, and pronounced it well worth making over. "It's best to buy a good thing while you're about it, if it does cost a little more," said Imogen.

"Yes, that's true," assented her sister. "Now I shouldn't be a mite surprised if Ann paid as much as one an' sixpence for this silk when 'twas new; but look at it now — there ain't a break in it. It's as good as your blue-and-yellow changeable silk, Imogen."

"Dun'no' but 'tis," said Imogen, reflectively.

Sarah went with Elmira to the mantua-maker's, who lived in the next house, to get the dress cut, while Imogen prepared the dinner. In the afternoon the two sisters gave Elmira an hour's work on her new gown, one stitching up the body, the other sewing breadths; then they borrowed the neighbor's horse and wagon and drove her home to Upham.

Elmira was glad to ride; she thought that she should die of shame should she walk home and meet Lawrence Prescott again.

Imogen drove. She was the older, but the larger and stronger of the two. Elmira sat in the rear gloom of the covered wagon with Sarah, holding her silk gown spread carefully over her knees. She thought of nothing all the way but the possibility of meeting Lawrence. She made up her mind that if she did she would sit far back in the wagon and not thrust her head forward at all. "If he acts as if he thought I might be in here, and looks real hard, then it will be time for me to do my part," she thought.

Whenever she saw a man or a team in the distance, her heart beat violently, but it was never Lawrence. All her sweet panic of expectation would have been quieted had she known that he was at that very time seated in Miss Camilla Merritt's arbor, drinking tea and eating fruit cake with her and pretty Lucina.

"Didn't you think Elmira seemed dreadful kind of flighty today — still as a mouse one minute and carryin' on the next?" Sarah asked Imogen, as they were driving home in the evening. They had waited, staying to tea and letting the horse rest, until the full moon arose.

"Yes, I did," said Imogen, "but Ann was just like her at her age. That silk is well enough, but it ain't no such quality as my blue an' yellow changeable one."

"Well, I dun'no' as it is. I dun'no' as it's as good as my figured brown one."

It was a beautiful spring night; the moon was one for lovers to light their fondest thoughts and fancies into reality. The two old sisters driving home met and passed many young couples on the country road. "If they don't look out I shall run over some of them fellars an' girls," said Imogen. "I don't b'lieve Elmira has ever had anybody waitin' on her, do you, Sarah?"

"Never heard of anybody," replied Sarah. "Well, anyhow, she's goin' to have a real handsome dress out of that silk."

"Yes, she is," said Imogen, and just then from before the great plunging feet of her horse a pair of young lovers sprang with a laugh, having seen nothing of team nor the old sisters nor yet of the little side lamps of happiness they bore, in the great dazzling circle of their own.

Elmira finished her dress Saturday. She had sat up nearly two nights stitching on it, but nobody would have dreamed it when she came down out of her chamber Sunday morning all ready for meeting. Her mother was sitting in the parlor beside a window, with her Bible on her knees. The window was opened wide, and the room was full of the reverberations of the meeting bell. Always on a pleasant Sunday morning in summer-time Ann Edwards sat with her Bible at the open window and listened to the meeting bell.

As Elmira entered, the bell tolled again, and the long wavering and dying of its sweet multiple tones commenced afresh. Elmira stood before her mother, and turned slowly about that she might view her on all sides in her new attire.

Elmira whirled slowly, in a whispering, shimmering circle of pale green silk; a little wrought-lace cape, which also had been part of her mother's bridal array, covered her bare neck, for the dress was cut low. She had bought a new ribbon of green and white, like the striped grass of the gardens, for her bonnet, and tied it in a crisp and dainty bow under her chin. This same bonnet, of a fine Florence braid, had served her for best for nearly ten years. She had worn a bright ribbon on it in the winter season and a delicate-hued one in summer-time, but it was always the same bonnet.

Elmira had not had a new summer ribbon for three years, and now, in addition, she had purchased some rosebuds, and arranged them in little clusters in a frilling of lace inside the brim. Her pretty face looked out of this little millinery halo with an indescribably mild and innocent radiance. One caught one's self looking past her fixed shining eyes for the brightness which they saw and reflected.

"Well," said her mother, "I guess you look as well as some other folks, if you didn't lay out quite so much money. I guess folks will have to give in you do."

Ann Edwards's little nervous face wore rather an expression of antagonistic triumph than a smile of motherly approval; so hostile had been all her conditions of life that she never laid down her weapons, and went with spear in rest, as it were, even into her few by-paths of delight.

She pulled Elmira's skirts here and there to be sure they hung evenly; she bade her stand close, and picked out the ribbon bow under her chin. "Now you'd better run along," said she, "or the bell will stop tollin'."

She watched the girl, in her own old bridal array, step down the front path, with more happiness than she had known since her husband's disappearance. Elmira had told her mother that Lawrence Prescott was coming to see her, and she had immediately leaped to furthest conclusions. Ann Edwards had not a doubt that Lawrence and Elmira would be married. She had, when it was once awakened, that highest order of ambition which ignores even the existence of obstacles.

As Elmira's green skirts fluttered out of sight behind some lilac-bushes pluming to the wind with purple blossoms Jerome came in, and his mother turned to him. "I guess Elmira will do about as well as any of the girls," said she, with her tone of blissful yet half vindictive triumph.

Jerome looked at her wonderingly. "Why shouldn't she?" said he.

Immediately Mrs. Edwards put forth her feminine craft like an involuntary tentacle of protection for her excess of imagination, against the masculine practicality of her son. Neither she nor Elmira had said anything about Lawrence Prescott to him; both knew how he would regard the matter. It seemed to Mrs. Edwards that she had fairly heard him say: "Marry Doctor Prescott's son! You know better, mother." Now she, with her Bible on her knees, shunted rapidly the whole truth behind a half truth.

"I guess she'll cut full as good a figure in my old silk and her old bonnet with a new ribbon on it as any of the girls," said she. Then she added, with a skilful swerve from whole truths and half truths alike: "You'd better hurry, Jerome, or you'll be late to meetin'. Elmira is out of sight, an' the bell's 'most stopped tollin'."

"I am not going this morning," said Jerome.

"Why not, I'd like to know?"

"John Upham sent his oldest boy over here this morning to tell me the baby's sick. I am going over there and see if I can do anything."

"I should think John Upham had better send for Doctor Prescott instead of taking you away from meeting."

"You know he won't, mother. I believe he'd let the baby die before he would. I've got to go there and do the best I can."

"Well, all I've got to say is, he ought to be ashamed of himself if he'd let his own baby die before he'd call in the doctor, I don't care how bad he's treated him. I shouldn't wonder if John Upham was some to blame about that; there's always two sides to a story."

Jerome made no reply. He would have been puzzled several times lately, had he considered it of sufficient moment, by his mother's change of attitude towards Doctor Prescott. He went to the china-closet beside the chimney. On the upper shelves was his mother's best china tea-set; on the lower a little array of cloudy bottles; some small bunches of herbs, all nicely labelled, were packed in the wide space at the bottom.

His mother's antagonistic eyes followed him. "I dun'no' as I can have them herbs in my china-closet much longer," said she; "they're scentin' up the dishes too much. If I want to have a little company to tea, I ain't goin' to have the tea all flavored with spear-mint an' catnip."

"Well, I'll move them when I come home," said Jerome, with his usual concession, which always aggravated his mother more than open rebellion, although she admired him for it. "I only brought those little bundles down from the barn loft to have them handy. I'll rig up a cupboard for them in the woodshed."

Jerome tucked a bottle or two in his pocket, and rolled up a little bouquet of herbs in paper.

"I should think it would be time for you to go and see that young one after meeting," said his mother, varying her point of attack when she met with no resistance.

"I'll go to meeting this afternoon," replied Jerome, in the tone with which he might have pacified a fretful child. There was no self-justification in it.

"I s'pose Doctor Prescott will be mad if he hears of your goin' there, an' I dun'no' but I should be in his place," she said, as Jerome went out. Then, as he did not answer, she added, calling out shrilly:

"I don't see why John Upham can't call in Lawrence, if he wants a doctor; he's begun to study with his father; he can't have nothin' against him. I guess he knows as much as you do."

"Mother's queer," Jerome told himself as he went down the road, and then dismissed the matter from his mind, for the con-sideration of the Upham baby and the probable nature of its ailment, upon which, however, he did not allow himself to dwell too long. Early in his amateur practice Jake Noyes had inculcated one precept in his mind, upon which he always acted.

"There's one thing I want to tell ye, J'rome, and I want ye to remember it," Jake Noyes had said, "and that is, a doctor had ought to be like jurymen — he'd ought to be sworn in to be unprejudiced when he goes to see a patient, just as a juryman is when he goes to court. If you don't know what ails 'em, don't ye go to speculatin', as to what 'tis an' what ye'll do, on the way there. Ten chances to one, if you're workin' up measles in your mind an' what you'll do for them, you'll find it's mumps, an' then you've got to cure your own measles afore you cure their mumps; an' if you're hard-bitted an' can't stop yourself easy when you're once headed, you may give saffron tea to bring out the measles whether or no. Think of the prospect, or the gals, or your soul's salvation, or anythin' but the sick folks, before you get to 'em the first time and don't know what ails 'em."

In girls Jerome had, so far, no interest; in his soul's salvation he had little active concern. The revivals which were occasionally upstirred in the community by prayer, and the besom of threatened destruction, passed over him like a hot wind, for which he had no power of sensation, sometimes to his own wonder. Probably the cause lay in the fact that he was too thoroughly, without knowing it, rooted and grounded in his own creed to be emotionally moved by religious appeals. Jerome had, as most have, consciously or not, and vitally or not, his own creed. He believed simply in the unquestionable justice of the intent of God, the thwarting struggles against it by free man, and that his duty to apply his small strength towards furthering what he could, if no more than an atom, of the eternal will lay plain before him.

Jerome, who had not yet been disturbed by love of woman, who fretted not over the salvation of his own soul, had therefore, in order to follow his mentor's advice, to turn his attention to the prospect. His way led in an opposite direction from the church, and he was late, so met none of the worshippers bound to meeting. He was rather glad of that. After he left the village the road lay through the woods, and now and then between blueberry-fields or open spaces of meadow, with green water-lines and shadows purple with violets in the hollows. Red cows in the meadows stared at him as he passed, with their mysterious abstraction from all reflection, then grazed again, moving in one direction from the sun. The blueberry-patches spread a pale green glimmer of blossoms, like a sheen of satin in a high light; young ferns curled beside the road like a baby's fingers grasping at life; the trees, which were late in leafing, also reached out towards the sun little rosy clasping fingers whereby to hold fast to the motherhood of the spring. The air was full of that odor so delicate that it is scarcely an odor at all, much less a fragrance, which certain so-called scentless plants give out, and then only to wide recognition when they bloom in multitudes — it was only the simplest evidence of life itself. Through that came now and then great whiffs of perfume from some unseen flowering bush, calling, as it were, from its obscurity, with halloos of fragrance, to the careless passer-by, to search it out.

Jerome passed along, seeing and comprehending all the sweet pageant of the spring morning, yet as an observer merely. Nature had as yet not established her fullest relationship to himself, and he knew not that her secret glory of meaning was like his own.

CHAPTER XXI

John Upham's farm, or rather what had been John Upham's farm (Doctor Prescott owned it now), began at the end of a long stretch of woods, with some fine fields sloping greenly towards the west. Farther on, behind a row of feathery elm-trees, stood the old Upham homestead.

John Upham did not live there now; his mortgage had been foreclosed nearly a year before, about the time the last baby was born. People said that the mother had been cruelly hurried out of her own house into the little shanty, which her husband was forced to rent for a shelter. Poor John Upham had lost all his ancestral acres to Doctor Prescott now, and did not fairly know himself how it had happened. There had been heavy bills for medicines and attendance, and the doctor had loaned him money oftentimes, with his land as security, for other debts. A little innocent saying of one of his six children to another was much repeated to the village, "Father bought you of Doctor Prescott, and paid for you with all the clover-field he had left, and you must be very good, for you came very dear."

It was known positively that John Upham had gone to Doctor Prescott's the day after he had left his old home, and told him to his face what he thought of him. "You have planned and manœuvred to get all my property into your hands from the very first of it," said John Upham. "You've drained me dry, an' now I hope you're satisfied."

"You had full value in return," replied the doctor, calmly.

"I haven't had time. In nine cases out of ten, if you had given me a little time, I could have got myself out, and you know it. You've screwed me down to the very second."

"I cannot afford to give my debtors longer time than that regulated by the laws of the commonwealth."

Then a sudden strange gleam had come into John Upham's blue eyes. "Thank the Lord," he cried out, in a trembling fervor of wrath — "thank the Lord, He gives all the time there is to His debtors, an' no commonwealth on the earth can make laws agin it." He had actually then raised a great fist and shaken it before the doctor's face. "Now, don't you ever darse to darken my doors again, Doctor Seth Prescott!" he had cried out. "If my wife or my children are sick, I'll let them lay and die before I'll have you in the house!" So saying, John Upham had stridden forth out of the doctor's yard, where he had held the conversation with him, with Jake Noyes and two other men covertly listening.

After that Jake Noyes had given surreptitious advice, with sly shoving of medicine-vials into John Upham's or his wife's hands when the children were ailing, and lately Jerome had taken his place.

"Guess you had better go there instead of me when the young ones are out of sorts," Jake Noyes had told Jerome. Then he had added, with a crafty twist and wink: "When ye can quarrel with your own bread an' butter with a cat's-paw might as well do it, especially when you're gettin' along in years. You 'ain't got anything to lose if you do set the doctor again ye, and I have."

The house in which the Uphams had taken shelter was in sight of the old homestead, some rods farther on, on the opposite side of the road. It stood in a sandy waste of weeds on the border of an old gravel-pit — an ancient cottage, with a wretched crouch of humility in its very roof. It had been covered with a feeble coat of red paint years ago, and cloudy lines of it still survived the wash of old rains and the beat of old sunbeams.

Behind it on the north and west rose the sand-hill, dripping with loose gravel as with water, hollowed out at its base until its crest, bristling with coarse herbage, magnified against the sky, projected far out over the cottage roof. The sun was reflected from the sand in a great hollow of arid light. Jerome, nearing it, felt as if he were approaching an oven. The cottage door was shut, as were all the windows. However, he heard plainly the shrill wail of the sick baby.

John Upham opened the door. "Oh, it's you, Jerome!" said he. "Good-day."

"Good-day," returned Jerome. "How is the baby?"

"Well, he seems kind of ailin'. Laury has been up with him all night. Thought maybe you might give him something. Come in, won't ye?"

There were only two rooms on the lower floor of the cottage — one was the kitchen, the other the bedroom where John Upham and his wife slept with the three youngest children.

Jerome followed Upham across the kitchen to the bedroom beyond. The kitchen was littered with all John Upham's poor household goods, prostrate and unwashed, degraded even from their one dignity of use. One of the kitchen windows opened towards the sand-hill; the room was full of its garish glare of reflected sunlight, and the revelations were pitiless. Laura Upham, once a model housekeeper, had lost all ambition and domestic pride, now she had such a poor house to keep and so many children to tend.

Upham muttered an apology as Jerome picked his way across the room.

"Laury has been up all night with the baby, an' she hasn't had any time to redd up the room," he said. "The children have been in here all the mornin', too, an' they've stirred things up some. I've just sent 'em out to pick flowers to keep 'em quiet."

As he spoke he gathered up awkwardly, with a curious over-motion of his broad shoulders, as if he would conceal the action, various articles in his path. When he opened the door into the bedroom he crammed them behind it with a quick, shifty motion.

The kitchen had been repulsive, but the bedroom fairly shocked with the very indelicacy of untidiness. Jerome felt an actual modesty about entering this room, in which so many disclosures of the closest secrets of the flesh were made. The very dust and discolorations of the poor furnishings, the confined air, made one turn one's face aside as from too coarse a betrayal of personal reserve. The naked indecency of domestic life seemed to display and vaunt itself, sparing none of its homely and ungraceful details, to the young man on the threshold of the room.

"Laury 'ain't had a chance to redd up this, either," poor John Upham whispered in his ear, and gathered up with a furtive swoop some linen from the floor.

"Oh, that's all right!" Jerome whispered back, and entered boldly, shutting as it were all the wretched disclosures of the room out of his consciousness, and all effort to do was needless when he saw Mrs. Upham's face.

Laura Upham's great hollow eyes, filled with an utter passiveness of despair, stared up at him out of a sallow gloom of face. She had been pretty once, and she was not an old woman now, but her beauty was all gone. Her slender shoulders rounded themselves over the little creature swathed in soiled flannel on her lap. Just then it was quiet; but it began wailing again, distorting all its miserable little face into a wide mouth of feeble clamor as Jerome drew near.

Mrs. Upham looked down at it hopelessly. She did not try to hush it. "It's cried this way all night," she said, in a monotonous tone. "It's goin' to die."

"Now, Laury, you know it ain't any sicker than it was before," John said, with a kind of timid conciliation; but she turned upon him with a fierce gleam lighting her dull eyes to life.

"You needn't talk to me," said she — "you needn't talk to me, John Upham, when you won't have the doctor when it's your own flesh an' blood that's dyin'. I don't care what he's done. I don't care if he has taken the roof from over our heads. My child is worth more than anything else. He'd come if you asked him, he couldn't refuse — you know he couldn't, John Upham!"

John Upham's face was white; his forehead and his chin got a curious hardness of outline. "He won't have a chance," he said, between his teeth.

"Let your own flesh and blood die, then!" cried his wife; but the fierceness was all gone from her voice; she had no power of sustained wrath, so spent was she. She gave a tearless wail that united with the child's in her lap in a pitiful chord of woe.

"Now, Laury, you know J'rome gave Minnie somethin' that helped her, and she seemed every mite as sick as the baby," her husband said, in a softer voice. But she turned her hopeless eyes again upon the little, squalid, quivering thing in her lap, and paid no more heed to him. She let Jerome examine the child, with a strange apathy. There was no hope, and consequently no power of effort, left in her.

When Jerome brought some medicine in a spoon, she assisted him to feed the child with it, but mechanically, and as if she had no interest. Her sharp right elbow shone like a knob of ivory through a great rent in her sleeve; her dress was unfastened, and there was a gleam of white flesh through the opening; she neither knew nor cared. There was no consciousness of self, no pride and no shame for self, in her; she had ceased to live in the fullest sense; she was nothing but the concentration of one emotion of despairing motherhood.

She heard Jerome and her husband moving about in the next room, she heard the crackling of fire in the stove, the clinking din of dishes, the scrape of a broom, not realizing in the least what the sounds meant. She heard with her mind no sound of earth but the wail of the sick baby in her lap.

Jerome Edwards could tidy a house as well as a woman, and John Upham followed his directions with clumsy zeal. When the kitchen was set to rights Mrs. Upham went in there, as she was bidden, with the baby, and sat down in a rocking-chair by the open window towards the road, through which came a soft green light from some opposite trees, and a breath of apple-blossoms.

"We've got the room all redd up, Laury," John Upham said, pitifully, stooping over her and looking into her face. She nodded vaguely, looking at the baby, who had stopped crying.

Jerome dropped some more medicine, and she took the spoon and fed it to the baby. "I think it will go to sleep now," said Jerome. Mrs. Upham looked up at him and almost smiled. Hope was waking within her. "I think it is nothing but a little cold and fever-ishness, Mrs. Upham," Jerome added. He had a great pitiful imag-ination for this unknown woe of maternity, which possibly gave him as great a power of sympathy as actual knowledge.

"You are a good fellow, Jerome, an' I hope I shall be able to do somethin' to pay you some day," John Upham said, huskily, when they were in the bedroom putting that also in order.

"I don't want any pay for what I give," Jerome returned.

When Jerome started for home, Mrs. Upham and the baby were both asleep in the clean bedroom. Retracing his steps along the pleasant road, he was keenly happy, with perhaps the true hap-piness of his life, to which he would always turn at last from all others, and which would survive the death and loss of all others.

He pictured John Upham's house as he found it and as he left it with purest self-gratulation. He had not gone far before he heard a clamor of childish voices; there were two, but they sounded like a troop. John Upham's twin girls broke through the wayside bushes like little wild things. Their hands were full of withering flowers. He called them, and bade them be very still when they went home, so as not to waken their mother and the baby, and they hung their heads with bashful assent. They were pretty children in spite of their soiled frocks, with their little, pink, moist faces and curling crops of yellow hair.

"If you keep still and don't wake them up, I will bring you both some peppermints when I come tomorrow," said Jerome. He had nearly reached the village when he met the two eldest Upham children. They were boys, the elder twelve, the younger eight, sturdy little fellows, advancing with a swinging trot, one behind the other, both chewing spruce-gum. They had been in the woods, on their way home, for a supply. Jerome stopped them, and repeated the charge he had given to the little girls, then kept on. The bell was ringing for afternoon meeting — in fact, it was almost done. Jerome walked faster, for he intended to go. He drew near the little white-steepled meeting-house standing in its small curve of greensward, with the row of white posts at the side, to which were tied the farmers' great plough-horses harnessed to covered wagons and dusty chaises, and then he caught a glimpse of something bright, like a moving flower-bush, in the road ahead. Squire Eben Merritt, his wife, his sister Miss Camilla, and his daughter Lucina, were all on their way to afternoon meeting.

The Squire was with them that day, leaving heroically his trout-pools and his fishing-fields; for was it not his pretty Lucina's second Sunday only at home, and was he not as eager to be with her as any lover? Squire Eben had gained perhaps twenty pounds of flesh to his great frame and a slight overcast of gray to his golden beard; otherwise he had not changed in Jerome's eyes since he was a boy. The Squire's wife Abigail, like many a small, dark woman who has never shown in her looks the true heyday of youth, had apparently not aged nor altered at all. Little and keenly pleasant, like some insignificant but brightly flavored fruit, set about with crisp silk flounced to her trim waist, holding her elbows elegantly aslant under her embroidered silk shawl, her small head gracefully alert in her bright-ribboned bonnet, she stepped beside her great husband, and then came Lucina with Miss Camilla.

Miss Camilla glided along drooping slenderly in black lace and lilac silk, with a great wrought-lace veil flowing like a bride's over her head, and shading with a black tracery of leaves and flowers her fair faded face; but Jerome saw her no more than he would have seen a shadow beside Lucina.

If Lucina's parents had changed little, she had changed much, with the wonderful change of a human spring, and this time Jerome saw her as well as her gown. She wore that same silken gown of a pale-blue color, spangled with roses, and the skirts were so wide and trained over a hoop and starched petticoats that they swung and tilted like a great double flower, and hit on this side and that with a quick musical slur. Over Lucina's shoulders, far below her waist, fell her wonderful fair hair, in curls, and every curl might well have proved a twining finger of love. Lucina wore a bonnet of fine straw, trimmed simply enough with a white ribbon, but over her face hung a white veil of rich lace, and through it her pink cheeks and lips and great blue eyes and lines of golden hair shone and bloomed and dazzled like a rose through a frosted window.

Lucina Merritt was a rare beauty, and she knew it, from her looking-glass as well as the eyes of others, and dealt with herself meekly wherewithal, and prayed innocently that she might consider more the embellishment of her heart and her mind than her person, and not to be too well pleased at the admiring looks of those whom she met. Indeed, it was to this end that she wore the white veil over her face, though not one of the maiden mates would believe that. She fancied that it somewhat dimmed her beauty, and that folk were less given to staring at her, not realizing that it added to her graces that subtlest one of suggestion, and that folk but stared the harder to make sure whether they saw or imagined such charms.

Jerome Edwards saw this beautiful Lucina coming, and it was suddenly as if he entered a new atmosphere. He did not know why, but he started as if he had gotten a shock, and his heart beat hard.

Squire Merritt made as if he would greet him in his usual hearty fashion, but remembering the day, and hearing, too, the first strains of the opening hymn from the meeting-house, for the bell had stopped tolling, he gave him only a friendly nod as he passed on with his wife. Miss Camilla inclined her head with soft graciousness; but Jerome looked at none of them except Lucina. She did not remember him; she glanced slightly at his face, and then her long fair lashes swept again the soft bloom of her cheeks, and her silken skirts fairly touched him as she passed. Jerome stood still after they had all entered the meeting-house; the long drone of the hymn sounded very loud in his ears.

He made a motion towards the meeting-house, hesitated, made another, then turned decidedly to the road. It seemed suddenly to him that his clothes must be soiled and dusty after his work in John Upham's house, that his hair could not be smooth, that he did not look well enough to go to meeting. So he went home, yielding for the first time, without knowing that he did so, to that decorative impulse which comes to men and birds alike when they would woo their mates.

CHAPTER XXII

The next morning Jerome went early to his uncle Ozias Lamb for some finished shoes, which he was to take to Dale. For the first time in his life, when he entered the shop, he had an impulse to avert his eyes and not meet his uncle's fully. Ozias had grown old rapidly of late. He sat, with his usual stiff crouch, on his bench and hammered away at a shoe-heel on his lapstone. His hair and beard were white and shaggy, his blue eyes peered sharply, as from a very ambush of old age, at Jerome loading himself with the finished shoes.

After the usual half grunt of greeting, which was scarcely more than a dissyllabic note of salutation between two animals, Ozias was silent until Jerome was going out.

"Ain't ye well this mornin'?" he asked then.

"Yes," replied Jerome, "I'm well enough."

"When a man's smart," said Ozias Lamb, "and has got money in his pocket, and don't want folks to know it, he don't keep feelin' of it to see if it's safe. He acts as if he hadn't got any money, or any pocket, neither. I s'pose that's what you're tryin' to do."

"Don't know what you mean," returned Jerome, coloring.

"Oh, nothin'. Go along," said his uncle.

But he spoke again before Jerome was out of hearing. "There ain't any music better than a squeak, in the grind you an' me have got to make out of life," said he, "an' don't you go to thinkin' there is. If you ever think you hear it, it's only in your own ears, an' you might as well make up your mind to it."

"I made up my mind to it as long ago as I can remember," Jerome answered back, yet scarcely with bitterness, for the very music which his uncle denied was too loud in his ears for him to disbelieve it.

When Jerome was returning from Dale, an hour later, his back bent beneath great sheaves of newly cut shoes, like a harvester's with wheat, he heard a hollow echo of hoofs in the road ahead, then presently a cloud of dust arose like smoke, and out of it came two riders: Lawrence Prescott, on a fine black horse — which his father used seldom for driving, he was so unsuited for standing patiently at the doors of affliction, yet kept through a latent fondness for good horse-flesh — and Lucina Merritt, on his pretty bay mare. Lucina galloped past at Lawrence's side, with an eddying puff of blue riding-skirt and a toss of yellow curls and blue plumes. Jerome stood back a little to give them space, and the dust settled slowly over him after they were by. Then he went on his way, with his heart beating hard, yet with no feeling of jealousy against Lawrence Prescott. He even thought that it would be a good match. Still, he was curiously disturbed, not by the reflection that he was laden with sheaves of leather — he would have been more ashamed had he been seen idling on a work-day — but because he feared he looked so untidy with the dust of the road on his shoes. She might have noticed his clothes, although she had galloped by so fast.

The first thing Jerome did, when he reached home, was to brush and blacken his shoes, though there was no chance of Lucina's seeing them. He felt as if he ought not to think of her when he had on dusty shoes.

The greater part of the next day Jerome passed, as usual, soling shoes in Ozias Lamb's shop. When he came home to supper, he noticed something unusual about his mother and sister. They had the appearance of being strung tightly with repressed excitement, like some delicate musical instruments. To look at or to speak to them was to produce in them sensitive vibrations which seemed out of proportion to the cause.

Jerome asked no questions. These disturbances in the feminine current always produced a corresponding stiffness of calm in his masculine one, as if by an instinct to maintain the equilibrium of dangerous forces for the safety of the household.

Elmira and her mother kept looking at each other and at him, pulses starting up in their delicate cheeks, flushes coming and going, motioning each other with furtive gestures to speak, then countermanding the order with sharp negatory shakes of the head.

At last Mrs. Edwards called back Jerome as he was going to his chamber, books under arm and lighted candle in hand.

"Look here," said she; "I want to show you something."

Jerome turned. Elmira was extending towards him a nicely folded letter, with a little green seal on it.

"What is it?" asked Jerome.

"Read it," said his mother. Jerome took it, unfolded it, and read, Elmira and his mother watching him. Elmira was quite pale. Mrs. Edwards's mouth was set as if against anticipated opposition, her nervously gleaming eyes were fierce with ready argument. Jerome knit his brows over the letter, then he folded it nicely and gave it back to Elmira.

"You see what it is?" said his mother.

"Yes, I see," replied Jerome, hesitatingly. He looked confused before her, for one of the few times of his life.

"An invitation for you an' Elmira to Squire Merritt's — to a party; it's Lucina's birthday," said his mother, and she fairly smacked her lips, as if the words were sweet.

Elmira looked at her brother breathlessly. Nobody knew how eager she was to go; it was the first party worthy of a name to which she had been bidden in her whole life. She and her mother had been speculating, ever since the invitation had arrived, upon the possibility of Jerome's refusing to accept it.

"Nobody can tell what he'll do," Mrs. Edwards had said. "He's just as likely to take a notion not to go as to go."

"I can't go if he doesn't," said Elmira.

"Why can't you, I'd like to know?"

Elmira shrank timidly. "I never went into Squire Merritt's house in my life," said she.

"I guess there ain't anything there to bite you," said her mother. "I'm goin' to say all I can to have your brother go; but if he won't, you can put on your new dress an' go without him." However, Mrs. Edwards privately resolved to use as an argument to Jerome, in case he refused to attend the party, the fact that his sister would not go without him.

She used it now. Mrs. Edwards's military tactics were those of direct onslaught, and no saving of powder. "Elmira's afraid to go unless you do," said she. "You'll be keepin' her home, an' she ain't had a chance to go to many parties, poor child!"

Jerome met Elmira's beseeching eyes and frowned aside, blushing like a girl. "Well, I don't know," said he; "I'll see."

That was the provincial form of masculine concession to feminine importunity. Mrs. Edwards nodded to Elmira when Jerome had shut the door. "He'll go," said she.

Elmira smiled and quivered with half fearful delight. Lawrence Prescott was coming to see her the next day, and the day after that she would be sure to meet him again at Squire Merritt's. She trembled before her own happiness, as before an angel whose wings cast shadows of the dread of delight.

"You'd better go to bed now," said her mother, with a meaning look; "you want to look bright tomorrow, and you've got a good deal before you."

The next day not a word was said to Jerome about Lawrence Prescott's expected call. He noticed vaguely that something unusual seemed to be going on in the parlor; then divined, with a careless dismissal of the subject, that it was house-cleaning. He had a secret of his own that day which might have rendered him less curious about the secrets of others. There were scarcely enough shoes finished to take to Dale, only a half lot, but Jerome announced his intention of going, to Ozias Lamb, with assumed carelessness.

"Why don't ye wait till the lot is finished?" asked Ozias.

"Guess I'll take a half lot this time," replied Jerome.

Ozias eyed him sharply, but said nothing.

Jerome had in his room a little iron-bound strong-box which had belonged to his father, though few treasures had poor Abel Edwards ever had occasion to store in it. After dinner that noon Jerome went up-stairs, unlocked the strong-box, took out some coins, handling them carefully lest they jingle, and put them in his leather wallet. Then he went down-stairs and out the front door as stealthily as if he had been thieving. Elmira and her mother were at work in the parlor, and saw him go down the walk and disappear up the road.

"I'll tell you what 'tis," said Mrs. Edwards, with one of her sharp, confirmatory nods, "J'rome's been takin' out some of that money, an' he's goin' to Dale to get him some new clothes."

"What makes you think so?"

"Oh, you see if he 'ain't. He 'ain't got a coat nor a vest fit to wear to that party, an' he knows it. If he's taken some of that money he's savin' up towards the mortgage I'm glad of it. Folks ought to have a little somethin' as they go along; if they don't, first thing they know they'll get past it."

Jerome did not start for Dale until it was quite late in the afternoon, working hard meanwhile in the shop. The day was another of those typical ones of early spring, which had come lately, drooping as to every leaf and bud with that hot languor which forces bloom. The door and windows of the little shop were set wide open. The honey and spice-breaths of flowers mingled with the rank effluvia of leather like a delicate melody with a harsh bass. Jerome pegged along in silence with knitted brow, yet with a restraint of smiles on his lips.

Ozias Lamb also was silent; his old face bending over his work was a concentration of moody gloom. Ozias was not as outspoken as formerly concerning his bitter taste of life, possibly because it had reached his soul. Jerome sometimes wondered if his uncle had troubles that he did not know of. He started for Dale so late that it was after sunset when he returned with a great parcel under his arm. He felt strangely tired, and just before he reached Upham village he sat down on a stone wall, laid his parcel carefully at his side, and looked about him.

The spring dusk was gathering slowly, though at first through an enhanced clearness of upper lights. All the gloom seemed to proceed from the earth in silvery breathings of meadows and gradual stealings forth of violet shadows from behind forest trees. The sky was so full of pure yellow light that even the feathery spring foliage was darkly outlined against it, and one could see far within it the fanning of the wings of the twilight birds. The air was cooler. The breaths of new-turned earth, and rank young plants in marshy places and woodland ponds were in it, overcoming somewhat those of sun-steeped blossoms, which had prevailed all day.

The road from Dale to Upham lay through low land, and however dry the night elsewhere, there was always a damp freshness. The circling clamor of birds overhead seemed wonderfully near. In the village the bell had begun to ring for an evening prayer-meeting, and one could have fancied that the bell hung in one of the neighboring trees. The clearness of sight seemed to enhance hearing, and possibly also that imagination which is beyond both senses. Jerome had a vague impression which he did not express to himself, that he had come to a door wide open into spaces beyond all needs and desires of the flesh and the earthly soul, and had a sense of breathing new air. Suddenly, now that he had gained this clear outlook of spirit, the world, and all the things thereof, seemed to be at his back, and grown dim, even to his retrospective thought. The image even of beautiful Lucina, which had dwelt with him since Sunday, faded, for she was not yet become of his spirit, and pertained scarcely to his flesh, except through the simplest and most rudimentary of human instincts. Jerome glanced at the parcel containing the fine new vest and coat which he had purchased, and frowned scornfully at this childish vanity, which would lead him to perk and plume and glitter to the sun, like any foolish bird which would awake the desire of the eyes in another.

"What a fool I am!" he muttered, and looked at the great open of sky again, and was half minded to take his purchases back to Dale.

However, when the clear gold of the sky began to pale and a great star shone out over the west, he rose, took up his parcel, and went home.

There was a light in the parlor. He thought indifferently that Paulina Maria Judd or his aunt Belinda might be in there calling on his mother; but when he went into the kitchen his mother sat there, and both the other women were with her.

The supper-table was still standing. "Where have you been,

Jerome Edwards?" cried his mother. She cast a sharp look at his parcel, but said nothing about it. Jerome laid it on top of the old desk which had belonged to his father. "I have been over to Dale," he replied; "I didn't start very early."

His aunt Belinda looked at him amiably. She had not changed much. Her face, shaded by her long curls, had that same soft droop as of a faded flower. Once past her bloom of the flesh, there was, in a woman so little beset by storms of the spirit as Belinda Lamb, little further change possible until she dropped entirely from her tree of life. She looked at Jerome with the amiable light of a smile rather than a smile itself, and said, with her old, weak, but clinging pounce upon disturbing trifles, "Why, Jerome, you 'ain't been all this time gettin' to Dale an' back?"

"I didn't hurry," replied Jerome, coldly, drawing a chair up to the supper-table. He had always a sensation of nervous impatience with this mild, negatively sweet woman which he could not overcome, though he felt shamed by it. He preferred to see Paulina Maria, though between her and himself a covert antagonism survived the open one of his boyhood — at least, he could dislike her without disliking himself.

The candle-light fell full upon Paulina Maria's face, which was even more transparent than formerly; so transfused was her clear profile by the candle-light that the outlines seemed almost to waver and be lost. She was knitting a fine white cotton stocking in an intricate pattern, and did not look at Jerome, or speak to him, beyond her first nod of recognition when he entered.

Presently, however, Jerome turned to her. "How is Henry?" he inquired.

"About the same," she replied, in her clear voice, which was unexpectedly loud, and seemed to have a curious after-tone.

"His eyes are no worse, then?"

"No worse, and no better."

"Can't he do any more than he did last year?" asked Mrs. Edwards.

"No, he can't. He hasn't been able to do a stitch on shoes since last Thanksgiving. He can't do anything but sit at the window and knit plain knittin'. I don't know how he would get along, if I hadn't showed him how to do that. I believe he'd go crazy."

"Don't you think that last stuff Doctor Prescott put in his eyes did him any good?" asked Mrs. Edwards.

"No, I don't. He didn't think it would, himself. He said all there was to do was to go to Boston and see that great doctor there and have an operation, an' it's goin' to cost three hundred dollars. Three hundred dollars! — it's easy enough to talk — three hundred dollars! Adoniram has been laid up with jaundice half the winter. I've bound shoes, and I've knit these fine stockin's for Mis' Doctor Prescott. They go towards the doctor's bill, but they're a drop in the bucket. She'd allow considerable on them, but it ain't *her* say. Three hundred dollars!"

"It's a sight of money," said Belinda Lamb. "I s'pose you could mortgage the house, Paulina Maria, and then when Henry got his eyesight back he could work to pay it off."

A deep red transfused Paulina Maria's transparent pallor, but before she could speak Ann Edwards interposed. "Mortgage!" said she, with a sniff of her nostrils, as if she scented battle. "Mortgage! Load a poor horse down to the ground till his legs break under him, set a baby to layin' a stone wall till he drops, but don't talk to me of mortgages; I guess I know enough about them. My poor husband would have been alive and well today if it hadn't been for a mortgage. It sounds easy enough — jest a little interest money to pay every year, an' all this money down; but I tell you 'tis like a leech that sucks at body and soul. You get so the mortgage looks worse than your sins, an' you pray to be forgiven that instead of them. I know. Don't you have a mortgage put on your house, Paulina Maria Judd, or you'll rue the day. I'd — steal before I'd do it!"

Paulina Maria made no response; she was quite pale again.

"I should think you'd be afraid Henry would go entirely blind if you didn't have something done for him," said Belinda Lamb.

"I be," replied Paulina Maria, sternly. She rose to go, and Belinda also, with languid response of motion, as if Paulina Maria were an upstirring wind.

When Paulina Maria opened the outer door there was a rush of dank night air.

"Don't you want me to walk home with you and Aunt Belinda?" asked Jerome. "It's pretty dark."

"No, thank you," replied Paulina Maria, grimly, looking back, a pale, wavering shape against the parallelogram of night; "the things I'm afraid of walk in the light as much as the dark, an' you can't keep 'em off."

"You make me creep, talkin' so," Belinda Lamb said, as she and Paulina Maria, two women of one race, with their souls at the antipodes of things, went down the path together.

"I hope Paulina Maria won't put a mortgage on her house; Henry 'd better be blind," said Ann Edwards, when they had gone.

Jerome, finishing his supper, said nothing, but he knew, and Paulina Maria knew that he knew, there was already a mortgage on her house. When Jerome rose from the table his mother pointed at the parcel on the desk.

"What's that?" she asked.

"I had to buy a coat and vest if I was going to that party," replied Jerome, with a kind of dogged embarrassment. He had never felt so confused before his mother's sharp eyes since he was a child. If she had blamed him for his purchase, he would have been an easy victim, but she did not.

"What did you get?" she asked.

"I'll show you in the morning — you can see them better."

"Well, you needed them, if you are goin' to the party. You've got to look a little like folks. Where you goin'?" for Jerome had started towards the door.

"Into the parlor to get a book." He opened the door, but his mother beckoned him back mysteriously, and he closed it softly.

"What is it?" he asked, wonderingly. "Who is there? Has Elmira got company?"

"Belinda Lamb begun quizzin' as soon as she got in here; said she thought she heard a man talkin', an' asked if it was you; an' when I said it wa'n't, wanted to know who it was. I told her right to her face it was none of her business."

"Who is it in there, mother?" asked Jerome.

"It ain't anybody to make any fuss about."

"Who is it in there with Elmira?"

"It's Lawrence Prescott, that's who it is," replied his mother, who was more wary in defence than attack, yet defiant enough when the struggle came. She looked at Jerome with unflinching eyes.

"Lawrence Prescott!"

"Yes, what of it?"

"Mother, he isn't going to pay attention to Elmira!"

"Why not, if he wants to? He's as likely a young fellow as there is in town. She won't be likely to do any better."

Jerome stared at his mother in utter bewilderment. "Mother, are you out of your senses?" he gasped.

"I don't know why I am," said she.

"Don't you know that Doctor Prescott would turn Lawrence out of house and home if he thought he was going to marry Elmira?"

"I guess she's good enough for him. You can run down your own sister all you want to, Jerome Edwards."

"I am not running her down. I don't deny she's good enough for any man on earth, but not with the kind of goodness that counts. Mother, don't you know that nothing but trouble can come to Elmira from this? Lawrence Prescott can't marry her."

"I'd like to know what you mean by trouble comin' to her," demanded his mother. A hot red of shame and wrath flashed all over her little face and neck as she spoke, and Jerome, perceiving his mother's thought, blushed at that, and not at his own.

"I meant that he would have to leave her, and make her miserable in the end, and that is all I did mean," he said, indignantly. "He can't marry her, and you know it as well as I. Then there is something else," he added, as a sudden recollection flashed over his mind: "he was out riding horseback with Lucina Merritt Monday."

"I don't believe a word of it," his mother said, hotly.

"I saw him."

"Well, what of it if he did? She's the only girl here that rides horseback, an' I s'pose he wanted company. Mebbe her father asked him to go with her in case her horse got scared at anything. I shouldn't be a mite surprised if he had to go and couldn't help himself. He wouldn't like to refuse if he was asked."

"Mother, you know that Lucina Merritt is the only girl in this town that Doctor Prescott would think was fit to marry his son, and you know his family have always had to do just as he said."

"I don't know any such thing," returned his mother; her voice of dissent had the shrill persistency of a cricket's. "Doctor Prescott always took a sight of notice of Elmira when she was a little girl and he used to come here. He never took to you, I know, but he always did to Elmira."

Jerome said no more. He lighted a candle, took his parcel of new clothes, and went up-stairs to his chamber.

It was twelve o'clock before Lawrence Prescott went home. Jerome had not gone to bed; he was waiting to speak to his sister. When he heard her step on the stairs he opened his door. Elmira, candle in hand, came slowly up the stair, holding her skirt up lest she trip over it. When she reached the landing her brother confronted her, and she gave a little startled cry; then stood, her eyes cast down before him, and the candle-light shining over the sweet redness and radiance of her face, which was at that moment nothing but a sign and symbol of maiden love.

All at once Jerome seemed to grasp the full meaning of it. His own face deepened and glowed, and looked strangely like his sister's. It was as if he began to learn involuntarily his own lesson from another's text-book. Suddenly, instead of his sister's face he seemed to see Lucina Merritt's. That look of love which levels mankind to one family was over his memory of her.

"What did you want?" Elmira asked, at length, timidly, but laughing before him at the same time like a foolish child who cannot conceal delight.

"Nothing," said her brother; "good-night," and went into his chamber and shut his door.

CHAPTER XXIII

The most intimate friends in unwonted gala attire are always something of a revelation to one another. Butterflies, meeting for the first time after their release from chrysalis, might well have the same awe and confusion of old memories.

On the night of the party, when they were dressed and had come down-stairs, Jerome, who had seen his sister every day of his life, looked at her as if for the first time, and she looked in the same way at him. Elmira's Aunt Belinda Lamb had given her, some time before, a white muslin gown of her girlhood.

"I 'ain't got any daughter to make it over for," said she, "an' you might as well have it." Belinda Lamb had looked regretfully at its voluminous folds, as she passed it over to Elmira. Privately she could not see why she should not wear it still, but she knew that she would not dare face Paulina Maria when attired in it.

Elmira, after much discussion with her mother, had decided upon refurbishing this old white muslin, and wearing that instead of her new green silk to the party.

"It will look more airy for an evenin' company," said Mrs. Edwards, "an' the skirt is so full you can take out some of the breadths an' make ruffles."

Elmira and her mother had toiled hard to make those ruffles and finish their daily stent on shoes, but the dress was in readiness and Elmira arrayed in it before eight o'clock on Thursday night. Her dress had a fan waist cut low, with short puffs for sleeves. Her neck, displaying, as it did, soft hollows rather than curves, and her arms, delicately angular at wrists and elbows, were still beautiful. She was thin, but her bones were so small that little flesh was required to conceal harsh outlines.

She wore a black velvet ribbon tied around her throat, and from it hung a little gold locket — one of the few treasures of her mother's girlhood. Elmira had tended a little pot of rose-geranium in a south window all winter. This spring it was full of pale pink bloom. She had made a little chaplet of the fragrant leaves and flowers to adorn her smooth dark hair, and also a pretty knot for her breast. Her skirt was ruffled to her slender waist with tiniest frills of the diaphanous muslin. Elmira in her party gown looked like a double white flower herself.

As for Jerome, he felt awkwardly self-conscious in his new clothes, but bore himself so proudly as to conceal it. It requires genuine valor to overcome new clothes, when one seldom has them. They become, under such circumstances, more than clothes — they are at least skin-deep. However, Jerome had that valor. He had bought a suit of fine blue cloth, and a vest of flowered white satin like a bridegroom's. He wore his best shirt with delicate cambric ruffles on bosom and wristbands, and his throat was swathed in folds of sheerest lawn, which he kept his chin clear of, with a splendid and stately lift. Jerome's hair, which was darker than when he was a boy, was brushed carefully into a thick crest over his white forehead, which had, like a child's, a bold and innocent fulness of curve at the temples. He had not usually much color, but that night his cheeks were glowing, and his black eyes, commonly somewhat stern from excess of earnestness, were brilliant with the joy of youth.

Mrs. Edwards looked at one, then the other, with the delighted surprise of a mother bird who sees her offspring in their first gayety of full plumage. She picked a thread from Jerome's coat, she put back a stray lock of Elmira's hair, she bade them turn this way and that.

When they had started she hitched her chair close to the window, pressed her forehead against the glass, looked out, and watched the white flutter of Elmira's skirts until they disappeared in the dark folds of the night.

There was, that night, a soft commotion of air rather than any distinct current of wind, like a gentle heaving and subsidence of veiled breasts of nature. The tree branches spread and gloomed with deeper shadows; mysterious white things with indeterminate motions were seen aloof across meadows or in door-yards, and might have been white-clad women, or flowering bushes, or ghosts.

Jerome and Elmira, when one of these pale visions seemed floating from some shadowy gateway ahead, wondered to each other if this or that girl were just starting for the party, but when they drew near the whiteness stirred at the gate still, and was only a bush of bridal-wreath. Jerome and Elmira were really the last on the road to the party; Upham people went early to festivities.

"It is very late," Elmira said, nervously; she held up her white skirts, ruffling softly to the wind, with both hands, lest they trail the dewy grass, and flew along like a short-winged bird at her brother's side. "Please walk faster, Jerome," said she.

"We'll have time enough there," returned Jerome, stepping high and gingerly, lest he soil his nicely blacked shoes.

"It will be dreadful to go in late and have them all looking at us, Jerome."

"What if they do look at us," Jerome argued, manfully, but he was in reality himself full of nervous tremors. Sometimes, to a soul with a broad outlook and large grasp, the great stresses of life are not as intimidating as its small and deceitful amenities.

When they reached Squire Merritt's house and saw all the windows, parallelograms of golden light, shining through the thick growth of trees, his hands and feet were cold, his heart beat hard. "I'm acting like a girl," he thought, indignantly, straightened himself, and marched on to the front door, as if it were the postern of a fortress.

But Elmira caught her brother by the long, blue coat-tail, and brought him to a stand.

"Oh, Jerome," she whispered, "there are so many there, and we are so late, I'm afraid to go in."

"What are you afraid of?" demanded Jerome, with a rustic brusqueness which was foreign to him. "Come along." He pulled his coat away and strode on, and Elmira had to follow.

The front door of Squire Merritt's house stood open into the hall the night was so warm, some girls in white were coming down the wide spiral of stair within, pressing softly together like scared white doves, in silence save for the rustle of their starched skirts. From the great rooms on either side of the hall, however, came the murmur of conversation, with now and then a silvery break of laughter, like a sudden cascade in an even current.

Flower-decked heads and silken-gleaming shoulders passed between the windows and the light, outlining vividly every line and angle and curve — the keen cut of profiles, the scallops of perked-up lace, the sharp dove-tails of ribbons. Before one window was upreared the great back and head of a man, still as a statue, yet with the persistency of stillness, of life.

That dogged stiffness, which betrays the utter self-abasement of resticity in fine company, was evident in his pose, even to one coming up the path. This party at Squire Merritt's was democratic, including many whose only experiences in social gatherings of their neighbors had come through daily labor and worship. All the young people in Upham had been invited; the Squire's three boon companions, Doctor Prescott and his wife, and the minister and his daughter, were the only elders bidden, since the party was for Lucina.

"The door's open," Elmira whispered, nervously. "Is it right to knock when the door's open, or walk right in, O Jerome?"

Jerome, for answer, stepped resolutely in, reached the knocker, raised it, and let it fall with a great imperious clang of brass, defying, as it were, his own shyness, like a herald at arms.

The white-clad girls on the stairs turned as with one accord their innocently abashed faces towards the door, then pushed one another on, and into the parlor, with soft titters and whispers.

Squire Eben Merritt's old servant, Hannah, gravely ponderous in purple delaine, with a wide white apron enhancing her great front, came forward from the room in the rear and motioned Jerome and Elmira to the stairs. She stared wonderingly after Jerome; she did not recognize him in his fine attire, though she had known him since he was a child.

When Jerome and Elmira came down-stairs he led the way at once into the north parlor, where the most of the guests were assembled. There were the village young women in their best attire, decked as to heads and bosoms with sweet drooping flowers, displaying all their humble stores of lace and ribbons and trinkets, jostling one another with slurring hisses of silk and crisp rattle of muslins, speaking affectedly with pursed lips, ending often a sibilant with a fine whistle, or silent, with mouths set in conscious smiles and cheeks hot with blushes. There were the village young men, in their Sunday clothes, standing aloof from the girls, now and then exchanging remarks with one another in a bravado of low bass. In the rear of the north parlor were Lucina and her parents, Mrs. Doctor Prescott and Lawrence, Miss Camilla Merritt, and the Squire's friends, Colonel Lamson, John Jennings, and Lawyer Means.

Jerome, with Elmira following, made his way slowly through the outskirts towards this fine nucleus of the party. Lawrence Prescott was talking gayly with Lucina, but when he saw Jerome and his sister approaching he stood back, with a slight flush and start, beside his mother, who with Miss Camilla was seated on the great sofa between the north windows. Mrs. Prescott fanned herself slowly with a large feather fan, and beamed abroad with a sweet graciousness. Her handsome face seemed to fairly shed a mild light of approval upon the company. She stirred with opulent foldings of velvet, shaking out vague musky odors; a brooch in the fine lace plaits over her high maternal bosom gave out a dull white gleam of old brilliants. Mrs. Prescott was more sumptuously attired than the Squire's wife, in her crimson and gold shot silk, which became her well, but was many seasons old, or than Miss Camilla, in her grand purple satin, that also was old, but so well matched to her own grace of age that it seemed like the garment of her youth, which had faded like it, in sweet communion with peaceful thoughts and lavender and rose-leaves.

Squire Eben Merritt stood between his wife and daughter.

Lucina had fastened a pretty posy in his button-hole, and he wore his fine new broadcloths, to please her, which he had bought for this occasion.

The Squire, though scarcely at home in his north parlor, nor in his grand apparel, which had never figured in haunts of fish or game, was yet radiant with jovial and hearty hospitality, and not even impatient for the cards and punch which awaited him and his friends in the other room, when his social duties should be fulfilled.

Lucina herself had set out the cards and the tobacco, and made a garland of myrtle-leaves and violets for the punch-bowl in honor of the occasion. "I want you to have the best time of anybody at my party, father," she had said, "and as soon as all the guests have arrived, you must go and play cards with Colonel Lamson and the others."

No other in the whole world, not even her mother, did Lucina love as well as she loved her father, and the comfort and pleasure of no other had she so deeply at heart.

At the Squire's elbow, standing faithfully by him until he should get his release, were his three friends: John Jennings and Lawyer Eliphalet Means in their ancient swallow-tails — John Jennings's being of renowned London make, though nobody in Upham appreciated that — and Colonel Jack Lamson in his old dress uniform. Colonel Lamson, having grown stouter of late years, wore with a mighty discomfort of the flesh but with an unyielding spirit his old clothes of state.

"I'll be damned if I thought I could get into 'em at first, Eben," he had told the Squire when he arrived. "Haven't had them on since I was pall-bearer at poor Jim Pell's funeral. I was bound to do your girl honor, but I'll be damned if I'll dance in 'em — I tell you it wouldn't be safe, Eben."

The Colonel looked with intense seriousness at his friend, then laughed hoarsely. His laugh was always wheezy of late, and he breathed hard when he took exercise.

Sometime in his dim and shady past Colonel Lamson was reported to have had a wife. She had never been seen in Upham, and was commonly believed to have died at some Western post during the first years of their marriage. Probably the beautiful necklace of carved corals, which the Colonel had brought that night for a present to Lucina, had belonged to that long-dead young wife; but not even the Squire knew.

As for John Jennings, he had never had a wife, and the trinkets he had bestowed upon sweethearts remained still in their keeping;

but he brought a pair of little pearly ear-rings for Lucina, and never wore his diamond shirt-button again. Lawyer Eliphalet Means brought for his offering a sandal-wood fan, a veritable lacework of wood, spreading it himself in his lean brown hand, which matched in hue, and eying it with a sort of dryly humorous satisfaction before he gave it into Lucina's keeping.

Squire Eben, despite his gratification for his daughter's sake, burst into a great laugh. "By the Lord Harry!" cried he; "you didn't go into a shop yourself and ask for that folderol?"

"Got it through a sea-captain, from India, years ago," replied the lawyer, laconically.

"Wouldn't she take it?" inquired Colonel Lamson, with sly meaning, his round, protruding eyes staring hard at his friend and the fan.

"Never gave her the chance," said Means, with a shrewd twinkle. Then he turned to Lucina, with a stiff but courtly bow, and presented the sandal-wood fan, and not one of them knew then, nor ever after, its true history.

Lucina had joyfully heard the clang of the knocker when Jerome arrived, thinking that they were the last guests, and her father could have his pleasure. Doctor Prescott had been called to Granby and would not come until late, if at all; the minister, it was reported, was ill with influenza — she and her mother had agreed that the Squire need not wait for them.

When Lucina saw the throng parting for the new-comers, she assumed involuntarily her pose of sweet and gracious welcome; but when Jerome and his sister stood before her, she started and lost composure.

Lucina remembered Elmira well enough, and had thought she remembered Jerome since last Sunday, when her father, calling to mind their frequent meetings in years back, had chidden her lightly for not speaking to him.

"He has grown and changed so, father," Lucina had said; "I did not mean to be discourteous, and I will remember him another time."

Lucina had really considered afterwards, saying nothing to her father or her mother, that the young man was very handsome. She had sat quite still that Sunday afternoon in the meeting-house, and, instead of listening to the sermon, had searched her memory for old pictures of Jerome. She had recalled distinctly the tea-drinking in her aunt Camilla's arbor, his refusal of cake, and gift of sassafras-root in the meadow; also his repulse of her childish generosity when she would have given him her little savings for the purchase of shoes. Old stings of the spirit can often be revived with thought, even when the cause is long passed. Lucina, sitting there in meeting, felt again the pang of her slighted benevolence. She was sure that she would remember Jerome at once the next time they met, but for a minute she did not. She bowed and shook hands prettily with Elmira, then turned to Jerome and stared at him, all unmindful of her manners, thinking vaguely that here was some grand young gentleman who had somehow gotten into her party unbidden. Such a fool do externals make of the memory, which needs long training to know the same bird in different feathers.

Lucina stared at Jerome, at first with grave and innocent wonder, then suddenly her eyes drooped and a soft blush crept over her face and neck, and even her arms. Lucina, in her short-sleeved India muslin gown, flowing softly from its gathering around her white shoulders to her slender waist, where a blue ribbon bound it, and thence in lines of transparent lights and blue shadows to her little pointed satin toe, stood before him with a sort of dumb-maiden appealing that he should not look at her so, but he was helpless, as with a grasp of vision which he could not loosen.

Jerome looked at her as the first man might have looked at the first woman; the world was empty but for him and her. The voices of the company were ages distant, their eyes dim across eternal spaces. The fragrance of sweet lavender and dried rose-leaves from Lucina's garments, and, moreover, a strange Oriental one, that seemed to accent the whole, from her sandal-wood fan, was to him, as by a transposing into a different key of sense, like some old melody of life which he had always known, and yet so forgotten that it had become new.

Jerome never knew how long he stood there, but suddenly he felt the Squire's kindly hand on his shoulder, and heard his loud, jovial voice in his ear. "Why, Jerome, my boy, what is the matter? Don't you remember my daughter? Lucina, where are your manners?"

And then Lucina curtesied low, with her fair curls drooping forward over her blushing face and neck, as pink as her corals, and Jerome bowed and strove to say something, but he knew not what, and never knew what he said, nor anybody else.

"'Twas the new clothes, boy," said the Squire in his ear. "By the Lord Harry, 'twas much as ever I knew you myself at first! I took you for an earl over from the old country. Lucina meant no harm. Go you now and have a talk with her."

Jerome wondered anxiously afterwards if he had spoken properly to the Squire's wife, to Mrs. Doctor Prescott, to Miss Camilla, and the others — if he had looked, even, at anybody but Lucina. He remembered the party as he might have remembered a kaleidoscope, of which only one combination of form and color abided with him. He realized all beside, as a broad effect with no detail. The card-playing and punch-drinking in the other room, the preliminary tuning of fiddles in the hall, the triumphant strains of a country dance, the weaving of the figures, the gay voices of the village youths, who lost all their abashedness as the evening went on, the supper, the table gleaming with the white lights of silver and the rainbow lustre of glass, the golden points of candles in the old candelabra, the fruity and spicy odors of cake and wine, were all as a dimness and vagueness of brilliance itself.

He did not know, even, that Lawrence Prescott was at Elmira's side all the evening, and after his father arrived, and that Elmira danced every time with him, and set people talking and Doctor Prescott frowning. He knew only that he had followed Lucina about, and that she seemed to encourage him with soft, leading smiles. That they sat on a sofa in a corner, behind a door, and talked, that once they stepped out on the stoop, and even strolled a little down the path, under the trees, when she complained of the room being hot and close. Then, without knowing whether he should do so or not, he bent towards her, with his arm crooked, and she slipped her hand in it, and they both trembled and were silent for a moment. He knew every word that Lucina had spoken, and gave a thousand different meanings to each. For the first time in his life, he tasted the sweets of praise from girlish lips. Lucina had heard of his good deeds from her father, how kind he was to the poor and sick, how hard he had worked, how faithful he had been to his mother and sister. Jerome listened with bliss, and shame that he should find it bliss. Then Lucina and he remembered together, with that perfect time of memory which is as harmonious as any duet, all the episodes of their childhood.

"I remember how you gave me sassafras," said Lucina, "and how you would not take the nice gingerbread that Hannah made, and how sad I felt about it."

"I will get some more sassafras for you tomorrow," said Jerome.

"And I will give you some more gingerbread if you will take it," said she, with a sweet coquettishness.

"I will, if you want me to," said Jerome.

They were out in the front yard then, a gust of wind pressed under the trees, and seemed to blow them together. Lucina's white muslin fluttered around Jerome's knees, her curls floated across his breast.

"Oh," murmured Lucina, confusedly, "this wind has come all of a sudden," and she stood apart from him.

"You will take cold; we had better go in," said Jerome. They went into the house, Jerome being a little hurt that Lucina had shrunk away from him so quickly, and Lucina disappointed that Jerome was so solicitous lest she take cold. Then they sat down again in the corner, and remembered that Jerome ate two pieces of cake at Miss Camilla's tea-party and she two and a half.

Somehow, before the party broke up that night, it was understood that Jerome was to come and see her the next Sunday night. And yet Lucina had not invited him, nor he asked permission to come.

CHAPTER XXIV

Jerome's mind, during the two days after the party, was in a sort of dazzle of efflorescence, and could not precipitate any clear ideas for his own understanding. Love had been so outside his calculation of life, that his imagination, even, had scarcely grasped the possibility of it.

He worked on stolidly, having all the time before his mental vision, like one with closed eyes in a bright room, a shifting splendor as of strange scenes and clouds.

He could not sleep nor eat, his spirit seemed to inhabit his flesh so thoroughly as to do away with the material needs of it. Still, all things that appealed to his senses seemed enhanced in power, becoming so loud and so magnified that they produced a confusion of hearing and vision. The calls of the spring birds sounded as if in his very ear, with an insistence of meaning; the spring flowers bloomed where he had never seen them, and the fragrance of each was as evident to him as a voice.

Jerome wondered vaguely if this strange exaltation of spirit were illness. Sunday morning, when he could not eat his breakfast, his mother told him that there were red spots on his cheeks, and she feared he was feverish.

He laughed scornfully at the idea, but looked curiously at himself in his little square of mirror, when he was dressing for meeting. The red spots were there, burning in his cheeks, and his eyes were brilliant. For a minute he wondered anxiously if he were feverish, if he were going to be ill, and, if so, what his mother and sister would do. He even felt his own pulse as he stood there, and discovered that it was quick. Then, all at once, his face in the glass looked out at him with a flash as from some sub-state of consciousness in the depths of his own being, which he could not as yet quite fathom.

"I don't know what ails me," he muttered, as he turned away. He felt as he had when puzzling over the unknown quantity in an algebraic equation. It was not until he was sitting in meeting, looking forward at Lucina's fair profile, cut in clear curves like a lily, that the solution came to him.

"I'm what they call in love," Jerome said to himself. He turned very pale, and looked away from Lucina. He felt as if suddenly he had come to the brink of some dread abyss of nature.

"That is why I want to go to see her tonight," he thought. "I won't go; I won't!"

Just before the bell stopped tolling, Doctor Prescott's family went up the aisle in stately file, the doctor marching ahead with an imperious state which seemed to force contributions from followers and beholders, as if a peacock were to levy new eyes for his plumage from all admiration along his path. The doctor's wife, in her satins and Indian cashmeres, followed him, moving with massive gentleness, a long ostrich plume in her bonnet tossing softly. Last came Lawrence, slight and elegantly erect, in his city broadcloth and linen, a figure so like his father as to seem almost his double, and yet with a difference beyond that of age, so palpable that a child might see it — a self-spelled word, with a different meaning in two languages.

The Merritt pew was just behind Doctor Prescott's. Lawrence had not been seated long before he turned slightly and cast a smiling glance around at beautiful Lucina, who inclined her head softly in response. Jerome had thus far never felt on his own account jealousy of any human being, he had also never been made ignominious by self-pity; now, both experiences came to him. Seeing that look of Lawrence Prescott's, he was suddenly filled with that bitterness of grudging another the sweet which one desires for one's self which is like no other bitterness on earth; and he who had hitherto pitied only the deprivations of others pitied his own, and so became the pauper of his own spirit. "He likes her," he told himself; "of course she'll like him. He's Doctor Prescott's son. He's got everything without working for it — I've got nothing."

Jerome looked at neither of them again. When meeting was over, he strode rapidly down the aisle, lest he encounter them.

"What ailed you in meeting, Jerome?" Elmira asked as they were going home.

"Nothing."

"You looked so pale once I thought you were going to faint away."

"I tell you nothing ailed me."

"You were dreadfully pale," persisted Elmira. She was so happy that morning that she had more self-assertion than usual. Lawrence Prescott had looked around at her three times; he had smiled at her once, when he turned to leave the pew at the close of meeting. Jerome had not noticed that, and she had not noticed Lawrence's smile at Lucina. She had been too fluttered to look up when Lawrence first entered.

That afternoon Jerome and Elmira set out for meeting again, but when they reached the turn of the road Jerome stopped.

"I guess I won't go this afternoon," said he.

"Why, what's the matter? Don't you feel well?" Elmira asked.

"Yes, I feel well enough, but it's warm. I guess I won't go." Elmira stared at him wonderingly. "Run along; you'll be late," said he, trying to smile.

"I'm afraid you are sick, Jerome."

"I tell you I am not. You'll be late."

Finally Elmira went on, though with many backward glances. Jerome sat down on the stone wall, behind a huge growth of lilac. He could see through a leafy screen the people in the main road wending their way to meeting. He had suddenly resolved not to go, lest he see Lucina Merritt again.

Presently there was out in the main road a graceful swing of light skirts and a gliding of shoulders and head which made his heart leap. Lucina was going to meeting with her mother. The moment she stirred the distance with dim advances of motion, Jerome knew her. It seemed to him that he would have known her shadow among a nightful, her step among a thousand. It was as if he had developed ultimate senses for her recognition.

Jerome, when he had once glimpsed her, looked away until he was sure that she had passed. When the bell had stopped ringing, he arose and climbed over the stone wall, then went across a field to the path skirting the poor-house which he had used to follow to school.

When he came opposite the poor-house in the hollow, he looked down at it. The day was so mild that the paupers were swarming into evidence like insects. Many of the house windows were wide open, and old heads with palsied nods, like Chinese toys, appeared in them; some children were tumbling about before the door.

Old Peter Thomas — who seemed to have become crystallized, as it were, in age and decrepitude, and advanced no further in either — was pottering around the garden, eying askant, like an old robin, the new plough furrows. Pauper women humped their calico backs over the green slopes of the fields, searching for dandelion greens, but not digging, because it was Sunday.

Their shrill, plaintive voices, calling to one another, came plainly to Jerome. When he reached the barn, there sat Mindy Toggs, as of old, chanting his accusatory refrain, "Simon Basset, Simon Basset."

Hitherto Jerome had viewed all this humiliation of poverty from a slight but no less real eminence of benefaction; today he had a miserable sense of community with it. "It is not having what we want that makes us all paupers," he told himself, bitterly; "I'm as much a pauper as any of them. I'm in a worse poor-house than the town of Upham's. I'm in the poor-house of life where the paupers are all fed on stones."

Then suddenly, as he went on, a brave spirit of revolt seized him. "It is wanting what we have not that makes us paupers," he said, "and I will not be one, if I tear my heart out."

Jerome climbed another stone wall into a shrubby pasture, and went across that to a pine wood, and thence, by devious windings and turnings, through field and forest, to his old woodland. It was his now; he had purchased it back from the Squire. Then he sat himself down and looked about him out of his silence and self-absorption, and it was as if he had come into a very workshop of nature. The hummings of her wheels and wings were loud in his ear, the fanning of them cool on his cheek. The wood here was very light and young, and the spring sun struck the roots of the trees.

Little swarms of gossamer gnats danced in the sunlit spaces; when he looked down there was the blue surprise of violets, and anemones nodded dimly out of low shadows. There was a loud shrilling of birds, and the tremulousness of the young leaves seemed to be as much from unseen wings as wind. However, the wind blew hard in soft, frequent gusts, and everything was tilting and bowing and waving.

Jerome looked at it all, and it had a new meaning for him. The outer world is always tinctured more or less to the sight by one's mental states; but who can say, when it comes to outlooks from the keenest stresses of spirit, how impalpable the boundary-lines between beholder and object may grow? Who knows if a rose does not really cease to be, in its own sense, to a soul in an extremity of joy or grief?

Whatever it might be for others, the spring wood was not today what it had ever been before to Jerome. All its shining, and sweetening, and growing were so forced into accord with himself that the whole wood took, as it were, the motion of his own soul. Jerome looked at a fine young poplar-tree, and saw not a tree but a maid, revealing with innocent helplessness her white body through her skirts of transparent green. The branches flung out towards him like a maiden's arms, with shy intent of caresses. Every little flower upon which his idle gaze fell was no flower, but an eye of love — a bird called to his mate with the call of his own heart. Every sight, and sound, and sweetness of the wood wooed and tempted him, with the reflex motion of his own new ardor of love and passion. He had not gone to meeting lest he see Lucina

Merritt again, and wished to drive her image from his mind, and here he was peopling his solitude with symbols of her which were bolder than she, and made his hunger worse to bear.

A childlike wonder was over him at the whole. "Why haven't I ever felt this way before?" he thought. He recalled all the young men he knew who had married during the last few years, and thought how they must have felt as he felt now, and he had no conception of it. He had been secretly rather proud that he had not encumbered himself with a wife and children, but had given his best strength to less selfish loves. He remembered his scorn of the school-master and his adoring girls, and realized that his scorn had been due, as scorn largely is, to ignorance. Instead of contempt, a fierce pity seized him for all who had given way to this great need of love, and yet he felt strange indignation and shame that he himself had come into the common lot.

"It is no use; I can't," he said, quite out loud, and set a hard face against all the soft lights and shadows which moved upon him with the motion of his own desires.

When he said "I can't," Jerome meant not so much any ultimate end of love as love itself. He never for a second had a thought that he could marry Lucina Merritt, Squire Eben Merritt's daughter, nor indeed would if he could. He never fancied that that fair lady in her silk attire could come to love him so unwisely as to wed him, and had he fancied it the fierce revolt at receiving so much where he could give so little, which was one of his first instincts, would have seized him. Never once he thought that he could marry Lucina, and take her into his penury or profit by her riches. All he resolved against was the love itself, which would make him weak with the weakness of all unfed things, and he made a stand of rebellion.

"I'm going to put her out of my mind," said Jerome, and stood up to his full height among the sweet spring growths, flinging back his head, as if he defied Nature herself, and went pushing rudely through the tremulous outreaching poplar branches, and elbowed a cluster of white flowering bushes huddling softly together, like maidens who must put themselves in a man's way, though to their own shaming.

CHAPTER XXV

Jerome decided that he would not go to see Lucina Merritt that Sunday night. He knew that she expected him, though there had been no formal agreement to that effect; he knew that she would wonder at his non-appearance, and, even though she were not disappointed, that she would think him untruthful and unmannerly.

"Let her," he told himself, harshly, fairly scourging himself with his resolution. "Let her think just as badly of me as she can. I'll get over it quicker."

The ineffable selfishness of martyrdom was upon him. He considered only his own glory and pain of noble renunciation, and not her agony of disillusion and distrust, even if she did not care for him. That last possibility he did not admit for a moment. In the first place, though he had loved her almost at first sight, the counter-reasoning he did not imagine could apply to her. It had been as simple and natural in his case as looking up at a new star, but in hers — what was there in him to arrest her sweet eyes and consideration, at a moment's notice, if at all? As well expect the star to note a new eye of admiration upon the earth.

In all probability, Lucina's heart had turned already to Lawrence Prescott, as was fitting. She had doubtless seen much of him — he was handsome and prosperous; both families would be pleased with such a match. Jerome faced firmly the jealousy in his heart. "You've got to get used to it," he told himself.

He did not think much of his sister in this connection, but simply decided that his mother, and possibly Elmira, had over-rated Lawrence Prescott's attention, and jumped too hastily at conclusions. It was incredible that any one should fancy his sister in preference to Lucina. Lawrence had merely called in a friendly way. He did not once imagine any such feeling on Elmira's part for young Prescott, as on his for Lucina, and had at the time more impatience than pity. However, he resolved to remonstrate if Lawrence should stay so late again with his sister.

"She may think he means more than he does, girls are so silly," he said. He did not class Lucina Merritt among girls.

That Sunday night, after dark, though he was resolved not to visit Lucina, he strolled up the road, past her house. There was no light in the parlor. "She doesn't expect me, after all," he thought, but with a great pang of disappointment rather than relief. He judged such proceedings from the rustic standpoint. Always in Upham, when a girl expected a young man to come to spend an evening with her, she lighted the best parlor and entertained him there in isolation from the rest of her family. He did not know how different a training in such respects Lucina had had. She never thought, since he was not her avowed lover, of sequestering herself with him in the best parlor. She would have been too proudly and modestly fearful as to what he might think of her, and she of herself, and her parents of them both. She expected, as a matter of course, to invite him into the sitting-room, where were her father and mother and Colonel Jack Lamson.

However, she permitted herself a little innocent manœuvre, whereby she might gain a few minutes of special converse with him without the presence of her elders. A little before dusk Lucina seated herself on the front door-step. Her mother brought presently a little shawl and feared lest she take cold, but Lucina said she should not remain there long, and there was no wind and no dampness.

Lucina felt uneasy lest she be deceiving her mother, but she could not bring herself to tell her, though she did not fairly know why, that she expected a caller.

The dusk gathered softly, like the shadow of brooding wings. She thought Jerome must come very soon. She could just see a glimmer of white road through the trees, and she watched that eagerly, never taking her eyes from it. Now and then she heard an approaching footstep, and a black shadow slanted athwart the road. Her heart sank, though she wondered at it, when that happened.

When Jerome came up the road she made sure at once that it was he. She even stirred to greet him, but after an indefinable pause he passed on also; then she thought she had been mistaken.

He saw the flutter of pale drapery on the door-step, but never dreamed that Lucina was actually there watching for him. After a while he went back. Lucina, who was still sitting there, saw him again, but this time did not stir, since he was going the other way.

When, at half past eight, she saw the people from the evening prayer-meeting passing on the road, she made sure that Jerome would not come that night.

She gave a soft sigh, leaned her head back against the fluted door-post, and tried to recall every word he had said to her, and every word she had said to him, about his coming. She began to wonder if she had possibly not been cordial enough, if she could have made him fear he would not be welcome. She repeated over and over, trying to imagine him in her place as listener, all she had said to him. She gave it the furthest inflections of graciousness and coolness of which she could have been capable, and puzzled sorely as to which she had used.

"It makes so much difference as to how you say a thing," thought poor Lucina, "and I know I was afraid lest he think me too glad to have him come. I wonder if I did not say enough, or did not say it pleasantly."

It did not once occur to Lucina that Jerome might mean to slight her, and might stay away because he wished to do so. She had been so petted and held precious and desirable during her whole sweet life, that she could scarcely imagine any one would flout her, though so timid and fearful of hurting and being hurt was she by nature, that without so much love and admiration she would have been a piteous thing.

She decided that it must be her fault that Jerome had not come. She reflected that he was very proud; she remembered, and the memory stung her with something of the old pain of the happening, how he would not take the cakes when she was a child, how he would not take her money to buy shoes. She shrank even then, remembering the flash with which he had turned upon her.

"I did not say enough, I was so afraid of saying too much, and that is why he has not come," she told herself, and sadly troubled her gentle heart thereby.

The tears came into her eyes and rolled slowly down her fair cheeks as she sat there in the dusk. She did not yet feel towards Jerome as he towards her. She had been too young and childish when she had known him for love to have taken fast root in her heart; and she was not one to love fully until she felt her footing firm, and her place secure in a lover's affections. Still, who can tell what may be in the heart of the gentlest and most transparent little girl, who follows obediently at her mother's apron-strings? In those old days when Abigail had put her little daughter to bed, heard her say her prayers for forgiveness of her sins of innocence, and blessings upon those whom she loved best, then kissed the fair baby face sunken in its white pillow, she never dreamed what happened after she had gone down-stairs. Every night, for a long time after she had first spoken to Jerome, did the small Lucina, her heart faintly stirred into ignorant sweetness with the first bloom of young romance, slip out of her bed after her mother had gone, kneel down upon her childish knees, and ask another blessing for Jerome Edwards.

"Please, God, bless that boy, and give him shoes and ginger-bread, because he won't take them from me," Lucina used to pray, then climb into bed again with a little wild scramble of hurry.

Sometimes, when she was a little girl, though her mother never knew it, Lucina used to be thinking about Jerome, and building artless air-castles when she bent her grave childish brow over her task of needle-work. Sometimes, on the heights of these castles reared by her innocent imagination, she and Jerome put arms around each other's necks and embraced and kissed, and her mother sat close by and did not know.

She also did not know that often, when she had curled Lucina's hair with special care on the Sabbath day, and dressed her in her best frock, that her little daughter, demurely docile under her maternal hands, was eagerly wondering if Jerome would not think her pretty in her finery.

Of course, when Lucina was grown up, and went away to school, these childish love-dreams seemed quite lost and forgotten, in her awakening under the light of older life. In those latter days Lucina had never thought about Jerome Edwards. She had even, perhaps, had her heart touched, at least to a fancy of love, by the admiration of others. It was whispered in the village that Lucina Merritt had had chances already. However, if she had, she had waved them back upon the donors before they had been fairly given, with that gentlest compassion which would permit no need of itself. Lucina, however her heart might have been swerved for a season to its natural inclination of love, had never yet admitted a lover, for, when it came to that last alternative of open or closed doors, she had immediately been seized with an impulse of flight into her fastness of childhood and maidenhood.

But now, though she scarcely loved Jerome as yet, the power of her old dreams was over her again. No one can over-estimate the tendency of the human soul towards old ways of happiness which it has not fully explored.

Lucina had begun, almost whether she would or not, to dream again those old sweet dreams, whose reality she had never yet tasted. Had life ever broken in upon the dreams, had a word or a caress ever become a fact, it is probable she would have looked now upon it all as upon some childish fruit of delight, whose sweetness she had proved and exhausted to insipidity. And this, with no disparagement to her, for the most faithful heart is in youth subject to growth and change, and not free as to the exercise of its own faithfulness.

Lucina that Sunday evening had put on one of her prettiest muslin frocks, cross-barred with fine pink flowers set between the bars. She tied a pink ribbon around her waist, too, and wore her morocco shoes. She looked down at the crisp flow of muslin over her knees, and thought if Jerome had known that she had put on that pretty dress, he would have been sure she wanted him to come. Still, she would not have liked him to know she had taken as much pains as that, but she wished so she had invited him more cordially to come.

The tears rolled down her cheeks and dropped on the fair triangle of neck between the folds of her lace tucker; she was weeping for Jerome's hurt, but it seemed strangely like her own. She was half minded to go into the house and tell her mother all about it, repeat that miserable little dialogue between herself and Jerome, which was troubling her so, and let her decide as to whether she had been lacking in hospitality or not, and give her advice. But she could not quite bring herself to do that.

The moon arose behind the house, she could not see it, but she knew it was there by the swarming of pale lights under the pine-trees, and the bristling of their tops as with needles of silver. She heard a whippoorwill in the distance calling as from some undiscovered country; there was an undertone of frogs from marshy meadows swelling and dying in even cadences of sound.

Lucina's mother came to the door and put her hand on the girl's head. "You must come in," she said; "your hair feels quite damp. You will take cold. Your dress is thin, too."

Lucina rose obediently and followed her mother into the sitting-room, where sat Squire Eben and Colonel Lamson in swirling clouds of tobacco smoke.

Lucina's cheeks had a wonderful clear freshness of red and white from the damp night air. There were no traces of tears on her sweet blue eyes. She came into the bright room with a smiling shrinking from the light, which gave her the expression of an angel. Both men gazed at her with a sort of passion of tenderest admiration, and also a certain sadness of yearning — the Squire because of that instinct of insecurity and possibility of loss to which possession itself gives rise, the Colonel because of the awakening of old vain longings in his own heart.

The Squire reached out a hand towards Lucina, caught her first by her flowing skirt, then by her fair arm, and drew her close to his side and pulled down her soft face to his. "Well, Pretty, how goes the world?" he said, with a laugh, which had almost the catch of a sob, so anxiously tender he was of her, and so timid before his own delight in her.

When she had kissed him and bade him good-night, Lucina went up to her own chamber and her mother with her.

"Abigail follows the child, since she came home, like a hen

with one chicken," the Squire said, smiling almost foolishly in his utter pride of this beautiful daughter.

The Colonel nodded, frowning gravely over his pipe at the opposite window. "She makes me think a little of my wife at her age," he said.

The Squire started. It was the first time he had ever heard the Colonel mention his wife. He sighed, looked at him, and hesitated with a delicacy of reticence. "It must have been a hard blow," he ventured, finally.

The Colonel nodded.

"Any children?" asked the Squire, after a little.

"No," replied Colonel Lamson. He puffed at his pipe, his face was redder than usual. "Well, Eben," he said, after a pause, during which the two men smoked energetically, "I hope you'll keep her a while."

"You don't think she looks delicate?" cried the Squire, turning pale. "Her mother doesn't think so."

The Colonel laughed heartily. "When a girl blossoms out like that there'll be plenty trying the garden-gate," said he.

The Squire flushed angrily. "Let 'em try it and be damned!" he said.

"You can't lock the gate, Eben; if you do, she'll open it herself, and no blame to her."

"She won't, I tell you. She's too young, and there's not a man I know fit to tie her little shoes."

"How's young Prescott?"

"Young Prescott be damned!"

The Colonel hesitated. He had seen with an eye, sharpened with long and thorough experience, Jerome Edwards and Lucina the night of the party. "How's that young Edwards?"

Squire Merritt stared. "The smartest young fellow in this town," he said, with a kind of crusty loyalty, "but when it comes to Lucina — Lucina!"

"I've liked that boy, Eben, ever since that night in Robinson's store," said the Colonel, with a curious gravity.

"So have I," returned the Squire, defiantly, "and before that — ever since his father died. He was the bravest little rascal. He's a hero in his way. I was telling Lucina the other day what he'd done. But when it comes to his lifting his eyes to her, to her — by the Lord Harry, Jack, nobody shall have her, rich or poor, good or bad. I don't care if he's a prince, or an angel from heaven. Don't I know what men are? I'm going to keep my angel of a child a while myself. I'll tell you one thing, sir, and that is, Lucina thinks more today of her old father than any man living; I'll bet you a thousand she does!" Squire Eben's voice fairly broke with loving emotion and indignation.

"Can't take you up, Eben," said the Colonel, dryly; "I'd be too darned sure to lose, and I couldn't pay a dollar; but — tomorrow's coming."

Squire Eben Merritt stood looking at his friend, a frown of jealous reverie on his open face. Suddenly, with no warning, as if from a sudden uplifting of the spirit, it cleared away. He laughed out his great hearty laugh. "Well, by the Lord Harry, Jack," said he, "when the girl does lose her heart, though I hope it won't be for many a day yet, if it's to a good man that can take care of her and fight for her when he's gone, her old father won't stand in the way. Lucina always did have what she wanted, and she always shall."

CHAPTER XXVI

For three weeks after that Jerome never saw Lucina at all. He avoided the sight of her in every way in his power. He went to Dale and returned after dark; he stayed away from meeting. He also strove hard to drive, even the thought of her, from his mind. He got out his algebra and Latin books again; every minute during which he was not at work, and even during his work, he tried to keep his mind so full that Lucina's image could not enter. But sometimes he had a despairing feeling, that her image was so incorporated with his very soul, that he might as well strive to drive away a part of himself.

He had no longer any jealousy of Lawrence Prescott. One day Lawrence had come to the shop when he was at work, and asked to speak to him a moment outside. He told him how matters stood between himself and Elmira. "I like your sister," Lawrence had said, soberly and manfully. "I don't see my way clear to marrying her yet, and I told her so. I want you to understand it and know just what I mean. I've got my way to make first. I don't suppose — I can count on much encouragement from father in this. You know it's no disparagement to Elmira, Jerome. You know father."

"Does your father know about it?" asked Jerome.

"I told mother," Lawrence answered, "and she advised me to say nothing about it to father yet. Mother thought I had better go on and study medicine, and get ready to practice, and perhaps then father might think better of it. She says we are both young enough to wait two or three years."

Jerome, in his leather apron, with his grimy hands, and face even, darkened with the tan of the leather, looked half suspiciously and bitterly at this other young man in his fine cloth and linen, with his white hands that had never done a day's labor. "You know what you are about?" he said, almost roughly. "You know what you are, you know what she is, and what we all are. You know you can't separate her from anything."

"I don't want to," cried Lawrence, with a great blush of fervor. "I'll be honest with you, Jerome. I didn't know what to do at first. I knew how much I thought of your sister, and I hoped she thought something of me, but I knew how father would feel, and I was dependent on him. I knew there was no sense in my marrying Elmira, or any other girl, against his wishes, and starving her."

"There are others he would have you marry," said Jerome, a pallor creeping through the leather grime on his face.

Lawrence colored. "Yes, I suppose so," he said, simply; "but it's no use. I could never marry any other girl than Elmira, no matter how rich and handsome she was, nor how much she pleased father, even if she cared about me, and she wouldn't."

"You have been — going a little with some one else, haven't you?" Jerome asked, hoarsely.

Lawrence stared. "What do you mean?"

"I — saw you riding —"

"Oh," said Lawrence, laughing, "you mean I've been horse-back-riding with Lucina Merritt. That was nothing."

"It wasn't nothing if she thought it was something," Jerome said, with a flash of white face and black eyes at the other.

Lawrence looked wonderingly at him, laughed first, then responded with some indignation, "Good Lord, Jerome, what are you talking about?"

"What I mean. My sister doesn't marry any man over another woman's heart if I know it."

"Good Lord!" said Lawrence. "Why, Jerome, do you suppose I'd hurt little Lucina? She doesn't care for me in that way, she never would. And as for me — why, look here, Jerome, I never so much as held her hand. I never looked at her even, in any way —" Lawrence shook his head in emphatic reiteration of denial.

"I might as well tell you that Lucina was the one I meant when I said father would like others better," continued Lawrence, "but Lucina Merritt would never care anything about me, even if I did about her, and I never could. Handsome as she is, and I do believe she's the greatest beauty in the whole county, she hasn't the taking way with her that Elmira has — you must see that yourself, Jerome."

Jerome laughed awkwardly. Nobody knew how much joy those words of Lawrence Prescott's gave him, and how hard he tried to check the joy, because it should not matter to him except for Elmira's sake.

"Did you ever see a girl with such sweet ways as your sister?" persisted Lawrence.

"Elmira is a good girl," Jerome admitted, confusedly. He loved his sister, and would have defended her against depreciation with his life, but he compared inwardly, with scorn, her sweet ways with Lucina's.

"There isn't a girl her equal in this world," cried her lover, enthusiastically. "Don't you say so, Jerome? You're her brother, you know what she is. Did you ever see anything like that cunning little face she makes, when she looks up at you?"

"Elmira's a good girl," Jerome repeated.

Lawrence had to be contented with that. He went on, to tell Jerome his plans with regard to the engagement between himself and Elmira. He was clearly much under the wise influence of his mother. "Mother says, on Elmira's account as well as my own, I had better not pay regular attention to her," he said, ruefully, yet with submission. "She says to go to see her occasionally, in a way that won't make talk, and wait. She's coming to see Elmira herself. I've talked it over with her, and she's agreed to it all, as, of course, she would. Some girls wouldn't, but she — Jerome, I don't believe when we've been married fifty years that your sister will ever have refused to do one single thing I thought best for her."

Jerome nodded with a puzzled and wistful expression, puzzled because of any man's so exalting his sister when Lucina Merritt was in the world, wistful at the sight of a joy which he must deny himself.

When he went home that night he saw by the way his mother and sister looked up when he entered the room that they were wondering if Lawrence had told him the news, and what he thought of it. Elmira's face was so eager that he did not wait. "Yes, I've seen him," he said.

Elmira blushed, and quivered, and bent closer over her work.

"What did I tell you?" said his mother, with a kind of tentative triumph.

"You don't know now what Doctor Prescott will say," said Jerome.

"Lawrence says his mother thinks his father will come round by-and-by, when he gets started in his profession; he always liked Elmira."

"Well, there's one thing," said Jerome, "and that is — of course you and Elmira are not under my control, but no sister of mine will ever enter any family where she is not welcome, with my consent."

"Lawrence says he knows his father will be willing by-and-by," said Elmira, tremulously.

"You know Doctor Prescott always liked your sister," said Ann Edwards.

"Well, if he likes her well enough to have her marry his son, it's all right," said Jerome, and went out to wash his hands and face before supper.

That night Lawrence stole in for a short call. When Elmira came up-stairs after he had gone, Jerome, who had been reading in his room, opened his door and called her in.

"Look here, Elmira," said he, "I don't want you to think I

don't want you to be happy. I do."

Elmira held out her arms towards him with an involuntary motion. "Oh, Jerome!" she whispered.

The brother and sister had always been chary of caresses, but now Jerome drew Elmira close, pressed her little head against his shoulder, and let her cry there.

"Don't, Elmira," he said, at length, brokenly, smoothing her hair. "You know brother wants you to be happy. You are the only little sister he's got."

"Oh, Jerome, I couldn't help it!" sobbed Elmira.

"Of course you couldn't," said Jerome. "Don't cry — I'll work hard and save, and maybe I can get enough money to give you a house and furniture when you're married, then you won't be quite so beholden."

"But you'll — get married yourself, Jerome," whispered Elmira, who had built a romance about her brother and Lucina after the night of the party.

"No, I shall never get married myself," said Jerome, "all my money is for my sister." He laughed, but that night after Elmira was fast asleep in her chamber across the way, he lay awake tasting to the fullest his own cup of bitterness from its contrast with another's sweet.

The longing to see Lucina, to have only the sight of her dear beautiful face to comfort him, grew as the weeks went on, but he would not yield to it. He had, however, to reckon against odds which he had not anticipated, and they were the innocent schemes of Lucina herself. She had hoped at first that his call was only deferred, that he would come to see her of his own accord, but she soon decided that he would not, and that all the advances must be from herself, since she was undoubtedly at fault. She had fully resolved to make amends for any rudeness and lack of cordiality of which she might have been guilty, at the first opportunity she should have. She planned to speak to him going home from meeting, or on some week day on the village street — she had her little speech all ready, but the chance to deliver it did not come.

But when she went to meeting Sunday after Sunday, dressed in her prettiest, looking like something between a rose and an angel, and no Jerome was there for her soft backward glances, and when she never met him when she was alone on the village street, she grew impatient.

About this time Lucina's father bought her a beautiful little white horse, like the milk-white palfrey of a princess in a fairy tale, and she rode every day over the county. Usually Squire Eben accompanied her on a tall sorrel which had been in his possession for years, but still retained much youthful fire. The sorrel advanced with long lopes and fretted at being reined to suit the pace of the little white horse, and Squire Eben had disliked riding from his youth, unless at a hard gallop with gun on saddle, towards a distant lair of game. Both he and the tall sorrel rebelled as to their nerves and muscles at this ladylike canter over smooth roads, but the Squire would neither permit his tender Lucina to ride fast, lest she get thrown and hurt, or to ride alone.

Lawrence Prescott never asked her to ride with him in those days. Lucina in her blue habit, with a long blue plume wound round her hat and floating behind in the golden blowing of her curls, on her pretty white horse, and the great booted Squire on his sorrel, to her side, reined back with an ugly strain on the bits, were a frequent spectacle for admiration on the county roads. No other girl in Upham rode.

It was one day when she was out riding with her father that Lucina made her opportunity to speak with Jerome. Now she had her horse, Jerome was finding it harder to avoid the sight of her. The night before, returning from Dale by moonlight, he had heard the quick tramp of horses' feet behind him, and had had a glimpse of Lucina and her father when they passed. Lucina turned in her saddle, and her moon-white face looked over her shoulder at Jerome. She nodded; Jerome made a stiff inclination, holding himself erect under his load of shoes. Lucina was too shy to ask her father to stop that she might speak to Jerome. However, before they reached home she said to her father, in a sweet little contained voice, "Does he go to Dale every night, father?"

"Who?" said the Squire.

"Jerome Edwards."

"No, I guess not every day; not more than once in three days, when the shoes are finished. He told me so, if I remember rightly."

"It is a long walk," said Lucina.

"It won't hurt a young fellow like him," the Squire said, laughing; but he gave a curious look at his daughter. "What set you thinking about that, Pretty?" he asked.

"We passed him back there, didn't we, father?"

"Sure enough, guess we did," said the Squire, and they trotted on over the moonlit road.

"Looks just like the back of that dapple-gray I had when you were a little girl, Pretty," said the Squire, pointing with his whip at the net-work of lights and shadows.

He never thought of any significance in the fact that for the two following days Lucina preferred riding in the morning in another direction, and on the third day preferred riding after sundown on the road to Dale. He also thought nothing of it that they passed Jerome Edwards again, and that shortly afterwards Lucina professed herself tired of riding so fast, though it had not been fast for him, and reined her little white horse into a walk. The sorrel plunged and jerked his head obstinately when the Squire tried to reduce his pace also.

"Please ride on, father," said Lucina; her voice sounded like a little silver flute through the Squire's bass whoas.

"And leave you? I guess not. Whoa, Dick; whoa, can't ye!"

"Please, father, Dick frightens me when he does so."

"Can't you ride a little faster, Pretty? Whoa, I tell ye!"

"In just a minute, father, I'll catch up with you. Oh, father, please! Suppose Dick should frighten Fanny, and make her run, I could never hold her. Please, father!"

The Squire had small choice, for the sorrel gave a fierce plunge ahead and almost bolted. "Follow as fast as you can, Pretty!" he shouted back.

There was a curve in the road just ahead, the Squire was out of sight around it in a flash. Lucina reined her horse in, and waited as motionless as a little equestrian statue. She did not look around for a moment or two — she hoped Jerome would overtake her without that. A strange terror was over her, but he did not.

Finally she looked. He was coming very slowly; he scarcely seemed to move, and was yet quite a distance behind. "I can't wait," Lucina thought, piteously. She turned her horse and rode back to him. He stopped when she came alongside. "Good-evening," said she, tremulously.

"Good-evening," said Jerome. He made such an effort to speak that his voice sounded like a harsh trumpet.

Lucina forgot her pretty little speech. "I wanted to say that I was sorry if I offended you," she said, faintly.

Jerome had no idea what she meant; he could, indeed, scarcely take in, until later, thinking of them, the sense of her words. He tried to speak, but made only an inarticulate jumble of sounds.

"I hope you will pardon me," said Lucina.

Jerome fairly gasped. He bowed again, stiffly.

Lucina said no more. She rode on to join her father. That night, after she had gone to bed, she cried a long while. She reflected how she had never even referred to the matter in question, in her suit for pardon.

CHAPTER XXVII

Lucina in those days was occupied with some pieces of embroidery in gay wools on cloth. There were varied designs of little dogs with bead eyes, baskets of flowers, wreaths, and birds on sprays. She had an ambition to embroider a whole set of parlor-chairs, as some young ladies in her school had done, and there was in her mind a dim and scarcely admitted fancy that these same chairs might add state to some future condition of hers.

Lucina had always innocently taken it for granted that she should some day be married and have a house of her own, and very near her father's. When she had begun the embroidery she had furnished a shadowy little parlor of a shadowy house with the fine chairs, and admitted at the parlor door a dim and stately presence, so shadowy to her timid maiden fancy that there was scarcely a suggestion of substance.

Now, however, the shadow seemed to deepen and clear in outline. Lucina fell to wondering if Jerome Edwards thought embroidered chairs pretty or silly. Often she would pause in her counting and setting even cross-barred stitches, lean her soft cheek on her slender white hand, and sit so a long while, with her fair curls drooping over her gentle, brooding face. Her mother often noticed her sitting so, and thought, partly from quick maternal intuition, partly from knowledge gained from her own experience, that if it were possible, she should judge her to have had her heart turned to some maiden fancy. But she knew that Lucina had cared for none of her lovers away from home, and at home there were none feasible, unless, perhaps, Lawrence Prescott. Lawrence had not been to see her lately; could it be possible the child was hurt by it? Abigail sounded cautiously the depths of her daughter's heart, and found to her satisfaction no image of Lawrence Prescott therein.

"Lawrence is a good boy," said Lucina; "it is a pity he is no taller, and looks so like his father; but he is very good. I do think, though, he might go to ride with me sometimes and save father from going. I would rather have father, but I know he does not like to ride. Lawrence had been planning to go to ride with me all through the summer. It was strange he stopped — was it not, mother?"

"Perhaps he is busy. I saw him driving with his father the other day," said Abigail.

"Well, perhaps he is," assented Lucina, easily. Then she asked advice as to this or that shade in the ears of the little poodle-dog which she was embroidering.

"Lucina is as transparent as glass," her mother thought. "She could never speak of Lawrence Prescott in that way if she were in love with him, and there is no one else in town."

Abigail Merritt, acute and tender mother as she was, settled into the belief that her daughter was merely given to those sweetly melancholy and wondering reveries natural to a maiden soul upon the threshold of discovery of life. "I used to do just so, busy as I always was, before Eben came," she thought, with a little pang of impatient shame for herself and her daughter that they must yield to such necessities of their natures. Abigail Merritt had never been a rebel, indeed, but there had been unruly possibilities within her. She remembered well what she had told her mother when her vague dreams had ended and Eben Merritt had come a-wooing. "I like him, and I suppose, because I like him I've got to marry him, but it makes me mad, mother."

Looking now at this daughter of hers, with her exceeding beauty and delicacy, which a touch would seem to profane and soil as much as that of a flower or butterfly, she had an impulse to hide her away and cover her always from the sight and handling of all except maternal love. She took much comfort in the surety that there was as yet no definite lover in Lucina's horizon. She did not reflect that no human soul is too transparent to be clouded to the vision of others, and its own, by the sacred intimacy with its own desires. Her daughter, looking up at her with limpid blue eyes, replying to her interrogation with sweet readiness, like a bird that would pipe to a call, was as darkly unknown to her as one beyond the grave. She could not even spell out clearly her hieroglyphics of life with the key in her own nature.

The day after Lucina had met Jerome on the Dale road, and had failed to set the matter right, she took her embroidery-work over to her Aunt Camilla's. She had resolved upon a plan which was to her quite desperate, involving, as it did, some duplicity of manœuvre which shocked her.

The afternoon was a warm one, and she easily induced, as she had hoped, her Aunt Camilla to sit in the summer-house in the garden. Everything was very little changed from that old summer afternoon of years ago. If Miss Camilla had altered, it had been with such a fine conservation of general effect, in spite of varying detail, that the alteration was scarcely visible. She wore the same softly spreading lilac gown, she wrote on her portfolio with the same gold pencil presumably the same thoughts. If her softly drooping curls were faded and cast lighter shadows over thinner cheeks, one could more easily attribute the dimness and thinness to the lack of one's own memory than to change in her.

The garden was the same, sweetening with the ardor of pinks and mignonette, the tasted breaths of thyme and lavender, like under-thoughts of reason, and the pungent evidence of box.

Lucina looked out of the green gloom of the summer-house at the same old carnival of flowers, swarming as lightly as if untethered by stems, upon wings of pink and white and purpling blue, blazing out to sight as with a very rustle of color from the hearts of green bushes and the sides of tall green-sheathed stalks, in spikes and plumes, and soft rosettes of silken bloom. Even the yellow cats of Miss Camilla's famous breed, inheriting the love of their ancestors for following the steps of their mistress, came presently between the box rows with the soft, sly glide of the jungle, and established themselves for a siesta on the arbor bench.

Lucina was glad that it was all so like what it had been, even to the yellow cats, seeming scarcely more than a second rendering of a tune, and it made it possible for her to open truthfully and easily upon her plan. She herself, whose mind was so changed from its old childish habit of simple outlook and waiting into personal effort for its own ends, and whose body was so advanced in growth of grace, was perhaps the most altered of all. However, there was much of the child left in her.

"Aunt Camilla," said she, in almost the same tone of timid deprecation which the little Lucina of years before might have used.

Camilla looked up, with gentle inquiry, from her portfolio.

"I have been thinking," said Lucina, bending low over her embroidery that her aunt might not see the pink confusion of her face, which she could not, after all, control, "how I came here and spent the afternoon, once, years ago; do you remember?"

"You came here often — did you not, dear?"

"Yes," said Lucina, "but that once in particular, Aunt Camilla?"

"I fear I do not remember, dear," said Camilla, whose past had been for years a peaceful monotone as to her own emotions, and had so established a similar monotone of memory.

"Don't you remember, Aunt Camilla? I came first with a stent to knit on a garter, and we sat out here. Then the yellow cats came, and father had been fishing, and he brought some speckled trout, and — then — the Edwards boy —"

"Oh, the little boy I had to weed my garden! A good little boy,"

Camilla said.

Lucina winced a little. She did not quite like Jerome to be spoken of in that mildly reminiscent way. "He's grown up now, you know, Aunt Camilla," said she.

"Yes, my dear, and he is as good a young man as he was a boy, I hear."

"Father speaks very highly of him," said Lucina, with a soft tremor and mounting of color, to which her aunt responded sensitively.

People said that Camilla Merritt had never had a lover, but the same wind can strike the same face of the heart.

"I have heard him very highly spoken of," she agreed; and there was a betraying quiver in her voice also.

"We had plum-cake, and tea in the pink cups — don't you remember, Aunt Camilla?"

"So many times we had them — did we not, dear?"

"Yes, but that one time?"

"I fear that I cannot distinguish that time from the others, dear."

There was a pause. Lucina took a few more stitches on her embroidery. Miss Camilla poised her gold pencil reflectively over her portfolio. "Aunt Camilla," said Lucina then.

"Well, dear?"

"I have been thinking how pleasant it would be to have another little tea-party, here in the arbor; would you have any objections?"

"My dear Lucina!" cried Miss Camilla, and looked at her niece with gentle delight at the suggestion.

The early situation was not reversed, for Lucina still admired and revered her aunt as the realization of her farthest ideal of ladyhood, but Miss Camilla fully reciprocated. The pride in her heart for her beautiful niece was stronger than any which she had ever felt for herself. She pictured Lucina instead of herself to her fancy; she seemed to almost see Lucina's face instead of her own in her looking-glass. When it came to giving Lucina a pleasure, she gave twofold.

"Thank you, Aunt Camilla," said Lucina, delightedly, and yet with a little confusion. She felt very guilty — still, how could she tell her aunt all her reasons for wishing the party?

"Shall we have your father and mother, or only young people, dear?" asked Miss Camilla.

"Only young people, I think, aunt. Mother comes any time, and as for father, he would rather go fishing."

"You would like the Edwards boy, since he came so long ago?"

"Yes, I think so, aunt."

"He is poor, and works hard, and has not been in fine company much, I presume, but that is nothing against him. He will enjoy it all the more, if he is not too shy. You do not think he is too shy to enjoy it, dear?"

"I should never have known from his manners at my party that he had not been in fine company all his life. He is not like the other young men in Upham," protested Lucina, with a quick rise of spirit.

"Well, I used to hear your grandfather say that there are those who can suit their steps to any gait," her aunt said. "I understand that he is a very good young man. We will have him and —"

"I think his sister," said Lucina; "she is such a pretty girl — the prettiest girl in the village, and it will please her so to be asked."

"The Edwards boy and his sister, and who else?"

"No one else, I think, Aunt Camilla, except Lawrence Prescott. There will not be room for more in the arbor."

Lucina did not blush when she said Lawrence Prescott, but her aunt did. She had often romanced about the two. "Well, dear," she said, "when shall we have the tea-party?"

"Day after tomorrow, please, Aunt Camilla."

"That will give 'Liza time to make cake," said Camilla. "I will send the invitations tomorrow, dear."

"'Liza will be too busy cake-making to run on errands," said Lucina, though her heart smote her, for this was where the true gist of her duplicity came in; "write them now, Aunt Camilla, and give them to me. I will see that they are delivered."

The afternoon of the next day Lucina, being out riding, passed Doctor Prescott's house, and called to Jake Noyes in the yard to take Miss Camilla's little gilt-edged, lavender-scented note of invitation. "Please give this to Mr. Lawrence," said she, prettily, and rode on. The other notes were in her pocket, but she had not delivered them when she returned home at sunset.

"I am going to run over to Elmira Edwards and carry them," she told her mother after supper, and pleaded that she would like the air when Mrs. Merritt suggested that Hannah be sent.

Thus it happened that Jerome Edwards, coming home about nine o'clock that night, noticed, the moment he opened the outer door, the breath of roses and lavender, and a subtle thrill of excitement and almost fear passed over him. "Who is it?" he thought. He listened, and heard voices in the parlor. He wanted to pass the door, but he could not. He opened it and peered in, white-faced and wide-eyes, and there was Lucina with his mother and sister.

Mrs. Edwards and Elmira looked nervously flushed and elated; there were bright spots on their cheeks, their eyes shone. On the table were Miss Camilla's little gilt-edged missives. Lucina was somewhat pale, and her face had been furtively watchful and listening. When Jerome opened the door, her look changed to one of relief, which had yet a certain terror and confusion in it. She rose at once, bowed gracefully, until the hem of her muslin skirt swept the floor, and bade Jerome good-evening. As for Jerome, he stood still, looking at her.

"Why, J'rome, don't you see who 'tis?" cried his mother, in her sharp, excited voice, yet with an encouraging smile — the smile of a mother who would put a child upon its best behavior for the sake of her own pride.

Jerome murmured, "Good-evening." He made a desperate grasp at his self-possession, but scarcely succeeded.

Lucina pulled a little fleecy white wrap over her head, and immediately took leave. Jerome stood aside to let her pass. Elmira followed her to the outer door, and his mother called him in a sharp whisper, "J'rome, come here."

When he had reached his mother's side she pinched his arm hard. "Go home with her," she whispered.

Jerome stared at her.

"Do ye hear what I say? Go home with her."

"I can't," he almost groaned then.

"Can't? Ain't you ashamed of yourself? What ails ye? Lettin' of a lady like her go home all alone this dark night."

Elmira ran back into the parlor. "Oh, Jerome, you ought to go with her, you ought to!" she cried, softly. "It's real dark. She felt it, I know. She looked real sober. Run after her, quick, Jerome."

"When she came to invite you to a party, too!" said Mrs. Edwards, but Jerome did not hear that, he was out of the house and hurrying up the road after Lucina.

She had not gone far. Jerome did not know what to say when he overtook her, so he said nothing — he merely walked along by her side. A great anger at himself, that he had almost let this tender and beautiful creature go out alone in the night and the dark, was over him, but he knew not what to say for excuse.

He wondered, pitifully, if she were so indignant that she did not like him to walk home with her now. But in a moment Lucina spoke, and her voice, though a little tremulous, was full of the utmost sweetness of kindness.

"I fear you are too tired to walk home with me," she said, "and

I am not afraid to go by myself."

"No, it is too dark for you to go alone; I am not tired," replied Jerome, quickly, and almost roughly, to hide the tumult of his heart.

But Lucina did not understand that. "I am not afraid," she repeated, in a little, grieved, and anxious way; "please leave me at the turn of the road, I am truly not afraid."

"No, it is too dark for you to go alone," said Jerome, hoarsely, again. It came to him that he should offer her his arm, but he dared not trust his voice for that. He reached down, caught her hand, and thrust it through his arm, thinking, with a thrill of terror as he did so, that she would draw it away, but she did not.

She leaned so slightly on his arm that it seemed more the inclination of spirit than matter, but still she accepted his support and walked along easily at his side. So far from her resenting his summary taking of her hand, she was grateful, with the humble gratitude of the primeval woman for the kindness of a master whom she has made wroth.

Lucina had attributed Jerome's stiffness at sight of her, and his delay in accompanying her home, to her unkind treatment of him. Now he showed signs of forgiveness, her courage returned. When they had passed the turn of the road, and were on the main street, she spoke quite sweetly and calmly.

"There is something I have been wanting to say to you," said she. "I tried to say it the other night when I was riding and met you, but I did not succeed very well. What I wanted to say was — I fear that when you suggested coming to see me, the Sunday night after my party, I did not seem cordial enough, and make you understand that I should be very happy to see you, and that was why you did not come."

"O—h!" said Jerome, with a long-drawn breath of wonder and despair. He had been thinking that he had offended her beyond forgiveness and of his own choice, and she, with her sweet humility, was twice suing him for pardon.

"I am very sorry," Lucina said, softly.

"That was not the reason why I did not," Jerome gasped.

"Then you were not hurt?"

"No; I — thought you spoke as if you would like to have me come —"

"Perhaps you were ill," Lucina said, hesitatingly.

"No, I was not. I did not —"

"Oh, it was not because you did not want to come!" Lucina cried out, quickly, and yet with exceeding gentleness and sad wonder, that he should force such a suspicion upon her.

"No, it was not. I — wanted to come more than — I wanted to come, but — I did not think it — best." Jerome said the last so defiantly that poor Lucina started.

"But it was because of nothing I had said, and it was not because you did not want to?" she said, piteously.

"No," said Jerome. Then he said, again, as if he found strength in the repetition. "I did not think it best."

"I thought you were coming that night," Lucina said, with scarcely the faintest touch of reproach but with more of wonder. Why should he not have thought it best?

"I am sorry," said Jerome. "I wanted to tell you, but I had no reason but that to give, and I — thought you might not understand."

Lucina made no reply. The path narrowed just there and gave her an excuse for quitting Jerome's arm. She did so with a gentle murmur of explanation, for she could do nothing abruptly, then went on before him swiftly. Her white shawl hung from her head to her waist in sharp slants. She moved through the dusk with the evanescent flit of a white moth.

"Of course," stammered Jerome, painfully and boyishly, "I — knew — you would not care if — I did not come. It was not as if — I had thought you — would."

Lucina said nothing to that either. Jerome thought miserably that she did not hear, or, hearing, agreed with what he said.

Soon, however, Lucina spoke, without turning her head. "I can understand," said she, with the gentlest and yet the most complete dignity, for she spoke from her goodness of heart, "that a person has often to do what he thinks best, and not explain it to any other person, because it is between him and his own conscience. I am quite sure that you had some very good reason for not coming to see me that Sunday night, and you need not tell me what it was. I am very glad that you did not, as I feared, stay away because I had not treated you with courtesy. Now, we will say no more about it." With that, the path being a little wider, she came to his side again, and looked up in his face with the most innocent friendliness and forgiveness in hers.

Jerome could have gone down at her feet and worshipped her.

"What a beautiful night it is!" said Lucina, tilting her face up towards the stars.

"Beautiful!" said Jerome, looking at her, breathlessly.

"I never saw the stars so thick," said she, musingly. "Everybody has his own star, you know. I wonder which my star is, and yours. Did you ever think of it?"

"I guess my star isn't there," said Jerome.

"Why, yes," cried Lucina, earnestly, "it must be!"

"No, it isn't there," repeated Jerome, with a soft emphasis on the last word.

Lucina looked up at him, then her eyes fell before his. She laughed confusedly. "Did you know what I came to your house tonight for?" said she, trying to speak unconsciously.

"To see Elmira?"

"No, to give both of you an invitation to tea at Aunt Camilla's tomorrow afternoon at five o'clock."

"I am very much obliged to you," said Jerome, "but —"

"You cannot come?"

"No, I am afraid not."

"The tea is to be in the arbor in the garden, the way it was that other time, when we were both children; there is to be plum-cake and the best pink cups. Nobody is asked but you and your sister and Lawrence Prescott," said Lucina, but with no insistence in her voice. Her gentle pride was up.

"I am very much obliged, but I am afraid I can't come," Jerome said, pleadingly.

Lucina did not say another word.

Jerome glanced down at her, and her fair face, between the folds of her white shawl, had a look which smote his heart, so full it was of maiden dignity and yet of the surprise of pain.

A new consideration came to Jerome. "Why should I stay away from her, refuse all her little invitations, and treat her so?" he thought. "What if I do get to wanting her more, and get hurt, if it pleases her? There is no danger for her; she does not care about me, and will not. The suffering will all be on my side. I guess I can bear it; if it pleases her to have me come I will do it. I have been thinking only of myself, and what is a hurt to myself in comparison with a little pleasure for her? She has asked me to this tea-party, and here I am hurting her by refusing, because I am so afraid of getting hurt myself!"

Suddenly Jerome looked at Lucina, with a patient and tender smile that her father might have worn for her. "I shall be very happy to come," said he.

"Not unless you can make it perfectly convenient," Lucina replied, with cold sweetness; "I would rather not urge you."

"It will be perfectly convenient," said Jerome. "I thought at first I ought not to go, that was all."

"Of course, Aunt Camilla and I will be very happy to have you come, if you can," said Lucina. Still, she was not appeased. Jerome's hesitating acceptance of this last invitation had hurt her more than all that had gone before. She began to wish, with a great pang of shame, that she had not gone to his house that night, had not tried to see him, had not proposed this miserable party. Perhaps he did mean to slight her, after all, though nobody ever had before, and how she had followed him up!

She walked on very fast; they were nearly home. When they reached her gate, she said good-night, quickly, and would have gone in without another word, but Jerome stopped her. He had begun to understand her understanding of it all, and had taken a sudden resolution. "Better anything than she should think herself shamed and slighted," he told himself.

"Will you wait just a minute?" he said; "I've got something I want to say."

Lucina waited, her face averted.

"I've made up my mind to tell you why I thought I ought not to come, that Sunday night," said Jerome; "I didn't think of telling you, but I can see now that you may think I meant to slight you, if I don't. I did not think at first that you could dream I *could slight anybody like you, and not want to go to see you, but I begin to see that you don't just know how every one looks at you.*"

"I thought I ought not to come, because all of a sudden I found out that I was — what they call in love with you."

Lucina stood perfectly still, her face turned away.

"I hope you are not offended," said Jerome; "I knew, of course, that there is no question of — your liking me. I would not want you to. I am not telling you for that, but only that you may not feel hurt because I slighted your invitation the other night, and because I thought at first I could not accept this. But I was foolish about it, I guess. If you would like to have me come, that is enough."

"You have not known me long enough to like me," said Lucina, in a very small, sweet voice, still keeping her face averted.

"I guess time don't count much in anything like this," said Jerome.

"Well," said Lucina, with a soft, long breath, "I cannot see why your liking me should hinder you from coming."

"I guess you're right; it shouldn't if you want me to come."

"Why did you ever think it should?" Lucina flashed her blue eyes around at him a second, then looked away again.

"I was afraid if — I saw you too often I should want to marry you so much that I would want nothing else, not even to help other people," said Jerome.

"Why need you think about marrying? Can't you come to see me like a friend? Can't we be happy so?" asked Lucina, with a kind of wistful petulance.

"I needn't think about it, and we can —"

"I don't want to think about marrying yet," said Lucina; "I don't know as I shall ever marry. I don't see why you should think so much about that."

"I don't," said Jerome; "I shall never marry."

"You will, some time," Lucina said, softly.

"No; I never shall."

Lucina turned. "I must go in," said she.

Her hand and Jerome's found each other, with seemingly no volition of their own. "I am glad you didn't come because you didn't like me," Lucina said, softly; "and we can be friends and no need of thinking of that other."

"Yes," Jerome said, all of a tremble under her touch; "and — you won't feel offended because I told you?"

"No, only I can't see why you stayed away for that."

CHAPTER XXVIII

The next afternoon Jerome went to Miss Camilla's tea-party. Sitting in the arbor, whose interior was all tremulous and vibrant with green lights and shadows, as with a shifting water-play, sipping tea from delicate china, eating custards and the delectable plum-cake, he tasted again one of the few sweet savors of his childhood.

Jerome, in the arbor with three happy young people, taking for the first time since his childhood a holiday on a work-day, seemed to comprehend the first notes of that great harmony of life which proves by the laws of sequence the last. The premonition of some final blessedness, to survive all renunciation and sacrifice, was upon him. He felt raised above the earth with happiness. Jerome seemed like another person to his companions. The wine of youth and certainty of joy stirred all the light within him to brilliancy. He had naturally a quicker, readier tongue than Lawrence Prescott, now he gave it rein.

He could command himself, when he chose and did not consider that it savored of affectation, to a grace of courtesy beyond all provincial tradition. In his manners he was not one whit behind even Lawrence Prescott, with his college and city training, and in face and form and bearing he was much his superior. Lawrence regarded him with growing respect and admiration, Elmira with wonder.

As for Miss Camilla, she felt as if tripping over her own inaccuracy of recollection of him. "I never saw such a change in any one, my dear," she told Lucina the next day. "I could scarcely believe he was the little boy who used to weed my garden, and with so few advantages as he has had it is really remarkable."

"Father says so, too," remarked Lucina, looking steadily at her embroidery.

Miss Camilla gazed at her reflectively. She had a mild but active imagination, which had never been dispelled by experience, for romance and hearts transfixed with darts of love. "I hope he will never be so unfortunate as to place his affections where they cannot be reciprocated, since he is in such poor circumstances that he cannot marry," she sighed, so gently that one could scarcely suspect her of any hidden meaning.

"I do not think," said Lucina, still with steadfast eyes upon her embroidery, "that a woman should consider poverty if she loves." Then her cheeks glowed crimson through her drooping curls, and Miss Camilla also blushed; still she attributed her niece's tender agitation to her avowal of general principles. She did not once consider any danger to Lucina from Jerome; but she had seen, on the day before, the young man's eyes linger upon the girl's lovely face, and had immediately, with the craft of a female, however gentle, for such matters, reached half pleasant, half melancholy conclusions.

It was gratifying and entirely fitting that her beautiful Lucina should have a heart-broken lover at her feet; still, it was sad, very sad, for the poor lover. "When the affections are enlisted, one should not hesitate to share poverty as well as wealth," she admitted, with a little conscious tremor of delicacy at such pronounced views.

"I do not think Jerome himself wants to be married," said Lucina, quickly.

Miss Camilla sighed. She remembered again the young man's fervent eyes. "I hope he does not, my dear," she said.

"*I* do not intend to marry either. I am never going to be married at all," said Lucina, with a seeming irrelevance which caused Camilla to make mild eyes of surprise and wonder sadly, after her niece had gone home, if it were possible that the dear child had, thus early, been crossed in love.

Lucina, ever since Jerome's confession of love, had experienced a curious revulsion from her maiden dreams. She had such instinctive docility of character that she was at times amenable to influences entirely beyond her own knowledge. Not understanding in the least Jerome's attitude of renunciation, she accepted it for herself also. She no longer builded bridal air-castles. She still embroidered her chair-covers, thinking that they would look very pretty in the north parlor, and some of the old chairs could be moved to the garret to make room for them. She gazed at her aunt Camilla with a peaceful eye of prophecy. Just so would she herself look years hence. Her hair would part sparsely to the wind, like hers, and show here and there silver instead of golden lustres. There would be a soft rosetted cap of lace to hide the thinnest places, and her cheeks, like her aunt's, would crumple and wrinkle as softly as old rose leaves, and, like her aunt, in this guise she would walk her path of life alone.

Lucina seemed to see, as through a long, converging tunnel of years, her solitary self, miniatured clearly in the distance, gliding on, like Camilla, with that sweet calm of motion of one who has left the glow of joy behind, but feels her path trend on peace.

"I dare say it may be just as well not to marry, after all," reasoned Lucina, "a great many people are not married. Aunt

Camilla seems very happy, happier than many married women whom I have seen. She has nothing to disturb her. I shall be happy in the way she is. When I am such an old maid that my father and mother will have died, because they were too old to live longer, I will leave this house, because I could not bear to stay here with them away, and go to Aunt Camilla's. She will be dead, too, by that time, and her house will be mine. Then I, in my cap and spectacles, will sit afternoons in the summer-house, and — perhaps — he — he will be older than I then, and white-haired, and maybe stooping and walking with a cane — perhaps — he will come often, and sit with me there, and we will remember everything together."

In all her forecasts for a single life, Lucina could not quite eliminate her lover, though she could her husband. She and Jerome were always to be friends, of course, and he was to come and see her. Lucina, when once Jerome had begun to visit her, never contemplated the possibility of his ever ceasing to do so. He did not come regularly — the wisdom of that was tacitly understood between them; since there was to be no marriage, there could necessarily be no courtship. There was never any sitting up together in the north parlor, after the fashion of village lovers. Jerome merely spent an hour or two in the sitting-room with the Squire and his wife and Lucina. Sometimes he and the Squire talked politics and town affairs while Lucina and her mother sewed. Sometimes the four played whist, or bezique, for in those days Jerome was learning to take a hand at cards, but he had always Mrs. Merritt for his partner, and the Squire Lucina. Indeed, Lucina would have considered herself highly false and treacherous had she manifested an inclination to be the partner of any other than her father. Sometimes the Squire sat smoking and dozing, and sometimes he was away, and in those cases Mrs. Merritt sewed, and Jerome and Lucina played checkers.

It tried Jerome sorely to capture Lucina's men and bar her out from the king-row, and she sometimes chid him for careless playing.

Sometimes, after Jerome was gone and Lucina in bed, Abigail Merritt, who had always a kind but furtively keen eye upon the two young people, talked a little anxiously to the Squire. "I know that he does not come regularly and he sees us all, but — I don't know that it is wise for us to let them be thrown so much together," she would say, with a nervous frown on her little dark face.

The Squire's forehead wrinkled with laughter, but he was finishing his pipe before going to bed, and would not remove it. He rolled humorously inquiring eyes through the cloud of smoke, and his wife answered as if to a spoken question. "I know Jerome Edwards doesn't seem like other young men, but he is a young man, after all, and, if we shouldn't say it, I am afraid somebody will get hurt. We both know what Lucina is —"

"You don't mean to say you're afraid Lucina will get hurt," spluttered the Squire, quickly.

"It isn't likely that a girl like Lucina could get hurt herself," cried Abigail, with a fine blush of pride.

"I suppose you're right," assented the Squire, with a chuckle. "I suppose there's not a young fool in the country but would think himself lucky for a chance to tie the jade's shoestring. I guess there'll be no hanging back of dancers whenever she takes a notion to pipe, eh?"

"She has not taken a notion to pipe, and I doubt if she will at present," said Abigail, with a little bridle of feminine delicacy, "and — he is a good young man, though, of course, it would scarcely be advisable if she did fancy him, but she does not. Lucina has never concealed anything from me since she was born, and I know —"

"Then it's the boy you're worrying about?"

Abigail nodded. "He's a good young man, and he has had a hard struggle. I don't want his peace of mind disturbed through any means of ours," said she.

The Squire got up, shook the ashes out of his pipe, and laid it with tender care on the shelf. Then he put his great hands one upon each of his wife's little shoulders, and looked down at her. Abigail Merritt had a habit of mind which corresponded to that of her body. She could twist and turn, with the fine adroitness of a fox, round sudden, sharp corners of difficulty, when her husband might go far on the wrong road through drowsy inertia of motion; but, after all, he had sometimes a clearer view than she of ultimate ends, past the petty wayside advantages of these skilful doublings and turnings.

She could deal with details with little taper-finger touches of nicety, but she could not judge as well as he of generalities and the final scope of combinations. It was doubtful if Abigail ever fairly appreciated her own punch.

"Abigail," said the Squire, looking down at her, his great bearded face all slyly quirked with humor — "Abigail, look here. There are a good many things that you and I can do, and a few that we can't do. I can fish and shoot and ride with any man in the county, and bluster folks into doing what I want them to mostly, if

I keep my temper; and as for you — you know what you can do in the way of fine stitching, and punch-making, and house-keeping, and you and I together have got the best, and the handsomest, and the most blessed" — the Squire's voice broke — "daughter in the county, by the Lord Harry we have. I can shoot any man who looks askance at her, I can lie down in the mud for her to walk over to keep her little shoes dry, and you can fix her pretty gowns and keep her curls smooth, and watch her lest she breathe too fast or too slow of a night, but there we've got to stop. You can't make the posies in your garden any color you have a mind, my girl, and I can't change the spots on the trout I land. We can't, either of us, make a sunset, or a rainbow, or stop a thunder-storm, or raise an east wind. There are things we run up blind against, and I reckon this is one of 'em. It's got to come out the way it will, and you and I can't hinder it, Abigail."

"We can hinder that poor boy from having his heart broken."

The Squire whistled. "Lock the stable-door after the colt is stolen, eh?"

"Eben Merritt, what do you mean?"

"I mean that the boy comes here now an then, not courting the girl, as I take it, at all, and shows so far no signs of anything amiss, and had, in my opinion, best be let alone. Lord, when I was his age, if a girl like Lucina had been in the question, and anybody had tried to rein me up short, I'd have kicked over the breeches entirely. I'd have either got her or blown my brains out. That boy can take care of himself, anyhow. He'll stop coming here of his own accord, if he thinks he'd better."

Abigail sniffed scornfully with her thin nostrils.

"Wait and see," said the Squire.

"I shall wait a long time before I see," she said, but she was mistaken. The very next week Jerome did not come, then a month went by and he had not appeared once at the Squire's house.

CHAPTER XXIX

One Sunday afternoon, during the latter part of July, Lucina Merritt strolled down the road to her aunt Camilla's. The day was very warm — droning huskily with insects, and stirring lazily with limp leaves.

There had been no rain for a long time, and the road smoked high with white dust at every foot-fall. Lucina raised her green and white muslin skirts above her embroidered petticoat, and set her little feet as lightly as a bird's. She carried a ruffled green silk parasol to shield herself from the sun, though her hat had a wide brim and flapped low over her eyes.

Her mother had remonstrated with her for going out in the heat, since she had not looked quite well of late. "You will make your head ache," said she.

"It is so cool in Aunt Camilla's north room," pleaded Lucina, and had her way.

She walked slowly, as her mother had enjoined, but it was like walking between a double fire of arrows from the blazing white sky and earth; when she came in sight of her aunt Camilla's house her head was dizzy and her veins were throbbing.

Lucina had not been happy during the last few weeks, and sometimes, in such cases, physical discomfort acts like a tonic poison. For the latter part of the way she thought of nothing but reaching the shelter of Camilla's north room; her mind regarding all else was at rest.

Miss Camilla's house was closed as tightly as a convent; not a breath of out-door air would she have admitted after the early mornings of those hot days. Lucina entered into night and coolness in comparison with the glare of day outside. When she had her hat removed, and sat in the green gloom of the north parlor, sipping a glass of water which Liza had drawn from the lowest depths of the well, then flavored with currant-jelly and loaf-sugar, she felt almost at peace with her own worries.

Her aunt Camilla, clad in dimly flowing old muslin, sat near the chimney-place, swaying a feather fan. She had her Bible on her knees, but she had not been reading; the light was too dim for her eyes. The fireplace was filled with the feathery green of asparagus, which also waved lightly over the gilded looking-glass, and was reflected airily therein. Asparagus plumes waved over all the old pictures also. The whole room from this delicate garnishing, the faded green tone of the furniture covers and carpet, from the wall-paper in obscure arabesques of green and satiny white, appeared full of woodland shadows. Miss Camilla, swaying her feather fan, served to set these shadows slowly eddying with a motion of repose. She had dozed in her chair, and her mind had lapsed into peaceful dreams before her niece arrived. Now she sat beaming gently at her. "Do you feel refreshed, dear?" she asked, when Lucina had finished her tumbler of currant-jelly water.

"Yes, thank you, Aunt Camilla."

"I fear you were not strong enough to venture out in such heat, glad as I am to see you, dear. Had you not better let 'Liza bring you a pillow, and then you can lie down on the sofa and perhaps have a little nap?"

"No, thank you, Aunt Camilla, I am not sleepy. I am quite well. I am going to sit by the window and read."

With that Lucina rose, got a book bound in red and gold from the stately mahogany table, and seated herself by the one window whose shutters were not tightly closed. It was a north window, and only one leaf of the upper half of the shutter was open. The aperture disclosed, instead of burning sky, a thick screen of horse-chestnut boughs. The great fanlike leaves almost touched the window-glass, and tinted all the dim parallelogram of light.

Even Lucina's golden head and fair face acquired somewhat of this prevailing tone of green, being transposed into another key of color. All her golden lights, and her roses, were lost in a delicate green pallor, which might have beseemed a sea-nymph. Her aunt, sitting aloof in that same green shaft of day filtered through horse-chestnut leaves, and also changed thereby, kept glancing at her uneasily. She knew that her brother and his wife had been anxious lately about Lucina. She ventured a few more gently solicitous remarks, which Lucina met sweetly, still with a little impatience of weariness, scarcely lifting her face from her book; then she ventured no more.

"The child does not like to have us so anxious over her," she thought, with that unfailing courtesy and consideration which would spare others though she torment herself thereby. She longed exceedingly to offer Lucina a wineglass of a home-brewed cordial, compounded from the rich juice of the blackberry, the finest of French brandy, and sundry spices, which was her panacea, but she abstained, lest it disturb her. Miss Camilla set a greater value upon peace of mind than upon aught else.

Lucina bent her face over her book, and turned the leaves quickly, as if she were reading with absorption. Presently Miss Camilla thought she looked better. The soft lapping as of waves, of the Sabbath calm, began again to oversteal her body and spirit.

Visions of her peaceful past seemed to confuse themselves with the present. "You — must stay to tea, and — not — go home until — after sunset, when it is cooler," she murmured, drowsily, and with a dim conviction that this was a Sabbath of long ago, that Lucina was a little girl in a short frock and pantalettes; then in a few minutes her head drooped limply towards her shoulder, and all her thoughts relaxed into soft slumberous breaths.

When her aunt fell asleep, Lucina looked up, with that quick, startled sense of loneliness which sometimes, in such case, comes to a sensitive consciousness. "Aunt Camilla is asleep," she thought; she turned to her book again. It was a copy of Mrs. Hemans's poems. Somehow the vivid sentiment of the lines failed to please her, though she, like her young lady friends, had heretofore loved them well. Lucina read the first stanza of "The warrior bowed his crested head" with no thrill of her maiden breast; then she turned to "The Bride of the Greek Isles," and that was no better.

She arose, tiptoed softly over to the table, and examined the other books thereon. There were volumes of the early English poets, an album, and *A Souvenir of Friendship, in red and gold, like the Hemans. She opened the souvenir, and looked idly at the small, exquisitely fine steel engravings, the alliterative verses, the tales of sentiment beginning with long preambles couched in choicest English. She shut the book with a little weary sigh, and looked irresolutely at her sleeping aunt, then at the chair by the north window.*

Lucina felt none of the languor which is sometimes caused by extreme heat. Instead, there was a fierce electric tension through all her nerves. She was weary almost to death, the cool of this dark room was unutterably grateful to her, yet she could not remain quiet. She had left her parasol and hat on the hall-table. She stole out softly, with scarcely the faintest rustle of skirts, tied on her hat, took her parasol, and went through the house to the back-garden door.

Looking back, she saw the old servant-woman's broadly interrogatory face in a vine-wreathed kitchen-window. "I am going out in the garden a little while, 'Liza," said Lucina.

The garden was down-crushed, its extreme of sweetness pressed out beneath the torrid sunbeams as under flaming hoofs. Lucina passed between the wilting ranks and flattened beds of flowers, and the breath of them in her face was like the rankest sweetness of love, when its delicacy, even for itself, is all gone. The pungent odor of box was like a shameless call from the street.

Lucina went into the summer-house and sat down. It was stifling, and the desperate sweetnesses of the garden seemed to have collected there, as in a nest.

Lucina, after a minute, sprang up, her face was a deep pink, she had a gentle distracted frown on her sweet forehead, her lips were pouting; she did not look in the least like the Lucina of the early spring.

She went out of the summer-house, and down the garden paths, and then over a stone wall, into the rear field, which bounded it. This field had been mowed not long before, and the stubble was pink and gold in the afternoon light.

The field was broad, and skirted on the west by a thick wood. Lucina, holding her green parasol, crossed the field to the wood. The stubble was hot to her feet, white butterflies flew in her face, rusty-winged things hurled themselves in her path, like shrill completions from some mill of insect life.

All along the wood there was a border of shadow. Lucina kept close to the trees, and so down the field. A faint, cool dampness stole out from the depths of the wood and tempered the heat for the width of its shade. Lucina put down her parasol; she was walking quite steadily, as if with a purpose.

The wood extended the length of many fields, running parallel with the main village street, behind the houses. Lucina, passing the Prescott house from the rear, instead of the front, seeing the unpainted walls and roof-slopes of barn and woodsheds, and the garden, had a curious sense of retroversion in material things which suited well her mind. She felt that day as if she were turned backward to her own self.

The fields were divided from one another by stone walls. Lucina crossed these, and kept on until she reached a field some distance beyond Doctor Prescott's house. Then she left the shadow of the wood, and crossed the field to the main road. In crossing this she kept close to the wall, slinking along rapidly, for she felt guilty; this field was all waving with brown heads of millet which should not have been trampled.

She got to the road and nobody had seen her. She crossed it, entered a rutty cart-path, and was in the Edwards' woodland.

For the first time in her life, Lucina Merritt was doing something which she acknowledged to herself to be distinctly unmaidenly. She had come to this wood because she had heard Jerome say that he often strolled here of a Sunday afternoon. Her previous little schemes for meeting him had been innocent to her own understanding, but now she had tasted the fruit of knowledge of her own heart.

She felt fairly sick with shame at what she was doing, she blushed to her own thoughts, but she had a helpless impulse as before, some goading spur in her own nature which she could not withstand.

She hurried softly down the cart-path between the trees, then suddenly stood still, for under a great pine-tree on the right lay Jerome. His hat was off, one arm was thrown over his head, his face was flushed with heat and slumber. Lucina, her body bent aloof with an indescribable poise of delicacy and the impulse of flight, yet looked at her sleeping lover until her whole heart seemed to feed itself through her eyes.

Lucina had not seen him for more than six weeks, except by sly glimpses at meeting and on the road. She thought, pitifully, that he had grown thin; she noticed what a sad droop his mouth had at the corners. She pitied, loved, and feared him, with all the trifold power of her feminine heart.

As she looked at him, her remembrance of old days so deepened and intensified that they seemed to close upon the present and the future. Love, even when it has apparently no past, is at once a memory and a revelation. Lucina saw the little lover of her innocent childish dreams asleep there, she saw the poor boy who had gone hungry and barefoot, she saw the young man familiar in the strangeness of the future. And, more than that, Lucina, who had hitherto shown fully to her awakening heart only her thought of Jerome, having never dared to look at him and love him at the same time, now gazed boldly at him asleep, and a sense of a great mystery came over her. In Jerome she seemed to see herself also, the unity of the man and woman in love dawned upon her maiden imagination. She felt as if Jerome's hands were her hands, his breath hers. "I never knew he looked like me before," she thought with awe.

Then suddenly Jerome, with no stir of awaking, opened his eyes and looked at her. Often, on arousing from a deep sleep, one has a sense of calm and wonderless observation as of a new birth. Jerome looked for a moment at Lucina with no surprise. In a new world all things may be, and impossibilities become commonplaces.

Then he sprang up, and went close to her. "Is it you?" he said, in a sobbing voice.

Lucina looked at him piteously. She wanted to run away, but her limbs trembled, her little hands twitched in the folds of her muslin skirt. Jerome saw her trembling, and a soft pink suffusing her fair face, even her sweet throat and her arms, under her thin sleeves. He knew, with a sudden leap of tenderness, which would have its way in spite of himself, why she was there. She had wanted to see him so, the dear child, the fair, wonderful lady, that she had come through the heat of this burning afternoon, stealing away alone from all her friends, and even from her own decorous self, for his sake. He pointed to the clear space under the pine where he had been lying. "Shall we sit down there — a minute?" he stammered.

"I — think I — had better go," said Lucina, faintly, with the quick impulse of maidenhood to flee from that which it has sought.

"Only a few minutes — I have something to tell you."

They sat down, Lucina with her back against the pine-tree, Jerome at her side. He opened his mouth as if to speak, but instead it widened into a vacuous smile. He looked at Lucina and she at him, then he came closer to her and took her in his arms.

Neither of them spoke. Lucina hid her face on his breast, and he held her so, looking out over her fair head at the wood. His mouth was shut hard, his eyes were full of fierce intent of combat, as if he expected some enemy forth from the trees to tear his love from him. For the first time in his life he realized the full might of his own natural self. He felt as if he could trample upon the needs of the whole world, and the light of his own soul; to gain this first sweet of existence, whose fragrance was in his face.

The strongest realization of his nature hitherto, that of the outreaching wants of others, weakened. He was filled with the insensate greed of creation for himself. He held Lucina closer, and bent his head down over hers. Then she turned her face a little, and their lips met.

Lucina had never since her childhood kissed any man but her father, and as for Jerome, he had held such things with a shame of scorn. This meant much to both of them, and the shock of such deep meaning caused them to start apart, as if with fear of each other. Lucina raised her head, and even pushed Jerome away, gently, and he loosened his hold and stood up before her, all pale and trembling.

"You must forgive me — I — forgot myself," he said, with quick gasps for breath, "I won't — sit — down there again." Then he went on, speaking fast: "I have been — wanting to tell you, but there was no chance. I could not come to see you any longer. I could not. I thought a man could go to see a woman when he was in love with her, and could bear it when the love was all on his side, and there was no — chance of marriage. I thought I could bear it if it pleased you, but — I didn't know it would be like this. I was never in love, and I did not know. I could think of nothing but wanting you. It was spoiling me for everything else, and there are other things in the world besides this. If I came much longer I should not be fit to come. I *could* not come any longer." Jerome looked down at Lucina, with an air of stern, yet wistful, argument. She sat before him with downcast, pale, and sober face, then she rose, and all her girlish irresolution and shame dropped from her, and left for a moment the woman in her unveiled.

"I love you as much as you love me," she said, simply.

Jerome looked at her. "You — don't mean — that?"

"Yes, I suppose I did when you told me first, but I did not know it then. Now I know it. I have been very unhappy because I feared you might be staying away because you thought I did not love you, but I dared not try to see you as I did before, because I had found myself out. Today I could not help it, whatever you might think of me, or whatever I might think of myself. I could not bear to worry any longer, lest you might be unhappy because you thought I did not love you. I do, and you need not stay away any more for that."

"Lucina — you don't mean —"

"Do you think I would have let you — do as you did a minute ago, if I had not?" said she, and a blush spread over her face and neck.

"I — thought — it was all — me — that — *you* — did not —"

"No, I let you," whispered Lucina.

"Oh, you don't mean that you — like me this same way that I do you — enough to marry me! You don't mean that?"

"Yes, I do," replied Lucina; she looked up at him with a curious solemn steadfastness. She was not blushing any more.

"I — never thought of this," Jerome said, drawing a long, sobbing breath. He stood looking at her, his face all white and working. "Lucina," he began, then paused, for he could not speak. He walked a little way down the path, then came back. "Lucina," he said, brokenly, "as God is my witness — I never thought of this — I never — thought that you — could — Oh, look at yourself, and look at me! You know that I could not have thought — oh, look at yourself, there was never anybody like you! I did not think that you could — care for or — be hurt by — *me*."

"I have never seen anybody like you, not even father," Lucina said. She looked at him with the shrinking yet loving faithfulness of a child before emotion which it cannot comprehend. She could not understand why, if Jerome loved her and she him, there was anything to be distressed about. She could not imagine why he was so pale and agitated, why he did not take her in his arms and kiss her again, why they could not both be happy at once.

"Oh, my God!" cried Jerome, and looked at her in a way which frightened her.

"Don't," she said, softly, shrinking a little.

"Lucina, you know how poor I am," he said, hoarsely. "You know I — can't — marry."

"I don't need much," said she.

"I couldn't — give you what you need."

"Father would, then."

"No, he would not. I give my wife all or nothing."

Lucina trembled. The same look which she remembered when Jerome would not take her little savings was in his eyes.

"Then — I would not take anything from father," she said, tremulously. "I wouldn't mind — being — poor."

"I have seen the wives of poor men, and you shall not be made one by me. If I thought I had not strength enough to keep you from that, as far as I was concerned, I would leave you this minute, and throw myself in the pond over there."

"I am not afraid to be the wife of — a poor man — if I love him. I — could save, and — work," Lucina said, speaking with the necessity of faithfulness upon her, yet timidly, and turning her face aside, for her heart had begun to fear lest Jerome did not really love her nor want her, after all. A woman who would sacrifice herself for love's sake cannot understand the sacrifice, nor the love, which refuses it.

"You shall not be, whether you are afraid or not!" Jerome cried out, fiercely. "Haven't I seen John Upham's wife? Oh, God!"

Lucina began moving slowly down the path towards the road; Jerome followed her. "I must go," she said, with a gentle dignity, though she trembled in all her limbs. "I came across the fields from Aunt Camilla's. I left her asleep, and she will wake and miss me."

"Oh," cried Jerome, "I wish —" then he stopped himself. "Yes, she will, I suppose," he added, lamely.

"He does not want me to stay," thought Lucina, with a sinking of heart and a rising of maiden pride. She walked a little faster.

Jerome quickened his pace, and touched her shoulder. "You must not think about me — about this," he murmured, hoarsely. "*You* must not be unhappy about it!"

Lucina turned and looked in his face sadly, yet with a soft

stateliness. "No," said she, "I will not. I do not see, after all, why I should be unhappy, or you either. Many people do not marry. I dare say they are happier. Aunt Camilla seems happy. I shall be like her. There is nothing to hinder our friendship. We can always be friends, like brothers and sisters even, and you can come to see me —"

"No, I can't," said Jerome, "I can't do that even. I told you I could not."

Lucina said no more. She turned her face and went on. She said good-bye quickly when she reached the road, and was across it and under the bars into the millet.

Jerome did not attempt to follow her; he stood for a moment watching her moving through the millet, as through the brown waves of a shallow sea; then he went back into the woods. When he reached the place where he had sat with Lucina he stopped and spoke, as if she were still there.

"Lucina," he said, "I promise you before God, that I will never, so long as I live, love or marry any other woman but you. I promise you that I will work as I never did before — my fingers to the bone, my heart to its last drop of blood — to earn enough to marry you. And then, if you are free, I will come to you again. I will fight to win you, with all the strength that is in me, against the whole world, and I will love you forever, forever, but I promise you that I will never say this in your hearing to bind you and make you wait, when I may die and never come."

CHAPTER XXX

Lucina did not go into her aunt Camilla's house again that afternoon. She crossed the fields — her aunt's garden — skirted the house to the road — thence home.

When she entered the south door her mother met her. "Why didn't you wait until it was cooler?" she asked; then, before the girl could answer, "What is the matter? Why, Lucina, you have been crying!"

"Nothing," replied Lucina, piteously, pushing past her mother.

"Where are you going?"

"Up-stairs to my chamber." With that Lucina was on the stairs, and her mother followed.

The two were a long time in Lucina's chamber; then Abigail came down alone to her husband in the sitting-room.

The Squire, who was as alert as any fox where his beloved daughter was concerned, had scented something wrong, and looked up anxiously when his wife entered.

"She isn't sick, is she?" he asked.

"She will be, if we don't take care," Abigail replied, shortly.

"You don't mean it!" cried the Squire, jumping up. "I'll go for the doctor this minute. It was the heat. Why didn't you keep her at home, Abigail?"

"Sit down, for mercy's sake, Eben!" said Abigail. She sat down herself as she spoke, and crossed her little slender feet and hands with a quick, involuntary motion, which was usual to her. "It is as I told you," said she. Abigail Merritt, good comrade of a wife though she was, yet turned aggressively feminine at times.

The Squire sat down. "What do you mean, Abigail?"

"I mean — that I wish that Edwards boy had never entered this house."

"Abigail, you don't mean that Lucina — What *do* you mean, Abigail?" finished the Squire, feebly.

"I mean that I was right in thinking some harm would come from that boy being here so much," replied his wife. Then she went on and repeated in substance the innocent little confession which Lucina had made to her in her chamber.

The Squire listened, his bearded chin sunken on his chest, his forehead, under the crest of yellow locks, bent gloomily.

"It seems as if you and I had done everything that we could for the child ever since she was born," he said, huskily, when his wife had finished. His first emotion was one of cruel jealousy of his daughter's love for another man.

Abigail looked at him with quick pity, but scarcely with full understanding. She could never lose, as completely as he, their daughter, through a lover. She had not to yield her to another of the same sex, and in that always the truest sting of jealousy lies.

"So far as that goes, it is no more than we had to expect, Eben," she said. "You know that. I turned away from my parents for you."

"I know it, Abigail, but — I thought, maybe, it wouldn't come yet a while. I've done all I could. I bought her the little horse — she seemed real pleased with that, Abigail, you know. I thought, maybe, she would be contented a while here with us."

"Eben Merritt, you don't for a minute think that she can be anywhere but with us, for all this!"

"It's the knowledge that she's willing to be that comes hard," said the Squire, piteously — "it's that, Abigail."

"I don't know that she's any too willing to," returned Abigail, half laughing. "The principal thing that seems to trouble the child is that Jerome won't come to see her. I rather think that if he would come to see her she would be perfectly contented."

"And why can't he come to see her, if she wants him to — will you tell me that?" cried the Squire, with sudden fervor.

"Eben Merritt, would you have the poor child getting to thinking more of him than she does, when he isn't going to marry her?"

"And why isn't he going to marry her, if she wants him? By the Lord Harry, Lucina shall have whoever she wants, if it's a prince or a beggar! If that fellow has been coming here, and now —"

"Eben, listen to me and keep quiet!" cried Abigail, running at her great husband's side, with a little, wiry, constraining hand on his arm, for the Squire had sprung from his seat and was tramping up and down in his rage that Lucina should be denied what she wanted, even though it were his own heart's blood. "You know what I told you," Abigail said. "Jerome is behaving well. You know he can't marry Lucina — he hasn't a penny."

"Then I'll give 'em pennies enough to marry on. The girl shall have whom she wants; I tell you that, Abigail."

"How much have you got to give them until we are gone, even if Jerome would marry under such conditions; and I told you what he said to Lucina about it," returned his wife, quietly.

"I'll go to work myself, then," shouted the Squire; "and as for the boy, he shall swallow his damned pride before he gives my girl an anxious hour. What is he, to say he will or will not, if she lifts her little finger? By the Lord Harry, he ought to go down on his face like a heathen when she looks at him!"

"Eben," said Abigail, "will you listen to me? I tell you, Jerome is behaving as well as any young man can. I know he is, from what Lucina has told me. He loves her, and he is proving it by giving her up. You know that he cannot marry her unless he drags her into poverty, and you know how much you have to help them with. You know, too, good as Jerome is, and worthy of praise for what he has done, that Lucina ought to do better than marry him."

"He is a good boy, Abigail, and if she's got her heart set on him she shall have him."

"You don't know that her heart is set on him, Eben. I think the best thing we can do is to send her down to Boston for a little visit — she may feel differently when she comes home."

"I won't have her crossed, Abigail. Was she crying when you left her?"

"She will soon be quiet and go to sleep. I am going to make some toast for her supper. Eben, where are you going?" The Squire had set forth for the door in a determined rush.

"I am going to see that boy, and know what this work means," he cried, in a loud voice of wrath and pity.

However, Abigail's vivacious persistency of common-sense usually overcame her husband's clumsy headlongs of affection. She carried the day at last, and the Squire subsided, though with growls of remonstrance, like a partially tamed animal.

"Have your way, and send her down to Boston, if you want to, Abigail," said he; "but when she comes back she shall have whatever she wants, if I move heaven and earth to get it for her."

So that day week Jerome, going one morning to his work, stood aside to let the stage-coach pass him, and had a glimpse of Lucina's fair face in the wave of a blue veil at the window. She bowed, but the stage dashed by in such a fury of dust that Jerome could scarcely discern the tenor of the salutation. He thought that she smiled, and not unhappily. "She is going away," he told himself; "she will go to parties, and see other people, and forget me." He tried to dash the bitterness of his heart at the thought, with the sweetness of unselfish love, but it was hard. He plodded on to his work, the young springiness gone from his back and limbs, his face sternly downcast.

As for Lucina, she was in reality leaving Upham not unhappily. She was young, and the sniff of change is to the young as the smell of powder to a war-horse. New fields present always wide ranges of triumphant pleasure to youth.

Lucina, moreover, loved with girlish fervor the friend, Miss Rose Soley, whom she was going to visit in Boston. She had not seen her for some months, and she tasted in advance the sweets of mutual confidences. That morning Jerome's face was a little confused in Lucina's mind with that of a rosy-cheeked and dark-ringleted girl, and young passion somewhat dimmed by gentle affection for one of her own sex.

Then, too, Lucina had come, during the last few days, to a more cheerful and hopeful view of the situation. After all, Jerome loved her, and was not that the principal thing? Perhaps, in time, it would all come right. Jerome might get rich; in the meantime, she was in no hurry to be married and leave her parents, and if Jerome would only come to see her, that would be enough to make her very happy. She thought that after her return he would very probably come. She reasoned, as she thought, astutely, that he would not be able to help it, when he saw her after a long absence. Then she had much faith in her father's being able to arrange this satisfactorily for her, as he had arranged all other matters during her life.

"Now don't you fret, Pretty," he had said, when she bade him good-bye, "father will see to it that you have everything you want." And Lucina, all blushing with innocent confusion, had believed him.

In addition to all this she had in her trunks, strapped at the back of the stage-coach, two fine, new silk gowns, and one muslin, and a silk mantilla. Also she carried a large blue bandbox containing a new plumed hat and veil, which cheered her not a little, being one of those minor sweets which providentially solace the weak feminine soul in its unequal combat with life's great bitternesses.

Lucina was away some three months, not returning until a few days before Thanksgiving; then she brought her friend, Miss Rose Soley, with her, and also a fine young gentleman, with long, curling, fair locks, and a face as fair as her own.

While Lucina was gone, Jerome led a life easier in some respects, harder in others. He had no longer the foe of daily temptation to overcome, but instead was the steady grind of hunger. Jerome, in those days, felt the pangs of that worst hunger in the world — the hunger for the sight of one beloved. Some mornings when he awoke it seemed to him that he should die of mere exhaustion and starvation of spirit if he saw not Lucina before night. In those days he would rather have walked over fiery plough-shares than visited any place where he had seen Lucina, and where she now was not. He never went near the wood, where they had sat together; he would not pass even, if he could help it, the Squire's house or Miss Camilla's. His was one of those minds for whom, when love has once come, place is only that which holds, or is vacant of, the beloved. He was glad when the white frost came and burned out the gardens and the woodlands with arctic fires of death, for then the associations with old scenes were in a measure lost.

One Sunday after the frost, when the ground was shining stiff with it, as with silver mail, and all the trees thickened the distance as with glittering furze, he went to his woodland, and found that he could bear the sight of the place where he and Lucina had been together; its strangeness of aspect seemed to place it so far in the past.

Jerome threw up his head in the thin, sparkling air. "I will have her yet," he said, quite aloud; and "if I do not, I can bear that."

He felt like one who would crush the stings of fate, even if against his own heart. He had grown old and thin during the last weeks; he had worked so hard and resolutely, yet with so little hope; and he who toils without hope is no better than a slave to his own will. That day, when he went home, his eyes were bright and his cheeks glowing. His mother and sister noticed the difference.

"I was afraid he was gettin' all run down," Ann Edwards told Elmira; "but he looks better today."

Elmira herself was losing her girlish bloom. She was one who needed absolute certainties to quiet distrustful imaginations, and matters betwixt herself and Lawrence Prescott were less and less on a stable footing. Lawrence was working hard; she should not have suspected that his truth towards her flagged, but she sometimes did. He did not come to see her regularly. Sometimes two weeks went past, sometimes three, and he had not come. In fact, Lawrence endeavored to come only when he could do so openly.

"I hate to deceive father more than I can help," he told Elmira, but she did not understand him fully.

She was a woman for whom the voluntary absence of a lover who yet loves was almost an insoluble problem, and in that Lucina was not unlike her. She was not naturally deceptive, but, when it came to love, she was a Jesuit in conceiving it to sanctify its own ends.

The suspense, the uncertainty, as to her lover coming or not, was beginning to tell upon her. Every nerve in her slight body was in an almost constant state of tension.

It was just a week from that day that Jerome and Elmira, being seated in meeting, saw Lucina enter with her parents and her visiting friends. Jerome's heart leaped up at the sight of Lucina, then sank before that of the young man following her up the aisle. "He is going to marry her; she has forgotten me," he thought, directly.

As for Elmira, she eyed Miss Rose Soley's dark ringlets under the wide velvet brim of her hat, the crimson curve of her cheek, and the occasional backward glance of a black eye at Lawrence Prescott seated directly behind her. When meeting was over, she caught Jerome by the arm. "Come out quick," she said, in a sharp whisper, and Jerome was glad enough to go.

Lucina's guests spent Thanksgiving with her. Jerome saw them twice, riding horseback with Lawrence Prescott — Lucina on her little white horse, Miss Soley on Lawrence's black, the strange young man on the Squire's sorrel, and Lawrence on a gray.

Lucina colored when she saw Jerome, and reined her horse, lingering behind the others, but he did not seem to notice it, and never looked at her after his first grave bow; then she touched her horse, and galloped after her friends with a windy swirl of blue veil and skirts.

Jerome wondered if his sister would hear that Lawrence Prescott had been out riding with Lucina and her friends. When he got home that night, he met Belinda Lamb coming out of the gate; when he entered, he saw by Elmira's face that she had heard. She was binding shoes very fast; her little face was white, except for red spots on the cheeks, her mouth shut hard. Her mother kept looking at her anxiously.

"You'd better not worry till you know you've got something to worry about; likely as not, they asked him to go with them 'cause Lucina's beau don't know how to ride very well, and he couldn't help it," she said, with a curious aside of speech, as if Jerome, though on the stage, was not to hear.

He took no notice, but that night he had a word with his sister after their mother had gone to bed. "If he has asked you to marry him, you ought to trust him," said he. "I don't believe his going to ride with that girl means anything. You ought to believe in him until you know he isn't worthy of it."

Elmira turned upon him with a flash of eyes like his own. "Worthy!" she cried — "don't I think he would be worthy if he did leave me for her! Do you think I would blame him if he did leave anybody as poor as I am, worked 'most to skin and bone, of body and soul too, for anybody like that girl? I guess I wouldn't blame him, and you needn't. I don't blame him; it's true, I know, he'll never come to see me again, but I don't blame him."

"If he doesn't come to see you again he'll have me to hear from," Jerome said, fiercely.

"No, he won't. Don't you ever dare speak to him, or blame him, Jerome Edwards; I won't have it." Elmira ran into her chamber, leaving an echo of wild sobs in her brother's ears.

The day after Thanksgiving, Lucina's friends went away; when Jerome came home that night Elmira's face wore a different expression, which Mrs. Edwards explained with no delay.

"Belinda Lamb has been here," she said, "and that young man is that Boston girl's beau; he ain't Lucina's, and Lawrence Prescott ain't nothing to do with it. He was up there last night, but it wa'n't anything. Why, Jerome Edwards, you look as pale as death!"

Jerome muttered some unintelligible response, and went out of the room, with his mother staring after him. He went straight to his own little chamber, and, standing there in the still, icy gloom of the winter twilight, repeated the promise which he had made in summer.

"If you are true to me, Lucina," he said, in a straining whisper — "if you are true to me — but I'll leave it all to you whether you are or not, I'll work till I win you."

CHAPTER XXXI

On the evening of the next day Jerome went to call on Lawyer Eliphalet Means. Lawyer Means lived near the northern limit of the village, on the other side of the brook.

Jerome, going through the covered bridge which crossed the brook, paused and looked through a space between the side timbers. This brook was a sturdy little torrent at all times; in spring it was a river. Now, under the white concave of wintry moonlight, it broke over its stony bed with a fierce persistency of advance. Jerome looked down at the rapid, shifting water-hillocks and listened to their lapsing murmur, incessantly overborne by the gathering rush of onset, then nodded his head conclusively, as if in response to some mental question, and moved on.

Lawyer Eliphalet Means lived in the old Means house. It upreared itself on a bare moon-silvered hill at the right of the road, with a solid state of simplest New England architecture. It dated back to the same epoch as Doctor Prescott's and Squire Merritt's houses, but lacked even the severe ornaments of their time.

Jerome climbed the shining slope of the hill to the house door, which was opened by Lawyer Means himself; then he followed him into the sitting-room. A great cloud of tobacco smoke came in his face when the sitting-room door was thrown open. Through it Jerome could scarcely see Colonel Jack Lamson, in a shabby old coat, seated before the blazing hearth-fire, with a tumbler of rum-and-water on a little table at his right hand.

"Sit down," said Means to Jerome, and pulled another chair forward. "Quite a sharp night out," he added.

"Yes, sir," replied Jerome, seating himself.

Lawyer Means resumed his own chair and his pipe, at which he puffed with that jealous comfort which comes after interruption. Colonel Lamson, when he had given a friendly nod of greeting to the young man, without removing his pipe from his mouth, leaned back his head again, stretched his legs more luxuriously, and blew the smoke in great wreaths around his face. This sitting-room of Lawyer Means's was a scandal to the few matrons of Upham who had ever penetrated it. "Don't look as if a woman had ever set foot in it," they said. The ancient female relative of Lawyer Means who kept his house had not been a notable housekeeper in her day, and her day was nearly past. Moreover, she had small control over this particular room.

The great apartment, with the purple clouds of tobacco

smoke, which were settling against its low ceiling and in its far corners, transfused with golden gleams of candles and rosy flashes of fire-light, dingy as to wall-paper and carpet, with the dust of months upon all shiny surfaces, seemed a very fortress of bachelorhood wherein no woman might enter.

The lawyer's books in the tall cases were arranged in close ranks of strictest order, as were also the neatly ticketed files of letters and documents in the pigeon-holes of the great desk; otherwise the whole room seemed fluttering and protruding out of its shadows with loose ends of paper and corners of books. All the free lines in the room were the tangents of irrelevancy and disorder.

The lawyer, puffing at his pipe, with eyes half closed, did not look at Jerome, but his attitude was expectant.

Jerome stared at the blazing fire with a hesitating frown, then he turned with sudden resolution to Means. "Can I see you alone a minute?" he asked.

The Colonel rose, without a word, and lounged out of the room; when the door had shut behind him, Jerome turned again to the lawyer. "I want to know if you are willing to sell me two hundred and sixty-five dollars' worth of your land," said he.

"Which land?"

"Your land on Graystone brook. I want one hundred and thirty-two dollars and fifty cents' worth on each side."

"Why don't you make it even dollars, and what in thunder do you want the land on two sides for?" asked the lawyer, in his dry voice, threaded between his lips and pipe.

Jerome took an old wallet from his pocket. "Because two hundred and sixty-five dollars is all the money I've got saved," he replied, "and —"

"You haven't brought it here to close the bargain on the spot?" interrupted the lawyer.

"Yes; I knew you could make out the deed."

Means puffed hard at his pipe, but his face twitched as if with laughter.

"I want it on both sides of the brook," Jerome said, "because I don't want anybody else to get it. I want to build a saw-mill, and I want to control all the water-power."

"I thought you said that was all the money you had."

"It is."

"How are you going to build a saw-mill, then? That money won't pay for enough land, let alone the mill."

"I am going to wait until I save more money; then I shall buy more land and build the mill," replied Jerome.

"Why not borrow the money?"

Jerome shook his head.

"Suppose I let you have some money at six per cent.; suppose you build the mill, and I take a mortgage on that and the land."

"No, sir."

"Why not? If I am willing to trust a young fellow like you with money, what is your objection to taking it?"

"I would rather wait until I can pay cash down, sir," replied Jerome, sturdily.

"You'll be gray as a badger before you get the money."

"Then I'll be gray," said Jerome. His handsome young face, full of that stern ardor which was a principle of his nature, confronted the lawyer's, lean and dry, deepening its shrewdly quizzical lines about mouth and eyes.

Means looked sharply at Jerome. "What has started you in this? What makes you think it will be a good thing?" he asked.

"No saw-mill nearer than Westbrook, good water-power, straight course of brook, below the falls can float logs down to the mill from above, then down to Dale. People in Dale are paying heavy prices for lumber on account of freight; then the railroad will go through Dale within five years, and they will want sleepers, and —"

"Perhaps they won't take them from you, young man."

"I have been to Squire Lennox, in Dale; he is the prime mover in the railroad, and will be a director, if not the president; he has given me the refusal of the job."

"Where will you get your logs?"

"I have bargained with two parties."

"Five years is a long time ahead."

"It won't be, if I wait long enough."

"You are a damned fool not to borrow the money. The railroad may go through in another year, and all the standing wood in the county may burn down," said Means, quietly.

"Let it then," said Jerome, looking at him.

The lawyer laughed, silently.

When Jerome went home he had in his pocket a deed of the land, but on the right bank of the brook only, the lawyer having covenanted not to sell or build upon the left bank. Thus he had enough land upon which to build his mill when he should have saved the money. He felt nearer Lucina than he had ever done before. The sanguineness of youth, which is its best stimulant for advance, thrilled through all his veins. He had mentioned five years as the possible length of time before acquisition; secretly he laughed at the idea. Five years! Why, he could save enough money in three years — in less than three years — in two years! It had been only a short time since he had made the last payment on the mortgage, and he had saved his two hundred and sixty-five dollars. A saw-mill would not cost much. He could build a great part of it himself.

That night Jerome truly counted his eggs before they were hatched. All the future seemed but a nest for his golden hopes. He would work and save — he was working and saving. He would build his mill; as he thought further, the foundation-stones were laid, the wheel turned, and the saw hissed through the live wood. He would marry Lucina; he saw her in her bridal white —

All this time, with that sublime cruelty which man can show towards one beloved when working for love's final good, and which is a feeble prototype of the Higher method, Jerome gave not one thought to the fact that Lucina knew nothing of his plans, and, if she loved him, as she had said, must suffer. When, moreover, one has absolute faith in, and knowledge of, his own intentions for the welfare of another, it is difficult to conceive that the other may not be able to spell out his actions towards the same meaning.

Jerome really felt as if Lucina knew. The next Sunday he watched her come into meeting with an exquisite sense of possession, which he imagined her to understand.

When he did not go to see her that night, but, instead, sat happily brooding over the future, it never once occurred to him that it might be otherwise with her.

All poor Lucina's ebullition of spirits from her pleasant visit, her pretty gowns, and her fond belief that Jerome could not have meant what he said, and would come to see her after her return, was fast settling into the dregs of disappointment.

Night after night she put on one of her prettiest gowns, and waited with that wild torture of waiting which involves uncertainty and concealment, and Jerome did not come. Lucina began to believe that Jerome did not love her; she tried to call her maidenly pride to her aid, and succeeded in a measure. She stopped putting on a special gown to please Jerome should he come; she stopped watching out for him; she stopped healing her mind with hope in order that it might be torn open afresh with disappointment, but the wound remained and gaped to her consciousness, and Lucina was a tender thing. She held her beautiful head high and forced her face to gentle smiles, but she went thin and pale, and could not sleep of a night, and her mother began to fret about her, and her father to lay down his knife and fork and stare at her across the table when she could not eat.

Squire Eben at that time ransacked the woods for choice game, and himself stood over old Hannah or his wife, broiling the delicate birds that they be done to a turn, and was fit to weep when his pretty Lucina could scarcely taste them. Often, too, he sent surreptitiously to Boston for dainties not obtainable at home — East India fruits and jellies and such — to tempt his daughter's appetite, and watched her with great frowns of anxious love when they were set before her.

One afternoon, when Lucina had gone up to her chamber to lie down, having left her dinner almost untasted, though there was a little fat wild bird and guava jelly served on a china plate, and an orange and figs to come after, the Squire beckoned his wife into the sitting-room and shut the door.

"D'ye think she's going into a decline?" he whispered. His great frame trembled all over when he asked the question, and his face was yellow-white. Years ago a pretty young sister of his, whose namesake Lucina was, had died of a decline, as they had termed it, and, ever since, death of the young and fair had worn that guise to the fancy of the Squire. He remembered just how his young sister had looked when she was fading to her early tomb, and today he had seemed to see her expression in his daughter's face.

Abigail laid her little hand on his arm. "Don't look so, Eben," she said. "I don't think she is in a decline; she doesn't cough."

"What ails her, Abigail?"

Mrs. Merritt hesitated. "I don't know that much ails her, Eben," she said, evasively. "Girls often get run down, then spring up again."

"Abigail, you don't think the child is fretting about — that boy again?"

"She hasn't mentioned his name to me for weeks, Eben," replied Abigail, and her statement carried reassurance, since the Squire argued, with innocent masculine prejudice, that what came not to a woman's tongue had no abiding in her mind.

His wife, if she were more subtle, gave no evidence of it. "I think the best plan would be for her to go away again," she added.

The Squire looked at her wistfully. "Do you think it would, Abigail?"

"I think she would brighten right up, the way she did before."

"She did brighten up, didn't she?" said the Squire, with a sigh.

"Well, maybe you're right, Abigail, but you've got to go with her this time. The child isn't going away, looking as she does now, without her mother."

So it happened that, a week or two later, Jerome, going to his work, met the coach again, and this time had a glimpse of Abigail Merritt's little, sharply alert face beside her daughter's pale, flowerlike droop of profile. He had not been in the shop long before his uncle's wife came with the news. She stood in the doorway, quite filling it with her voluminosity of skirts and softly palpitating bulk, holding a little fluttering shawl together under her chin.

"They've gone out West, to Ohio, to Mis' Merritt's cousin, Mary Jane Anstey, that was; she married rich, years ago, and went out there to live, and Abigail 'ain't seen her since. She's been teasin' her to come for years; her own folks are all dead an' gone, an' her husband is poorly, an' she can't leave him to come here. Camilla, she paid the expenses of one of 'em out there. Lucina's been real miserable lately, an' they're worried about her. The Squire's sister, that she was named for, went down in a decline in six months; so her mother has taken her out there for a change, an' they're goin' to make a long visit. Lucina is real poorly. I had it from 'Lizy Wells. Camilla told her."

Jerome shifted his back towards his aunt as he sat on his bench. His face, bent over his work, was white and rigid.

"You're coldin' of the shop off, Belindy," said Ozias.

"Well, I s'pose I be," said she, with a pleasant titter of apology, and backed off the threshold and shut the door.

"That's a woman," said Ozias, "who 'ain't got any affairs of her own, but she's perfectly contented an' happy with her neighbors', taken weak. That's the kind of woman to marry if you ain't got anythin' to give her — no money, no interests in life, no anythin'."

Jerome made no reply. His uncle gave a shrewd glance at him. "When ye can't eat lollypops, it's jest as well not to have them under your nose," he remarked, with seemingly no connection, but Jerome said nothing to that either.

He worked silently, with fierce energy, the rest of the morning. He had not heard before of Lucina's ill health; she had not been to church the Sunday previous, but he had thought of nothing serious from that. Now the dreadful possibility came to him — suppose she should die and leave his world entirely, of what avail would all his toil be then? When he went home that noon he ate his dinner hastily, then, on his way back to the shop, left the road, crossed into a field, and sat down in the wide solitude, on a rock humping out of the dun roll of sere grass-land. Always, in his stresses of spirit, Jerome sought instinctively some closet which he had made of the free fastnesses of nature.

The day was very dull and cold; snow threatened, should the weather moderate. Overhead was a suspended drift of gray clouds. The earth was stark as a corpse in utter silence. The still-ness of the frozen air was like the stillness of death and despair. A fierce blast would have given at least the sense of life and fighting power. "Suppose she dies," thought Jerome — "suppose she dies."

He tried to imagine the world without Lucina, but he could not, for with all his outgoing spirit his world was too largely within him. For the first time in his life, the conception of the death of that which he loved better than his life was upon him, and it was a conception of annihilation. "If Lucina is not, then I am not, and that upon which I look is not," was in his mind.

When he rose, he staggered, and could scarcely see his way across the field. When he entered his uncle's shop, Ozias looked at him sharply. "If you're sick you'd better go home and go to bed," he said, in a voice of harsh concern.

"I am not sick," said Jerome, and fell to work with a sort of fury.

As the days went on it seemed to him that he could not bear life any longer if he did not hear how Lucina was, and yet the most obvious steps to hear he did not take. It never occurred to him to march straight to the Squire's house, and inquire of him con-cerning his daughter's health. Far from that, he actually dreaded to meet him, lest he read in his face that she was worse. He did not go to meeting, lest the minister mention her in his prayer for the sick; he stayed as little as possible in the company of his mother and sister, lest they repeat the sad news concerning her; if a neighbor came in, he got up and left the room directly. He never went to the village store of an evening; he ostracized himself from his kind, lest they stab him with the confirmation of his agonizing fear. For the first time in his life Jerome had turned coward.

One day, when Lucina had been gone about a month, he was coming home from Dale when he heard steps behind him and a voice shouting for him to stop. He turned and saw Colonel Jack Lamson coming with breathless quickening of his stiff military gait.

When the Colonel reached him he could scarcely speak; his wheezing chest strained his coat to exceeding tightness, his face was purple, he swung his cane with spasmodic jerks. "Fine day," he gasped out.

"Yes, sir," said Jerome.

It was near the end of February, the snow was thawing, and for the first time there was a suggestion of spring in the air which caused one, with the recurrence of an old habit of mind, to listen and sniff as for birds and flowers.

The two men stepped along, picking their way through the melting snow. "The doctor has ordered me out for a three-mile march every day. I'm going to stent myself," said the Colonel, still breathing hard; then he looked keenly at Jerome. "What have you been doing to yourself, young fellow?" he asked.

"Nothing. I don't know what you mean," answered Jerome.

"Nothing! Why, you have aged ten years since I last saw you!"

"I am well enough, Colonel Lamson."

"How about that deed I witnessed? Have you got enough money to build the mill yet?"

"No, I haven't," replied Jerome, with a curious tone of defiance and despair, which the Colonel interpreted wrongly.

"Oh, don't give up yet," he said, cheerfully. "Rome wasn't built in a day, you know."

Jerome made no reply, but trudged on doggedly.

"How is she?" asked the Colonel, suddenly.

Jerome turned white and looked at him. "Who?" he said.

The Colonel laughed, with wheezy facetiousness. "Why, she — *she*. Young men don't build nests or saw-mills unless there is a she in the case."

"There isn't —" began Jerome. Then he shut his mouth hard and walked on.

"It's only my joke, Jerome," laughed the Colonel, but there was no responsive smile on Jerome's face. Colonel Lamson eyed him narrowly. "The Squire had a letter from his wife yesterday," he said, with no preface. Then he started, for Jerome turned upon him a face as of one who is braced for death.

"How — is she?" he gasped out.

"Who? Mrs. Merritt? No, confound it all, my boy, she's better! Hold on to yourself, my boy; I tell you she's better."

Jerome gave a deep sigh, and walked ahead so fast that the Colonel had to quicken his pace. "Wait a minute," he panted; "I want a word with you."

Jerome stopped, and the Colonel came up and faced him. "Look here, young man," he said, with sudden wrath, "if I thought for a minute you had jilted that girl, I wouldn't stop for words; I would take you by the neck like a puppy, and I'd break every bone in your body."

Jerome squared his shoulders involuntarily; his face, confronting the Colonel's, twitched. "I'll kill you or any other man who dares to say I did," he cried out, fiercely.

"If I hadn't known you didn't I would have seen you damned before I'd spoken to you," returned the Colonel; "but what I want to ask now is, what in — are you doing?"

"I'd like to know what business 'tis of yours!"

"What in — are you doing, my boy?" repeated the Colonel.

There was something ludicrous in the contrast between his strong language and his voice, into which had come suddenly a tone of kindness which was almost caressing. Jerome, since his father's day, had heard few such tones addressed to him, and his proudly independent heart was softened and weakened by his anxiety and relief over Lucina.

"I am — working my fingers to the bone — to win her, sir," he blurted out, brokenly.

"Does she know it?"

"Do you think I would say anything to her to bind her when I might never be able to marry her?" said Jerome, with almost an accent of wonder.

The Colonel whistled and said no more, for just then Belinda Lamb and Paulina Maria came up, holding their petticoats high out of the slush.

The two men walked on to Upham village, the Colonel straight, as if at the head of a battalion, though his lungs pumped hard at every step, holding back his square shoulders, protruding his tight broadcloth, swinging his stick airily, Jerome at his side, burdened like a peasant, with his sheaf of cut leather, but holding up his head like a prince.

CHAPTER XXXII

Lucina and her mother were away some three months; it was late spring when they returned. It had been told in Upham that Lucina was quite well, but when people saw her they differed as to her appearance. "She looks dreadful delicate now, accordin' to my way of thinkin'," some of the women, spying sharply upon her from their sitting-room windows and their meeting-house pews, reported.

Jerome saw her for the first time after her return when she followed her father and mother up the aisle one Sunday in May when all the orchards were white. He thought, with a great throb of joy, that she looked quite well, that she must be well. If the red and white of her cheeks was a little too clear, he did not appreciate it. She was all in white, like the trees, with some white blossoms and plumes on her hat.

After meeting, he lingered a little on the porch, though Elmira was walking on, with frequent pauses turning her head and looking for him. However, when Lucina appeared, he did not get the kindly glance for which he had hoped. She was talking so busily with Mrs. Doctor Prescott that she did not seem to see him, but the color on her cheeks was deeper. Jerome joined his sister hastily and went home quite contented, thinking Lucina was very well.

However, in a few weeks' time he began to hear whispers to the contrary. Sometimes Lucina did not go to meeting; still, she was seen out frequently riding and walking. When Jerome caught a glimpse of her he strove to shut away the knowledge that she did not look well from his own consciousness. But when Lucina had been at home six weeks she took a sudden turn for the better, which could have been dated accurately from a certain morning when she met Colonel Jack Lamson, she being out riding and he walking. He kept pace with the slow amble of her little white horse for some distance, sometimes grasping the bridle and stopping in a shady place to talk more at ease.

When Lucina got home that noon her mother noticed a change in her. "You look better than you have done for weeks," said she.

"I enjoyed my ride," Lucina said, with a smile and a blush which her mother could not fathom. The girl ate a dinner which gladdened her father's heart; afterwards she went up to her chamber, and presently came down with her hat on and her silk work-bag on her arm.

"I am going to take one of my chair-covers over to Aunt Camilla's," said she.

"Well, walk slowly," said her mother, trying to conceal her delight lest it betray her past anxiety. Lucina had not touched her embroidery for weeks, nor stepped out-of-doors of her own accord.

When she was gone her father and mother looked at each other. "She's better," Eben said, with a catch in his voice.

"I haven't seen her so bright for weeks," replied Abigail. She had a puzzled look in spite of her satisfaction. That night she ascertained through wariest soundings that Lucina had not met Jerome when riding in the morning. She had suspected something, though she scarcely knew what. Lucina's secrecy lately had deceived even her mother. She had begun to think that the girl had not been as much in earnest in her love affair as she had thought, and was drooping from some other cause.

When Lucina revealed with innocent readiness that she had met Colonel Lamson that morning and talked with him, and with no one else, Abigail could make nothing of it.

However, Lucina from that day on improved. She took up her little tasks; she seemed quite as formerly, only, possibly, somewhat older and more staid.

The Squire thought that her recovery was due to a certain bitter medicine which Doctor Prescott had given her, and often extolled it to his wife. "It is singular that medicine should work like a flash of lightning after she had been taking it for weeks with no effect," thought Abigail, but she said nothing.

One afternoon, not long after her talk with Colonel Lamson, Lucina met Jerome face to face in the road, and stopped and held out her hand to him. "How do you do?" she said, paling and blushing, and yet with a sweet confidence which was new in her manner.

Jerome bowed low, but did not offer his hand. She held out hers persistently.

"I can't shake hands," he said, "mine is stained with leather; it smells of it, too."

"I am not afraid of leather," Lucina returned, gently.

"I am," Jerome said, with a defiance in which there was no bitterness. Then, as Lucina still looked at him and held out her hand, with an indescribable air of pretty, childish insistence and womanly pleading, her blue eyes being sober almost to tears, he motioned her to wait a moment, and swung over the fence and down the road-side, which was just there precipitous, to the brook-bed. He got down on his knees, plunged his hands into the water, like a golden net-work in the afternoon light, washed his hands well, and returned to Lucina. She laid her little hand in his, but she shook her head, smiling. "I liked it better the other way," said she.

"I couldn't touch your hand with mine like that."

"You would give me more if you let me give you something sometimes," said Lucina, with a pretty, sphinxlike look at him as she drew her hand away.

Jerome wondered what she had meant after they had separated. Acute as he was, and of more masterly mind than she, he was at a loss, for she had touched that fixed idea which sways us all to greater or less degree and some to delusion. Jerome, with his one principle of giving, could not even grasp a problem which involved taking.

He puzzled much over it, then decided, not with that lenient slighting, as in other cases when womankind had vexed him with blind words, but with a fond reverence, as for some angelic mystery, that it was because Lucina was a girl. "Maybe girls are given to talking in that riddlesome kind of way," thought Jerome.

He was blissfully certain upon one point, at all events. Lucina's whole manner had given evidence to a confidence and understanding upon her part.

"She knows what I am doing," he told himself. "She knows how I am working, and she is contented and willing to wait. She knows, but she isn't bound." Jerome had not dreamed that Lucina's indisposition had had aught to do with distress of mind upon his account.

Now he fell upon work as if it had been a veritable dragon of old, which he must slay to rescue his princess. He toiled from earliest dawn until far dark, and not with hands only. Still he did not neglect his gratuitous nursing and doctoring. He saved like a miser, though not at his mother's and sister's expense. He himself would taste, in those days, no butter, no sugar, no fresh meat, no bread of fine flour, but he saw to it that is mother and Elmira were well provided.

When winter came again, he used to hasten secretly along the road, not wishing to meet Lucina for a new reason — lest she discover how thin his coat was against the wintry blast, how thin his shoes against the snow.

"I never thought Jerome was so close," Elmira sometimes said to her mother.

"He ain't close, he's got an object," returned Ann, with a

shrewd, mysterious look.

"What do you mean, mother?"

"Nothin'."

Elmira's and Lawrence's courtship progressed after the same fashion. If Doctor Prescott suspected anything he made no sign. Lawrence was attending patients regularly with his father and reading hard.

Sometimes, during his occasional calls upon Elmira, he saw Jerome. The two young men, when they met on the road, exchanged covertly cordial courtesies; a sort of non-committal friendship was struck up between them. Lawrence was the means of introducing Jerome to a new industry, of which he might otherwise never have heard.

"Father and I were on the old Dale road this morning," he said, "and there is a fine cranberry-meadow there on the left, if anybody wants to improve it. There's plenty of chance for drainage from that little stream that runs into Graystone, and it's sheltered from the frost. Old Jonathan Hawkins owns it; we went there — his wife is sick — and he said he used to sell berries off it, but it had run down. He said he'd be glad to let somebody work it on shares, just allowing him for the use of the land. He's too old to bother with it himself, and he is pretty well straitened for money. There's money in it, I guess."

Jerome listened, and the next day went over to Jonathan Hawkins's place, on the old Dale road, and made his bargain. Some of his work on the cranberry-meadow was done before light, his lantern moving about the misty expanse like a marsh candle. When the berries were ripe he employed children to pick them, John Upham's among the rest. He cleared quite a sum by this venture, and added it to his store. In two years' time he had saved enough money for his mill, and early in the fall had the lumber all ready. He had engaged one carpenter from Dale; he thought that he could build the mill himself with his help, and that of some extra hands for raising.

On the evening before the day on which he expected to begin work he went to see Adoniram Judd. The Judds lived off the main road, in a field connected with it by a cart-path. Their house, after the commonest village pattern — a long cottage with two windows on either side of the front door — stood closely backed up against a wood of pines and larches. The wind was cold, and the sound of it in the evergreens was like a far-off halloo of winter. The house had a shadowy effect in waning moonlight, the walls were mostly gray, being only streaked high on the sheltered sides with old white paint.

Since Paulina Maria could not afford to have a coat of new paint on her house, she had a bitter ambition, from motives of tidiness and pride, to at least remove all traces of the old. She felt that the chief sting of present deprivation lay in the evidence of its contrast with former plenty. She hated the image in her memory of her cottage glistening with the white gloss of paint, and would have weakened it if she could. Paulina Maria accordingly, standing on a kitchen-chair, had scrubbed with soap and sand the old paint-streaks as high as her long arms would reach, and had, at times, when his rheumatism would permit, set her tall husband to the task. The paint, which was difficult to remove by any but its natural effacers — the long courses of nature — was one of those minor material antagonisms of life which keep the spirit whetted for harder ones.

Paulina Maria Judd had many such; when the pricks of fate were too firm set against her struggling feet she saved herself from the despair of utter futility by taking soap and water and sand, and going forth to attack the paint on her house walls, and also the front door-stone worn in frequent hollows for the collection of dirt and dust.

This evening, when Jerome drew near, he saw a long rise of back over the door-step, and a swiftly plying shoulder and arm. Paulina Maria looked up without ceasing when Jerome stood beside her.

"You're working late," he said, with an attempt at pleasantry.

"I have to do my cleanin' late or not at all," replied Paulina Maria, in her cold, calm voice. She rubbed more soap on her cloth.

"Uncle Adoniram at home?" Jerome had always called Adoniram "Uncle," though he was his father's cousin.

"Yes."

"I want to see him a minute about something."

"You'll have to go round to the back door. I can't have more dirt tracked into this while it's wet."

Jerome went around the house to the back door. As he passed the lighted sitting-room windows he saw a monstrous shadow with steadily moving hands on the curtain. He fumbled his way through the lighted room, in which sat Adoniram Judd closing shoes and his son Henry knitting. When the door opened Henry, whose shadow Jerome had seen on the window-pane, looked up with the vacant peering of the blind, but his fingers never ceased twirling the knitting-needles.

"How are you?" said Jerome.

Adoniram returned his salutation without rising, and bade him take a chair. Henry spoke not at all, and bent his dim eyes again over his knitting without a smile. Henry Judd had the lank height of his father, and his blunt elongation of face and features, informed by his mother's spirit. The result in his expression was an absolute ferocity instead of severity of gloom, a fury of resentment against his fate, instead of that bitter leaning towards it which is the acme of defiance.

Henry Judd bent his heavy, pale brows over the miserable feminine work to which he was forced. His long hands were white as a girl's, and revealed their articulation as they moved; his face, transparently pale, showed a soft furze of young beard on cheek and chin.

"How are you, Henry?" asked Jerome.

Henry made no reply, only scowled more gloomily. Paulina Maria's ardent severity of Christianity had produced in her son, under his first stress of life, a fierce rebound. To no word of Scripture would Henry Judd resort for comfort; he never bent knee in prayer, and would not be led, even by his mother's authority, to meeting on Sunday. The voice of his former mates, who had with him no sympathy of like affliction, filled him with a sullen rage of injury. He was somewhat younger than Jerome, but had seemed formerly much attracted to him. Now he had not spoken to him for a year.

Jerome, when he entered, had looked happy and eager, as if he was burdened with some pleasant news. Now his expression changed; he looked at Adoniram, then at Henry, then at Adoniram again, and motioned an inquiry with his lips. Adoniram shook his head sadly.

Paulina Maria came in through the kitchen, where she had left her scrubbing utensils, got an unfinished shoe, and sat down to her binding. She did not notice Jerome again, and he sat frowning moodily at the floor.

"It is a cold night for the season," remarked Adoniram, at length, with an uneasy attempt at entertainment, to which Jerome did not respond with much alacrity. He acted at first as if he did not hear, then collected himself, said that it was cold, and there might be a frost if the wind went down, and rose.

"You ain't goin' so soon?" asked Adoniram, with slow surprise.

"I only ran over for a minute; I've got some work to do," muttered Jerome, and went out.

He went along the ridgy cart-path across the field to the road, but when he reached it he stopped short. He stood for ten minutes or more, motionless, thinking so intently that it was as if his body stood aside from his swift thought, then he returned to the Judd house.

He went around to the back door, but when he reached it he stopped again. After a little he crept noiselessly back to the cart-path, and so to the road again.

But it was as if, when he reached the road, he met some unseen and mighty arm of denial which barred it. He stopped there for the second time. Then he went back again to the Judd house, and this time when he reached the door he opened it and went in.

When he entered the sitting-room, where Adoniram and Paulina Maria and Henry were, they all looked up in astonishment.

"Forgot anything?" inquired Adoniram.

"Yes," replied Jerome. Then he went on, speaking fast, in a strained voice, which he tried hard to make casual. "There was something I wanted to say. I've been thinking about Henry's eyes. If — you want to take him to Boston, to that doctor, I've got the money. I've got five hundred dollars you're welcome to. I believe you said it would take that." He looked straight at Paulina Maria as he spoke, and she dropped her work and looked at him.

Adoniram made a faint, gasping noise, then sat staring at them both. Henry started, but knitted on as remorselessly as his own fate.

"How did you come by so much money?" asked Paulina Maria, in her pure, severe voice.

"I saved if from my earnings."

"What for?"

"You'll be welcome to take it, and use it for Henry."

"That ain't answering my question."

Jerome was silent.

"You needn't answer if you don't want to," said Paulina Maria, "for I know. You've kept it dark from everybody but Lawyer Means and your mother and Elmira, but your mother told me a year ago. I haven't told a soul. You've been saving up this money to build a mill with and — I've been over to your mother's this afternoon — you are going to start it tomorrow."

"I am not obliged to start it tomorrow," said Jerome.

"You're obliged to for all me. Do you think I'll take that money?"

Jerome turned to Henry. "Henry, it's for you, and not your mother," said he. "Will you take it?"

Henry, still knitting, shook his head.

"I tell you there is no hurry about the mill. I can wait and earn more. I give it to you freely."

"We shouldn't take it unless I give you a note of hand, Jerome," Adoniram interposed, in a quavering voice.

Paulina Maria looked at her husband. "What is your note of hand worth?" she asked, sternly.

"Won't you take it, Henry? I've always thought a good deal of you, and I don't want you to be blind," Jerome said.

Henry shook his head; there was an awful inexorableness with himself displayed in his steady knitting.

"There are things worse than blindness," said Paulina Maria. "Nobody shall sacrifice himself for my son. If our own prayers and sacrifices are not sufficient, it is the will of the Lord that he should suffer, and he will suffer."

"Take it, Henry," pleaded Jerome, utterly disregarding her.

"Would you take it in my son's place?" demanded Paulina Maria, suddenly. She looked fixedly at Jerome. "Answer me," said she.

"That has nothing to do with it!" Jerome cried, angrily. "He is going blind, and this money will cure him. If you are his mother —"

"Don't ask anybody to take even a kindness that you wouldn't take yourself," said Paulina Maria.

Jerome flung out of the room without another word. When he got out-of-doors, he found Adoniram at his elbow.

"I want ye to know that I'm much obliged to ye, J'rome," he whispered. He felt for Jerome's hand and shook it. "Thank ye, thank ye, J'rome," he repeated, brokenly.

"I don't want any thanks," replied Jerome. "Can't you take the money and make Henry go with you to Boston and see the doctor, if she won't?"

"It's no use goin' agin her, J'rome."

"I believe she's crazy."

"No, she ain't, J'rome — no, she ain't. She knows how you saved up that money, an' she won't take it. She's made so she can't take anybody else's sufferin' to ease hers, an' so's Henry — he's like his mother."

"Can't you make her take it, Uncle Adoniram?"

"She can't make herself take it; but I'm jest as much obliged to ye, J'rome."

Adoniram was about to re-enter the house. "She'll wonder where I be," he muttered, but Jerome stopped him. "If I do begin work on the mill tomorrow," said he, "I sha'n't be able to fetch and carry to Dale, nor to do as much work in Uncle Ozias's shop. Do you suppose you can help out some?"

"I can, if I'm as well as I be now, J'rome."

"Of course, you can earn more than you do now," said Jerome. That was really the errand upon which he had come to the Judds that evening. He had been quite elated with the thought of the pleasure it would give them, when the possibility of larger service — Henry's cure by means of his cherished hoard — had suddenly come to him.

He arranged with Adoniram Judd that he should go to the shop the next morning, then bade him good-night, and turned his own steps thither.

When he came in sight of Ozias Lamb's shop, its window was throwing a long beam of light across the field creeping with dry grass before the frosty wind. When Jerome opened the door, he started to see Ozias seated upon his bench, his head bowed over and hidden upon his idle hands. Jerome closed the door, then stood a moment irresolute, staring at his uncle's dejected figure. "What's the matter, Uncle Ozias?" he asked.

Ozias did not speak, but made a curious, repellent motion with his bowed shoulders.

"Are you sick?"

Again Ozias seemed to shunt him out of the place with that speaking motion of his shoulder.

Jerome went close to him. "Uncle Ozias, I want to know what is the matter?" he said, then started, for suddenly Ozias raised his face and looked at him, his eyes wild under his shaggy grizzle of hair, his mouth twisted in a fierce laugh. "Want to know, do ye?" he cried — "want to know? Well, I'll tell ye. Look at me hard; I'm a sight. Look at me. Here's a man, 'most threescore years and ten, who's been willin' to work, an' has worked, an' 'ain't been consid-ered underwitted, who's been strugglin' to keep a roof over his head an' his wife's, an' bread in their two mouths; jest that, no more. He 'ain't had any children; nobody but himself an' his wife, an' she contented with next to nothin'. Jest a roof an' bread for them — jest that; an' he an able-bodied man, that's worked like a dog — jest that; an' he's got to give it up. Look at him, he's a sight for wise men an' fools." Ozias laughed.

"What on earth do you mean, Uncle Ozias?"

"Simon Basset is goin' to foreclose tomorrow."

Jerome stared at his uncle incredulously. "Why, I thought you had earned plenty to keep the interest up of late years!" he said.

"There was more than present interest to pay; there was back interest, and I've been behind on taxes, and there was an old doctor bill, when I had the fever; an' that wa'n't all — I never told ye, nor anybody. I was fool enough to sign a note for George Henry Green, in Westbrook, some years ago. He come to me with tears in his eyes, said he wouldn't care so much if it wa'n't for his wife an' children; he'd got to raise the money, an' couldn't get nobody to sign his note. I lost every dollar of it. It's been all I could do to pay up, an' I couldn't keep even with the interest. I knew it was comin'."

"How much interest do you owe?" asked Jerome, in an odd voice. He was very pale.

"Two hundred an' seventy dollars — it's twelve per cent."

"And you can't raise it?"

"Might as well try to raise the dead."

"Well, I can let you have it," said Jerome.

"You?"

"Yes."

His uncle looked at him with his sharp, strained eyes; then he made a hoarse noise, between a sob and a cough. "Rob you of that money you've been savin' to build your mill! We'll take to the woods first!" he cried.

"I've saved a good deal more than two hundred and seventy dollars."

"You want every dollar of it for your mill. Don't talk to me."

"I'd want every dollar if I was going to build it, but I am not," said Jerome.

"What d'ye mean? Ain't ye goin' to start it tomorrow?"

"No, I've decided not to."

"Why not, I'd like to know?"

"I'm going to wait until the Dale railroad seems a little nearer. I shouldn't have much business for the mill now if I built it, and there's no use in its standing rotting. I'm going to wait a little."

Poor Ozias Lamb looked at him with his keen old eyes, which were, perhaps, dulled a little by the selfishness of his sore distress. "D'ye mean what ye say, J'rome?" he asked, wistfully, in a tone that was new to him.

"Yes, I do; you can have the money as well as not."

"I'll give ye my note, an' ye can have this piece of land an' the shop — this ain't mortgaged — as security, an' I'll pay ye — fair per cent.," Ozias said, hesitatingly.

"All right," returned Jerome.

"An'," Ozias faltered, "I'll work my fingers to the bone; I'll steal — but you shall have your money back before you are ready to begin the mill."

"That may be quite a while," Jerome said, laughing as openly as a child. His uncle suspected nothing, though once he could scarcely have been deceived.

"I've been round to Uncle Adoniram's tonight," Jerome added, "to get him to come here tomorrow and help with that lot of shoes. I'm going to take up with an offer I've had to cut some wood on shares. I think I can make some money out of it, and it'll be a change from so much shoemaking, for a while."

"You never was the build for a shoemaker," said his uncle.

CHAPTER XXXIII

Jerome gave his mother the same reason which he had given Ozias for the postponement of the mill.

"It seems to me it's dreadful queer you didn't find out it wa'n't best till the day before you were goin' to start work on it," said she, but she suspected nothing.

As for Elmira, she manifested little interest in that or anything else. She was not well that autumn. Elmira's morbidly sensitive temperament was working her harm under the trial of circumstances. Extreme love, sensitiveness, and self-depreciation in some natures produce jealousy as unfailingly as a chemical combination its given result. Elmira, though constantly spurring herself into trust in her lover, was again jealous of him and Lucina Merritt.

Lawrence had been seen riding and walking with Lucina. He had called at the Squire's on several evenings, when Elmira had hoped that he might visit her. She was too proud to mention the matter to Lawrence, but she began to be galled into active resentment by her clandestine betrothal. Why should not everybody know that she had a beau like other girls; that Lawrence was hers, not Lucina Merritt's? Elmira wished, recklessly and defiantly, that people could find out every time that Lawrence came to see her. Whenever she heard a hint to the effect that he was attentive to her, she gave it significance by her bearing. Possibly in that way she herself precipitated matters.

She had not been feeling well for some time, having every afternoon a fever-ache in her limbs and back, and a sensation of weariness which almost prostrated her, when, one evening, Lawrence came, and, an hour afterwards, his father.

Elmira never forgot, as long as she lived, Doctor Prescott's handsome, coldly wrathful old face, as he stood in the parlor door looking at her and Lawrence. He had come straight in, without knocking. Mrs. Edwards had gone to bed, Jerome was not at home.

Lawrence had been sitting on the sofa with Elmira, his arm around her waist. He arose with her, still clasping her, and confronted his father. "Well, father," he said, with an essay at his gay laugh, though he blushed hotly, and then was pale. As for Elmira, she would have slipped to the floor had it not been for her lover's arm.

Doctor Prescott stood looking at them.

"Father, this is the girl I am going to marry," Lawrence said, finally, with a proudly defiant air.

"Very well," replied the doctor; "but when you marry her, it will be without one penny from me, in realization or anticipation. You will have only what your wife brings you."

"I can support my wife myself," returned Lawrence, with a look which was the echo of his father's own.

"So you can, before long, at the expense of your father's practice, which he himself has given you the ability to undermine," said the doctor, in his cold voice. "I bid you both good-evening. You, my son, can come home within a half hour, or you will find the doors locked." With that the doctor went out; there was a creak of cramping wheels, and a lantern-flash in the window, then a roll, and clatter of hoofs.

Elmira showed more decision of spirit than her lover had dreamed was in her. She drove him away, in spite of his protestations. "All is over between us, if you don't go at once — at once," said she, with a strange, hysterical force which intimidated him.

"Elmira, you know I will be true to you, dear. You know I will marry you, in spite of father and the whole world," vowed Lawrence; but he went at her insistence, not knowing, indeed, what else to do.

The next day Elmira wrote him a letter setting him free. When she had sent the letter she sat working some hours longer, then she went up-stairs and to bed. That night she was in a high fever.

Lawrence came, but she did not know it. He had a long talk with Jerome, and almost a quarrel. The poor young fellow, in his wrath and shame of thwarted manliness, would fain have gone to that excess of honor which defeats its own ends. He insisted upon marrying Elmira out of hand. "I'll never give her up — never, I'll tell you that. I've told father so to his face!" cried Lawrence. When he went up-stairs with Jerome and found Elmira in the uneasy stupor of fever, he seemed half beside himself.

"I'm to blame, father's to blame. Oh, poor girl — poor girl," he groaned out, when he and Jerome were down-stairs again.

That night Lawrence had a stormy scene with his father. He burst upon him in his study and upbraided him to his face. "You've almost killed her; she's got a fever. If she lives through it I am going to marry her!" he shouted.

The doctor was pounding some drugs in his mortar. He brought the pestle down with a dull thud, as he replied, without looking at his son. "You will marry her or not, as you choose, my son. I have not forbidden you; I have simply stated the conditions, so far as I am concerned."

The next morning, before light, Lawrence was over to see Elmira. After breakfast his mother came and remained the greater part of the day. Elmira grew worse rapidly. Since Doctor Prescott was out of the question, under the circumstances, a physician from Westbrook was summoned. Elmira was ill several weeks; Lawrence haunted the house; his mother and Paulina Maria did much of the nursing, as Mrs. Edwards was unable. Neither Lawrence nor Mrs. Prescott ever fairly knew if Doctor Prescott was aware that she nursed the sick girl. If he was, he made no sign. He also said nothing more to Lawrence about his visits.

It was nearly spring before Elmira was quite recovered. Her illness had cost so much that Jerome had not been able to make good the deficit occasioned by his loan to Ozias Lamb, as he would otherwise have been. He postponed his mill again until autumn, and worked harder than ever. That summer he tried the experiment of raising some of the fine herbs, such as summer savory, sweet-marjoram, and thyme, for the market. Elmira helped in that. There is always a relief to the soul in bringing it into intimate association with the uniformity of nature. Elmira, bending over the bed of herbs, with the sweet breath of them in her nostrils, gained a certain quiet in her unrest of youth and passion. It was as if she kept step with a mightier movement which tended towards eternity. She had persisted, in spite of Lawrence's entreaties, in her determination that he should cease all attention to her. He had gone away, scarcely understanding, almost angry, with her, but she was firm, with a firmness which she herself had not known to be within her capacity.

She looked older that summer, and there was a staidness in her manner. She always worked over the herb-beds with her back to the road, lest by any chance she should see Lawrence riding by with Lucina.

"I know what you're working so extra hard for," she told Jerome one day, with wistful, keen eyes upon his face.

"I've always worked hard, haven't I?" he said, evasively.

"Yes, you've worked hard, but this is extra hard. Jerome Edwards, you think, maybe, if you can earn enough, you can marry her by-and-by."

Jerome colored, but he met his sister's gaze freely. "Well, suppose I do," said he.

"Oh, Jerome, do you suppose it's any use — do you suppose she will?" Elmira cried out, in a kind of incredulous pity.

"I know she will."

"Did she say so — did she say she would wait? Oh, Jerome!"

"Do you think I would bind her to wait?"

"But she must have owned she liked you. Did she?"

"That's between her and me."

"Don't you feel afraid that she may turn to somebody else? Don't you, Jerome?" Elmira questioned him with a feverish eagerness which puzzled him.

"Not with her," he answered.

Elmira felt comforted by his faith in a way which he did not suspect. It strengthened her own. Perhaps, after all, Lawrence would not care for Lucina; perhaps he would work and wait for her, as, indeed, he had vowed to do. After that Elmira worked over the herb-beds with her face to the road. When Belinda Lamb reported that Lawrence and Lucina had been out riding, and Ann said, with a bitter screw of her nervous little face, "Fish in shallow waters bites easy, especially when there's gold on the hook," she was not much disturbed.

Ann fully abetted her daughter in her resolution to dismiss her suitor, after his father's manifestation. "I guess there's as good fish in the sea as ever was caught," said she, "and I guess Doctor Seth Prescott 'll find out that. If there's them he don't think fit to tie his son's shoestrings, there's them that feels above tyin' 'em."

In September Jerome began work on his mill. He had never been so hopeful in his life. It cost him more self-denial not to go to Lucina and speak out his hope than ever before. He queried with himself if he could not go, then shut his heart, opening like a mouth of hunger for happiness, hard against it. "The mill may burn down; they may not buy the logs. I've got to wait," he told himself.

By early spring the mill was in full operation. The railroad through Dale was surveyed, and work was to be commenced on it the next fall, and Jerome had the contract for the sleepers. Again he wondered if he should not go to Lucina and tell her, and again he resolved to wait. He had made up his mind that he would not speak until a fixed income was guaranteed by at least a year's test.

"I wish they would put railroads through for us every year," he said to the man whom he had secured to help him. He was an elderly man from Granby, who had owned a mill there, which had been sold three years before. He had a tidy sum in bank, and people wondered at his going to work again.

"I 'ain't got so very many years to work," he told Jerome when he sought to hire him, "an' I thought I'd give up for good three years ago; thought I'd take it easy, an' have a comfortable old age. I got fifty dollars more'n I expected when I sold out the mill, an' I laid it out for extras for mother an' me; bought her a sofy an' stuffed rockin'-chair, a new set of dishes, an' some teaspoons, an' some strainers for the windows agin fly-time. 'Now, mother,' says I, 'we'll jest lay down in the daytime, an' rock, an' eat with our new spoons out of our new dishes, an' keep the flies out, the rest of our lives.'

"But mother she looked real sober. 'What's the matter?' says I.

"'Nothin',' says she, 'only I was thinkin' about your father.'

"'What about him?' says I.

"'Nothin',' says she, 'only I remember mother's sayin', when he quit work, he wouldn't live long. She always said it was a bad sign.'

"That settled me. I remembered father didn't live six months after he quit work, an' grandfather before him, an' I'd every reason to think it run in the family. So says I to mother, 'Well, I'm havin' too good a time livin' to throw it away settin' in rockin'-chairs an' layin' down in the daytime. If work is goin' to keep up the picnic a while longer, why, I'm goin' to work.'

"So the very next day I hired out to the man that bought my mill, an' there I've worked ever since, till now, when he's got his son he wants to give the job to. I'll go with ye, an' welcome, for a spell. Mother ain't afeard to stay alone, an' I'll go home over Sundays. Ye need somebody who knows somethin' about a mill, if ye're green at it yourself."

This man, whose name was Martin Cheeseman, was hoary with age, but far from being past his prime of work. He had a large and shambling strength of body and limb, like an old bear, and his sinews were, of their kind, as tough as those of the ancient woods which he severed.

One afternoon, when the mill had been in operation about two months, Squire Eben Merritt, John Jennings, and Colonel Lamson came through from the thick woods into the clearing. The Squire bore his fishing-rod and dangled a string of fine trout. John Jennings had a book under his arm.

When they emerged into the clearing, the Colonel sat down upon a stump and wiped his red face. The veins in his forehead and neck were swollen purple, and he breathed hard. "It's hotter than seven devils," he gasped.

"Devils are supposed to be acclimated," John Jennings remarked, softly. He stood looking about him. The Squire had gone into the mill, where Jerome was at work.

Martin Cheeseman was outside, shearing from lengths of logs some last straggling twigs before they were taken into the mill for sawing. The old man's hat had lost its brim, and sat back on his head like a crown; some leaves were tangled in his thick, gray fleece of hair and beard. His shaggy arms were bare; he wielded his hatchet with energy, grimacing at every stroke.

"He might be the god Pan putting his fallen trees out of their last agonies," said Jennings, dreamily, and yet half laughing, as if at himself, for the fancy.

The Colonel only groaned in response. He fanned himself with his hat. Jennings stood, backed up against a tree, surveying things, his fine, worn face full of a languid humor and melancholy.

The place looked like a sylvan slaughter-field. The ground was thick-set with the mangled and hacked stumps of great chestnut-trees, and strewn with their lifeless limbs and trunks, as with members of corpses; every stump, as Jennings surveyed it with fanciful gaze, looked with its spread of supporting roots upon the surface, curiously like a great foot of a woody giant, which no murderer could tear loose from its hold in its native soil.

All the clearing was surrounded with thickets of light-green foliage, amidst which clouds of white alder unfolded always in the soft wind with new surfaces of sweetness.

However, all the fragrant evidence of the new leaves and blossoms was lost and overpowered here. One perceived only that pungent aroma of death which the chestnut-trees gave out from their fresh wounds and their spilled sap of life. One also could scarcely hear the spring birds for the broad whir of the saw-mill, which seemed to cut the air as well as the logs. Even the gurgling rush of the brook was lost in it, but not the roar of water over the dam.

The Squire came out of the mill, whither he had been to say a good word to Jerome, and stood by Martin Cheeseman. "Lord," he said, "think of the work those trees had to grow, and the fight they made for their lives, and then along comes a man with an axe, and breaks in a minute what he can never make nor mend! What d'ye mean by it, eh?"

Martin Cheeseman looked at him with shrewd, twinkling eyes. He was waist-deep in the leafy twigs and boughs as in a nest. "Well," he said, "we're goin' to turn 'em into somethin' of more account than trees, an' that's railroad-sleepers; an' that's somethin' the way Natur' herself manages, I reckon. Look at the caterpillar an' the butterfly. Mebbe a railroad-sleeper is a butterfly of a tree, lookin' at it one way."

"That's all very well, but how do you suppose the tree feels?" said the Squire, hotly.

"Not bein' a tree, an' never havin' been a tree, so's to remember it, I ain't able to say," returned the old man, in a dry voice; "but, mebbe, lookin' at it on general principles, it ain't no more painful for a tree to be cut down into a railroad-sleeper than it is for a man to be cut down into an angel."

John Jennings laughed.

"You'd make a good lawyer on the defence," said the Squire, good-naturedly, "but, by the Lord Harry, if all the trees of the earth were mine, men might live in tents and travel in caravans till doomsday for all I'd cut one down!"

The Colonel and Jennings did not go into the mill, but they nodded and sang out good-naturedly to Jerome as they passed. He could not leave — he had an extra man to feed the saw that day, and had been rushing matters since daybreak — but he looked out at them with a radiant face from his noisy interior, full of the crude light of fresh lumber and sawdust.

The Squire's friendly notice had pleased his very soul.

"That's a smart boy," panted the Colonel, when they had passed.

"Yes, sir; he's the smartest boy in this town," assented the Squire, with a nod of enthusiasm.

Not long after they emerged from the woods into the road they reached Jennings's house, and he left his friends.

The Colonel lived some quarter of a mile farther on. He had reached his gate, when he said, abruptly, to the Squire, "Look here, Eben, you remember a talk we had once about Jerome Edwards and your girl?"

The Squire stared at him. "Yes; why?"

"Nothing, only seeing him just now set me to wondering if you were still of the same mind about it."

"If being willing that Lucina should have the man she sets her heart on is the same mind, of course I am; but, good Lord, Jack, that's all over! He hasn't been to the house for a year, and Lucina never thinks of him!"

Colonel Lamson laughed wheezily. "Well, that's all I wanted to know, Eben."

"What made you ask me that?" asked the Squire, suspiciously.

"Nothing; seeing Jerome and his mill brought it to mind. Well, I'll be along tonight."

"That's all over," the Squire called out again to the Colonel, going slowly up the hill to the house door. However, when he got home, he questioned Abigail.

"I haven't heard Lucina mention Jerome Edwards's name for

months," said she, "and he never comes here; but she seems perfectly contented and happy. I think that's all over."

"I thought so," said Eben.

Abigail was preparing the punch, for the Squire expected his friends that evening. Jennings came first; some time after Means and Lamson arrived. They had a strange air of grave excitement and elation.

When the game of cards was fairly under way, the Colonel played in a manner which confused them all.

"By the Lord Harry, Jack, this is the third time you've thrown away an honor!" the Squire roared out, finally. "Is it the punch that's gone to your head?"

"No, Eben," replied the Colonel, in a hoarse voice, with solemn and oratorical cadences, as if he rose to address a meeting. "It is not the punch. I am *used to punch. It is money. I've just had word that — that old mining stock I bought when I was in the service, and haven't thought worth more than a New England sheep farm, has been sold for sixty-five thousand dollars.*"

CHAPTER XXXIV

The next week Colonel Lamson went to Boston, and took his friend John Jennings with him. Whether the trip was purely a business one, or was to be regarded in the light of a celebration of the Colonel's good fortune, never transpired.

Upham people exchanged wishes to the effect that John Jennings and Colonel Lamson might not take, in their old age, to sowing again the wild oats of their youth. "John Jennings drank himself most into his grave; an' as for Colonel Lamson, it's easy enough to see that he's always had his dram, when he felt like it. If they get home sober an' alive with all that money, they're lucky," people said. It was the general impression in Upham that the Colonel had gone to Boston with his sixty-five thousand dollars in his pocket. Lawyer Means's ancient relative, who served as housekeeper, was reported to have confessed that she was on tenterhooks about it.

However, in a week the Colonel and his friend returned, and the most anxious could find nothing in their appearance to justify their gloomy fears. They had never looked so spick and span and prosperous within the memory of Upham, for both of them were clad in glossiest new broadcloth, of city cut, and both wore silk bell-hats, which gave them the air of London dandies. Jennings, moreover, displayed in his fine shirt-front a new diamond pin, and the Colonel stepped out with stately flourishes of a magnificent gold-headed cane.

Soon it was told on good authority that the lawyer's housekeeper, and John Jennings's also, had a present from the Colonel of a rich black satin gown, that the lawyer had a gold-headed cane — which he was, indeed, seen to carry, holding it stiff and straight, like a roll of parchment, with never a flourish — and the Squire a gun mounted in silver, and such a fishing-rod as had never been seen in the village. When Lucina Merritt came to meeting the Sunday after the Colonel's return, there glistened in her little ears, between her curls, some diamond ear-drops, and Abigail wore a shawl which had never been seen in Upham before.

Lawyer Means's female relative, and Jennings's housekeeper, said, emphatically, that they didn't believe that either of them drank a drop of anything stronger than water all the time they were gone.

The Colonel was radiant with satisfaction; he went about with his face beaming as unreservedly as a child's who has gotten a treasure. He often confided to Means his perfect delight in his new wealth. "Hang it all, Means," he would say, "I wouldn't find a word of fault, not a word, I'd strut like a peacock, if that poor little girl I married was only alive, and I could buy her a damned thing out of it; then there's something else, Means —" the Colonel's face would take on an expression of mingled seriousness and humor — "Means," he would conclude, in a hoarse, facetious whisper, "I bought those stocks when I was first married; thought I'd got to pitch in and provide for my family, and in order to save enough money to get them I ran in debt for a new uniform and some cavalry boots and a pony, and damned if I know if I ever paid for them."

Jerome, going to the mill one day shortly afterwards, reached the Means house as the Colonel was coming down the hill. "Stop a moment," the Colonel called, and Jerome waited until he reached him. "Fine day," said the Colonel.

"Yes, sir, 'tis," replied Jerome; then he added, "I was glad to hear of your good fortune, sir."

"Suppose," said the Colonel, abruptly, "that twenty-five thousand of it had come to you, what would you have done with it?"

Jerome looked at him in a bewildered fashion. "It wasn't mine, and there's no use talking about it," he said.

"What would you do with it? Out with it! Would you stick to that bargain you made in Robinson's that evening?"

Jerome hesitated.

"You needn't be afraid to speak," urged the Colonel. "If you'd stick to it, say so. I sha'n't call it any reflection upon me; I haven't the slightest intention of giving twenty-five thousand dollars to the poor, and if you've changed your mind, say so."

"I haven't changed my mind, and I would stick to it," Jerome replied then.

"And," said the Colonel, "you are sticking to that other resolution of yours, to work until you win a certain fair lady, are you?"

Jerome colored high. He was inclined to be indignant, but there was a strange earnestness in the Colonel's manner.

"I'm not the sort of fellow not to stick to a resolution of that kind when I've once made it," he replied, shortly.

The Colonel chuckled. "Well, I didn't think you were," he returned — "didn't think you were, Jerome. That's all. Good-day." With that, to Jerome's utter astonishment, Colonel Lamson trudged laboriously up the hill to the Means house again.

"He must have come down just to ask me those questions," thought Jerome, and thought with more bewilderment still that the Colonel must even have been watching for him. He had no conception of his meaning, but he laughed to himself at the bare fancy of twenty-five thousand dollars coming to him, and also at the suggestion that he would not be true to his resolution to win Lucina. Jerome was beginning to feel as if she were already won. The next spring, if he continued to prosper, he had decided to speak to her, and, as the months went on, nothing happened to discourage him.

The next winter the snows were uncommonly heavy. They began before Thanksgiving and came in thick storms. There were great drifts in all the door-yards, the stone walls and fences were hidden, the trees stood in deep, swirling hollows of snow. Now and then a shed-roof broke under the frozen weight; one walked through the village street as through clear-cut furrows of snow, all the shadows were blue, there was a dazzle of glacier light over the whole village when the sun arose. However, it was a fine winter for Jerome, as far as his work was concerned. Wood is drawn easily on sleds, and the snow air nerves one for sharp labors. Jerome calculated that by May he should be not only doing a prosperous business, but should have a snug little sum clear. Then he would delay no longer.

On the nineteenth day of March came the last snow-storm, and the worst of the season. Martin Cheeseman went home early. Jerome did not stay in the mill long after he left. The darkness was settling down fast, and he could do little by himself.

Moreover, an intense eagerness to be at home seized him. He began to imagine that something had happened to his mother or Elmira, and imagination of evil was so foreign to him that it had almost the force of conviction.

He fell also to thinking of his father, inconsequently, as it seemed, yet it was not so, for imagined disasters lead back by retrograde of sequence to memories of real ones.

He lived over again his frenzied search for his father, his discovery of the hat on the shore of the deep pond. "Poor father!" he muttered.

All the way home this living anxiety for his mother and sister, and this dead sorrow haunted him. He thought as he struggled through the snow, his face bent before the drive of the sleet as before a flail of ice, how often in all weathers his father had traversed this same road, how his own feet could scarcely step out of his old tracks. He thought how many a night, through such a storm as this, his father had toiled wearily home, and with no such fire of youth and hope in his heart to cheer him on. "Father must have given up a long time before he died," he said to himself.

The imagination of his father plodding homeward in his old harness of hopeless toil grew so strong that his own identity paled. He seemed to lose all ambition and zeal, a kind of heredity of discouragement overspread him. "I don't know but I'll have to give up, finally, the way he did," he muttered, panting under the buffeting of the snow wind.

He met no one on his way home. Once a loaded wood-sled came up behind him with a faint creak and jingle of harness, then the straining flanks of the horse, the cubic pile of wood shaded out of shape by the snow, the humped back of the driver on the top, passed out of sight, as behind a slanting white curtain. The village houses receded through shifting distances of pale gloom; one could scarcely distinguish the white slants of their roofs, and the lamp-lights which shone out newly in some of the windows made rosy nimbuses.

When Jerome drew near his own home he looked eagerly, and saw, with relief, that the white thickness of the storm was suffused with light opposite the kitchen windows.

"Everything all right?" he asked, when he entered, stamping and shaking himself.

Elmira was toasting bread, and she turned her flushed face wonderingly. "Yes; why shouldn't it be?" she said.

"No reason why. It's an awful storm."

Ann was knitting fast, sitting over against a window thick with clinging shreds of snow. Her face was in the shadow, but she looked as if she had been crying. She did not speak when Jerome entered.

"What ails mother?" he whispered to Elmira, following her into the pantry when he had a chance.

"She's been telling a dream she had last night about father, and it made her feel bad. Hush!"

When they were all seated at the supper-table, Ann, of her own accord, began to talk again of her dream.

"I've been tellin' your sister about a dream I had last night," said she, with a curious, tearful defiance, "an' I'm goin' to tell you. It won't hurt you any to have your poor father brought to mind once in a while."

"Of course you can tell it, mother, though I don't need that to bring father to mind. I was thinking about him all the way home," Jerome answered.

"Well, I guess you don't often think about him all the way home. I guess you and your sister both don't think about your poor father, that worked and slaved for you, enough to hurt you. I had a dream last night that I 'ain't been able to get out of my mind all day. I dreamt that I was in this room, an' it was stormin', jest as it is now. I could hear the wind whistlin' an' howlin', an' the windows were all thick with snow. I dreamt I had a little baby in my arms that was sick; it was cryin' an' moanin', an' I was walkin' up an' down, up an' down, tryin' to quiet it. I didn't have my rheumatism, could walk as well as anybody. All of a sudden, as I was walkin', I smelt flowers, an' there on the hearth-stone was a rose-bush, all in bloom. I went up an' picked a rose, an' shook it in the baby's face to please it, an' then I heard a strange noise, that drowned out the wind in the chimney an' the baby's cryin'. It sounded like cattle bellowing, dreadful loud and mournful. I laid the baby down in the rockin'-chair, an' first thing I knew it wasn't there. Instead of it there was a most beautiful bird, like a dove, as white as snow. It flew 'round my head once, and then it was gone. I thought it went up chimney.

"The cattle bellowing sounded nearer, an' I could hear them trampin'. I run to the front door, an' there they were, comin' down the road, hundreds of 'em, horns a-tossin' an' tails a-lashin', flingin' up the snow like water. I clapped to the front door, an' bolted it, an' run into the parlor, an' looked out of the window, an' there on the other side, as plain as I ever see it in my life, was your father's face — there was my husband's face.

"He didn't look a day older than when he left, an' his eyes an' his mouth were smilin' as I hadn't seen 'em since he was a young man.

"'Oh, Able!' says I. 'Oh, Abel!' An' then the face wa'n't there, an' I heard a noise behind me, an' looked around.

"I couldn't believe my eyes when I saw that parlor. All the chairs an' the sofa were covered with my weddin'-dress, that was made over for Elmira; the window-curtains were made of it, an' the table-spread. Thinks I, 'How was there enough of that silk, when we had hard work to get Elmira's dress out?'

"Then I saw, in the middle of the room, a great long thing, all covered over with silk, an' I thought it was a coffin. I went up to it, an' there was Abel's hat on it, the one he wore when he went away. I took the hat off, an' the weddin'-silk, an' there was a coffin.

"I thought it was Abel's. I raised the lid and looked. The coffin was full of beautiful clear water, an' I could see through it the bottom, all covered with bright gold dollars. I leant over it, and there was my own face in the water, jest as plain as in a lookin'-glass, an' there was Abel's beside it. Then I turned around quick, an' there was Abel — there was my husband, standin' there alive an' well. Then I woke up."

Ann ended with a hysterical sob. Jerome and Elmira exchanged terrified glances.

"That was a beautiful dream, mother," Jerome said, soothingly. "Now try to eat your supper."

"It's been so real all day. I feel as if — your father had come an' gone again," Ann sobbed.

"Try and eat some of this milk-toast, mother; it's real nice," urged Elmira.

But Ann could eat no supper. She seemed completely unstrung, for some mysterious reason. They persuaded her to go to bed early; but she was not asleep when they went up-stairs, about ten o'clock, for she called out sharply to know if it was still snowing.

"No, mother," Jerome answered, "I have just looked out, and there are some stars overhead. I guess the storm is over."

"Oh, Jerome, you don't suppose mother is going to be sick, do you?" Elmira whispered, when they were on the stairs.

"No, I guess she's only nervous about her dream. The storm may have something to do with it, too."

"Oh, Jerome, I feel exactly as if something was going to happen!"

"Nonsense," said Jerome, laughing. "You are nervous yourself. I'll give you and mother some valerian, both of you."

"Jerome, I am *sure* something is going to happen."

"It would be strange if something didn't. Something is happening all over the earth with every breath we draw."

"Jerome, I mean to *us!*"

Jerome gave his sister a little push into her room. "Go to bed, and to sleep," said he, "and leave your door open if you're scared, and I'll leave mine."

Jerome himself could not get to sleep soon; once or twice Elmira spoke to him, and he called back reassuringly, but his own nerves were at a severe tension. "What has got into us all?" he thought, impatiently. It was midnight before he lost himself, and he had slept hardly an hour when he wakened with a great start.

A wild clamor, which made his blood run cold, came from below. He leaped out of bed and pulled on his trousers, hearing all the while, as in a dream, his mother's voice shrilling higher and higher. "Oh, Abel, Abel, Abel! Oh, Abel!"

Elmira, with a shawl over her night-gown, bearing a flaring candle, rushed across the landing from her room. "Oh," she gasped, "what is it? what is it?"

"I guess mother has been dreaming again," Jerome replied, hoarsely, but the thought was in his mind that his mother had gone mad.

"There's — cold air — coming — in," Elmira said, in her straining voice. "The front door is — wide open."

At that Jerome pushed her aside and rushed down the stairs and into the kitchen.

There stood his mother over an old man, seated in her rocking-chair. There she stood, pressing his white head against her breast, calling over and over again in a tone through whose present jubilation sounded the wail of past woe, "Oh, Abel, Abel, Abel!"

Jerome looked at them. He wondered, dazedly, if he were really there and awake, or asleep and dreaming up-stairs in his bed. Elmira came close beside him and clutched his arm — even that did not clear his bewildered perceptions into certainty. It is always easier for the normal mind, when confronted by astonishing spectacles, to doubt its own accuracy rather than believe in them. "Do *you* see him?" he whispered, sharply, to Elmira.

"Yes; who is it? *Who* is it?"

Then Jerome, in his utter bewilderment, spoke out the secret which he had kept since childhood.

"It can't be father," said he — "it can't be. I found his hat on the shore of the Dead Hole. Father drowned himself there."

At the sound of his voice Ann turned around. "It's your father!" she cried out, sharply — "it's your father come home. Abel, here's the children."

Jerome eyed a small japanned box, or trunk, on the floor, a stout stick, and a handkerchief parcel. He noted then clots of melting snow where the old man had trod. Somehow the sight of the snow did more to restore his faculties than anything else. "For Heaven's sake, let us go to work!" he cried to Elmira, "or he'll die. He's exhausted with tramping through the snow. Get some of that brandy in the cupboard, quick, while I start up the fire."

"Is it father? Oh, Jerome, is it father?"

"Mother says so. Get the brandy, quick."

Jerome stirred the fire into a blaze, and put on the kettle, then he went to his mother and laid his hand on her shoulder. "Now, mother," he said, "he must be put into a warm bed."

"Yes, put him into his own bed — his own bed!" shrieked his mother. "Oh, Abel, dear soul, come and sleep in your own bed again, after all these years! Poor man, poor man, you've got home to your own bed!"

Jerome gave his mother's thin, vibrating shoulder a firm shake. "Mother," he said, "tell me — you must tell me — is this man father?"

"Don't you know him? Don't you know your own father? Look at him." Ann threw back her head and pointed at the old worn face on her breast.

Jerome stared at it. "Where — did he come — from?" he panted.

"I don't know. He's come. Oh, Abel, Abel, you've come home!"

"Give me some of that brandy, quick," Jerome called to Elmira, who stood trembling, holding the bottle and glass. He poured out some brandy, and, with a teaspoon, fed the old man, a few drops at a time. Presently he raised his head feebly, but it sank back. He tried to speak. "Don't try to talk," said Jerome; "wait till you're rested. Mother, let him alone now; sit down there. Elmira, you must try and help me a little."

"If you've got to be helped, I'll help," cried Ann, fiercely.

With that his mother, who had not walked since he could remember, ran into the bedroom, and began spreading the sheets smooth and shaking the pillows.

The old man was a light-weight. Jerome almost carried him into the bedroom, and laid him on the bed. He fed him with more brandy, and put hot-water bottles around him. Presently he breathed evenly in a sweet sleep. Ann sat by his side, holding his hand, and would not stir, though Jerome besought her to go upstairs to Elmira's room.

"I guess I don't leave him to stray away again," said she.

Out in the kitchen, Elmira pressed close to Jerome. "Is it," she whispered in his ear — "is it father?"

Jerome nodded.

"How do you know?"

"I remember."

"Are you sure?"

"Yes, he's grown old, but I remember."

"Where — did he — come from?"

"I don't know. We must wait till he wakes up."

The brother and sister huddled close together over the fire, and waited. Elmira held Jerome's hand fast in her little cold one.

"What's in that little tin trunk?"

"Hush; I don't know."

"Jerome, mother *walked!*"

"Hush; I saw her."

It was an hour before they heard a sound from the bedroom. Then Ann's voice rang out clearly, and another, husky and feeble, sounded in response. Jerome and Elmira went into the room, and stood beside the bed.

"Here's the children, Abel," said Ann.

The face on the pillow looked stranger than before to Jerome. When half unconscious it had worn a certain stern restraint, which coincided with his old memories; now it was full of an innocent pleasantness, like a child's, which puzzled him. The old man began talking eagerly too, and Jerome remembered his father as very slow-spoken, though it might have been the slowness of self-control, not temperament.

"How they've grown!" he said, looking at his children and then at Ann. "That's Jerome, and that's Elmira. How I've lotted on this day." He held out a feeble hand; Elmira took it, timidly, then leaned over and kissed him. Jerome took it then, and it seemed to him like a hand from the grave. His doubt passed; he knew that this man was his father.

"I hadn't got asleep," Ann said; "I was thinkin' about him. I heard somebody at the front door; I got up and went; I knew it was him."

The old man smiled at them all. "I'll tell you where I've been," he said. "It won't take long. I was behindhand in that interest money. I couldn't earn enough to get ahead nohow. I was nothin' but a drag on you all, nothin' but a drag. All of a sudden, that day when I went away, I reasoned of it out. Says I, that mortgage will be foreclosed; my stayin' where I be won't make no difference about that. I ain't doin' anythin' for my family, anyway. I'm wore out tryin', and it's no use. If I go away, I can do more for 'em than if I stay. I can save every cent I earn, till I get enough to pay that mortgage up. I'll get a chance that way to do somethin' for 'em. So I went."

The utter inconsequence of his father's reasoning struck Jerome like a chill. "His mind isn't just right," he thought.

"Where did you go, Abel?" asked his mother.

"To West Linfield."

"What!" cried Jerome. "That's only twenty miles away."

Abel Edwards laughed with childlike cunning. "I know it," he said. "I went to work on Jabez Summers's farm there. It's way up the hill-road; nobody ever came there that knew me. I took another name, too — called myself Ephraim Green. I've saved up fifteen hundred dollars. It's there in that little tin chist. I bought that of Summers for a shillin', to keep my money in. There's five hundred in gold, an' the rest in bank-bills. You needn't worry now, mother. We'll pay that mortgage up tomorrow."

"The mortgage is all paid. We've paid it, Abel," cried Ann.

"Paid! The mortgage ain't paid!"

"Yes, we've paid it. We all earnt money an' paid it."

"Then we can keep the money," said the old man, happily. "We can keep it, mother; I thought it would go kinder hard partin' with it. I've worked so hard to save it. I 'ain't had many clothes, an' I 'ain't ever been to meetin' lately, my coat got so ragged."

Elmira was crying.

"How did you get here tonight, father?" Jerome asked, huskily.

"I walked from West Linfield; started yesterday afternoon. I come as far as Westbrook, an' it began to snow. I put up at Hayes's Tavern."

"At Hayes's Tavern, with all that money!" exclaimed Elmira.

"Why, ain't they honest there?" asked the old man, quickly.

"Yes, father, they're all right, I guess. Go on."

"They seemed real honest," said his father. "I told 'em all about it, and they acted real interested. Mis' Hayes she fried me some slapjacks for supper. I had a good room, with a man who was goin' to Boston this mornin'. He started afore light; he was gone when I woke up. I stayed there till afternoon, then I started out. I got a lift as far as the Corners, then I walked a spell and went into a house, where they give me some supper, and give me another lift as far as the Stone Hill Meetin'-house. I've been trampin' since. It was ruther hard, on account of the roads bein' some drifted, but it's stopped snowin'."

"Why didn't you come on the coach, Abel, when you had all that money?" asked Ann, pitifully. "I wonder it hadn't killed you."

"Do you suppose I was goin' to spend that money for coach hire? You dun'no' how awful hard it come, mother," replied the old man. He closed his eyes as he spoke; he was weary almost to death.

"He'll go to sleep again if you don't talk, mother," Jerome whispered.

"Well, I'll lay down side of him, an' mebbe we'll both go to sleep," his mother said, with a strange docility. Jerome assisted her into the bed, then he and Elmira went back to the kitchen.

Jerome motioned to Elmira to be quiet, and cautiously lifted the little japanned trunk and passed it from one hand to the other, as if testing its weight. Elmira watched him with her bewildered, tearful eyes. Finally he tiptoed softly out with it, motioning her to follow with the candle. They went into the icy parlor and closed the door.

"What's the matter, Jerome?" Elmira whispered.

"I'm afraid there may be something wrong with the money. I'm going to find it out before he does, if there is."

There was a little padlock on the trunk, but it was tied together with a bit of leather shoestring, not locked. Jerome took out his jack-knife, cut the string, and opened the trunk. Elmira held the candle while he examined the contents. There was a large old wallet stuffed with bank-notes, also several parcels of them tied up carefully.

"It's just as I thought," Jerome muttered.

"What?"

"Some of the money is gone. The gold isn't here. It might have been the man who roomed with him at Hayes's Tavern. There have been queer things done there before now. All I wonder is, he didn't take it all."

"Oh, Jerome, it isn't gone?"

"Yes, the gold is gone. Here is the bag it was in. The thief left that. Suppose he thought he might be traced by it."

"Oh, poor father, poor father, what will he do!" moaned Elmira.

"He'll do nothing. He'll never know it," said Jerome.

"What do you mean?"

"Wait here a minute." Jerome went noiselessly out of the room and up-stairs. He returned soon with a leathern bag, which he carried with great caution. "I'm trying to keep this from jingling," he whispered.

"Oh, Jerome, what is it?"

Jerome laughed and untied the mouth of the bag. "You must help me put it into the other bag; every dollar will have to be counted out separately."

"Oh, Jerome, is it money you've saved?"

"Yes; and don't you ever tell of it to either of them, or anybody else, as long as you live. I guess poor father sha'n't know he's lost any of his money he's worked so hard to get, if I can help it."

CHAPTER XXXV

A stranger passing Abel Edwards's house the day after his return might have gotten the impression that one of the functions of village life — a wedding or a funeral — was going on there. From morning until late at night the people came down the road, wading through the snow, the men with trousers tucked into boots, the women with yarn-stockings over their shoes, their arms akimbo, pinning their kilted petticoats to their hips. Many drove there in sleighs, tilting to the drifts. The Edwards's door-yard was crowded with teams.

All the relatives who had come fourteen years before to Abel Edwards's funeral came now to his resurrection. They had gotten the news of it in such strange, untraceable ways, that it seemed almost like mental telegraphy. The Greens of Westbrook were there — the three little girls in blue, now women grown. One of them came with her husband and baby; another with a blushing lout of a lad, to whom she was betrothed; and the third, with a meek blue eye, on the watch for a possible lover in the company. The Lawson sisters, from Granby, arrived early in the day, being conveyed thither by an obliging neighbor. Amelia Stokes rode to Upham on the butcher's wagon, in lieu of another conveyance, and her journey was a long one, necessitating hot ginger-tea and the toasting of her slim feet at the fire upon her arrival. Amelia was clad in mourning for her old mother, who had died the year before. At intervals she wept furtively, incited to grief by recollections of her mother, which the place and occasion awakened.

"Every once in a while it comes over me how poor mother relished them hot biscuits and that tea at your funeral," she whispered softly to Abel, who smiled with childlike serenity in response.

All day Abel sat in state, which was, however, intensified in the afternoon by a new suit of clothes, which Jerome had purchased in Dale. As soon as Jerome returned with it, he was hustled into the bedroom with his father.

"Get your father into 'em quick, before anybody else comes," said Ann Edwards. She was dressed in her best, and Elmira had further adorned her with a little worked lace kerchief of her own, fastened at the bosom with a sprig of rose-geranium leaves and blossoms. Ann had confined herself to her chair since arising that morning. She made no allusion to her walking the night before, and seemed to expect assistance as usual.

"Do you suppose mother can't walk this morning?" Elmira

whispered to Jerome.

"Hush," he replied, "don't bother her with it unless she speaks of it herself. I have a book which gives instances of people recovering under strong excitement, and then going back to where they were before. I don't believe mother can walk, or she would."

Ann Edwards and Abel sat side by side on the sofa in the parlor, and the visitors came and greeted them, with a curious manner, which had in it not so much of the joy of greeting, as awe and a solemn perplexity. Always, after shaking hands with the united couple, they whispered furtively to one another that Abel Edwards was much changed, they should scarcely have known him. Yet, with their simple understandings, they could not have defined the change, which they recognized plainly enough, for it lay not so much in form and feature as in character. Abel Edwards's hair was white, he was somewhat fuller in his face, but otherwise he was little altered, so far as mere physical characteristics went. The change in him was subtler. Jerome had noticed it the night before, and it was evidently a permanent condition. Abel Edwards, from being a reserved man, with the self-containment of one who is buffeted by unfair odds of fate, yet will not stoop to vain appeals, but holds always to the front his face of dumb dissent and purpose, was become a garrulous and happy child. People hinted that Abel Edwards's mind was affected, but it was a question whether that was the case, or whether it was the simple result of his abandonment, fourteen years before, of the reins which had held an original nature in check. He might possibly have merely, when renouncing his toil over the up-grade of life, slipped back to his first estate, and thus have experienced in one sense no change at all.

Many of Abel's old friends and neighbors were not fully convinced of the desirability of his reappearance. When a man has been out of his foothold in the crowd for fourteen years, he cannot regain it without undue jostling of people's shoulders, and prejudices even. The resurrection of the dead might have, if the truth were told, uncomfortable and perplexing features for their nearest and dearest, and Abel Edwards had been practically dead and buried.

"They were gettin' along real well before he come; of course, they're glad to see him, but I dun'no' whether they'll get along as well with him or not," proclaimed Mrs. Green of Westbrook, with the very aggressiveness of frankness, and many looked assent.

Abel's wife had no question in her inmost heart of its utter blessedness at his return, but her grief at his loss had never healed. For that resolute feminine soul, which had fought on in spite of it, her husband had died anew every morning of those fourteen years when she awoke to consciousness of life; but it was different with his children. For both of them the old wounds had closed; it was now like tearing them asunder, for it is often necessary to revive an old pain to fully appreciate a present joy. Had Jerome and Elmira been older at the time of their father's disappearance, it would have been otherwise, but as it was, their old love for him had been obliterated, not merely by time and absence, but growth. It was practically impossible, though they would not have owned it to themselves, for them to love their father, when he first returned, as they had used. They were painfully anxious to be utterly faithful, and had an odd sort of tender but imaginative pity towards him, but they could grasp no more. Both of them hesitated when they said father; every time they returned home and found him there it was with a sensation of surprise.

Three days after Abel Edwards's return came one of the severest rain-storms ever known in Upham. The storm began before light; when people first looked out in the morning their windows were glazed with streaming wet, but it did not reach its full fury until eleven o'clock. Then the rain fell in green and hissing sheets.

"Gorry," Martin Cheeseman said, looking out of the mill door, which seemed to open into a solid wall of water, "looks as if the great deep was turned upsidedown overhead. If it keeps on this way long there'll be mischief."

"Think there'll be danger to the mill?" Jerome asked, quickly.

"No, I guess not, it's built strong; but I wouldn't resk the solid airth long under Niagry. Where you goin'?"

"Down to Robinson's store. I want to get something."

"Well, I should think you were halfwitted to go out in this soak if you could keep a roof over your head," cried Cheeseman, but Jerome was gone.

He bought strong rope at Robinson's store, and before night the mill was anchored to some stout trees and one great granite bowlder. Cheeseman helped grumblingly. "I shall get laid up with rheumatiz out of it," he said; "an' this rain can't keep on, it ain't in natur', out of the Old Testament."

But the rain continued all that day and night, and the next day, with almost unremitting fury. At times it seemed more than rain — there were liquid shafts reaching from earth to sky. By noon of the second day, half the cellars in the village were flooded; coops floated in slatted wrecks over fields; the roads were knee-deep in certain places; the horses drew back — it was like fording a stream. People began to be alarmed.

"If this keeps on an hour longer, there'll be the devil to pay," Squire Eben Merritt said, when he came home to dinner. He had been down to Lawyer Means's and crossed the Graystone brook, which was now a swollen river.

"What will happen?" asked Abigail.

"Happen? The Main Street bridge will go, and the saw-mill, and the Lord knows what else."

Lucina turned pale.

"It will be hard on Jerome if he loses his mill," said her mother.

"Well, the boy will lose it if it keeps on," returned the Squire. "He's working hard, with four men to help him; they're loading it with stones and anchoring it with ropes, but it can't stand much more. I miss my guess, if the foundations are not undermined now."

Lucina said not a word, but as soon as she could she slipped up-stairs to her chamber and prayed that her Heavenly Father would save poor Jerome's mill, and stop the rain; but it kept on raining. When Lucina heard the fierce dash of it on her window-pane, like an angry dissent to her petition, she prayed more fervently, sobbing softly in the whiteness of her maiden bed; still it rained.

The mighty body of snow, pierced in a thousand places by the rain as by liquid fingers, settled with inconceivable rapidity. Great drifts which had slanted to the tops of north windows twelve hours before were almost gone. The wide snow-levels of the fields were all honey-combed and glistening here and there with pools. The trees dripped with clots of melting snow, there were avalanches from the village roofs, and even in the houses was heard the roar of the brook. It was, however, no longer a brook, not even a river, but a torrent. It over spread its banks on either side. Forest trees stood knee-deep in it, their branches swept it. At three o'clock Jerome's mill was surrounded, though on one side by only a rippling shallow of water. He had plenty of helpers all day; for if his dam and mill went, there was danger to the Main Street bridge. Now they had all taken advantage of the last firm footing, and left the mill. They had joined a watching group on a rise of ground beyond the flood. The rain was slacking somewhat, and half the male portion of the village seemed assembled, watching for the possible destruction of the mill. Now and then came a hoarse shout across the swelling water to Jerome. He alone remained in his mill, standing by the great door that overlooked the dam and the falls. He was high above it, but the spray wet his face.

The great yellow flood came leaping tumultuously over the dam, and rebounding in wild fountains of spray. Trees came with it, and joists — a bridge somewhere above had gone. Strange, uncanny wreckage, which could not be defined, bobbed on the torrent, and took the plunge of annihilation over the dam. Every now and then came a cry and a groan of doubt from the watchers, who thought this or that might be a drowned man.

Besides the thundering rush of the water there were other sounds, which Jerome seemed to hear with all his nervous system. The mill hummed with awful musical vibrations, it strained and creaked like a ship at sea.

The hoarse shouts from the shore for him to leave the mill were redoubled, but he paid no heed. He was on the other side, and knew nothing of a sudden commotion among the people when Jake Noyes came dashing through the trees and calling for Doctor Prescott, who had joined them some half hour before.

"Come quick, for God's sake!" he shouted; "you're wanted on the other side of the brook, and the bridge will be gone, and you'll have to go ten miles round. Colonel Lamson is down with apoplexy!"

Jerome did not know when the doctor followed Noyes hurriedly out to the road where his team was waiting, and Squire Eben Merritt went at a run after them, shouting back, "Don't let that boy stay in that mill too long; see to it, some of you."

There came a great barn-roof down-stream, followed by a tossing wake of hay and straw. The crowd on shore groaned. It broke when it passed the falls, and so the danger to the bridge below was averted, but a heavy beam slewed sidewise as it passed the mill, and struck it. The mill quivered in every beam, and the floor canted like the deck of a vessel. Martin Cheeseman rushed in and caught Jerome roughly by the arm. "For God's sake, what ye up to?" he shouted above the roar of the water, "Come along with ye. She's goin'!"

The old man had a rope tied to his middle; Jerome followed him, unresistingly, and they crossed, almost waist-deep and in danger of being swept from their foothold by the current. Cheeseman kept tight hold of Jerome's arm. "Bear up," he said, in a hoarse whisper, as they struggled out of the water; "life's more'n a mill."

"It's more than a mill that's going down," replied Jerome, in a dull monotone which Cheeseman did not hear. There were plenty of out-stretched hands to help them to the shore; the men pressed around with rude sympathy.

"It's darned hard luck," one and another said, with the defiant emphasis of an oath.

Then they turned from Jerome and riveted their attention upon the mill, which swayed visibly. Jerome stood apart, his back turned, looking away into the depths of the dripping woods. Cheeseman came up and clapped his shoulder hard. "Don't ye want to see it go?" he cried. "It's a sight. Might as well get all ye can out of it."

Jerome shook his head.

"Ye'd better. I tell ye, it's a sight. I've seen three go in my lifetime, an' one of 'em was my own. Lord, I looked on with the rest! Might as well get all the fun you can out of your own funeral. Hullo! There — there goes the dam, an' — there goes the mill!"

There was a wild chorus of shouts and groans. Jerome's mill went reeling down-stream, but he did not see it. He had heard the new spouting roar of water and the crash, and knew what it meant, but look he would not.

"Ye missed it," said Cheeseman.

Some of the men came up and wrung his hand hurriedly, then were off with the crowd to see the Main Street bridge go. Jerome sat down weakly on a pile of sodden logs, which the flood had not reached.

Cheeseman stared at him. "What on airth are you settin' down there for?" he asked.

"I'm going, pretty soon," Jerome replied.

"You'll catch your death, settin' there in those wet clothes. Come, git up and go home."

Jerome did not stir; his white face was set straight ahead; he muttered something which the other could not hear. Cheeseman looked at him perplexedly. He laid hold of his shoulder and shook him again, and ordered him angrily, with no avail; then set off himself. He was old, and the chill of his wet clothes was stealing through him.

Not long afterwards Jerome went down the road towards home. Half way there he met a hurrying man, belated for the tragic drama on the village stage.

"Hullo!" he called, excitedly. "Your mill gone?"

"Yes."

"Dam gone?"

"Yes."

"Gosh! Bridge gone?"

"Don't know."

"Gosh! if I ain't quick, I'll miss the whole show," cried the man, with a spurt ahead; but, after all, he stopped a moment and looked back curiously at Jerome plodding down the flooded road, his weary figure bent stiffly, with the slant of his own dejectedness, athwart the pelting slant of the storm.

CHAPTER XXXVI

Jerome, when his mill went down, felt that his dearest hope in life went with it. His fighting spirit did not fail him; he had not the least inclination to settle back for the buffets of fate; but the combat henceforth would be for honor only, not victory. He felt that his defeats had established themselves in an endless ratio to his efforts.

"I shall go to work again, and save up money for a new mill. I shall build it after a long while; but something will always happen to put me back, and I shall never marry her," he told himself.

Had he the money with which he had made good his father's loss, he could have rebuilt in a short time, but he did not consider the possibility of taking that and, perhaps, supplementing it by a loan from his father. "It would break the old man's heart to touch his money," he said, "and the mill might go again, and it would all be lost."

On the morning after the destruction of his mill, Squire Eben Merritt came to Jerome's door, and gave him a daintily folded little note. "Lucina sent this to you," he said, and eyed him with a sort of sad keenness as he took it and thanked him in a bewildered fashion, his haggard face reddening.

The Squire himself looked as if he had passed a sleepless night, his fresh color had faded, his face was elongated. "I'm sorry enough about your loss, my boy," he said, "but I can't say as much as I might, or feel as much as I might, if my old friend hadn't gone down in — a deeper flood." The Squire's voice broke. Jerome looked away from his working face. He had scarcely, in his own selfishness of loss, grasped the news of Colonel Lamson's death, which had taken place before the bridge went down and before the doctor arrived. He muttered something vaguely sympathetic in response. Lucina's little letter seemed to burn his fingers.

The Squire dashed his hand across his eyes, coughed hard, then glanced at the letter. "Lucina has been talking to her mother," he said, abruptly. "It seems the — Colonel Lamson had told her something that you said to him. We didn't know how matters stood. By-and-by you and I will have a talk. Don't be too down-hearted over the mill — there's more than one way out of that difficulty. In the meantime, there's her letter — I've read it. She's cried all night because your damned mill has gone, and looks sick enough to call the doctor this morning, and, by the Lord Harry! sir, you can think yourself a lucky fellow!" With that the Squire shook his head fiercely and strode down the path with bowed shoulders. Jerome went up-stairs with his letter.

"What did the Squire want?" his mother called, but he did not heed her.

It was his first letter from Lucina. He opened it and read; there were only a few delicately formed lines, but for him they were as finely cut, with all possible lights of meaning, as a diamond:

"Dear Friend" [wrote Lucina], — "I beg you to accept my sympathy in the disaster which has befallen your property, and I implore you not to be disheartened, and not to consider me unmaidenly for signing myself your ever faithful and constant friend, through all the joys or vicissitudes of life.
"Lucina Merritt."

This letter, modelled after the fashion which Lucina had learned at school, whereby she bound and laced over with set words and phrases, as with a species of emotional stays, her love and pity, not considering it decorous to give them full breath, filled Jerome with happiness and despair. He understood that Colonel Lamson had betrayed him, that Lucina, all unasked, had bound herself in love and faithfulness to him through all his failing efforts.

"I won't have it — I won't have it!" he muttered, fiercely, but he kissed the little letter with exulting rapture. "I've got this much, anyhow," he thought.

He wondered if he should answer it. How could he refuse her dear constancy and affection, yet how could he accept it? He had no hope of marrying her, he reasoned that it would be better for her should he even repulse her rudely. It would be like screwing the rack for his own body to do that, but he declared to himself that he ought. "She'll never marry at all, if she waits for you; it'll hinder her looking at somebody else; she'll be an old maid, she'll be all alone in the world, with no husband or children, and you know it," he told himself, with a kind of mental squaring of his own fists in his face. All the time, with that curious, dogmatic selfishness which has sometimes its roots in unselfishness itself, he never considered the effect upon poor Lucina of the repulse of her love and constancy. Such was his ardor for unselfishness that, in its pursuit, he would have made all others selfish nor cared.

That day the sun shone in a bright, windy sky. The snow was nearly gone, the brook still leaped in a furious torrent, but there was no more danger from it. The waters were, in fact, receding slowly. Jerome worked all day near the ruinous site of his mill, and

Martin Cheeseman with him. He had a quantity of logs and lumber, which had escaped the flood, to care for. Cheeseman inquired if he was going to rebuild the mill.

"When I get money enough," Jerome replied, with a sturdy fling of a log.

"'Ain't ye got most enough?"

"No."

"Ye ought to have. What ye done with it?"

"Put it to a good use," Jerome said, with no resentment of the other's curiosity.

"Why don't ye hire money, if ye 'ain't got enough?"

"I don't hire money," answered Jerome, and heaved another log with a splendid swing from his shoulders.

Cheeseman looked at him doubtfully. "Well," he said, "I 'ain't got none to hire. I've got my money out of mills on the banks of roarin' streams, an' I'm goin' to keep it out. I believe in Providence, but I don't believe in temptin' of it. I 'ain't got no money to hire."

"And I don't want to hire, so we sha'n't quarrel about that," Jerome replied, shortly.

"I don't say that I wouldn't let ye have a little money, if you needed it, an' it was for somethin' safe for both of us," said Cheeseman, uneasily, "but, as I said before, I don't believe in temptin' of Providence, especially when it seems set agin you."

"I am not going to shirk any blame off on to Providence," Jerome responded, scornfully. "It was Stimson's weak dam up above."

"Mebbe the dam was weak, but Providence took advantage of it," insisted Cheeseman, who, in spite of his cheerful temperament, had a gloomy theology. "I'd like to know why ye think your mill went down; do ye think ye done anything to deserve it?" he said, further, in an argumentative tone.

"If I thought I had, I'd do it again," Jerome returned, and went off to a distant pile of lumber out of sound of Cheeseman's voice.

He felt a proud sensitiveness, almost a shame, over his calamity, which he would have been at a loss to explain. All day long, when men came to view the scene of disaster, he tried to avoid them. He shrank in spirit even from their sympathy.

"No worse for me than for anybody else," he would reply, when told repeatedly, with gruff condolence, that it was hard luck. His sensitiveness might have arisen from some hereditary taint from his orthodox ancestors of their belief that misfortune is the whip-lash for sin, or from his native resentment of pity. At home he could not talk of it either with his mother or Elmira; as for his father, he sat in the sun and dozed. It was doubtful if he fully realized what had happened.

Jerome worked in the woods that day until after dark; when he went home he found that the Squire had been there with a request for him to be one of the bearers at the Colonel's funeral. That was considered a post of melancholy honor, and his mother looked sadly important over it.

"I s'pose as long as the poor Colonel is gone himself, an' there's only three left that he used to be so intimate with, that they thought you would be a good one," said she.

"It is strange they did not ask some one nearer his age," Jerome said, wonderingly.

The funeral was appointed for the next afternoon. Jerome sat in the parlor of the Means house with the mourners, who were few, as the dead man had no kin in Upham. Indeed, there was nobody except his three old friends, his house-keeper, and Abigail Merritt and Lucina.

Jerome did not look at Lucina, nor she at him; as the service went on, he heard her weeping softly. The minister, Solomon Wells, standing near the black length of the coffin, lifted his voice in eulogy of the dead. The parlor door-way and that of the room beyond, were set with faces straining with attention.

The minister's voice was weak; every now and then people looked inquiringly at one another, and there were fine hisses of interrogation. This parlor of the Means house had never been used since the time of the lawyer's mother. Women had been hard at work there all day, but still there was over everything a dim, filmy effect, as of petrified dust and damp. A great pier-glass loomed out of the gloom of a wall like a sheet of fog, with scarcely a gleam of gold left in its tarnished frame. The steel engravings over the mantel-shelf and between the windows showed blue hazes of mildew. The mahogany and rosewood of the furniture was white in places; there had been a good fire all day, but all the covers and the carpet steamed in one's face with cold damp. However, scarcely a woman in Upham but would have been willing to be a legitimate mourner for the sake of investigating the mysterious best-room, which had had a certain glory in the time of the lawyer's mother.

A great wreath of white flowers lay on the coffin. Its breathless sweetness clung to the nostrils and seemed to fill the whole house. Now and then a curl of pungent smoke floated from the door-cracks of the air-tight stove. All the high lights in the room were the silver of the coffin trimmings and the white wreath.

Solomon Wells had a difficult task. The popular opinion of Colonel Jack Lamson in Upham was that he had led a hard life, and had hastened his end by strong drink. He could neither tell the commonly accepted truth out of respect to the deceased, nor lies out of regard to morality. However, one favorable point in the character of the deceased, upon which people were agreed, was his geniality and bluff heartiness of good-humor. That the minister so enlarged and displayed to the light of admiration that he almost made of it the aureole of a saint. He was obliged then to take refuge in the broad field of generalities, and discourse upon his text of "All flesh is as grass," until his hearers might well lose sight of the importance of any individual flicker of a grass blade to this wind or that, before the ultimate end of universal hay.

Solomon Wells was not a brilliant man, but he had a fine instinct for other people's corns and prejudices. Everybody agreed that his remarks were able; there were no dissenting voices. He concluded with an apt and solemnly impressive reference to the wheat and the chaff, the garnering and the casting into furnace, leaving the application concerning the deceased wholly to his audience. That completed his success. When he sat down there was a heaving sigh of applause.

All through the discourse, the hymns, and the concluding prayer, Lucina sobbed softly at intervals, her face hidden in her cambric handkerchief. Somehow it went to her tender soul that the poor Colonel should be lying there with no wife or child to mourn him; then she had loved him, as she had loved everybody and everything that had come kindly into her life. Every time she thought of the corals and the beautiful ear-rings which the Colonel had given her she wept afresh. Moreover, the motive for tears is always complex; hers may have been intensified somewhat by her anxiety about her lover and his misfortune. Now and then her mother touched her arm remonstratingly. "Hush; you'll make yourself sick, child," she whispered, softly; but poor Lucina was helpless before her grief.

The Squire, John Jennings, and Lawyer Means all sat by the dead body of their friend, with pale and sternly downcast faces. Jerome looked scarcely less sad. He remembered as he sat there every kind word which the Colonel had ever spoken to him, and every one seemed magnified a thousand-fold. This call to lend his living strength towards the bearing of the dead man to his last home seemed like a call to a labor of love and gratitude, though he was still much perplexed that he should have been selected.

"There's Doctor Prescott and Cyrus Robinson and Uncle Ozias — any one of them nearer his own age," he thought. It was not until the next day but one that the mystery was solved. That night Lawyer Eliphalet Means came to see Jerome, and informed him that the Colonel had left a will, whereby he was entitled to a legacy of twenty-five thousand dollars.

CHAPTER XXXVII

Colonel Lamson's will divided sixty-five thousand dollars among five legatees — ten thousand was given to John Jennings, five thousand to Eliphalet Means, five thousand to Eben Merritt, twenty thousand to Lucina Merritt, and twenty-five thousand to Jerome Edwards.

Upham was not astonished by the first four bequests; the last almost struck it dumb. "What in creation did he leave twenty-five thousand dollars to that feller for? He wa'n't nothin' to him," Simon Basset stammered, when he first heard the news on Tuesday night in Robinson's store. His face was pale and gaping, and folk stared at him.

Suddenly a man cried out, "By gosh, J'rome promised to give the hull on't away! Don't ye remember?"

"That's so," cried another; "an' Doctor Prescott an' Basset have got to hand out ten thousand apiece if he does. Fork over, Simon."

"Guess ye'll wait till doomsday afore J'rome sticks to his part on't," said Basset, with a sneer; but his lips were white.

"No, I won't; no, I won't," responded the man, hilariously. "J'rome's goin' to do it; Jake here says he heard so; it come real straight." He winked at the others, who closed around, grinning maliciously.

Basset broke through them with an oath and made for the door. "It's a damned lie, I tell ye!" he shouted, hoarsely; "an' if J'rome's sech a G— d— fool, I'll see ye all to h—, and him too, afore I pay a dollar on't."

When the door had slammed behind him, the men looked at one another curiously. "You don't s'pose J'rome will do it," one said, meditatively.

"He'll do it when the river runs uphill an' crows are white," answered another, with a hard laugh.

"I dun'no'," said another, doubtfully. "J'rome Edwards 's always been next-door neighbor to a fool, an' there's no countin' on what a fool 'll do!"

"S'pose you'd calculate on comin' in for some of the fool's money, if he should give it up," remarked a dry and unexpected voice at his elbow.

The man looked around and saw Ozias Lamb. "Ye don't think he'll do it, do ye?" he cried, eagerly.

"'Ain't got nothin' to say," replied Ozias. "I s'pose when a fool does part with his money, there's always wise men 'nough to take it."

John Upham, who, with some meagre little purchases in hand, had been listening to the discussion, started for the door. When he had opened it, he turned and faced them. "I'll tell ye one thing, all of ye," he said, "an' that is, *he'll* do it."

There was a clamor of astonishment. "How d'ye know it? Did he tell ye so?" they shouted.

"Wait an' see," returned John Upham, and went out.

Plodding along his homeward road, a man passed him at a rapid stride. John Upham started. "Hullo, J'rome," he called, but getting no response, thought he had been mistaken.

However, the man was Jerome, but the tumult of his soul almost deafened him to voices of the flesh. He was, for the time, out of the plane of purely physical sounds on one of the spirit, full of unutterable groanings and strivings.

When Jerome had received the news of his legacy, he had felt, for the first time in his whole life, the joy of sudden acquisition and possession. His head reeled with it; he was, in a sense, intoxicated. "Am I rich? *I* —?" he asked himself. Pleasures hitherto out of his imagination of possession seemed to float within his reach on this golden tide of wealth.

He would have been more than man had not this first grasp of the divining-rod of the pleasures of earth filled him with the lust of them. Even his love for Lucina, and his parents and sister, seemed for a while subverted by that love for himself, to which the chance of its gratification gave rise. Vanities which he had never known within his nature, and petty emulations, rose thick, like a crop of weeds on a rich soil. He saw himself in broadcloth and fine linen, with a great festoon of gold chain on his breast and a gold watch in pocket, walking with haughty flourishes of a cane, or riding in his own carriage. He saw himself in a new house, grander than Doctor Prescott's; he saw his parlor more richly furnished, *his* wife, *his* mother and sister more finely attired than any women in the village, *his* father throned like a king in the late sunshine of life. Jerome had usually sound financial judgment and conservative estimate of the value of money, but now he thought of twenty-five thousand dollars as almost unlimited wealth.

That night, after he had the news from Lawyer Means, he could not sleep until nearly morning. He lay awake, spending, mentally, principal and interest of his little fortune over and over, and spending, besides that, much of the singleness and unselfishness of his own heart.

However, after an hour or two of sleep, which seemed to turn, as sleep sometimes will, the erratic currents of his mind back into the old channels, from which it had been forced by this earthquake stress of life, he experienced a complete revulsion.

He remembered — what he had either forgotten or ignored — the scene in the store, his vow, the drawing up of the document which registered it. He awoke into this memory as into a chilling atmosphere, and went down-stairs with a grave face. He met his mother's and sister's almost hysterical delight, which had not abated overnight, his father's childlike wonder and admiration, soberly; as soon as he could, he got away to his work, which was still in the wood where his mill had stood. Cheeseman had gone home, still Jerome was not alone much of the day. People came to congratulate him, also out of curiosity. The little village was wild over the legacy, and the document concerning its division among the poor.

There were two distinct factions, one upholding the belief that Jerome would remain true to his promise, the other full of scoffing and scorn at the insanity of it. Both factions invaded Jerome, and while neither broached the matter directly, strove by indirect and sly methods to ascertain his mind.

"S'pose ye'll quit work now, J'rome; s'prised to see ye here this mornin'," said one.

"When ye goin' to run for Congress, J'rome?" asked another.

Still another inquired, meaningly, with a sly wink at his comrades, how much money he was going to allow for home missions? and another, when he was going to Boston to buy his gold watch and chain? Until he went home at night he was haunted by the doubtful attention of the idle portion, just now large, of the village population.

It was too early for planting, and quite recently the supply of work from the Dale shoe-dealer had been scanty. People were at a loss to account for it, as the business had increased during the last two years, and many Upham men had been employed. Lately there had been a rumor as to the cause, but few had given it credence.

This afternoon, however, it was confirmed. Just before dark, a man, breathless, as if he had been running, joined the knot of loafers. "Well," he said, panting, "I've found out why the shoes have been so scarce."

The others stared at him, inquiringly.

"That — durned varmint, over to Dale, he's bought the old meetin'-house, an' — sent down to Boston fer — some machines, an' — he's goin' to have a factory. There's no more handwork to be done; that's the reason he's been holdin' it back."

"How'd ye find it out? Who told ye?" asked one and another, scowling.

"Saw 'em, with my own eyes, unloadin' of the new machines at the railroad, an' saw the gang of men he's got to work 'em hangin' round his store. It's the railroad that's done it. It's made freight to Boston cheap enough so's he can make it pay. Robinson's goin' to give up shoes here. I had it straight. He don't want to compete with machine-work, and he don't want to put in machines himself. It was an unlucky day for Upham when that railroad went through Dale."

"Curse the railroad, an' curse all the new ideas that take the bread out of poor men's mouths to give it to the rich," said a bitter voice, and there was a hoarse amen from the crowd.

"I'd give ten years of my life if I could raise enough money, or, if a few of us together could raise enough money, to start a factory in Upham," cried a man, fiercely, "then we'd see whether it was brains as good as other men's that were lacking!"

The man, who had not been there long, was quite young, not much older than Jerome, and had a keen, thin face, with nervous red spots coming and going in his cheeks, and fiery, deep-set eyes. He had the reputation of being very smart and energetic, and having considerable self-taught book-knowledge. He had a wife and two babies, and was, if the truth were told, staying away from home that day that his wife, who was a delicate, anxious young thing, might think he was at work. He had eaten nothing since morning.

"We shouldn't be no better off, if you put machines in your factory," said a squat, elderly man, with a surly overhanging brow and a dull weight of jaw.

"I guess we who are not too old to learn could run machines as well as anybody, if we tried," returned the young man, scornfully; "and as for the rest, handwork is always going to have a market value, and there'll always be some sort of a demand for it. It would go hard if we couldn't give those that couldn't run machines something to do, if we had the factory; but we haven't, and, what's more, we sha'n't have." As he spoke, he went over to Jerome, who was prying up a heavy log, and lifted with him.

"Do you think you could form a company, if you had enough money between you?" Jerome asked him.

"Yes, of course; we'd be fools if we didn't," he said.

"I say, curse the railroads and the machines! I wish every railroad track in the country was tore up! I wish every train of cars was kindlin'-wood, an' all the engine wheels an' the machine wheels would lock, till the crack of doom!" shouted the bitter voice again.

"There's no use in damning progress because we happen to be in the way of it. I'd rather be run over than lock the wheels myself," Jerome said, suddenly.

"It remains to be seen whether ye would or not," the voice returned, with sarcastic meaning. There was a smothered chuckle from the crowd, which began to disperse; the shadows were getting thick in the wood.

After supper that night, Jerome went up to his room, and sat down at his window. His curtain was pulled high. He looked out into the darkness and tried to think, but directly a door slammed, and a shrill babble of feminine tongues began in the room below. Belinda Lamb had arrived.

Jerome got his hat, stole softly down-stairs, and out of the front door. "I've got to be alone somewhere, where I can think," he said to himself, and forthwith made for the site of his mill; he could be sure of solitude there at that hour.

When he arrived, he sat down on a pile of logs and gazed unseeingly at the broad current of the brook, silvering out of the shadows to the light of a young moon. The roar of it was loud in his ears, but he did not seem to hear it. There are times when the spirit of the living so intensifies that it comes into a silence and darkness of nature like death.

Jerome, in the solitude of the woods, without another human soul near, could concentrate his own into full action. As he sat there, he began to defend his own case like a lawyer against a mighty opponent, whom he recognized from the dogmas of orthodoxy, and also from an insight inherited from generations of Calvinistic ancestors, as his own conscience.

Jerome presented his case tersely, the arguments were all clearly determined beforehand. "This twenty-five thousand dollars," he said, "will lift me and mine out of grinding poverty. If I give it up, my father and mother and sister will have none of it. Father has come home unfit for any further struggles; mother has aged during the last few days. She was nerved up to bear trouble, the shock of joy has taken her last strength. She can do little now. This money will make them happy and comfortable through their last days. If I give up this money, they may come to want. I have lost my work in Dale, like the rest; I may not be able to get a living, even; we may all suffer. This money will give my sister a marriage-portion, and possibly influence Doctor Prescott to favor his son's choice. If that does not, my failure to carry out my part of the agreement, and the doctor's consequent release from his, may influence him to make no further opposition. If I give the money, and so force the doctor to give his, or put him to shame for refusing, Elmira can never marry Lawrence. I can give more to Uncle Ozias than he would receive as his share of a common division. I can send Henry Judd to Boston to have his eyes cured. And — I can marry Lucina Merritt. She loves me, she is waiting for me. I have not answered her letter. She is wondering now why I do not come. If I give up the money, I can never marry her — I can never come."

Then the great still voice, which was, to his conception, within him, yet without, through all nature, had its turn, and Jerome listened.

Then he answered, fiercely, as to spoken arguments. "I know the whole is greater than the parts; I know that to make a whole village prosperous and happy is more than the welfare of three or four, but the three and the four come first, and that which I would have for myself is divine, and of God, and I cannot be what I would be without it, for no man who hungers gets his full strength. If I give this, it is all. I can make no more of my life."

He looked as if he listened again for a moment, and then stood up. "Well," he said, "it is true, if a man gives his all he can do no more, and no more can be asked of him. What I have said I will do, I will do, and I will save neither myself nor mine by a lie which I must lie to — my own soul!"

Jerome went down the path to the road, but stopped suddenly, as if he had got a blow. "Oh, my God!" he cried, "Lucina!" All at once a consideration had struck him which had never fully done so before. All at once he grasped the possibility that Lucina might suffer from his sacrifice as much as he. "I can bear it — myself," he groaned, "but Lucina, Lucina; suppose — it should kill her — suppose it should — break her heart. I am stronger to suffer than she. If I could bear hers and mine, if I could bear it all. Oh, Lucina, I cannot hurt *you* — I cannot, I cannot! It is too much to ask. God, I *cannot*!"

Jerome stood still, in an involuntary attitude of defiance. His arm was raised, his fist clinched, as if for a blow; his face uplifted with stern reprisal; then his arm dropped, his tense muscles relaxed. "I could not marry her if I did not give it up," he said. "I should not be worthy of her; there is no other way."

CHAPTER XXXVIII

Jerome went to Lawyer Means's that night. Means, himself, answered his knock, and Jerome opened abruptly upon the subject in his mind. "I want to give away that money, as I said I would," he declared.

The lawyer peered above a flaring candle into the darkness. "Oh, it is you, is it! Come in."

"No, I can't come in. It isn't necessary. I have nothing to say but that. I want to give away the money, according to that paper you drew up, and I want you to arrange it."

"You've made up your mind to keep that fool's promise, have you?"

"Yes, sir."

"Look here, young man, have you thought this over?"

"Yes, sir."

"You know what you're going to lose. You remember that your own family — your father and mother and sister — can't profit by the gift?"

"Yes, sir; I have thought it all over."

"Do you realize that if you stick to your part of the bargain, it does not follow that the doctor and Basset will stick to theirs?"

Jerome stared at him. "Didn't they sign that document before witnesses?"

The lawyer laughed. "That document isn't worth the paper it's written on. It was all horse-play. Didn't you know that, Jerome?"

"Did the doctor and Basset know it?"

"The doctor did. He wouldn't have signed, otherwise. As for Basset — well, I don't know, but if he comes and asks me, as he will before he unties his purse strings, I shall tell him the truth about it, as I'm bound to, and not a dollar will he part with after he finds out that he hasn't got to. You can judge for yourself whether Doctor Seth Prescott is likely to fling away a fourth of his property in any such fool fashion as this."

"Well, I don't know that it makes any difference to me whether they give or not," said Jerome, proudly.

"Do you mean that you will abide by your part of the agreement if the others do not abide by theirs?"

"I mean, that I keep my promise when I can; and if every other man under God's footstool breaks his, it is no reason why I should break mine."

"That sounds very fine," said the lawyer, dryly; "but do you realize, my young friend, how far your large fortune alone would go when divided among the poor of this village?"

"Yes, sir; I have reckoned it up. There are about one hundred who would come under the terms of the agreement. My money alone, divided among them, would give about two hundred and fifty dollars apiece."

"That is a large sum."

"It is large to a man who has never seen fifty dollars at once in his hand, and it is large when several unite and form a company for a new factory, with machines."

"Do you think they will do that?"

"Yes, sir. Henry Eames will set it going; give him a chance."

"Why don't you, instead of parting with your money, set up the factory yourself, and employ the whole village?"

"That is not what I said I would do, and it is better for the village to employ itself. I might fail, or my factory might go, as my mill has."

"How long do you suppose it will be that every man will have his two hundred and fifty dollars after you have given it to him? Tell me that, if you can."

"That isn't my lookout."

"Why isn't it your lookout? A careless giver is as bad as a thief, sir."

"I am not a careless giver," replied Jerome, stoutly. "I can't tell, and no man can tell, how long they will keep what I give them, or how long it will be before the stingiest and wisest get their shares away from the weak; but that is no more reason why I should not give this money than it is a reason why the Lord Almighty should not furnish us all with fingers and toes, and our five senses, and our stomachs."

"You might add, our immortal souls, which the parsons say we'll get snatched away from us if we don't watch out," said Means, with a short laugh. "Well, Jerome, it is too late for me to attend to this business tonight. I am worn out, too, by what I have been through lately. Come tomorrow, and, if you are of the same mind, we'll fix it up."

Somewhat to Jerome's surprise, the lawyer extended a lean, brown hand for his, which he shook warmly, with a hearty "Good-night, sir."

"I don't believe he was trying to hinder me from giving it, after all," Jerome thought, as he went down the hill.

Eliphalet Means, shuffling in loose slippers, returned to his sitting-room, where were John Jennings and Eben Merritt. There were no cards, and no punch, and no conviviality for the three bereaved friends that night. The three sat before the fire, and each smoked a melancholy pipe, and each, when he looked at or spoke to the others, looked and spoke, whatever his words might be, to the memory of their dead comrade.

The chair in which the Colonel had been used to sit stood a little aloof, at a corner of the fireplace. Often one of the trio would eye it with furtive mournfulness, looking away again directly without a glance at the others.

When Means entered, he was smiling, for the first time that evening. "Well," he said, "I have seen something tonight that I have never seen before, that I shall never see again, and that no man in this town has ever seen before, or will see again, unless he lives till the millennium."

The others stared at him. "What d'ye mean?" asked the Squire.

"I have seen something rarer than a white black-bird, and harder to discover than the north pole. I have seen a poor man, clothed and in his right mind, give away every dollar of a fortune within three days after he got it."

The two men looked at him, speechless. "He hasn't!" gasped the Squire, finally.

"He has."

"By the Lord Harry!"

"Well," said John Jennings, slowly, "if I had started out on a search for such a man I should have wanted more than Diogenes's lantern."

"And I should have called for blue-lights and rockets, the aurora borealis, chain lightning, the solar system, and the eternal light of nature, but I discovered him with a penny dip," said Eliphalet Means, chuckling. He stood on the hearth before his two friends, his back to the fire; it was a cool night, and he had got chilled at the open door.

"He is going to give away the whole of it?" John Jennings said, with wondering rumination.

"Every dollar."

Means looked at them, all the shrewd humor faded out of his face. "I've got something to tell both of you," he said, gravely; "and, Eben, while I think of it, I have a letter that *he* wanted given to your daughter. Remind me to hand it over to you to take to her when you go home tonight. I've got something to tell you; the time has come; *he* said it would. I didn't half believe it, God forgive me. I tell you, I've got a keen scent for the bad in human nature, but he had a keen one for the good. He'd have made a sharp counsel on the right side. After *he* got his money, he used to talk day and night about the poverty of this town. He had a great heart. He — *wanted* and intended that twenty-five thousand dollars to go just the way it is going." The lawyer, with every word, shook his skinny right hand before the others' faces; he paused a second and looked at them with solemn impressiveness; then he continued: "He wanted to give that twenty-five thousand dollars, in equal parts, to the poor of this town, as indicated in that instrument which I drew up at Robinson's for Prescott and Basset, but instead of giving it himself he left it to Jerome Edwards to give. He said that it would amount to the same thing, and I tried to argue him out of it. I did not believe any man could stand the temptation of a fortune between his fingers, but *he* said Jerome Edwards could and would, and the money was as sure to go as he intended it to as if he doled it out himself in dollars and cents, and he was right. God bless him! And — that twenty-five thousand dollars is going just the way he meant it to go."

CHAPTER XXXIX

The next day Jerome went again to Lawyer Means's. It was near noon when he returned; he met many people on the road, and they all looked at him strangely. Men stood in knots, and the hum of their conversation died low when he drew near. They nodded to him with curious respect and formality; after he had passed, the rumble of voices began anew. One woman, whom he met just before he turned the corner of his own road, stopped and held out a slender, trembling hand.

"I want to shake hands with you, J'rome," she said, in a sweet, hysterical voice. Then she raised to his a worn face, with the piteous downward lines of old tears at mouth and eyes, and a rasped red, as of tears and frost, on thin cheeks. "That money is goin' to save my little home for me; I didn't know but I'd got to go on the town. God bless you, J'rome," she whispered, quaveringly.

"The Colonel's the one to be thanked," Jerome said.

"I come under that agreement, don't I?" she asked, anxiously. "They told me that lone women without anybody to support 'em came under it."

"Yes, you do, Miss Patch."

"Oh, God bless you, God bless you, J'rome Edwards!" she cried, with a fervor strange upon a New England tongue.

"Colonel Lamson is the one to have the thanks and the credit," Jerome repeated, pushing gently past her. His face was hot. He wondered, as he approached his house, if his own family had heard the news. As soon as he opened the door he saw that they had. Elmira did not lift a white, dumbly accusing face from her work; his father looked at him with curious, open-mouthed wonder; his mother spoke.

"I want to know if it's true," she said.

"Yes, mother, it is."

"You've given it all away?"

"Yes, mother."

"Your own folks won't get none of it?"

Jerome shook his head. He had a feeling as if he were denying his own flesh and blood; for the moment even his own conscience turned upon him, and accused him of injustice and lack of filial love and gratitude.

Ann Edwards looked at her son, with a face of pale recrimination and awe. She opened her mouth to speak, then closed it without a word. "I never had a black silk dress in my life," said she, finally, in a shaking voice, and that was all the reproach which she ever offered.

"You shall have a black silk dress anyhow, mother," Jerome replied, piteously. He went out of the room, and his father got up and followed him, closing the door mysteriously.

"That was a good deal to give away, J'rome," he whispered.

"I know it, father, and I'll work my fingers to the bone to make it good to you and mother. That's all I've got to live for now."

"J'rome," whispered the father, thrusting his old face into his son's, with an angelic expression.

"What is it, father?"

"*You shall have my fifteen hundred, an' build a new mill.*"

"Father, I'd *die* before I'd touch a dollar of your money!" cried Jerome, passionately, and, tears in his eyes, flung away out to the barn, whither he was bound, to feed the horse.

He watched all day for a chance to speak alone to Elmira, but she gave him none, until after supper that night. Then, when he beckoned her into the parlor, she followed him.

"Elmira," he said, "don't feel any worse about this than you can help. I had to do it."

"If you care more about strangers than you do about your own, that is all there is to it," she said, in a quiet voice, looking coldly in his face.

"Elmira, it isn't that. You don't understand."

"I have said all I have to say."

"Let me tell you —"

"I have heard all I want to."

"Elmira, don't give up so. Maybe things will be brighter somehow. I had to do my duty."

"It is a noble thing to do your duty," she said, with a bitter smile on her little face. Elmira, that night, seemed like a stranger to Jerome, and maybe to herself. Despair had upstirred from the depths of her nature strange, tigerish instincts, which otherwise might have slept there unmanifest forever. She also had not failed to appreciate Jerome's action in all its bearings upon herself and Lawrence Prescott, and, when she heard of it, had given up all her longing hope of happiness.

"You have to do it, whether it is noble or not," returned Jerome.

"Of course," said she, "and if your sister is in the way of it, trample her down; don't stop for that." She went out, but turned back, and added, harshly, "I saw Jake Noyes this afternoon on my way home. He was coming here to ask you to go up to Doctor Prescott's this evening; he wants to see you. If he says anything about me, you can tell him that as long as he and you do your duty, I am satisfied. I ask nothing more, not even his precious son." Elmira rushed across the entry, with a dry sob. Jerome stood still a moment; it seemed to him that he had undertaken more than he could bear. A dreadful thought came to him; suppose Lucina were to look upon him as his sister did. Suppose she were to take it all in the same way. It did not seem as if she could, but she was a woman, like his sister, and how could he tell?

Jerome got his hat and went to Doctor Prescott's. He wondered why he had been summoned there, and braced himself for almost anything in the way of contumely, but with no dread of it. The prospect of legitimate combat, where he could hit back, acted like a stimulant after his experience with his sister.

Lawrence Prescott answered his knock, and Jerome wondered, vaguely, at his radiant welcome. He shook his hand with warm emphasis. "Father is in the study," he said; "walk right in — walk right in, Jerome." Then he added, speaking close to Jerome's ear, "God bless you, old fellow!"

Jerome gave an astonished glance at him as he went into the study, whose door stood open. Doctor Prescott was seated at his desk, his back towards the entrance.

"Good-evening. Sit down," he said, curtly, without turning his head.

"Good-evening, sir," replied Jerome, but remained standing. He stood still, and stared, with that curious retrospection into which the mind can often be diverted from even its intensest channels, at the cases of leather-bound books and the grimy medicine-bottles, green and brown with the sediments of old doses, which had so impressed him in his childhood. He saw, with an acute throb of memory, the old valerian bottle, catching the light like liquid ruby. He had stepped back so completely into his past, of a little, pitiful suppliant, yet never wholly intimidated, boy, in this gloomy, pungent interior, that he started, as across a chasm of time, when the doctor arose, came forward, and spoke again. "Be seated," he said, with an imperious wave towards a chair, and took one for himself.

Jerome sat down; in spite of himself, as he looked at the doctor opposite, the same old indignant, yet none the less vital, sense of subjection in the presence of superiority was over him as in his childhood. He saw again Doctor Seth Prescott as the incarnation of force and power. There was, in truth, something majestic about the man — he was an autocrat in a narrow sphere; but his autocracy was genuine. The czar of a little New England village may be as real in quality as the Czar of all the Russias.

The doctor began to speak, moving his finely cut lips with clear precision.

"I understand," said he, "that you have fulfilled the promise which you made in my presence several years ago, to give away twenty-five thousand dollars, should such a sum be given to you. Am I right in so understanding?"

"Yes, sir."

"Do you know that the instrument, drawn up by Lawyer Means at that time is illegal, that no obligation stated therein could be enforced?"

"Yes, sir."

"Who told you — Mr. Means?"

"Yes, sir."

"Before you gave the money or after?"

"Before."

"You know that I am not under the slightest legal restriction to give the sum for which I stand pledged in that instrument, even though you have fulfilled your part of the agreement."

"It depends upon what you consider a legal restriction."

"What do you mean by that?"

"I mean that I make no promise which is not a legal restriction upon myself," replied Jerome, with a proud look at the other man.

"Neither do I," returned the doctor, with a look as proud; "but your remark is simply a quibble, which we will pass over. I say again, that I am under no legal restriction, in the common acceptance of that term, to give a fourth part of my property to the poor of this town. That you admit?"

Jerome nodded.

"Well, sir," said the doctor, "knowing that fact myself, having it admitted by you and all others, I have yet determined to abide by my part of that instrument, and relinquish one fourth part of the property of which I stand possessed."

Jerome started; he could scarcely believe his ears.

"But," the doctor continued, "since I am in no wise bound by the terms of the instrument, as drawn up by Lawyer Means, I propose to alter some of them, as I deem judicious for the public welfare. One-fourth of my property, which consists largely of real estate, cannot manifestly be given in ready money without great delay and loss. Therefore I propose giving to a large extent in land, and in a few cases liquidations of mortgage deeds; and — I also propose giving in such proportions and to such individuals as I shall approve and select; a strictly indiscriminate division is directly opposed to my views. I trust that you do not consider that this method is to be objected to on the grounds of any infringement upon my legal restrictions."

"No, sir, I don't," replied Jerome.

"There is one other point, then I have done," said Doctor Prescott. "I have withdrawn my objection to my son's marriage with your sister. That is all. I have said and heard all I wish, and I will not detain you any longer." Doctor Prescott looked at him with a pale and forbidding majesty in his clear-cut face. Jerome arose, and was passing out without a word, as he was bidden, when the old man held out his hand. He had the air of extending a sceptre, and a haughty downward look, as if the whole world, and his own self, were under his feet. Jerome shook the proffered hand, and went. His hand was on the latch of the outer door, when the sitting-room door on the left opened, and he felt himself enveloped, as it were, in a softly gracious feminine presence, made evident by wide rustlings of silken skirts, pointed foldings of lavender-scented white wool over out-stretched arms, and heaving waves of white lace over a high, curving bosom. Doctor Prescott's wife drew Jerome to her as if he were still a child, and kissed him on his cheek. "Give your sister my fondest love, and may God give you your own reward, dear boy," she said, in her beautiful voice, which was like no other woman's for sweetness and softness, though she was as large as a queen.

Then she was gone, and Jerome went home, with the scent of lavender from her laces and silks and white wools still in his nostrils, and a subtler sweetness of womanhood and fine motherhood dimly perceived in his soul.

When he got home, he knew, by the light in the parlor windows, that Lawrence was with his sister. He had been in bed some time before he heard the front door shut.

Elmira, when she came up-stairs, opened his door a crack, and whispered, in a voice tremulous with happiness, "Jerome, you asleep?"

"No."

"Do — you know — about Lawrence and me?"

"Yes; I'm real glad, Elmira."

"I hope you'll forgive me for speaking to you the way I did, Jerome."

"That's all right, Elmira."

CHAPTER XL

The next morning Jerome was just going out of the yard when he met Paulina Maria Judd and Henry coming in. Paulina Maria held her blind son by the hand, but he walked with an air of resisting her guidance.

"J'rome, I've come to see you about that money," said Paulina Maria. "I hear you're goin' to give us two hundred and fifty dollars. I told you once we wouldn't take your money."

"This is different. This is the money Colonel Lamson left me, that I'd agreed to give away."

"It ain't any different to us. You can keep it."

"I sha'n't keep it, anyway. For God's sake, aunt, take it! Henry, take it, and get your eyes cured!"

"I sha'n't take money that's given in any such way, and neither will my son. I haven't changed my mind about what I said the other night, and neither has he. You need this money yourself. If the money had been left to us, it would have been different; we sha'n't take it, and you needn't offer it to us; you can count us out in your division. We sha'n't take what Doctor Prescott has offered neither — to give us the mortgage on our house. It's an honest debt, and we don't want to shirk it. If we're paupers, we'll be paupers of God, but of no man!"

"Henry," pleaded Jerome, "just listen to me." But it was of no avail. His cousin turned his blind face sternly away from his pleading voice, and went out of the yard, still seeming to strive against his mother's leading hand.

Jerome followed them, still arguing with them; he even walked with them a little, after the turn of the road. Then he gave it up, and went on to the store, where he had an errand. He resolved to see Adoniram, and try to influence him to take the money for his blind son. He could not believe that he would not do so. Long before he reached the store he could hear the gabble of excited voices, and loud peals of rough laughter. "What's going on?" he thought. When he entered, he saw Simon Basset backed up against a counter, at bay, as it were, before a great throng of village men and boys. Basset was deathly white through his grime and beard-stubble, his gaunt jaws snapping like a wolf's, his eyes fierce with terror.

"Shell out, Simon," shouted a young man, with a butting motion of a shock head towards the old man. "Shell out, I tell ye, or ye'll have a writ served on ye."

"I tell ye I won't; ye don't know nothin' about it; I 'ain't got no property!" shrieked Simon Basset, amidst a wild burst of laughter.

"He 'ain't got no property, he 'ain't, hi!" shouted the boys on the outskirts, with peals of goblin merriment.

"I tell ye I 'ain't got more'n five thousand dollars to my name!"

"You 'ain't, eh? Where's all your land, you old liar?" asked the young man, who seemed spokesman for the crowd.

"It ain't wuth nothin'. I couldn't sell it today if I wanted to."

"Gimme the land, then, an' we'll take the risk," was the cry. "J'rome and the doctor have shelled out; now it's your turn, or you'll hev the officers after ye."

Jerome pushed his way through the crowd. "What are you scaring him for?" he demanded. "He's an old man, and you ought to be ashamed of yourselves."

"He ain't more'n seventy," replied the young man, "an' he's smart as a cricket — he's smart enough to gouge the whole town, old 's he is."

"That's so, Eph!" chorused his supporters.

Jerome grasped Basset by the shoulder. "Don't you know you are not obliged to give a dollar, if you don't want to?" he asked. "That paper wasn't legal."

The old man shrank before him with craven terror, and yet with the look of a dog which will snap when he sees an unwary hand. "Ye don't git me into none of yer traps," he snarled. "What made Doctor Prescott give anythin'?"

"He gave because he wanted to keep his promise, not because he was forced to by that paper."

"Likely story," said Simon Basset.

"I tell you it's so."

"Likely story, Seth Prescott ever give it if he wa'n't obliged to. Ye can't trap me."

"Go and ask him, if you don't believe me," said Jerome.

"Ye don't trap me, I'm too old."

"Go and ask Lawyer Means, then."

"I guess, when ye git me into that pesky lawyer's clutches, ye'll know it! Ye can't trap me. I guess I know more about law than ye do, ye damned little upstart ye! Why couldn't ye have kept your dead man's shoes to home, darn ye? Ye'll come on the town yerself, yet; ye won't have money enough to pay fer your buryin', an' I hope to God ye won't! Curse ye! I'll live to see ye in your pauper's grave yet, old 's I be. Ye *thief!* I tell ye, I 'ain't got no money. I 'ain't got more'n five thousand dollars, countin' everythin' in the world, an' I'll see ye all damned to hell afore I'll give ye a dollar. Let me out, will ye?" Simon Basset made a clawing, catlike rush through the crowd to the door.

"I tell you, Simon Basset, you haven't got to give a dollar," shouted Jerome; but he might as well have shouted to the wind.

"No use, J'rome," chuckled the shock-headed young man, "he's gone plumb crazy over it. You can't make him listen to nothin'."

"What do you mean, badgering him so?" cried Jerome, angrily.

"He's a mean old cuss, anyhow," said the young man, with a defiant laugh.

"That's so! Serves him right," grunted the others. They were all much younger than Jerome, and many of them were mere boys. It seemed strange that a man as sharp as Basset had taken them seriously.

Jerome, the more he thought it over, was convinced that Simon Basset was half crazed with the fear of parting with his money. When he came out of the store, he hesitated; he was half inclined to follow Basset home, and try to reason him into some understanding of the truth. Then, remembering his violent attitude towards himself, he decided that it would be useless, and went home. He planned to plough his garden that day.

"I've got to work at something," Jerome told himself; "if it isn't one thing, it's got to be another." He dwelt always upon Lucina: what she was thinking of him; if she thought that he did not love her, because he had given her up; if she would look at him, if she were to see him, as his sister had done the night before. Jerome had not yet answered Lucina's letter. He did not know how to answer it; but he carried it with him night and day.

He went home, got his horse and plough, and fell to work in his hilly garden ground. His father came out and sat on a stone and watched him happily. Jerome was scarcely accustomed to his father yet, but he treated him as tenderly as if he were a child, and the old man followed him like one. Indeed, he seemed to prefer his son to his wife, though Ann watched him with jealous affection. Ann Edwards had never walked since the night of her husband's return. She never alluded to it; sometimes her children thought that she had not known it herself.

Jerome was still ploughing in the afternoon when his uncle Ozias Lamb came.

Ozias stumped softly through the new-turned mould. He had a folded paper in his hand, and he extended it towards Jerome. "D'ye know anythin' about this?" he asked. His face was ashy.

Jerome brought his horse to a stand. "What is it?"

"Don't ye know?"

"No, I don't."

"Well, it's that mortgage deed that Basset held on my place, with — the signature torn off, cancelled —" Ozias said, in a hoarse voice. "D'ye know anythin' about it now?"

"No, I don't," replied Jerome, with emphasis.

"Well," said Ozias, "I found it under the front door-sill. Belindy said she heard a knock on the front door, but when she went there wa'n't nobody there, an' there was this paper. She come runnin' out to the shop with it. It was jest before noon. What d'ye s'pose it means?"

Jerome took the deed and examined it closely. "Have you read what's written above the heading of it?" he asked.

"No; what is it, J'rome?"

Ozias put on his spectacles; Jerome pointed to a crabbed line above the heading of the mortgage deed.

"I giv as present the forth part of my proputty, this morgidge to Ozier Lamm.
"Simon Basset."

"He's took crazy!" cried Ozias, staring wildly at it.

"Guess he's been crazy over dollars and cents all his life, and this is just an acute phase of it," replied Jerome, calmly, taking up his plough handles again.

"I b'lieve the hull town's crazy. I've heard that Doctor Prescott has give his place back to John Upham, an' Peter Thomas is comin' out of the poor-farm an' goin' back to his old house. J'rome, I declar' to reason, I b'lieve you're crazy, an' the hull town has caught it. What's that? Who's comin'?"

A wild-eyed little boy, with fair hair stiff to the breeze, came racing across the plough ridges. "Come quick! Come quick!" he gasped. "They've sent me — Doctor Prescott's ain't to home — he's most dead! Come quick!"

"Where to?" shouted Jerome, pulling the tackle off the horse.

"Come quick, J'rome!"

"Where *to*?"

"Speak up, can't ye?" cried Ozias, shaking the boy by his small shoulder.

"To Basset's!" screamed the boy, shrilly, jerked away from Ozias, and was off, clearing the ground like a hound, with long leaps.

"Lord," said Ozias, looking at the deed, "it's killed him!"

Jerome had freed the horse from the plough, and now sprang upon his back.

"Ye ain't goin' to ride him bare-back?" asked Ozias.

"I'm not going to stop for a saddle. G'long!" Jerome bent forward, slapped the horse on the neck, dug his heels into his sides, and was off at a gallop.

Ozias followed, still clutching the deed. Abel Edwards came out as he reached the house. "Where's J'rome goin' to?" he asked.

"Down to Basset's; somethin's happened. He's fell dead or somethin'. I'm goin' to see what the matter is."

"Wait till I git my hat, an' I'll go with ye."

The two old men went at a fast trot down the road, and many joined them, all hurrying to Simon Basset's.

They had reached Lawyer Means's house, which stood in sight of Basset's, before they met a returning company. "It's no use your goin'," shouted a man in advance. "He's gone. J'rome Edwards said so the minute he see him, an' now Doctor Prescott he's come, an' he says so. He was dead before they cut him down."

With the throng of excited men and boys came one pale-faced, elderly woman, with her cap awry and her apron over her shoulders. She was Miss Rachel Blodgett, Eliphalet Means's house-keeper.

She took up her position by the Means's gate, and the crowd gathered about her as a nucleus. Other women came running out of neighboring houses, and pressed close to her skirts. Cyrus Robinson's son pushed before her, and, when she began to speak in a strained treble, overpowered it with a coarse volume of bass. "Let me tell what I've got to first," he ordered, importantly. "My part comes first, then it's your turn. I've got to go back to the store. It was just about noon that Simon Basset come in ag'in and asked for a piece of rope. Said he wanted it to tie his cow with. I got out some rope, and he tried to beat me down on it; asked me if I hadn't got some second-hand rope I'd let him have a piece of. Finally I got mad, and asked him why, if he wasn't willing to pay for rope what it was worth, he didn't use a halter or his clothes-line.

"He whined out that his halter was broke, and he hadn't had a clothes-line for years. That last I believed, quick enough, for I knew he didn't ever have any washing done.

"Then I asked him why he didn't steal a rope if he was too poor to pay for it, and he said he was too poor. He wasn't worth more than five thousand dollars in the world, and he'd given away all he was going to of that. When he got started on that, he ripped and raved the way he did this morning; hang it, if I didn't begin to think he was out of his mind. Then he went off, about ten minutes past twelve, without his rope. I suppose there were pieces of rope enough around, but I got mad, he acted so darned mean about it, and wouldn't hunt it up for him, and I'm glad now I didn't."

Rachel Blodgett, who had been teetering with eagerness on her thin old ankles, interposing now and then sharp quavers of abortive speech, cut short Robinson's last words with the impetuosity of her delivered torrent. "I washed today," said she. "I didn't wash yesterday because it wasn't a good drying-day, and last week I had my clothes around three days in the tub, and I made up my mind I wouldn't do it again. So I washed today.

"I got my clothes all hung out before dinner. I had an uncommon heavy wash today, an extra table-cloth — Mr. Means tipped his coffee over yesterday morning — and the sheets of the spare chamber bed were in, so I put up a little piece of line I had, between those two trees, beside my regular clothes-line.

"About an hour ago I thought to myself the clothes ought to be dry, and I'd just step out and look. So I run out, and there were the clothes I'd hung on the little line — some dish-towels, and two of my aprons, and one of Mr. Means's shirts — down on the ground in the dirt, and the line was gone. Thinks I, 'Where's that line gone to?'

"I stood there gaping, I couldn't make head or tail of it. Then I see the little Crossman boy out in the yard, and I hollered to him — 'Willy,' says I, 'come here a minute.'

"He come running over, and I asked him if he'd seen anybody in our yard since noon. He said he hadn't seen anybody but Mr. Basset. He saw him coming out of our yard tucking something under his coat.

"That put me on the track. If I do say it of the dead, and one that's gone to his account in an awful way, Mr. Basset had been over here time and time again, and helped himself. I ain't going to say he stole; he helped himself. He helped himself to our kindling wood, and our hammer, and our spade, and our rake. After the spade went, I made a notch on the rake-handle so I could tell it, and when that went, I slipped over to Mr. Basset's one day when I knew he wasn't there, and there was our rake in his shed. I said nothing to nobody, but I just brought our rake home again, and I hid it where he didn't find it again. Mr. Means, though he's a lawyer, looks out sharper for other folks' belongings than he does for his own. He'd never say anything; he went and bought another spade and hammer, and he'd bought another rake if I hadn't got that.

"When that little Crossman boy said he'd seen Mr. Basset coming out of our yard tucking something under his coat, it put me right on the track, though I couldn't think what he wanted with that little piece of rope. I should have thought he wanted it to mend a harness with, but his old horse died last winter; folks said he didn't have enough to eat, but I ain't going to pass any judgment on that, and I knew he sold his old harness, because the man he sold it to had been to Mr. Means to get damages for being taken in. The harness had broke, and his horse had run away, and the man declared that that harness had been glued together in places.

"But I don't know anything about that. The poor man is dead, and if he glued his harness, it's for him to give account of, not me. I couldn't think what he wanted that rope for, but I felt mad. The rope wasn't worth much, but it was his helping himself to it, without leave or license, that riled me, and there were my clean clothes all down in the dirt — there they are now, you can see 'em there — and I knew I'd got to wash 'em over.

"So I made up my mind I'd got spunk enough, and I'd go right over there and tell Simon Basset I wanted my rope. So I took off my apron and clapped it over my shoulders — I've had a little rheumatism lately, and the wind's kind of cold today — and I run over there.

"I — don't know what came over me. When I got to the house, a chill struck all through my bones. I trembled like a leaf. I felt as if something had happened. I thought, at first, I'd turn around and go home, and then I thought I wouldn't be so silly, that it was just nerves, and nothing had happened. I went round to the side door, and I didn't see him puttering around anywhere, so I peeked into the wood-shed. I thought if I saw my rope there I'd just take it, and run home and say nothing to nobody.

"But I didn't see it, so I went back to the door and knocked. I knocked three times, and nobody came. Then I opened the door a crack, and hollered — 'Mr. Basset!' says I, 'Mr. Basset!'

"I called a number of times, then I got out of patience. I thought he'd gone away somewhere, and I might as well go in and see if I couldn't find my rope. So I opened the door wide and stepped in.

"It was awful still in there — somehow the stillness seemed to hit my ears. It was just like a tomb. That dreadful horror came over me again. I felt the cold stealing down my back. I made up my mind I'd just peek into the kitchen, and if I didn't see my rope, I wouldn't look any farther; I'd go home.

"So — the kitchen door was ajar, and I pushed it, and it swung open, and — I looked, and there — there!"

Suddenly the woman's shrill monologue was intensified by

hysteria. She pointed wildly, as if she saw again the awful sight which she had seen through that open door.

"There, there!" she shrieked — "there! He was — there — oh — Willy — the doctor — Jerome Edwards — Willy — oh, there, there!" She caught her breath with choking sobs, she laughed, and the laugh ended in a wailing scream; she clutched her throat, she struggled, she was beside herself for the time, run off her track of reason by her panic-stricken nerves."

Two pale, chattering women, nearly as hysterical as she, led her, weeping shrilly all the way, into the house, and the crowd dispersed; some, whose curiosity was not yet satisfied, to seek the scene of the tragedy, some to return home with the news. Two men of the latter, walking along the village street, discussed the amount of the property left by the dead man. "It's as much as fifty thousand dollars," said one.

"Every dollar of it," assented the other.

"It ain't likely he's made a will. Who's goin' to heir it? He 'ain't got a relation that I know of. All the folks I ever heard of his havin', since I can remember, was his step-father an' his brother Sam, an' they died twenty odd years ago."

"Adoniram Judd's father was Simon Basset's mother's cousin."

"He wa'n't."

"Yes, he was. They both come from Westbrook, where I was born."

"Now they can pay off the mortgage, and get Henry's eyes fixed."

"Adoniram Judd ain't goin' to get all that money!"

"I wouldn't sell ye his chance on 't for forty thousand dollars."

CHAPTER XLI

During Jerome's absence at Simon Basset's, Squire Eben Merritt's wife came across lots to the Edwardses' house. A little red shawl over her shoulders stood out triangularly to the gusts of spring wind; a forked end of red ribbon on her bonnet fluttered sharply. Abigail Merritt moved with nervous impetus across the fields, like an erratic thread of separate purpose through an even web. All the red of the spring landscape was in the swift passing of her garments. All that was not in straight parallels of accord with the universal yielding of nature to the simplest law of growth was in her soul. She passed on her own errand, cutting, as it were, a swath of spirit through the soft influence of the spring. Abigail Merritt's mouth was tightly shut, her eyes were narrow gleams of resolution, there were red spots on her cheeks. She had left Lucina weeping on the bed in her little chamber; she had said nothing to her, nor her husband, but she had resolved upon her own course of action.

"It is time something was done," said Abigail Merritt, nodding to herself in the glass as she tied on her bonnet, "and I am going to do it."

When she reached the Edwardses' house, she stepped briskly up the path, bowing to Mrs. Edwards in the window, and Elmira opened the door before she knocked.

"Good-afternoon; I would like to see your brother a moment," Abigail announced, abruptly.

"He isn't at home," said Elmira; "something has happened at Simon Basset's — I don't know what. A boy came after Jerome, and he hurried off. Father's gone too." Elmira blushed all over her face and neck as she spoke. "Jerome will be sorry he wasn't at home," she added. She had a curious sense of innocent confusion over the situation.

Mrs. Edwards blushed too, like an echo, though she gave her little dark head an impatient toss.

"Then please ask your brother if he will be so kind as to come to the Squire's after supper tonight," she returned, in her smart, prettily dictatorial way, and took leave at once, though Elmira urged her politely to come in and rest and wait for her brother's return.

She gave the message to Jerome when he came home. "What do you suppose she wants of you?" she asked, wonderingly. Jerome shook his head.

"Why, you look as white as a sheet!" said Elmira, staring at him.

"I've seen enough this afternoon to make any man look white," Jerome replied, evasively.

"Well, I suppose you have; it is awful about Simon Basset," Elmira assented, shudderingly.

Jerome had to force himself to his work after he had received Mrs. Merritt's message. The tragedy of Simon Basset had given him a terrible shock, and now this last set his nerves in a tumult in spite of himself.

"What can she want?" he questioned, over and over. "Shall I see Lucina? What can her mother have to say to me?"

One minute, thinking of Simon Basset, he stood convicted, to his shame, of the utter despicableness of all his desires pertaining to the earth and the flesh, by that clear apprehension of eternity which often comes to one at the sight of sudden death. He settled with himself that wealth and success and learning, and love itself even, where as nothing beside that one surety of eternity, which holds the sequence of good and evil, and is of the spirit.

Then, in a wild rebellion of honesty, he would own to himself that, whether he would have it so or not, to his understanding, still hampered by the conditions of the flesh, perhaps made morbid by resistance to them, but that he could not tell, love was the one truth and reality and source of all things; that life was because of love, not love because of life.

Jerome set his mouth hard as he ploughed. The newly turned sods clung to his feet and made them heavy, as the fond longings of the earth clung to his soul. It seemed to Jerome that he had never loved Lucina as he loved her then, that he had never wanted her so much. Also that he had never been so firmly resolved to give her up. If Lucina had seemed beyond his reach before, she seemed doubly so then, and her new wealth loomed between them like an awful golden flood of separation. "I have given away all my money," he said. "Shall I marry a wife with money, to make good my loss?" He laughed at himself with bitter scorn for the fancy.

After supper, he dressed himself in his best clothes, and set out for Squire Merritt's, evading as much as he could his mother's questions and surmises. Ann's bitterness at his disposal of his money was softened to loquacity by her curiosity.

"I s'pose," said she, "that if that poor girl goes down on her knees to you, an' tells you her heart is breakin', that you'll jest hand her over to the town poor, the way you did your money."

"Don't, mother," whispered Elmira, as Jerome went out, making no response.

"I'm goin' to say what I think 's best. I'm his mother," returned Ann. But when Jerome was gone, she broke down and cried, and complained that the poor boy hadn't eat any supper, and she was afraid he'd be sick. Abel, sitting near her, snivelled softly for sympathy, not fairly comprehending her cause for tears. When she stopped weeping, and took up her knitting-work again, he drew a sigh of relief and fell to eating an apple.

As for Elmira, she tried to comfort her mother, and she had an anxious curiosity about Jerome and his call at the Merritts'; but Lawrence Prescott was coming that evening.

Presently Ann heard her singing up-stairs in her chamber, whither she had gone to curl her hair and change her gown.

"I'm glad somebody can sing," muttered Ann; but in the depths of her heart was a wish that her son, instead of her daughter, could have had the reason for song, if it were appointed to one only. "Women don't take things so hard as men," reasoned Ann Edwards.

When Jerome knocked at Squire Merritt's door that evening, Mrs. Merritt opened it. For a minute everything was dark before him; he had thought that he might see Lucina. His voice sounded strange in his own ears when he replied to Mrs. Merritt's greeting; he almost reeled when he followed her into the parlor. It was a cool, spring night, and there was a fire on the hearth. A silver branch of candles on the mantel-shelf lit the room.

Mrs. Merritt looked anxiously at Jerome as she placed a chair. "I hope you are well," she said, in her quick way, but her voice was kind. Jerome thought it sounded like Lucina's. He stammered that he was quite well.

"You look pale."

When he made no response to that, she added, with a motherly cadence, that he had been through a great deal lately; that she had felt very sorry about the loss of his mill.

Jerome thanked her. He sat opposite, in a great mahogany armchair, holding himself very erect; but his pulses sang in his ears, and his downcast eyes scanned the roses in the carpet. He did not understand it, but he was for the moment like a school-boy before the aroused might of feminity of this little woman.

"It is partly about your mill that I want to see you," said Abigail Merritt. "The Squire has something which he wishes to propose, but he has begged me to do so for him. He thinks my chances of success are better. I don't know about that," she finished, smiling.

Jerome looked up then, with quick attention, and she came at once to the point. Abigail Merritt, her mind once made up, was not a woman to beat long about a bush. "The Squire has, as you know," she said, "a legacy of five thousand dollars from poor Colonel Lamson. He wishes to invest part of it. He would like to rebuild your mill."

Jerome colored high. "Thank him, and thank you," he said; "but —"

"He does not propose to give it to you," she interposed, quickly. "He would not venture to propose that, however much he might like to do so. His plan is to rebuild the mill, and for you to work it on shares — you to have your share of the profits for your labor. You could have the chance to buy him out later, when you were able."

Jerome was about to speak, but Abigail interrupted again. "I beg you not to make your final decision now," she said. "There is no necessity for it. I would rather, too, that you gave your answer to the Squire instead of me. I have nothing to do with it. It is simply a proposition of the Squire's for you to consider at your leisure. You know how much my husband has always thought of you since you were a child. He would be glad to help you, and help himself at the same time, if you will allow him to do so; but that can pass over. I have something else of more importance to me to say. Jerome Edwards," said she, suddenly, and there was a new tone in her voice, "I want you to tell me just how matters stand between you and my daughter, Lucina. I am her mother, and I have a right to know."

Jerome looked at her. His handsome young face was very white. "I — have been working hard to earn enough money to marry," he said, speaking quick, as if his breath failed him. "I lost my mill. I will not ask her to wait."

"You had a fortune, but you gave it away," returned Mrs. Merritt. "Well, we will not discuss that; that is not between you and me, or any human being, if you did what you thought right. Lucina has twenty thousand dollars, you know that?"

Jerome nodded. "Yes," he replied, hoarsely.

"What difference will it make whether you have the money or your wife?"

"It makes a difference to me," Jerome cried then, with that old flash of black eyes which had intimidated the little girl Lucina in years past.

"And yet you say you love my daughter," said Mrs. Merritt, looking at him steadily.

"I love her so much that I would lay down my life for her!"

Jerome cried, fiercely, and there was a flare of red over his pale face.

"But not so much that you would sacrifice one jot or one tittle of your pride for her," responded Abigail Merritt, with sharp scorn. Suddenly she sprang up from her chair and stood before the young man, every nerve in her slight body quivering with the fire of eloquence. "Now listen, Jerome Edwards," said she. "I know who and what you are, and I know who and what my daughter is. I give you your full due. You have traits which are above the common, and out of the common; some which are noble, and some which render you dangerous to the peace of any one who loves you. I give you your full due, and I give my daughter hers. I can say it without vanity — it is the simple truth — Lucina has had her pick and choice among many. She could have wedded, had she chosen, in high stations. She has a face and character which win love for her wherever she goes. I am not here to offer or force my daughter upon any unwilling lover. If I had not been sure, from what she has told me, and from what I have observed, that you were perfectly honest in your affection for her, I should not have sent for you tonight. I —"

She stopped, for Jerome burst out with a passion which startled her. "Honest! Oh, my God! I love her so that I am nothing without her. I love her more than the whole world, more than my own life!"

"Then give up your pride for her, if you love her," said Abigail, sharply.

"My pride!"

"Yes, your pride. You have given away everything else, but how dare you think yourself generous when you have kept the thing that is dearest of all? You generous — you! Talk of Simon Basset! You are a miser of a false trait in your own character. You are a worse miser than he, unless you give it up. What are you, that you should say, 'I will go through life, and I will give, and not take?' What are you, that you should think yourself better than all around you — that you should be towards your fellow-creatures as a god, conferring everything, receiving nothing? If you love my daughter, prove it. Take what she has to give you, and give her, what is worth more than money, if you had the riches of Crœsus, the pride of your heart."

Jerome stood before her, looking at her. Then, without a word, he went across the room to a window, and stood there, his back towards her, his face towards the moonlight night outside.

"Is it pride or principle?" he said, hoarsely, without turning his head.

"Pride."

Jerome stood silently at the window. Abigail watched him, her brows contracted, her fingers twitching; there were red spots on her cheeks. This had cost her dearly. She, too, had given up her pride for love of Lucina.

Jerome, with a sudden motion of his shoulders, as if he flung off a burden, left the window and crossed the room. He was very pale, but his eyes were shining. He towered over Mrs. Merritt with his splendid height, and she was woman enough, even then, to note how handsome he was. "Will you give me Lucina for my wife?" said he.

Tears sprang to Abigail's eyes, her little face quivered. She took Jerome's hand, pressed it, murmured something, and went out. Jerome understood that she had gone to call Lucina.

It was not long before he heard Lucina's step on the stairs, and the rustle of her skirts. Then there was a suspensive silence, as if she hesitated at the door; then the latch was lifted and she came in.

Lucina, in a straight hanging gown of blue silk, stood still near the door, looking at Jerome with a wonderful expression of love and modest shrinking and trust and fear, and a gentle dignity and graciousness withal, which only a maiden's face can compass. Lucina did not blush nor tremble, though her steady poise seemed rather due to the repression of tremors than actual calm of spirit. Though no color came into Lucina's smooth, pale curves of cheek, and though her little hands were clasped before her, like hands of marble, her blue eyes were dilated, and pulses beat hard in her delicate throat and temples.

Jerome, on his part, was for a minute unable to speak or approach her. An awe of her, as of an angel, was over him, now that for the first time the certainty of possession was in his heart. It often happens that one receiving for the first time a great and long-desired blessing, can feel, for the moment, not joy and triumph so much as awe and fear at its sudden glory of fairness in contact with his unworthiness.

But, all at once, as Jerome hesitated a soft red came flaming over Lucina's face and neck, and tears of distress welled up in her eyes. Far it was from her to understand how her lover felt, for awe of herself was beyond her imagination, and a dreadful fear lest her mother had been mistaken and Jerome did not want her after all, was in her heart. She gave him a little look, at once proud and piteously shamed, and put her hand on the door-latch; but with that Jerome was at her side and his arms were around her.

"Oh, Lucina," he said, "I am poor — I am poorer than when I spoke to you before. You must give all and I nothing, except myself, which seems to me as nothing when I look at you. Will you take me so?"

Then Lucina looked straight up in his face, and her blushes were gone, and her blue eyes were dark, as if from unknown depths of love and faithfulness. "Don't you know," she said, with an authoritative seriousness, which seemed beyond her years and her girlish experience — "don't you know that when I give you all I give to myself, and that if I did not give you all I could never give to myself, but should be poor all my life?

"And, and —" continued Lucina, tremulously, for she was beginning to falter, being nerved to such length of assertive speech only by her wish to comfort and reassure Jerome, "don't you know — don't you know, Jerome, that — a woman's giving is all her taking, and — you wouldn't take the gingerbread, dear, and the money for the shoes, when we were both children — but, maybe your — taking from — somebody who loves you is your — best giving —"

With that Lucina was sobbing softly on Jerome's shoulder, and he was leaning his face close to hers, whispering brokenly and kissing her hair and her cheek.

"It doesn't matter, after all, because you lost your mill, dear," Lucina said, presently, "because we have money enough for everything, now."

"It is your money, for your own needs always," Jerome returned, quickly, and with a sudden recoil as from a touch upon a raw surface, for the sensitiveness of a whole life cannot be hardened in a moment.

"No, it is yours, too; he meant it so," said Lucina, with a little laugh. "You wait a minute and I will show you."

With that Lucina fumbled in the pocket of her silken gown and produced a letter.

"Read this, dear," said she, "and you will see what I mean."

"What is it?" asked Jerome, wonderingly, staring at the superscription, which was, "For Mistress Lucina Merritt, to be opened and read by herself, at her pleasure and discretion, and to be read by herself and Jerome Edwards jointly on the day of their betrothal."

"Come over to the light and we will read it together," said Lucina.

Jerome and Lucina sat down on the sofa under the branching candlestick and read the letter with their heads close together.

The letter ran:

"Dear Mistress Lucina, — When this you read an old soldier will have fought his last battle, and his heart, which has held you as kindly as a father's, will have ceased to beat. But he prays that you will ever, in your own true and loving heart, save a place for his memory, and he begs you to accept as an earnest of his affection, with his fond wishes for your happiness, the sum of twenty thousand dollars, as specified in his last will and testament.

"And he furthermore begs that the said sum of twenty thousand dollars be regarded by you, when you wed Jerome Edwards, in the light of a dowry, to be employed by you both, for your mutual good and profit, during your married life. And this with my commendation for the wisdom of your choice, and my fervent blessing upon my foster son and daughter.

"I am, dear Mistress Lucina, your obedient servant to command, your devoted friend, and your affectionate foster father,

"John Lamson."

THE END